My Story

WAR STORIES FOR BOYS

Stories from the
Second World War

Scholastic Children's Books
Euston House, 24 Eversholt Street,
London, NW1 1DB, UK
A division of Scholastic Ltd
London ~ New York ~ Toronto ~ Sydney ~ Auckland
Mexico City ~ New Delhi ~ Hong Kong

First published in the UK in this edition by Scholastic Ltd, 2009

Battle of Britain
First published in the UK by Scholastic Ltd, 2002
Text copyright © Chris Priestley, 2002

Desert Danger
First published in the UK by Scholastic Ltd, 2005
Text copyright © Jim Eldridge, 2005

D-Day
First published in the UK by Scholastic Ltd, 2004
Text copyright © Bryan Perrett, 2004

ISBN 978 1407 10868 1

All rights reserved
Printed and bound in Germany by GGP Media GmbH, Poessneck
Cover image supplied by Corbis

2 4 6 8 10 9 7 5 3 1

Contents

Battle of Britain
1

Desert Danger
119

D-Day
255

BATTLE
OF
BRITAIN

Chris Priestley

England, 1941

Sometimes I can't remember a time when I didn't have the roar of engines or the rattle of machine-guns ringing in my ears. Sometimes it feels as though I've been a fighter pilot all my life – that I had no life before the RAF, before the War, before the Battle of Britain. But I did. Of course I did. Once I was just Harry Woods, a kid like any other kid. And I suppose that's when my story really begins. . .

1939

I wish I could say I joined the Volunteer Reserve of the RAF because I wanted to serve my country and all that rot, but really, when it comes right down to it, I just wanted to fly. I'd wanted to fly for as long as I could remember.

When I was a kid I used to watch swifts screeching round our house, or see swallows swooping over the summer cornfields and I'd dream of flying too. And then one day, I was up on Hunter's Hill, when a strange noise filled the air.

I looked and an aeroplane appeared over the copse – some sort of biplane, I've no idea what kind. It flew so low, its wheels almost brushed the tops of the beech trees and a dozen crows exploded from the branches in panic.

I chased after it, like a dog after a stick, running through the waist-high grass of the meadow cheering and whooping. The pilot pulled her round to the east and as he flew away he waved down at me and I waved back. *That* was the moment I decided that I had to be a pilot.

I watched him go, the sound of the engine dying away as he headed toward the horizon. I waved and waved, until my arm ached. Then I had the strangest feeling that there was someone behind me and I

4

turned round. The field was empty. A breeze shook the long grass and waves spread out over the meadow like ripples in water. When I turned back, the plane was gone.

The RAF Volunteer Reserve gave me the opportunity to fly and I took it. I joined in January 1939. I was eighteen years old. We were all given the rank of sergeant and the RAF paid the fees for our flying lessons as long as we took the evening classes in navigation and signals and so on.

As well as the RAFVR, there was another organisation of part-time pilots: the Auxiliary Air Force. These were spare-time squadrons, a bit like the Territorial Army, except they had a reputation for being filled with toffs who lined their jackets with red silk. They were all officers of course. The VR didn't have much time for the AAF. The regular RAF didn't have much time for either of us.

I learned to fly at weekends in Tiger Moth biplanes, taught by ex-RAF bods who all seemed like something out of *Biggles*. It was fantastic, taking to the air in an open cockpit under clear blue skies. It was a wonderful summer, that summer of '39, the summer before the War.

Mum and Dad never really understood the flying thing, though. My dad's a doctor and I know he wanted me to follow him into medicine. Even so, they both seemed pleased when I told them I'd like to be an architect. Flying was just a hobby to me really.

"They're not teaching you for fun," my dad would say, and he was right of course. The whole idea of the VR and the AAF was to build up a supply of trained pilots. We all kind of knew there would be a war, and I suppose I wanted to see some action – and not be stuck in some godforsaken trench like they were in the last one.

I was in London when war was declared. It was a Sunday morning. I was visiting my sister Edith, who was training to be a nurse. We heard the PM's speech together. Chamberlain sounded tired and sad. The wireless crackled and hissed. It was 3 September 1939.

"*This morning,*" he said. "*The British Ambassador in Berlin handed the German Government a final note stating that unless we heard from them by eleven o'clock that they were prepared at once to withdraw their troops from Poland, a state of war would exist between us.*" Edith reached out and grabbed my hand. "*I have to tell you now that no such undertaking has been received, and that consequently . . . this country is at war with Germany.*"

Almost immediately, air-raid sirens went off and barrage balloons took to the sky, looking like great fat silver fish. We all grabbed our gas masks and waited for the bombers to fill the sky . . . but none came. Not then, anyway. In fact nothing happened for so long that people called it the "Phoney War". Even so, buildings were sandbagged just in case, and a blackout was brought in, so bombers wouldn't have an easy target at night. Street lights were switched off and car headlights covered.

I was nearly killed by a tram when I was up in London. I only just jumped out of the way in time. Edith said that a doctor told her that road deaths had doubled since the blackout.

She also told me about all the accidents they had to deal with: people falling down flights of steps in the dark and walking into trees and lampposts – and each other. Eventually the powers that be painted white stripes on everything to make it a bit easier to see them.

I was called up to active service as soon as war broke out and spent the bitterly cold winter being knocked into shape by the RAF. We went to horribly dull lectures and learnt how to march and salute and all that rot. We learned to navigate. We learned to shoot. And of course we flew.

I flew Harts, Magisters, Harvards and Ansons, learning to fly in formation, learning how to do rolls and loops and spins, learning the stuff I would need in the months to come. At every stage we were tested and I was pleased to see I was pretty good. "Above Average" it said in my Log Book.

Some of the chaps were trained to fly bombers, of course, but me, I was going to be a fighter pilot. I suppose I should have been scared – a couple of chaps were killed just training – but I wasn't. I was just incredibly excited. *I just wanted to fly*.

In the spring they let me loose in a Hurricane, which was a whole different kettle of fish, faster than anything I'd ever flown before. It was fantastic! But it was nothing compared to the aircraft I was going to spend the war flying. It was nothing compared to the Spitfire.

May 1940

I arrived home on leave on Wednesday 15 May. When my mum opened the door and saw me in my uniform she burst into tears.

"Pilot Officer Harry Woods reporting for duty," I said. She hugged me so tightly I thought my lungs would collapse. I don't know whether she was proud or sad. A bit of both maybe. Mothers are a funny lot.

My dad was in the lounge listening to the wireless. He switched it off as I walked in, stood up and shook me firmly by the hand.

"So those are the wings you've worked so hard to get?" he said, looking at the badge on my tunic.

"Yes," I said with a grin. "Sewed them on myself."

"I'll go and make us all a nice cup of tea," said Mum.

Dad and I sat down, neither of us quite knowing what to say. The clock on the mantelpiece ticked away. Dad leaned forward, looking serious.

"You know the Germans broke through the French Line this morning?"

"Yes – heard about it at the station. Looks like this is it."

Dad nodded. "I suppose it is, son." The kettle began to whistle in the kitchen.

"What do you make of Churchill, Dad?" I said. Churchill had taken over as PM a few days before.

"Well he's got to be better than Chamberlain," he said. "You need an old bulldog like Churchill if there's going to be a scrap. And there is."

"Oh please don't let's talk about the War, dear," called Mum from the kitchen.

"You remember Bob Jenkins?" said Dad.

"Bob Jenkins. Of course I know Bob. I played cricket with him."

"Well he's with the British Expeditionary Force," said Dad.

"He's only nineteen," said Mum as she came in with the tea.

"So am I," I replied rather foolishly. Mum put the tea tray down, burst into tears and ran upstairs.

"I'm sorry . . . I just. . ." I babbled.

"Come and see what's going on in the garden," said Dad. I followed him out and through the side gate, round to the back of the house.

"What on earth?" I couldn't believe my eyes. Mum's beautiful flower borders were all dug up and the place looked like a building site. There were sheets of corrugated iron lying around and Dad seemed to be digging the whole place over.

The garden had always been so perfect. Mum spent every spare minute out there. It was her pride and joy. I suddenly remembered how, as a little boy, I used to follow her about with a toy wheelbarrow as she deadheaded the roses, until it was full of faded petals.

"What's all this, Dad?" I said.

"Well, the corrugated iron over there's an Anderson shelter

I've bought. We're not likely to be bombed, I know, but you can't be too careful, can you? And we're going to grow our own vegetables. Do our bit. Chickens too, actually."

"Good for you, Dad. But doesn't Mum mind? About the flowers, I mean? About the roses?"

"Her idea, son."

"Well good for her, too, then," I said. "It shouldn't be for too long, anyway, should it?

"Let's hope not," he said.

Dad lit his pipe and a robin hopped down from his perch on a spade handle to tug a worm from the earth. Dad looked up at the sky. I followed his gaze, but there was nothing there. Somewhere in the distance a cuckoo sounded off.

"We don't want a hero for a son, Harry," he said without turning round. "Your mother and I are quite happy with the one we've got."

"Message received, Dad. I'll be careful."

"Good lad. Now, how about that cup of tea?"

By the time we'd walked back into the house, Mum was in the lounge smiling as if nothing had happened, handing round the biscuits and asking what I thought about the garden. I heard all the latest gossip about the village – mostly about people I could hardly remember, and then Dad took pity on me and changed the subject.

"So, tell us about the Spitfire, son," said Dad. "Is it as good as they say?"

"Better," I said. "For a start it's the most beautiful plane in the world."

"Does that matter?" said Mum with a smile.

"Well I think in a way it does," I said. "It looks good because it's so well designed. It has these beautiful thin wings. Elliptical. It's a work of art really. Pilots have a saying, actually: 'If it looks right, it *is* right.'"

"And it's fast?" said Dad.

"I'll say. There's over a thousand horsepower of Rolls Royce engine inside – the Merlin III. It'll go over 360 miles per hour."

"But how can you bear to go so fast?" said Mum. My dad just shook his head in disbelief.

"It's fantastic! Taking off, climbing at 2,500 feet a minute, up, up, up to 20,000 feet. It gets jolly cold up there too, so you're glad of the fleecy boots and the gloves – and the oxygen of course. Oh, but when you're up there above the clouds, above the world, soaring like an eagle. . ."

I stopped because I saw them both looking at me, and I laughed self-consciously.

"You really do love it, don't you dear? Flying, I mean," said Mum with a smile.

"Yes," I said. "Yes, I do."

"But it's not just about flying, is it son?" said Dad. "You've got those Messer. . . Mesher. . ."

"Messerschmitts. Yes, that's true. It's the Me109s we really have to look out for, they're the really fast ones. They're the best fighters the Luftwaffe – the German Air Force – have got. But there's also a 110. They have a gunner in the cockpit as well as the pilot. So do all the bombers, actually. The Junkers 87 – you know, the Stuka. . ."

"Yes," said Dad. "I remember those from newsreels from Poland. Hateful things. They actually have sirens on them don't they?"

"Yes," I said. "Frightens the living daylights out of people when they swoop down, I shouldn't wonder." Dad shook his head.

"Then there's a Junkers 88. They have four chaps in them. There's the Dornier – they call that one the 'Flying Pencil' because it's skinny and looks a bit like . . . well, like a flying pencil, I suppose. They have four chaps too. Oh, and Heinkels. Heinkel 111s. They have four or five chaps and guns sticking out all over the shop." I was off. "Of course we all want to prove ourselves against the Me109 pilots. Show them who's boss, that kind of thing."

"And these Me109s, as you call them – they have guns too?"

"'Fraid so. Cannons and machine guns." Mum looked down at the table and put her hands in front of her face. "Of course, I've got some fire-power of my own. I've got eight .303 Browning machine-guns on my wings."

"Eight?" said Dad.

"Yes. Four on each wing. Three hundred rounds a piece. . ."

"Oh *please* can't we talk about something else?" shouted Mum. Dad stopped right there and turned to look at her. "Sorry," she said, smiling again. "All this talk about aircraft is very dull. You know I don't understand about machines."

"Sorry, Mum," I said. I held out my hand and she grabbed it tightly.

I arrived at base on 24 May, eager to do my bit. The place was pretty swish as they'd been doing a lot of work on it over the winter, getting it into shape for whatever was coming up.

My squadron was in 11 Group of Fighter Command, the group covering southeast England and the group closest to the German bases in France. We were going to be in the front line.

I stood and looked out across the runway, with the dispersal huts dotted around it, hangars full of Hurricanes and Spitfires. I felt myself getting a few inches taller just standing there taking it all in.

Hurricanes had already been sent to France and Norway, so I assumed it wouldn't be long before we'd be seeing some action as well. I was pretty keen, looking back. Horribly keen.

"At least the Phoney War is over," I said to a chap in the mess. He was sitting opposite me reading a newspaper. He didn't reply.

"I said, at least the Phoney War is over. Now we can get on with it." He peeped over the top of his paper and gave me a withering look.

"It can't have seemed like much of a Phoney War to the Poles," he said.

"No . . . I mean . . . that's not what I meant. . ." I said.

"Or to the Czechs, or the Danes or the Norwegians," he continued. I didn't reply this time.

"And I dare say that if you were a Jew fleeing for your life from the Nazis it must have seemed pretty darned real. . ."

"Look," I said. "I was only trying to be sociable." He disappeared back behind his paper.

"Don't mind him," said another of the chaps. "Lenny's always like that when he's reading the paper. Come on Lenny, be nice to the man, he's new to this madhouse."

Lenny lowered his paper and thrust out his hand.

"Pilot Officer Mike Leonard," he said.

"Pilot Officer Harry Woods," I said.

I was just about to say something else, when there was a low drone outside and he stood up. All round the mess, the chaps stopped what they were doing and walked outside. I followed them.

Aircraft were descending out of a pale grey sky. A Hurricane squadron coming back from France – or rather what was left of the squadron. As they landed and came to a halt, aircrew ran and helped the pilots out, calling for help for those who were injured.

One of the pilots walked towards me, hollow-eyed, and I held out my hand and said, "Well done. Come on, I'll buy you a drink?" I must have looked such a kid, all neat and clean and grinning like an idiot.

He pushed straight past me as if he hadn't seen me, nearly knocking me off my feet. We watched him walk silently to the quarters he'd vacated weeks before. We followed him in and found him slumped on the bed fully dressed. He slept for two days straight.

The British Expeditionary Force was in trouble, as we found out in our briefing from our CO on the 30th. He stood in front of a large map showing the southeast of England, the Channel and the coast of France.

"As you know," he said, "the Belgian army surrendered at midnight on the 27th. The boys of the BEF have been ordered to make for the coast. . ." He pointed to the map. "Here – at the port of Dunkirk. An operation code-named Operation Dynamo has been instigated to get as many of them as possible away by sea. The Germans will of course do everything in their power to stop it – and that's where we come in. The RAF have been ordered to supply air cover for the evacuation." An excited murmur went round the room.

"Now I know you Spitfire pilots have been chomping at the bit, eager to get involved – but frankly, the top brass feel that Spitfires are too darned valuable to lose by sending them to France." There were a few snorts from Hurricane pilots in the room. "In any event, that's all about to change. If we are going to get the better of the Luftwaffe, we shall have to use everything we've got. Thousands of Allied troops are staggering on to that 12-mile stretch of beach, exhausted, with the Germans snapping at their heels. The harbour has been bombed out of action and the beach shelves away so that big ships can't get close to the shore. It's going to be hard work getting them off, and they're going to need our help in trying to keep the Jerry bombers off their backs. Your squadron leaders will give you more details. Good luck, gentlemen."

It was the 31st. I'd flown many times before, but suddenly it dawned on me that this was it. The practice was over. This was the real thing. My guts suddenly felt cold and heavy, like I'd swallowed a rock. I felt dizzy, doubled up and vomited.

"No time for that, old chap," said a passing pilot cheerily, and I pulled myself together and made for my aircraft. I cringed with embarrassment but the sick feeling wore off as I walked towards my Spitfire. Then I noticed something odd: each of the other pilots in turn patted Lenny on the shoulder as they were passing. It was done almost absent-mindedly and there was no kind of reaction from Lenny at all. He just carried on getting his stuff together and climbing up into his aircraft.

As for me, I stepped up on to the wing, patted my Spit on the flank like I used to do with Blackie, our old horse, and I whispered to it. I can't tell you what I whispered, it was just stuff. It probably sounds like I'm crazy, I know, but it was just something I did. Everybody did something.

I put on my flying helmet and plugged in the R/T – the radio telephone – and my oxygen. I glanced nervously around me and checked my instrument panel over and over again. I signalled to the airman below and he yanked the chocks away from my wheels. We taxied off in formation and then gathered speed.

As we moved off across the grass in the early morning light, the clumsy bumping finally gave way to that great feeling of floating: dull old earth giving way to air and soaring flight. It got me every time, every single time.

Off over the rooftops and steeples, the orchards, the hedgerows in blossom, the hop fields; over the cliffs and the closed-off beaches, out across the sea to the War beyond the slate-grey waters of the Channel.

We flew in tight formation and I tried to concentrate on

maintaining my position as we approached the soot-black skies of Dunkirk. A huge wall of black smoke rose in front of us, a filthy cloak that turned day into night. Then a shaft of sunlight cut a slit through the clouds, hitting the sea like a searchlight. In the sea there were boats and big ships and wrecks sticking out of the waves like jawbones. Near the beach the water was flecked with the floating wreckage of ships and men, the beach studded with those who were waiting for escape. It was a Bible scene, if ever I saw one. Like the Israelites at the Red Sea with Pharaoh at their back, waiting for some kind of deliverance.

We patrolled the coast, but though we saw plenty of action going on on the ground, we saw no sign whatsoever of the Luftwaffe, though we could see evidence of their handiwork all around. We were at the limits of our range here and we got the order to return to base before we ran out of fuel.

I have to say I felt relieved. Good, I thought, it's over and not a scratch. I banged the inside of the cockpit and grinned. I'd heard of chaps in France who only went up the one time and got blasted; bang, end of story. Not me, though.

Then a Messerschmitt shot straight past in front of me, blasting away at the Spit to my starboard. Then there was another, and another. I looked wildly around me. The radio was full of shouting and swearing. "Behind you!" someone shouted. Behind who? Behind who?

Me109s were coming down on us from all over the place, dropping out of the clouds above us. I found myself ducking, ridiculously, inside my cockpit, twitching nervously as if I was being buzzed by hornets.

A sixth sense told me there was one on my tail and I lurched wildly to avoid it, almost crashing into another Spit as I did so. I decided to loop back and try and get some kind of view of what the heck was going on.

The sea and sky spun round together like a kaleidoscope until I righted myself. I tried to get my bearings, but I couldn't see a thing. I heard someone screaming. Screaming and screaming in my headphones.

I looked about, craning my neck. Nothing. Then I saw it: an Me109 coming straight at me from above. I rolled away as it blasted at me. A Spit shot by, coughing smoke, with flames in the cockpit. A German aircraft following behind, blasting like fury. I fired at him but missed by miles. Debris was flying past, clipping my wing.

They were all around me but never in my gun sight. I could feel myself almost crying with the frustration of it. It just felt like sooner or later I was going to get hit and go down. They were better than me. It was as simple as that. The Spitfire might have been the better plane, but not with me in the cockpit.

I swung round and suddenly a Messerschmitt shot across in front of me. I fired off a quick squirt and caught the tail fin. Then there was nothing to fire at. As fast as the Germans had come they were gone, and we were left to limp back to base.

When my plane came to a halt, I found that I couldn't move. I just sat there holding the stick. Then someone slid back the cockpit canopy.

"Are you hit?" he said, but I just sat there staring out through the gun sight.

"*Are you hit?*" he shouted.

"No," I said, suddenly coming to. "No, I'm fine. I'm OK."

I hurriedly clambered out of the cockpit and jumped down, eager to be back on the ground. My legs felt as though they belonged to someone else and I thought for one terrible moment that I was going to keel over. But I didn't.

"Hit anything?" said one of the chaps.

"Well, actually, I did get a crack at an Me109."

"You did? Fantastic!"

"Yes, just clipped its tail. No idea what happened after that. Fuel was getting so low, I had to get back."

"Good show!" he said. "I didn't hit a thing – not a sausage!" I grinned. "Good for you!" he said.

"Thanks. Listen," I said, "what's that business with Lenny? You know, that thing everyone does before the patrol?"

"What thing?" he laughed.

"You know. You all patted him as you passed. I saw you." He seemed a little embarrassed.

"It's for luck, old stick," he said.

"Luck?" I said. "But why Lenny?"

"Well," he said, "it all goes back to a little incident there was a week or so back. A few of the boys were up getting a bit of practice in – Lenny was one of them. Anyway, something happened to his Spit.

19

The engine cut out completely and it started to fall out of the sky. None of the controls would respond, and he had no choice but to get out.

"He slid back the hatch and climbed out, but somehow got caught up in the cockpit and he was stuck there, half in, half out. He could see the ground hurtling towards him as the Spit started to spin.

"As the plane turned over, he was thrown clear and managed to open his chute at about 1,000 feet. The Spit crashed into an empty field, Lenny hit a copse of trees at a fair old rate of knots, and that slowed him down. Then he tumbled through a thicket, through a hedge and into a pile of . . . well, manure, actually."

"Manure?" I asked, smiling.

"Yes – a ruddy great pile of the stuff. Broke his landing, that's for sure. And that's all that *was* broken. He didn't have a scratch on him."

"That's incredible," I said.

"And that's why, you see. A chap like that has got to have a bit of luck to spare, don't you think? We're a superstitious lot, I suppose, but ever since then it's been a habit to pat him as we leave. One of the young chaps started it and it just sort of caught on. Silly really, I suppose, but we need all the luck we can get in this game."

"And Lenny doesn't mind?"

"Well, I don't know," he said with a smile. "Never thought to ask, now you come to mention it." He walked off and I was left standing with some of the others, watching a kestrel fluttering over the edge of the airfield.

Just then I noticed a Hurricane pilot striding across the aerodrome towards us. He didn't look too happy either. It looked like someone was for it and I looked around to see who he was heading for. Then I realized it was me.

He grabbed my lapel with one hand and looked as if he was going to swipe me with the other. Lenny stepped in between us.

"I hope you're not thinking of striking a fellow officer," Lenny said. The Hurricane pilot looked at me, then looked at Lenny, then back at me. He let me go.

"Look," I said. "What am I supposed to have done?"

"You damn near shot my tail off, you silly idiot! Damned Spitfire pilots," he snorted. "You think you're God's gift, don't you?" He stormed off.

It turned out that it wasn't an Me109 I'd shot, but this chap's Hurricane. I could have killed him. I felt terrible. And despite the fact that I could not see anything remotely funny about this at all, I thought that Lenny might *never* stop laughing about it.

"Come on," he said, finally pulling himself together, "I'll buy you a drink."

We walked across to the mess, Lenny chuckling to himself most of the way. I was smiling a little myself, by now.

"I hear you're a lucky man," I said as we sat down.

"I hear you talk to your Spitfire," said Lenny. I laughed and went a little red. "Don't blush," he said. "Barnes over there carries a bit of cot blanket in his pocket from when he was a baby. And you've never seen so many lucky rabbits' feet"

"Never really understood that," I said.

"What? Rabbits' feet?" he said

"Well, if rabbits are so lucky," I said, "they wouldn't have lost their feet in the first place, would they?"

"Good point," said Lenny, laughing. "So," he said, "what were you going to do before the War came along?"

"Architecture," I said. "I was training to be an architect. How about you?"

"I was studying History, but I'm not sure what I want to do. My dad wants me to teach like him, but I'm not cut out for that. I don't know what I'll end up doing. Journalism maybe. Or maybe I'll go into politics, who knows? It's a bit hard to see very far ahead, isn't it?" I nodded.

"Listen, thanks for taking my side back there," I said.

"It was nothing," he said. "And sorry again about before. I just hate that 'Phoney War' business. There's nothing phoney about this war. Maybe if some of the chaps here read newspapers a little more and played ping-pong a little less. . ."

"They're not a bad lot," I said. "I'm not a great one for newspapers and politics myself."

He smiled. "I just think you ought to know what's going on, that's all," he said. "I think you should know what you're fighting for."

"I'm fighting for my family, I suppose," I said. "I can't say I think about anything much beyond that." He nodded.

"Yes, of course," he said. "Me too. But all I'm saying is this is not just about us and our families. We're fighting for something bigger than that, aren't we?"

"We are?" I said. "And what's that? King and Country, you mean?"

"No, no," he said with a smile. "I'm talking about freedom. Does that sound corny?"

"No," I said. "Of course not." His smile disappeared and he leant forward to whisper.

"Look," he said. "They think they're right. They are so sure they're right. The Nazis I mean. They think they're right about all this master-race business and the only way to prove they're not is to beat them. Do you know what I mean? They have to be stopped." I nodded. "And we are going to stop them, aren't we?"

"Yes," I said, raising my glass. "Yes we are."

"To freedom," he said.

"To freedom."

June 1940

On 1 June, we woke before first light. The ground crew already had the engines going on our Spits. I could see the blue glow of the exhaust flames glimmering from the familiar silhouettes. I shivered and flapped my arms up and down to get my circulation going.

My cup of tea was already cold and I tossed it on to the grass. A greasy rainbow shimmered in an oily puddle at my feet. I yawned so hard I almost dislocated my jaw.

"Get a move on, Woods," said my squadron leader.

I jogged over to my aircraft and hauled myself up on to the wing. I patted her and whispered to her and climbed into the cockpit. I checked my instruments, checked my R/T and oxygen. Everything OK. I looked around. Everyone was ready. I gave a thumbs-up to the crewman, who pulled out the chocks. We were off.

I pushed the throttle right forward, I kept the stick nice and central and eased her off the ground. Throttle back and there was the double thud of the wheels pulling up and tucking themselves in. Airborne.

The scene was amazing now. The Channel was flecked with all kinds of vessels – ordinary people bravely answering the call to come to the rescue of those stranded soldiers. As well as Royal Navy ships, there were now fishing boat and tugboats, yachts, pleasure steamers and Thames barges. It was an incredible sight.

I was over the Dunkirk beaches at 5.00 a.m. We patrolled in formation, heading east along the coast towards the new day rising. A few thousand feet below us the beach looked almost purple in that strange light and a mother-of-pearl sheen polished the sea.

Men and boats still crowded the scene, shadowy figures moved about in the sand and along the shore. Vessels of all shapes and sizes sat offshore, waiting for the Stukas to arrive. There was a click on the R/T and then my squadron leader's voice:

"Bandits dead ahead." Sure enough, there were a dozen Me110s heading away from us. "Tally ho!"

Then it was every man for himself. The Germans saw us and scattered and we scattered with them. It was all nerve now, all reflexes and adrenalin. The world speeded up and you had to go with it, like some crazy merry-go-round.

I span out of formation. There were Me109s above us but I ignored them as much as I could. I took after a 110 that had banked off to my starboard. It disappeared into a cloud, but I kept right after it. I wasn't going to be shaken off so easily. When the cloud broke again there it was.

I steered her into my gun sights and thumbed the firing button. Tracer shot out from my guns and headed off toward the German. At first nothing happened, but then smoke began to snake out from his port engine. I came in closer.

I fired off another blast and peeled away. A whole chunk of the cockpit canopy flew off and very nearly smacked straight into me. The Messerschmitt seemed to hang in the air for a second – then it exploded and broke into pieces. There was no chance for anyone to bale out. I saw it go down, down, down and smash into the sea.

"*The Royal Air Force engaged the main strength of the German Air Force, and inflicted upon them losses of at least four to one,*" drawled Churchill on 4 June. We were listening in the mess and there were a few sceptical snorts. Four to one? It hadn't felt like four to one. "*And the Navy, using nearly 1,000 ships of all kinds, carried over 335,000 men, French and British, out of the jaws of death and shame, to their native land and to the tasks which lie immediately ahead. We must be very careful not to assign to this deliverance the attributes of a victory.*"

"Not much chance of that!" shouted someone.

"*Wars are not won by evacuations. But there was a victory inside this deliverance, which should be noted. It was gained by the Air Force. Many of our soldiers coming back have not seen the Air Force at work; they saw only the bombers which escaped its protective attack. They underrate its achievements...*" A huge cheer went up. Churchill was trying to give the RAF some credit.

Soldiers were telling their families they hadn't seen the RAF at Dunkirk, but we were there all right. And they hadn't seen our losses.

To tell the truth, Churchill laid it on a bit thick – but we didn't complain. It felt good to be getting a pat on the back. He compared us to knights – to the Knights of the Round Table, even. It was fantastic.

"*Even though large tracts of Europe and many old and famous states have fallen or may fall into the grip of the Gestapo and all the odious apparatus of Nazi rule, we shall not flag or fail. We shall go on to the end, we shall fight in France, we shall fight on the seas and oceans, we shall fight with growing confidence and growing strength in the air, we shall defend our island, whatever the cost may be, we shall fight on the beaches, we shall fight on the landing grounds, we shall fight in the fields and in the streets, we shall fight in the hills; we shall never surrender. . .*" More cheers.

It was quite a speech all round. He could certainly talk, old Winston. One of the chaps in our squadron could do a terrific impersonation of him. Very funny. Not too respectful though, to tell the truth, so we had to make sure the CO wasn't about.

On Saturday the 8th I got a lift up to London with a couple of the chaps. They were off to a club, but I'd arranged to take Edith to the flicks in Leicester Square. *Confessions of a Nazi Spy* was on and we'd both heard it was good. I hadn't seen a film in ages.

I met Edith in the Strand and we walked up through Covent Garden. London was its usual lively self, despite the rationing and blackouts and all the other things that war had brought. The place was full of servicemen, soldiers, sailors – even a few RAF here and there.

Nobody really had any idea of what was going to happen next, except that whatever it was, it was unlikely to be pleasant. Everyone was out to have a good time in whatever way they could, because it might be the last good time they had.

Even so, I was a little edgy to tell the truth. Despite Churchill's speech, the RAF was coming in for a lot of stick over Dunkirk. As far as most people were concerned we had let the side down. I could see it in the faces of the people we passed as they looked at my uniform.

Edith didn't seem to notice – or if she did, she didn't say. She was a fully fledged nurse now. She looked pretty glamorous actually, hair up, tons of make-up. Mum wouldn't have approved, but I thought she looked great. I told her a little of what I'd been through since I last saw her.

"You poor thing, Harry," she said. "Is it really dreadful?"

"Yes, it is a bit. Can be, anyway," I said. "We've been fairly lucky. One squadron lost all its pilots on their very first sortie."

"Oh my God, Harry. I had no idea. . ."

"Why should you?" I said. "It's not going to do morale any good to hear what's really happening out there."

"What about you, Harry?" she said. "What about your morale?"

I smiled. "You get used to it somehow," I said. "But it is hard, seeing chaps you had breakfast with not turn up for lunch." She stopped and looked at me. I could hear jazz music rising up from a cellar bar.

"Are you frightened, Harry?" The question took me back a bit. It was one I'd always avoided asking myself.

"Frightened?" I said. "I suppose I am, yes. Sometimes. You'd have to be a fool not to be."

"Poor Harry," she said, and she hugged me. A couple of sailors nearby cheered drunkenly. "But it's not going to last long, is it? The War, I mean."

"Well. . ." I said. "The Germans have had a bit of practice at this game. They seem to have got the hang of it."

"But they shan't win. They must know that," she said.

I smiled again. "No," I said. "Of course not, sis," I said. "We'll show them a thing or two."

"One of our doctors says the Americans will come into the War soon and it'll all be over by Christmas."

"Could be," I lied.

Well, we were in the queue, laughing and joking. We were reminiscing about when I'd fallen out of the apple tree at home and been left dangling by my braces. Dad threatened to leave me there but I started crying, so Mum made him fetch a ladder and get me down.

"You were such a cry-baby," she said.

"I was not!" I protested, though it was all too true.

"And a mummy's boy," she said.

"That is such rot," I said, laughing. Just then, two soldiers walked past.

"Bloody, 'ell, Paddy," said one of them. "Look what we've got 'ere. One of those brave pilots we've 'eard so much about."

I told him I didn't want any trouble, but he grabbed me by the lapel. He was a big lad, I realized – a little too late. He pulled me close. His breath stank of booze. His voice reeked of contempt.

"I was at Dunkirk. I had to wade through dead bodies. Where were you, eh? Where were you?" I was about to answer, when he hit me – thwack – right in the jaw. It was a heck of a punch, actually. It was all I could do to stay on my feet. Before I could decide whether to risk hitting him back, Edith jumped in front of me.

"How dare you!" she yelled at him. "Call a policeman, someone."

"Come on, Paddy, let's get out of 'ere. 'E's not worth it." And the two soldiers walked away.

"What a horrible man," said Edith, but then I heard someone further back in the queue shout "RAF cowards!" I could see by people's faces that they took the soldier's part, not mine. I was only too happy when I reached the darkness of the cinema.

There was a newsreel about the Dunkirk evacuation. The soldiers looked grim and exhausted. On the wireless it said that they came off the boats smiling, but I didn't see anybody smiling. It was a miracle they'd got so many off, but it was still an awful mess.

All the pride I'd felt at bringing down that Me110 slipped away and I felt myself sinking lower and lower into my seat. To cap it all, the film wasn't up to much anyway. And the tickets had cost five bob!

Mum told me on the telephone that she and Dad had gone round to Mr Jenkins' house to congratulate him when they heard that his son Bob had got off Dunkirk beach unscathed. But Churchill's speech hadn't hit home with Mr Jenkins either.

"Just wanted to say how glad we were that Bob's home safe and sound," Dad had said.

"Hmmph!" snorted Mr Jenkins. He didn't invite them in.

"You must be so relieved," said Mum.

"My son was stuck on that Godawful beach for days. . ." said old Jenkins.

"It must have been terrible," said Mum. "But at least it's over. . ."

"Being strafed by Jerry aircraft, he was, and he says there was no sign of the RAF." Mum and Dad looked at each other. "Says he never saw a single British aircraft the whole time he was there. Plenty of German ones, though.

"Well I'm pleased Bob is home safe," said my dad, trying to keep the peace. "We just thought we ought to pop round."

"Yes," said Mum. "We're just happy he's home safe."

"No thanks to your son," added Mr Jenkins, poking Dad in the chest.

"Now just a minute. . ." said my dad, taking a step up towards the door.

"Don't you 'just a minute' me," said Mr Jenkins. "My son could have died on that beach. . ."

"And mine could die every time he takes off!" said my dad. "The army might be back home, but the RAF are still in France."

"Not your son, though, eh?" said Mr Jenkins. "Bunch of pansies."

"I beg your pardon?" said Dad.

"The RAF. A bunch of pansies! They're no match for Fritz and everybody knows it!"

"How dare you!" said Dad. "I ought to punch you on the nose!"

Mum had had to pull him away. She said she'd never seen him like that before. She said it was like he turned into Jimmy Cagney right before her eyes. I was proud of him. I'd have paid five bob to see him take on old Jenkins, any day of the week. Bob Jenkins was a rotten cricketer anyway.

On Monday 10 June, the Italians declared war on us as well – as if we didn't have enough on our plates with the Germans. Now we had to fight on two fronts, and we'd been stretched to the limit before. Thousands of Italians living in Britain were promptly rounded up and interned, just as the Germans had been at the start of the War.

Edith told me that an Italian restaurant in London had had its windows smashed the same night. The owner changed the flags outside, swapping them for Union Jacks. She passed by when he was doing it and she saw tears running down his cheeks. Her friends said they'd never eat there again, but she said she felt sorry for him. Typical Edith.

Four days later and the Nazis rolled into Paris. There was something about the idea of them goose-stepping about in that city that made me feel angry. I had always wanted to go there and now I felt they were spoiling it, that it would never be the same again. But then I supposed nothing would.

Then the French threw the towel in. The northern half of the country – the bit nearest to us – was occupied by the Germans. Captured Luftwaffe pilots were freed and put back in the cockpit to face us across the Channel. Now we were for it.

"*What General Weygand called the Battle of France is over,*" said

Winston on the 18th. I was sitting right by the wireless with Lenny. "*I expect the Battle of Britain is about to begin. . .*"

"We're ready for 'em, Winston!" shouted one of the chaps at the ping-pong table.

"*The whole fury and might of the enemy must very soon be turned on us. Hitler knows that he will have to break us in this island or lose the War. . .*"

"Never!" shouted someone at the back.

"*If we can stand up to him, all Europe may be free and move forward into broad, sunlit uplands. But if we fail, then the life of the whole world, including the United States. . .*"

"Come on, Yanks!"

"Shut up!"

"Shut up the lot of you!" said the CO.

"*Let us therefore brace ourselves to our duties, and so bear ourselves that, if the British Empire and its Commonwealth last for a thousand years, men will say: This was their finest hour.*"

Edith had sent me a cartoon from the *Evening Standard*. It was by someone called Low, showing a Tommy shaking his fist at a sky full of German bombers with the words "*Very well, alone.*" It seemed to capture that mood, that feeling of having our backs to the wall. I thought it was first rate, but Lenny was quick to point out that we weren't *quite* alone.

"How come?" I asked.

"Well, think about it," he said. "Just in the RAF, the Australians, New Zealanders and Canadians have all joined in. Then there are the Yank and Irish volunteers. And the South Africans. And what about the Czechs and the Poles. . ."

"OK, OK, I get the message!" I said, putting my hands over my ears.

Lenny had a point, though. 11 Group was commanded by a Kiwi, Air Vice-Marshal Keith Park, who was terrific, flitting about between bases in his Hurricane, wearing his trademark white helmet, and 10 Group – the group north of London – was commanded by a South African, Air Vice-Marshal Leigh-Mallory.

Canadian pilots had seen plenty of action in France, and now we had Czechs and Poles training to fly our aircraft. These chaps had managed to evade the Germans all across Europe. They had seen the power of the Luftwaffe at first hand and were out for revenge.

We even had some Yanks at the base. Some Americans were so fed up with the USA staying neutral, that they came and joined up anyway. We were glad to have them. Come to think of it, Churchill was half American himself!

July 1940

As I reached our front door, I heard an incredible racket coming from the hall, like a suit of armour falling down a flight of stairs. When the front door opened I saw Edith standing there with an armful of saucepans.

"Edith!" I shouted. "I didn't know you were home."

"Only arrived an hour ago. Can't stop. Mum's in frantic mode."

"Hello dear!" called Mum. "Get a move on, Edith."

I squeezed against the wall as Edith and Mum edged past with what looked like every kitchen utensil in the house. They tossed them all into an old pram and went clinking and clanking down the drive towards the village.

My dad was reading the paper in the sitting room.

"Good to see you, son. You're looking well." I looked terrible. "Sit yourself down."

"What's going on?" I said.

"Aluminium Fever," said Dad.

"Aluminium Fever?" I asked, picking up a copy of *Picture Post*. Dad handed me a scrap of paper torn from a newspaper. It showed a picture of a woman holding saucepans next to a picture of some Spitfires in flight. It was addressed to "The Women of Britain". It said:

GIVE US YOUR ALUMINIUM

We want it and we want it now. New and old, of every type and description, and all of it. We will turn your pots and pans into Spitfires and Hurricanes, Blenheims and Wellingtons. I ask therefore, that everyone who has pots and pans, kettles, vacuum cleaners, hat pegs, coat hangers, shoe trees, bathroom fittings and household ornaments, cigarette boxes, or any other articles made wholly or in part of aluminium, should hand them over to the local headquarters of the Women's Voluntary Services. The need is instant. The call is urgent. Our expectations are high.

The Daily Sketch had a headline saying, "*From the frying pan into the Spitfire!*"

"Clever that, don't you think?" said Dad, "From the frying pan into the Spitfire. Like out of the frying pan and into the fire. . ."

"Yes, I get it, Dad," I said, smiling. "They do know that this is all baloney, don't they?" I said. "None of those pans will ever be used in a Spit," I said. "They're precision machines, you know. They're not going to make them out of old saucepans. It's all propaganda."

"Keep that thought to yourself will you, son," said Dad. "Your mother is very keen on all this. She's head of the local Women's Voluntary Service you know."

"Really? Good for Mum. But it's true though," I said.

"Maybe so, maybe not. I don't know. What I do know is that it does your mother good to feel like she's doing her bit, so let her be. As far as she's concerned, she's building you a Spitfire. What harm can it do? Every little helps."

"Point taken."

"Good lad."

"Were those your fishing rods I saw being hauled off for scrap?" I said, picking up a copy of the *Radio Times*.

"Fishing rods?" said my father with a rather shell-shocked expression on his face. "My . . . my fly-fishing rods?"

"Every little helps," I said smiling behind my magazine.

Over lunch I entertained the family with tales of life in the RAF – heavily censored tales, of course. I couldn't really talk very much about the fighting, because I knew Mum just didn't want to hear about it. She had seen something in the paper showing our aircraft.

Mum asked me to describe the base, because she said I was always talking about it in my letters, but she had no idea what it was like.

"Well," I said, "there's a runway, of course – a grass one – and around that there are crew rooms and dispersal huts. That's where we sleep and sit around when we're at 'readiness'."

"Readiness?" said Edith.

"Stand-by. It means we're ready to scramble." I smiled. "Take off at the double."

"I know what scramble means," she said, slapping me round the shoulder.

"Then there's the anti-aircraft guns – ack-ack we call them – to protect the base. There's a parade ground, naturally, and a church. A mess for officers like myself and one for NCOs. Let me see ... barracks, armoury, parachute store. Most important, actually, is the Ops Room."

"Ops?" said Edith.

"Sorry," I said. "Operations Room. It's where all the info comes in about enemy positions and so forth. They get all the up-to-the-minute info, and telephone through to dispersal and send us on our way." I did an impression of someone talking into the telephone. "50 bandits, angels 20." I said. Everyone looked blank. Then Edith laughed.

"What on earth are you talking about?" she said.

"So bandits are Germans?" suggested Dad.

"Enemy aircraft, yes," I said. "Could be Italians of course, now."

"Well why don't you just say Germans?" said Edith. "It isn't any quicker to say 'bandits'."

"It isn't meant to be quicker. It's kind of a code." Edith shook her head.

"And angels are RAF aircraft?" said Mum.

"No," I said. "Angels are thousands of feet. Angels 20 means 20,000 feet. Fifteen thousand would be angels 15 and so on."

"I've never heard such nonsense," said Edith and everyone laughed.

Mum and Dad had seen a newsreel clip showing Goering, the head of the Luftwaffe. He'd been a crack pilot during the Great War, but looked like he would have a bit of a problem getting into a cockpit now.

"He's so fat," said Mum. "And so ugly."

"He is a bit of a sight," I agreed. "He's stinking rich apparently, though. He's got his own personal train."

"They're all a ghastly shower, if you ask me," said Dad. "Goebbels, Himmler . . . Hitler for that matter. Like something from a horror film. It beats me how anyone could ever listen to a word they say."

"I saw some of those WAFE girls at the cinema," said Mum. "They do look very smart, don't they?"

"WAAFs, Mum," I said. "They're called WAAFs. It stands for Women's Auxiliary Air Force. We've got them at our place of course. Some of them are not bad lookers, actually, but goodness knows what they are going to do if bombs start falling. . ."

"What on earth do you mean?" said Edith crossly.

"Well, I just mean . . . you know . . . girls aren't used to that kind of thing," I said, wishing I'd never started.

"And you are, I suppose?" said Edith.

"Yes . . . I mean, no. Look, it's what all the chaps are saying. . ."

"Oh do shut up," said Edith suddenly. "You are talking the most awful rot!"

"Edith's right, dear," said Mum. "You are talking rubbish." Dad laughed.

"OK! OK!" I said, holding up my hands. "It was a casual remark for goodness' sake; no need to shoot me down in flames!"

"Don't say that!" shouted Mum. I shrugged and laughed.

"It's just an expression. . ."

"Don't ever use it again," she said coldly and got up from her chair. "I'm going out into the garden." Edith and Dad looked at me.

"What?" I said.

"You idiot!" snapped Edith, and she got up to follow Mum.

"It's just an expression, Dad," I said. Dad just shook his head and sighed. Then he got up and went to his armchair to read the *Radio Times*.

"It's just an expression," I said quietly to myself.

Back at base it was the same mix of boredom and frantic activity. Jerry was launching attacks on convoys and ports on the south coast. Me109s would come over first, looking for a fight, and then Junkers 87 dive-bombers – Stukas – would swoop down on the ships in the Channel.

Most of the time we would get there too late and the damage would be done, with the Germans already high-tailing it back to France. It was frustrating to say the least. We all wanted to take on the 109s, but Fighter Command wanted us to save ourselves for the fight to come.

And when we weren't in the air we were engaged in endless debate...

"All I'm saying is, Vivien Leigh's all right. . ." I said.

"All right?" one of the chaps said. "All right? Have you seen *Gone With the Wind*?"

"Of course I have. But Merle Oberon is on a different level altogether."

"Rubbish!" he said.

"She is just *so* much better looking," I said. "Ask anyone."

"Absolute nonsense!" he said.

"What do you say, Lenny?" I said, giving Lenny a tap with my foot.

"What? About what?" he said, looking up from his book.

"Merle Oberon."

Lenny looked thoughtfully off in to the distance. We waited expectantly. Then he looked back at me. "And Merle Oberon is. . .?"

"Oh come on," I said. "You must know who Merle Oberon is. She's in *Wuthering Heights*."

"Well I've read the book," said Lenny. "But I can't remember anyone called. . ."

"The movie, you chump," I said. "She's an *actress*!"

"Ah, I see. She played Cathy presumably," he said.

"I don't remember who she played. We're not arguing about who she played, we're arguing about who is the most. . ."

"Hey, shut up you lot and listen to this!" shouted a chap over by the wireless. He turned the volume up.

"*Somebody's hit a German*," said the voice on the wireless. "*And he's coming down with a long streak . . . coming down completely out of control . . . and now a man's baled out by parachute. It's a Junker's 87 and he's going slap into the sea. There he goes – smash!*"

It turned out that a BBC reporter, Charles Gardner, had just set up his equipment on the cliffs at Dover when by complete fluke all this action started right in front of him. Out at sea, about 40 Stukas with an escort of Me109s were laying into a convoy. Antiaircraft guns on the coast were blasting away at them.

41

He described it just as if it was a football match or something. You could hear bombs; you could hear the rattle of machine-gun fire from the fighters. There was something so odd about listening to all this on the wireless. The whole mess went totally silent.

Dad told me later how he and Mum had listened to it on the wireless. My dad had reached over to switch it off, but my mum said, no, she wanted to hear. She said it made her feel closer to me. She held my dad's hand and carried on listening.

Gardner sounded a little disappointed when the bombers headed for home, but he got very excited again when the fighters reappeared. He was like a kid. He was almost giggling.

"There are three Spitfires chasing three Messerschmitts now. Oh boy! Look at them going! Oh yes. I've never seen anything so good as this. The RAF fighters have really got these boys taped."

When he finished we all cheered. We loved it, of course, but not everyone was so keen. Dad told me there were angry letters in newspapers complaining that this just wasn't the way to go on when lives were at stake. Gardner was rapped across the knuckles and told not to do it again. But I think it made the people at home feel part of it all. It did for my mum, anyway.

Then Adolf got up on his hind legs and made some crazy speech on the 19th, blaming the war on Jews and Freemasons and arms manufacturers – which was odd, because we'd all sort of thought *he* was to blame. The newsreel showed him ranting and snarling as always.

"A great Empire will be destroyed. An Empire which it was never my

intention to destroy or even to harm. . ." We could make peace, he said, or he would destroy the British Empire.

Well old Chamberlain had shown what happened if you gave in to bullies when he made the mistake of listening to Adolf in '39. Churchill wasn't about to make that mistake again and we told him where he could stick his peace offer.

I groaned as the airman orderly patted me on the shoulder. I gingerly opened my eyes. It wasn't yet light. I groaned again. My shoulder ached. I felt like I was a hundred years old.

"Oh hell," I said. "I was hoping it had all been some terrible dream."

"'Fraid not, Sir. War's still on. Jerry's still expecting you."

"OK," I said. "I'm – yawn – ready for action." Then I pulled the blanket back over my head for a couple more precious minutes.

I climbed reluctantly out of bed and I got dressed over my pyjamas and put my leather Irvin jacket on to fend off the cold. Then I pulled my flying boots on and tried to focus my tired eyes, squinting into the surrounding murk.

The sun was just beginning to send out a queasy glow to the east as I stepped outside to check my aircraft. The grass was covered in a heavy dew, so heavy it looked like frost. A cockerel was crowing somewhere off in the world beyond.

I said hello to the crew who were working on my Spit. I stepped up on to the wing and then into the cockpit. I checked all the instruments, making sure I had a full tank of fuel, connected the oxygen and R/T leads of my helmet and left it on the stick. OK, I was ready.

I jumped down and walked back to the hut. I warmed my hands by the stove. I looked around the hut at the pilots slumped about the place. A couple of them looked about fifteen.

Operational training had been dropped from six months to four weeks. A lot of these sprogs never got to fire their guns until they went on their first sortie. Sometimes this was the last time too. At nineteen, I felt like a veteran.

The press called us "Dowding's Chicks". The "Chick" part was because of our youth, the "Dowding" part was after our boss – Air Chief Marshal Sir Hugh Dowding, the head of Fighter Command. Dowding was a terrific fellow, actually, though he was a bit severe. They called him "Stuffy" Dowding, though not to his face, obviously.

Lenny was asleep in his favourite chair, snoring gently. I sat down, closed my eyes and instantly went back to sleep. Sleep just closed in over me, as if I was sinking into a deep black ocean. I felt as though I could have slept for a thousand years.

Off in the distance I heard a bell ringing. It sounded like the bell my teacher used to have in the playground to call us all back to the classroom. Ring, ring, ring. I saw her standing there, ringing the bell, faster and faster, more and more frantically.

Then I was running out over the wet grass, out into the cold dawn light. Chute on, harness on, gloves and helmet on. Engine roaring. Taxiing out. Taking off. I woke up somewhere over Maidstone.

This routine would happen day after day. Ten minutes later the sky would be heaving with aircraft, friends and foe, and we were all of us fighting for our lives. Ten minutes after that the fight would be won or lost. Then, back at base, we'd do a quick headcount to see who was missing.

Then I'd give my report and the crew would run all over the Spit checking for damage, refuelling her and the like. Armourers fed the guns. I'd go to the loo and wash. Then I'd sit back down in my chair, close my eyes and wait to go up again. This was how we lived then, patrol after patrol, scramble after scramble.

One day I was having a running battle with a wasp that was pestering me. Lenny was sitting next to me, reading a book (as always). I grabbed it off him and with one movement thwacked the wasp to the floor and squashed him with the heel of my flying boot.

"Do you mind?" said Lenny, grabbing his book back.

"Sorry. Wasps. Hate them."

"Can't imagine they're too keen on you either," he said looking down at the squashed wasp and snatching his book back.

"So – what's the book?" I asked.

"*Metamorphosis.*"

"Come again?"

"*Metamorphosis.*"

"Hmm," I said. "Any good?"

"It is rather, yes."

"What's it about?"

"Well, funnily enough, it's about a man who wakes up to find he's turned into an insect."

I raised an eyebrow. "Doesn't sound very funny," I said.

"Not your cup of tea, I shouldn't think," he said with a smile.

"Hmm. . . Who's it by, then, this book of yours?"

"Kafka. Franz Kafka."

"Sounds German."

"Czech, actually," he said.

"Oh," I said.

"He did write in German, though. Maybe you should turn me in."

"Very funny. You think you're so clev—"

"Squadron scramble!"

We were at 20,000 feet when we saw them. I came down out of the sun and let off a burst of fire at one of them. Smoke started out of its starboard engine. I saw the flicker of flames. The Me110 fell away, down towards the bank of clouds. But like an idiot I followed it down.

And like a complete and utter idiot I didn't break away. Suddenly there was series of bumps as the cannon on the back of the 110 hit home. I cursed myself long and loud, but had to face facts. The control column was useless. I would have to bale out.

I slid back the cockpit cover, undid my harness and pushed myself clear. The air seemed to scoop me up as the Spit fell away from me, sinking out of sight into the clouds below. I tumbled over and over, pulled the ripcord and up went my parachute.

I was swung about rather wildly for a while, but gradually things calmed down and I found myself floating down through the cloud layer, expecting any moment that a German plane would appear out of the swirling blankness like a shark in milky water.

Then the clouds began to break up and then, quite suddenly, I was looking down on the world, like a traveller looking at a map. I looked about me for Jerry aircraft but they were all heading back to France.

The patchwork of fields below me looked rather wonderful. The cloud shadow moved away to the east and I tugged at my chute to make sure I didn't drift out to sea. The fabric fluttered and flapped like a flag.

I pulled my mask off. I heard the all-clear sounding. I heard a whistle blowing. I looked up at the blue sky and whistled back. The sun was bright now and I saw a twinkling star-like glint as a windscreen of a distant vehicle caught the light. Two gulls flew by beneath my feet. A car horn tooted.

Houses loomed into view as I descended. Trees too. What had seemed like a map now seemed like a child's model – a toy tractor on a farm track, a hump-backed barn with some milk churns outside.

The field I was heading towards had a lone white horse in it. As I got closer it whinnied and shook its head and then set off around the field at a mad gallop. I saw a land girl standing by a car and I waved and shouted, "Hello!"

I landed well, sending up a fluttering skylark. It was very calm so I didn't get dragged along the ground by the chute. As I got to my feet the land girl walked up to me.

"You *are* English aren't you?" she asked nervously.

"I certainly am," I said. A huge smile lit up her freckled face. The skylark twittered above our heads. I had never felt so alive.

August 1940

I managed to persuade Lenny to get out and go to a local dance one summer night. It was great fun, actually. We were celebrities now. You couldn't open a newspaper without seeing a Spitfire pilot grinning back at you. We were a big hit with the girls and we danced ourselves dizzy.

We managed to get a lift as far as the crossroads, but forgot that they'd taken down all the signposts to foil any Jerry paratroopers. Our navigational training came to nothing and we ended up completely lost. Lenny blamed me, of course, for suggesting the dance in the first place.

"Happy now?" said Lenny.

"Look, it's not my fault, old chap," I said.

"You said you knew the way. Of course it's your fault."

"Look, if you moaned a little less and tried to help me find out where we are..."

"And how are you going to do that? It's pitch black and you haven't the faintest idea what direction we're heading in."

"Oh, will you please..."

Suddenly we heard a rumble, a drone, getting nearer and nearer. I couldn't see a thing, but I dived headlong into a ditch anyway and

Lenny followed close behind. The noise got louder and louder until whatever it was suddenly stopped right next to us.

I peered out. Instead of a Panzer division of invading Germans or whatever I'd expected, there was a tractor in the field next to me. The farmer had climbed down and was just lighting his pipe. I felt a complete fool. Still, at least he hadn't seen us.

"Er... Excuse me," I said, trying not to startle him.

"You lost?" he said with a smile.

"Yes. Yes we are."

"You're a young flyer, ain't you? One of them there Dowding's Chickens."

"Chicks," I said.

"You what?" said the farmer.

"Dowding's Chicks. It's on account of how we're so young," said Lenny.

"Not on account of how you can't fly then?" he said. He grinned. "Just kidding. Come on, I'll give you a lift."

"What are you doing, driving round in the middle of the night, if you don't mind me asking?" said Lenny.

"Doing my bit, ain't I," he said. "Doing my bit for productivity and all that. We all got to do our bit, now, eh?" We nodded. "Safer too, at night."

"You must see a lot of action from these fields," I said.

"Oh yes. I had one of those Hurricanes in my top field the other day. Made a right mess of my wheat."

"Sometimes we just have to land where we can, I'm afraid, Mr..."

"Oh 'e didn't land," he said. "'E just come down, if you get my drift."

50

Just then there was droning noise coming from the south and heading our way. There was no mistake this time. This time it was definitely a bomber. And it wasn't one of ours. Once again, Lenny and I jumped in the ditch and put our hands over our heads.

The droning got nearer and nearer until it was right over our heads. We closed our eyes, gritted our teeth and held our breath. Then it just as quickly moved away into the distance. Very slowly we climbed out of hiding.

The tractor driver hadn't moved, and was puffing quietly on his pipe.

"One of those Jerry bombers. Junkers they call 'em, don't they?" He pronounced Junkers with a hard "j", like in junk.

"Yunkers," said Lenny. "It's pronounced Yunkers."

"Junkers," repeated the farmer in the same way as before. "Even if those so-and-sos take over, I ain't going to be speaking no German."

Then, out of the corner of my eye, I became aware of a strange fluttering. There it was again. And again. Slowly, right in front of my face a piece of paper drifted back and forth like an autumn leaf. I plucked it from the air.

"What the..." said the farmer. "Let's 'ave a look at that there." He flicked his lighter and the three of us crowded round.

On the paper was written, in large capital letters A LAST APPEAL TO REASON BY ADOLF HITLER. Underneath was a reprint of the speech he'd made back in July. The farmer chuckled.

"'E's a rum 'n', ain't 'e though?" Then he set the leaflet on fire, dropped it on to the road and then stamped it out with his boot. "Come on, Chickens," he said. "Hop aboard."

The tractor rattled into life and off it went with us hanging on to the side. It wasn't much faster than walking but we weren't so very far away.

"I say!" I said suddenly. "How do you know we're not spies?"

"Oh," he said. "Those Jerrys is 'ard as nails. No, I knew you was English the minute I sees you jump in that ditch."

On Tuesday 13 August a fine drizzle fell from a cygnet-grey blanket of cloud. Jerry had been hitting some of the forward bases. I'd flown over one of them after a raid and they'd made quite a mess of it. Today, we'd hopefully get the jump on them.

We spent most of the day staving off boredom and thoughts of the next scramble, but at about four o'clock we were running hell-for-leather out of our dispersal hut and not long after we were up against a flock of Jerry aircraft – Stukas, Me109s, Me110s – the whole shooting match.

We climbed to 20,000 feet and watched the bombers sail by below us at about 15,000. The Squadron Leader shouted "Tally Ho!" and we arced around behind them and dropped out of the sun. They never even saw us coming.

The Me109s were higher as usual and dived across to meet us. I looped round and found myself jumping straight onto a 109's back. I gave him a quick squirt, the aircraft wobbled slightly, flipped on to its back and then burst into flames. It dropped out of the sky, spiralling crazily down, down, through the clouds and back to earth. My first 109!

I saw a Hurricane steaming towards an Me110, guns blazing. Then he just kept on going, ploughing straight into the German. Both planes exploded into each other, scattering flaming fragments across the crowded sky.

The sky was criss-crossed with vapour trails and snaking coils of black smoke. Planes flickered by like fish in a murky pond, darting this way and that. A parachute opened. A piece of wing fluttered by. Columns of smoke rose up along the horizon. I saw Stukas standing out white against it.

They were slow and I hared after them. I swept round behind one and came in from just below. I could see the big yellow bomb hanging underneath. I was so close I couldn't miss – but miss I did. Bringing down the 109 had made me cocky. I came in too fast, overshot and missed by miles. Out of ammo, I had no choice but to run for home. The Stuka carried on with its bomb.

"Just get it sorted out!" I snapped at the mechanic and stormed off. Lenny wandered up.

"Problems?" he asked.

"Just these idiots," I said. I heard the mechanic muttering to one of the other airmen and swung back round to face him. He actually looked a little frightened. Had I changed so much?

"Look, it's my life on the line up there!" I shouted, pointing up to the sky. "If you screw up, it's me that pays the price, not you. Just do your job, OK?" I saw Lenny raise an eyebrow and I turned towards him.

"Steady on, old chap. We're all on the same side, you know."

"Stay out of it, will you Lenny?" I said.

"OK, OK," he said, holding up his hands. "Don't shoot. I'm a hero too, remember?" He grinned, but I wasn't in the mood.

"Look, Lenny. . ." I began. BOOM! "What the. . .?" BOOM! The whole place shook.

"Scramble! Scramble! Protect base!"

A Junkers 88 roared past above us. We both dived as the bomb dropped. BOOM! We picked ourselves up and ran to a trench near the ack-ack guns. The crew were already getting our Spits going and we grabbed our gear and made a dash for our aircraft.

Pieces of shrapnel and stones were raining down, pinging off the aluminium of my Spit. The take-off was total chaos, with aircraft jinking this way and that, lit up by blinding flashes. BOOM! We got away, though. Up and away and at those blasted bombers.

Below us the airmen and WAAFs were making for their shelters. The Ops Room was hit. So was one of the hangars. Smoke blinded me for a second and then I was through and out into the fight.

I chased after a Junkers but lost him before I could even think about firing. A Hurricane zipped by me, white smoke pouring out of its exhaust and the pilot climbing out of the cockpit. Ack-ack fire burst all around me.

Then I spotted an Me109 in my mirror, homing in for me. I rolled away just as he opened fire and he must have missed me by inches. BOOM! Another bomb exploded well wide of the airfield, sending clods of earth into the air.

When I righted myself I saw a Hurricane blasting away at a Dornier. He roared in so close I thought he hadn't left enough time to pull out of his dive, but at the last instant he did and the Dornier wobbled and then flipped down, nose first.

But the bombers were getting through. Clouds of black smoke rose up from around the base. A Junkers suddenly appeared heading straight for me. Instinctively, I let off a burst. But I missed him by miles and then had to spin away.

Then, as always, they were gone and there was that gnawing frustration of not having done enough. When I got back to the base I found the place in chaos. A couple of the hangars were up in flames and there were pieces of aircraft scattered across the airfield. A dog went past, limping and whimpering.

I saw the mechanic I had torn a strip off, blood trickling from a head wound, trying desperately to fix a damaged Spit while fire-fighters tackled a blaze only yards away from him. A hanger roof collapsed to my left with an almighty crunch and clang.

An ambulance swung round in front of me, swerving to avoid the severed tailplane of a Hurricane. A German pilot parachuted slowly down into the midst of all this activity, but he was already dead, hanging limply from his harness. About 50 feet up, his chute caught a spark and burst into flames and he flopped to the ground.

One of our chaps was walking backwards and forwards along a stretch of about ten feet. He was wearing pyjamas with an Irvin jacket over the top and nothing on his feet. The all-clear wailed out over everything.

Civilians and Home Guard ran this way and that, carrying stretchers and buckets of water. Chaps from the Ops room, covered in dust, helped clear a bombed out trench with their bare hands. Spits and Hurricanes landed on the pot-holed strip.

A young WAAF staggered towards me supporting an airman whose face sparkled with broken glass.

"Well?" she yelled. "Are you just going to stand there, or are you going to give me a hand?"

"The gratitude of every home in our island," said Winston on the 20th, his voice growling out of the mess wireless, *"in our Empire, and indeed throughout the world, except in the abodes of the guilty, goes out to the British airmen who, undaunted by odds, unwearied in their constant challenge and mortal danger, are turning the tide of the World War by their prowess and by their devotion."*

"Cheers!" shouted one of the lads, raising a glass.

"Never in the field of human conflict was so much owed by so many to so few. . ."

"He must have been looking at our mess bills!" shouted someone at the back.

Later that week I spent half an hour chasing a Dornier across Kent, amazed at the speed it seemed to be doing – only to find that it was not a Dornier at all, but a fleck of dirt on my screen. I was in a foul mood and almost out of fuel when I got back to base. As I walked into the mess, I saw one of the chaps look at me and then nudge another. They all turned to face me. All except Lenny, who wasn't there.

He'd been jumped by an Me109 over the Thames estuary. He'd managed to haul his Spit back to base, but with a hole the size of a cricket ball in the side of the cockpit. He was unconscious by the time they'd got to him and he had been taken to hospital. He was in a bad way – but he'd live, they said.

It was a couple of days before I could get to see him. Hospitals always give me the shivers and this one was no exception. Sunlight poured through the high windows in diagonal shafts. The glass had been crisscrossed with tape to stop it from splintering in an air raid, and the tape cast crazy shadows on the corridor walls. I could see plum-coloured hollyhocks growing between the sandbags outside.

I asked an Aussie nurse for directions and I eventually found Lenny's room. He was sitting up in bed – reading a book as usual. I knocked and walked in.

"Harry," he said, looking up. "Good of you to come."

"Nonsense," I said. "How are you, old chap?"

"I've been better, I must say. But there are chaps a lot worse off than me." We'd talked about burns before and I knew that's what he meant. We all had a dread of being burnt to death in our aircraft. And maybe even more of a dread of being burnt and surviving.

"Your folks been in?"

"Just missed them, actually. My mother's in a bit of a state. You know what mothers are like."

"I do. I certainly do. Must be tough for them, though."

"Yes it must."

"How about your dad?"

"He never wanted me to go in the RAF in the first place, so it's difficult. He doesn't say much, but I know he thinks it's all my fault."

"I'm sure he doesn't, Lenny."

"So tell me about things. Are they coping without me back at base?

"Oh, just about," I said smiling.

"I hear things have been rather lively."

"I'll say. But look, you don't want to talk about all that, surely. . ."

"No I do, I really do," he said. "You've got no idea how boring it is here. Come on, what's been happening?"

So I gave him the gen on everything that had happened in the last few weeks. It was odd talking about it. I hadn't really had much of a chance to take it all in, but telling Lenny about it brought out what a wild time it had been.

"You know the RAF bombed Berlin again last night," said Lenny.

"Yes, I know. The Germans started it, though." Jerry bombers had hit the City of London on 24 August.

"Look, that had to be an accident, those bombs falling on the City," said Lenny. "If that had been the real target they'd have flattened it. And how many times do you think Hitler is going to put up with us bombing Berlin before he goes off? It's like hitting a hornet's nest with a stick."

"Maybe so," I said. "Maybe so."

Then a nurse popped her head round the door and said I ought to be leaving so Lenny could rest.

"I say," I said when she'd gone. "She's a bit of a stunner."

"Hands off," he said with a grin. "I saw her first."

"You take good care of yourself, my friend," I said, and reached out to shake his hand.

"And you," said Lenny. "Don't get stupid up there."

"I won't. You take care and I'll see you around." And then I left, walking through those long hospital corridors, in and out of the shadows, and into the waiting sunlight. Neither of us had mentioned Lenny's missing leg.

September 1940

It felt like the world was slowing down. I could feel my pulse in my thumb on the stick as it rested next to the red firing button. Tiny wisps of cloud were scudding across the front of my cockpit.

It was magical, like a dream. I didn't feel the harness that strapped me in, or even the cockpit around me. It just felt like I was flying up there, really flying. It was as if I had melted into the Spitfire. As if I had grown wings. I no longer had to think about turning, I just turned as a bird would, swooped as a bird would swoop.

We did our usual dance, the Luftwaffe and ourselves, round and round. Then I saw the Me109 below me, standing out against the mashed-potato clouds, the crippled cross of the swastika standing on its tail. I banked to port and dived down towards it. I could hear nothing but my own breath inside my mask. I could feel my pulse on the trigger.

I willed the German into the gun sight. Just a little more. Just a little more. Don't rush it. Wait. Wait. I could see the pilot in the cage of his cockpit. But he didn't see me.

"This is for Lenny," I said, but not out loud. Only in my head. "This one is for Lenny," I said and I pressed the fire button.

I spoke to Lenny the next day and told him about the 109. I didn't say it was for him, but he somehow seemed to know. Lenny was funny like that. It was as if he knew what I was thinking.

"Don't get sloppy up there, Harry, will you," he said. "Don't start getting sloppy."

"Who me?" I said. "Not a chance."

"You OK, Harry?" he asked.

"Me?" I said. "I'm fine. Well, maybe a little tired."

"Listen," he said, picking up a newspaper. "Have you seen this speech by Hitler? I told you that the Berlin raids would get his goat. Listen to this: '*If the British Air Force drops two or three or four thousand kilograms of bombs, then we will in one night drop 150, 250, 300 or 400 thousand kilograms. When they declare that they will increase their attacks on our cities, then we will raze their cities to the ground. We will stop the handiwork of these night air pirates, so help us God! In England they're filled with curiosity and keep asking, "Why doesn't he come?" Be calm. He's coming. He's coming!*'"

"He's a friendly sort of chap, isn't he?" I said. "What a madman. And mad enough to do it, Lenny," I said.

"Yes, Harry. He is."

On the 7th we busied ourselves on stand-by once again. Some of the chaps dozed, some read books or magazines, some played chess, or dominoes, or cards. Everyone had different ways of staving off the boredom and the nausea.

One of the chaps was reading *Picture Post*. It had a photo of a smiling RAF pilot on it. It was the issue from 31 August and had a heading "The Men Against Goering." The pilot on the cover was already dead.

At about 4.30 we were airborne again. It was a sunny autumn day. The afternoon sun was warming up the colours in the trees. As I climbed, I saw a game of cricket being played down below me on a village green. Someone in the crowd waved.

We assumed that Jerry was heading for our bases or maybe the aircraft factories they'd attacked a few days before. I was climbing to patrol height, the sun lighting up my rear-view mirror, when I saw them.

"What the..." I said out loud. I heard a string of stronger exclamations coming from others in the flight.

It was a vast swarm of hundreds of Heinkels, Dorniers and Me109s, a formation bigger than anything I'd ever seen – bigger than any of us had ever seen.

"London," I muttered to myself. "They're heading for London!" I thought of Edith.

I was still climbing as they dropped the bombs. I could see them tumbling towards the docks. We were too late; too late by half. We were spectators and great bursts of white light lit up the scene.

I flew straight at them and I let go with my guns. You couldn't miss really, there were just so many of them. I fired wildly into the mass. I just kept firing, like I was in some kind of trance. There was something overwhelming about the scale of it, something hypnotic.

I looked in my mirror. The Spit playing tail-end Charlie was weaving about at the back of us, checking for enemy fighters. A shadow passed across the cockpit. I looked up but there was nothing there. I looked back in my mirror. The tail-end Charlie was gone.

Me109s. They must have been up at 25,000 feet. All thoughts of attacking the bombers had to be forgotten. This was just about saving our own necks. There were just too many of them. I swung my Spit round and twisted away from them, turning and dodging for all I was worth. At least two stayed on my tail as I shot over Tower Bridge. I turned my Spit as sharply as I could and shook them off. As I turned back, going east past the dome of St Paul's, I saw it all. It was like hell. It was like looking into the mouth of hell.

Hundreds of bottle-shaped incendiary bombs were tumbling down, turning the docks into an inferno; raining down on to streets and houses. The sky was black with smoke and the horizon red with the glow of the fires. Bomb after bomb after bomb. It was unbelievable.

I saw a warehouse collapse in a ball of flame. I saw a roof explode, spraying tiles and bricks up into the air. Ack-ack positions pounded and flak crackled in the air below us. A barrage balloon blew up to my starboard, and sank away, trailing flames.

"Cowards! Dirty cowards!" I shouted, banging my fist on the side of my cockpit in sheer frustration.

We did our best, but it wasn't nearly good enough. I could see Hurricanes and Spits blasting away at the mass of German aircraft and making no impression at all. We were like sparrows pecking a huge flock of crows. I felt useless.

Another Me109 took after me, but gave up pretty soon. They'd done their job and were getting low on fuel. The Germans were heading back. I managed to let rip at a Heinkel but it carried on regardless. And now I was out of ammo. Bitterly, I returned to base.

The place was frantic; ground crew running about like crazy. I gave my report and got ready for the next battle. Meanwhile my Spit was refuelled and rearmed. There was another wave coming in, as big as the first. It was hard to believe really. I just tried to pull myself together and steel myself to do better next time. In 40 minutes I was back up.

Again, we were too late and still climbing when we met them. Even so, I shared in a Heinkel and did some damage to a Dornier. On another day I would have been proud, but that day it felt puny considering what we were up against. The second wave hit London at about 8.30pm and dropped as many bombs as the first.

And of all those hundreds of German planes, we found out later that we had managed to down just 41. *Forty-one!* And on top of that we'd lost 28 of *our* fighters. But at least we did better than the ack-ack guns. They didn't hit any Germans at all!

The papers said that hundreds of civilians and rescue workers were killed and hundreds more were badly injured. Thank God Edith wasn't one of them. She told me later what a time she'd had of it, though. People brought in with hideous injuries, terrible burns. Women. Children.

Edith had seen Churchill touring Silvertown, one of the worst affected areas. He did a little Chaplin-type thing, twirling his hat on the end of his cane. He shouted, "Are we downhearted?" and the answer from the crowd was very firmly, "No!" Morale was high. It needed to be. The very next day the bombers came back. And they came back again and again and again.

On Sunday morning, 15 September, I sat in a chair dozing after breakfast. There was a slight breeze blowing over the aerodrome and I closed my eyes. I dreamt I was back in the meadow up near Hunter's Hill, standing in the flowing yellow grass, running my hands back and forth across the grass seeds. I was nine, maybe ten.

Behind me I heard the drone of an engine and I looked round. Over the tops of the beech trees came an aircraft, swooping in low. Not a biplane this time, but a Spitfire. It swooped so low that it sent a ripple across the grass. I ran after it, shouting and whooping.

But then I heard another noise behind me. I stopped running and turned, staring into the sun. I squinted upwards and another aircraft burst from the blinding light. A Messerschmitt 109 shot across the field towards the Spit. I shouted, knowing it was futile. I yelled as the 109's canons erupted into life.

The sirens shrieked out and I was already running as I snapped awake. Then, booming out over the speakers: "Squadrons scramble, London angels 20!"

It was another bright, clear day and we chased our shadows across the grass to our planes. As usual I patted my Spitfire on its flank and whispered a few words of encouragement before I climbed into the cockpit.

Still half-asleep, I strapped myself in and got her going, swinging round into the dazzling sun and taking my place in the formation. Then we bumped over the airfield and up into the air, wood pigeons bursting from the trees. The gilt cockerel on the top of a church spire caught the late morning sun.

"Two hundred bandits crossing Dover flying north at angels 20," said the voice on the R/T, but at that moment the War seemed far, far away. I felt as though I was soaring above the whole sorry world. My love of flying seemed to flood back into me.

This time we ignored the instructions coming from the ground and headed in an arc to the west, climbing all the while. Height was the thing and we all knew it. You just didn't stand a chance if you caught them as you were still scrabbling for altitude, because you just didn't have the speed. The other thing was to hit the bombers, not the fighters.

But then there they were, like a flock of crows or a swarm of fat black flies: a big rectangular pack of Heinkels with their escorts of Me110s and 109s. Antiaircraft batteries were booming way below and shells were bursting all around.

This time we were early. This time we climbed above them, flying in the same direction, mirroring their formation. We each looked down at our targets. I shrugged my shoulders and took a deep breath. This one had to count. *This one had to count.*

Then we dived. The 110s screamed out to intercept us but they weren't quick enough. I flew towards the flank of a Heinkel, the rear gunner blasting away wildly. I fired a quick burst. The gunner stopped firing.

A Heinkel exploded to starboard and a piece of wing spun wildly towards me, missing my cockpit by inches. I sent out a burst and a Heinkel slumped out of formation with smoke pouring out of its engines.

RAF fighters buzzed the bombers, firing into the pack. All around me I could see our fighters climbing and diving and German planes falling and burning. We were getting through. We were finally getting through.

Edith told me later how she had stood in a crowd and watched the fight, cheering as German planes fell from the skies into the Thames and into the city they had attempted to destroy. All across London people did the same.

The battered German formation retreated back to France and I flew back to base. Fighter Command had lost over 50 planes. But we'd destroyed a quarter of theirs. If they thought we were going to roll over and die, they were wrong.

I got a letter from Mum and Dad telling me that they'd had a bit of excitement in the village. A German pilot had parachuted in to the field at the back of the churchyard and the local Home Guard had sent for Dad as the German had been a bit knocked about.

When Dad had got there they'd put a road block up and the Home Guard had asked Dad for his ID. Dad said it was ridiculous because he'd known the men who'd asked for it all their lives. In fact he'd helped to deliver one of them as a baby!

The pilot was being held in the church hall. A couple of old-timers had their guns trained on him, the local bobby was there, and the army was on its way.

He had a shrapnel wound on his elbow from the dogfight that brought him down, and a nasty crack on his forehead courtesy of the Home Guard. I told my dad on the telephone that it was typical – I shot them down and he patched them up.

Not that that pilot would be getting back into a Messerschmitt. He would be shipped off to Canada, double-quick, and he was lucky. At least if we came down we were on home soil – that's if we didn't end up in the drink of course!

Dad had been determined to hate him, but found himself thinking of me as he tended the wounds. He said he had been expecting to find some sort of monocled character in jackboots with a sneer on his lips and a scar down his cheek. Instead there was a young chap not much older than me, trying to look brave when in fact he had no idea what was going to happen next.

"Will I be shot?" the pilot had asked my father, apparently. My father told him that of course he wouldn't be shot and cleaned him up the best he could. The pilot thanked him and Dad told him about me being a fighter pilot.

One of the Home Guard told my dad that he shouldn't be telling Germans that sort of thing, but Dad told him not to talk such nonsense. The pilot asked what I flew.

"Spitfire," said Dad.

"Ah yes," said the German. "The famous Spitfire." Dad smiled proudly. "I shot one down only yesterday," said the pilot.

My folks also told me they'd taken in an evacuee. A kid called Peter. Edith asked Mum and Dad if they'd have him as his mum worked at the hospital and was frantic with worry. He'd already been evacuated once and had such a horrible time of it, they'd brought him back.

In fact, most of the kids who'd been evacuated at the beginning of the War were back by the following Christmas. No bombs fell, so they all came home. It made it all the worse when Jerry did start bombing, of course.

I got a chance to drop in on my folks for a day on the 22nd and the first person I saw when I opened the door was this evacuee of theirs. He was a funny-looking tike, thin as a rake with bony legs sticking out of his shorts. He stared at me from under a flop of blond hair.

"Peter, isn't it?" I said. He didn't reply. He just stood there staring at me. Mum came out of the kitchen.

"It's all right Peter," she said. "It's only Harry. Are you going to say hello?" But instead of saying hello, he turned on his heels and ran as fast as his little legs would take him up the stairs.

"He's still very shaken by all this," said Mum.

"It's good of you to take him in, Mum."

"Nonsense," she said. "Anyway, sit yourself down and relax. It's so lovely to see you." She gave me one of her bear-hugs. I swear she could crush an ox. "Your father will be back soon," she called from the kitchen. "And you look tired!"

I was tired, too. I flopped down in the armchair and closed my eyes. Then I realized Peter was standing in the doorway.

"You fly Spitfires, don'tcha?"

"That I do," I said. Peter walked a little closer.

"Shot down many Jerries?" he said.

"A few," I said.

"I'd like to be a Spitfire pilot, I really would."

"It's not as much fun as it probably seems," I said. "So how do you like living in the country?"

"It's great. All the fresh air an' that."

"Your parents must be glad to know you're safe, out of harm's way? With all the bombing I mean."

"Yeah," he said. "They're getting bombed every bleedin' night, they are."

"Not sure my mother would approve of the language, old chap," I said.

"She's a nice lady, your muvver," he said. "Kind an' that."

"She is. You must be missing yours," I said.

"Yeah," he said. "An' me dad, too. 'E says them Jews are in the shelters all day."

"Does he now," I said frowning.

"Yeah," he carried on. "Says they're all cowards an' all this is their fault. 'E says we shouldn't be fightin' Hitler at all, we shouldn't—" And then I just saw red. I suddenly thought of Lenny and what had happened to him fighting for the likes of this boy. It seemed a waste and it made me mad.

"Why you little. . ." I grabbed him by his jumper and pinned him against the wall. He was gasping and clawing at my wrists and his feet were six inches off the ground.

"Stop it! Stop that at once!" yelled my mother coming out from the kitchen. I let go and he dropped to the floor, slumped against the wall and the skirting board. I just stood there. I looked at Mum and I looked down at Peter. They both looked terrified. Terrified of me.

My mother darted forward and pulled the boy away to the other side of the room shielding him from me like I was a rabid dog. Now she looked angry.

"What do you think you're doing?" she shouted. "He's a boy! He's just a boy!"

"You didn't hear him." I muttered. "You didn't hear what he was saying!"

"*He's just a boy!*" she yelled again.

My mother turned her back on me and comforted Peter, who stared out from behind her arm in absolute terror. I turned on my heels and left the room; left the house and the garden, walked up over the back fields to Hunter's Hill.

I sat on the fence that borders the copse. What was happening to me? I looked down at my hands. I felt ashamed of myself. The whole thing with Lenny, the constant tension, the exhaustion – it was getting to me far more than I'd realized.

I looked up. Housemartins hunted for insects around the oaks and beeches. I'd never noticed before how much like fighters they were as they wheeled about together. It looked like a dogfight up there.

Two land girls were walking across the meadow below, talking and giggling. A farmer was feeding his horse in the shade of a huge ash tree. Suddenly Dad was standing next to me.

"Look Dad, I'm sorry about Peter. I was an ass, I'm sorry. But you should have heard what he said. . ."

"I think I can guess," said Dad. "His father is a Fascist, a Mosley supporter. By rights he ought to be in prison. Peter is just parroting his father's prejudices."

"Even so. How can you let him get away with that?"

"Look, do you think I only treat people I like?" said Dad. "There'd be fewer people round here if that was true, I can tell you. We don't get to choose who needs our help."

"I suppose not." I said with a shrug.

"And I've got news for you, son. You're in the same boat."

"How do you mean?" I asked.

"You're fighting for everyone, not just the people you know; not just the people you like. You don't get to choose, either." He grinned at me. "It's a pain isn't it?"

"Yes it is," I said, grinning back.

"And you'll apologize to Peter, won't you?" he said.

"Yes, I suppose so," I said

"Good lad. Shall we head back?"

"I'll follow you down. I just want a few minutes." Dad nodded and walked off down the hill.

My mother was standing in the kitchen washing up some cups and saucers. She didn't look round when I came to the door.

"I'm sorry, Mum," I said.

"So am I, dear," she said. She turned to face me with a weak smile.

"Just a bit tense at the moment," I said. "Things getting me down a bit."

"Then why won't you talk to me about them?"

"You'd only worry," I said.

"I worry anyway," she said. "Talk to me."

So I filled her in about Lenny. She wanted to cry, I could tell, but she stopped herself. When I'd finished she came over and kissed me on the cheek like she used to do when I was a little boy.

"How's Peter?" I asked.

"A little bruised. A little frightened. He'll be all right. But he's not as tough as he'd like to seem. This is hard for him."

"That doesn't give him the right to—"

"No," she said. "It doesn't. He's wrong and we tell him he's wrong. And maybe, just maybe, we can change his mind. I hope so." She paused and adjusted some flowers in a vase on the table. "Or, of course, we could just strangle him and have done with it."

I smiled. "Point taken, Mum," I said. "I'll try not to throttle him again."

"You'll do better than that, young man. You can take him to the pictures."

"But, Mum. . ."

"Never mind 'But, Mum'. *Pinocchio* is on at the Plaza. You know – the new Walt Disney film. Mrs Harris says it's marvellous."

"But, *Mum*. . ."

"Go on," she said, pushing me through the door towards the stairs. "It'll do you good. If you hurry, you'll make the next show."

I shrugged and began to climb the stairs, knowing full well that I was never going to get out of it. I stood in the doorway of the bedroom and Peter lay playing with a toy Spit and a toy Me109. He pretended that he hadn't heard me.

On the floor was a copy of *Picture Post*. The cover showed a mother hugging her young son, both looking terrified. The headline was "THE EAST END AT WAR: *Two of Hitler's enemies*."

"Peter?" I said.

"Yeah?" he said without looking up.

"Look, sport," I said. "Sorry about before, you know. Uncalled for."

Peter carried on playing with his toy planes. I almost walked away. There seemed no way he was going to go anywhere with me. But I owed it to Mum to give it a shot.

"Who's winning?" I said, watching the pretend dogfight.

"The Spit of course," he said without turning round. "Spits are the best."

"Me109s can fly higher."

"Spits can fly faster and turn quicker."

I smiled. "I say, fancy coming to the flicks with me to see *Pinocchio*?"

I'd hardly finished speaking when he was off his bed, barging past me and bounding down the stairs.

"Come on!" he shouted. "Or we'll miss the start!"

We didn't miss the start. When we were going to our seats, a couple of people shook me by the hand and a couple more patted me on the shoulder. Everyone loved the RAF now.

There was a newsreel showing Londoners getting on with it in spite of the bombers. It was pretty corny stuff, but it went down well and there were plenty of cheers at the mention of the "boys of the RAF" and plenty of boos every time the Germans were mentioned. It was like being at a panto.

Well, I have to say Mrs Harris was right for a change. It was pretty first rate, actually. Amazing to think that it was just a lot of drawings we were looking at, although I did think it was all a bit typical that while we were being blasted to Hell and back, the Yanks were making cartoons!

There was this terrific bit where a huge whale called Monstro was chasing Pinocchio and his father. Well, when that whale was bearing down on them, Peter squeezed up against me and peeped over my coat sleeves, grabbing my arm and jumping every time the whale made a move. Mum was right – Peter wasn't half as tough as he made out.

And when Jiminy Cricket sang "When You Wish Upon A Star" I thought the whole cinema was going to burst into tears. I felt a little tearful myself. Embarrassing really. I suppose we all had a lot to wish for.

"Here," I said, the next time I visited Lenny. "I brought you some books. I got them from that old secondhand place near the station. They looked dull so I thought you'd probably like them."

"Thanks," said Lenny. "You didn't have to waste your money on me, you know."

"What else am I going to spend it on?"

"Thought by now you'd be dating one of those WAAFs you're always talking about."

"No," I said. "Not while all this is going on."

"Live for today, old chap," he said. "You don't know what's going to happen." He glanced down at his leg.

"I know," I said. "But I don't want to think about anyone when I'm up there. I don't want to be careful. Being too careful is as bad as being careless. You just have to do what feels right, regardless. Otherwise you get. . . Sorry, Lenny, listen to me going on. . ."

"Don't worry about it. Honestly. I don't want you feeling sorry for me, Harry. I won't have it." I smiled. He smiled back, a little weakly.

"So," I said. "Are they treating you well? Any good-looking nurses?"

"Not bad," he said. "On both counts." Another weak smile. "How are things back at base? Are they managing without me?"

"Just about, just about."

"They're fixing me up with a desk job, you know."

"That's great. A brainbox like you should be running the show, not being a donkey like the rest of us."

"Thanks Harry. I'll be glad of the work. Too much time to think here, if you know what I mean." I nodded and put my hand on his shoulder. He turned away.

"Hey," I said. "We've got a film crew coming to the base – you know, one of those Ministry of Information set-ups."

"That's something I would like to see," laughed Lenny.

"Less of the giggling," I said. "Who knows. When all this is over I just may have a career as a movie star waiting for me."

Then a nurse came in with some food on a tray.

"Visiting time's over, I'm afraid." I got up.

"Sorry. I'll leave you to it, then," I said.

"What do you think, Nurse," said Lenny. "Can you see him in the movies?" She looked me up and down as she was leaving.

"Comedies maybe," she said, and disappeared through the door.

I rang Edith when I got back. She was having a pretty rough time of it, by all accounts. She sounded older.

She asked me how Lenny was – Mum and Dad had told her about him in their last letter. I said I had taken some books in for him. She asked what they were and I said the only one I could remember was *Moby Dick* because it had a picture of a whale on it. I suppose I had whales on the brain after *Pinocchio*.

"Oh no!" she said. "You idiot!"

"What do you mean?" I asked, a bit taken aback.

"*Moby Dick*, you twit! Captain Ahab! Captain Ahab!"

"Sorry, sis. What are you talking about?" She sighed a very big sigh.

"You don't have a clue, do you? Don't you ever read a book? Captain Ahab in *Moby Dick* only has one leg, you chump. The other is bitten off by a whale!"

"Oh no," I said. "What am I going to do? I... I... Oh no, Edith. What an idiot!"

But when I spoke to Lenny on the phone he could hardly stop laughing. He said it had cheered him up no end. He said only I could have done something *that* stupid.

"Glad to have been of service," I said. And he collapsed into laughter all over again.

October 1940

The film crew arrived on 5 October. It was a lark at first. All the attention was pretty head-swelling, I have to admit. We were like a bunch of school kids, clowning about. The director got rather cross actually and the CO came and tore a strip off us.

Well, all thoughts of Hollywood soon went out of my head. It was tedious in the extreme. The whole process was painfully slow. If this is what movie stars go through every day, then they can keep it, they really can.

The chaps from the film crew briefed us about what they were going to do and what they wanted us to do. It was all incredibly simple, but they still felt the need to tell us over and over again as if we were idiots or something.

They spent an age rearranging furniture and waiting for the light to be just right and so forth. One chap pointed out that he usually played a few hands of pontoon with some of the others, but the director said that chess would give a better impression.

All this nonsense was bad enough, but the filming itself was even worse. No sooner had the director yelled "Action!" than he yelled "Cut!" One minute he didn't like the way someone was standing, the next he didn't like the chair someone was sitting in.

One of the chaps had to pretend to be asleep until he heard the siren and then jump up and dash for his Spit. The director made the poor fellow do it over and over again. First he said he didn't look asleep. He said he looked like he was pretending.

"I am pretending!" the pilot said.

Then the director said he didn't look startled enough. Then he didn't like the way he ran. Eventually the chap snapped, and when he had been asked to do it for the umpteenth time, he jumped up from his bunk and yelled, "I hope you're not going to ask me to do it again when I ditch into the Channel!"

Then it was my go. In the next scene we had to sit around playing chess and whatever and then when he gave us the shout of "Go!" we had to run like crazy for our aircraft. I was right in front, looking very thoughtful, holding a knight, just ready to move.

"Go!" he shouted, and off we went.

"No, no, no!" he shouted, and brought us all back. He had his head in his hands and was groaning.

"Some of you are grinning. This is serious. This is for morale. This is for your folks back home. Now, let's do it properly, shall we?" We all shuffled back to our positions. "And . . . action!"

I picked up my knight again and tried to look even more thoughtful than before. Then the siren went off. We jumped up. I knocked the chess table over with my knee. Papers were thrown down, pipes dropped, half-finished cups of tea left on the ground.

"No, no, no!" the director shouted, apparently. He thought we were too over-the-top this time. In fact he was so busy trying to call us back that he missed filming us taking off. This was a real scramble.

When we got back, the crews met us and set to work on patching up the aircraft. I had a jagged hole in the port wing, and the airmen looked cross with me as usual, for giving them even more work to do. The film crew were still there. The director ran over to me as we walked away from the plane.

"I know this is going to seem a liberty, but we have to get back to the footage we were shooting. The light's changing all the time. . ."

"You're persistent, I'll say that for you," I said.

"Look, I've got my job to do, just like you. It may not be quite so glamorous. . ."

"Glamorous," I said. "Is that what it is?"

"Yes," he said, "As a matter of fact, I think it is."

"Not long ago this place was being bombed. I wonder how glamorous you'd have found that?"

"Listen, sonny," he said, walking a little closer. "I'm based in London. You may have heard on the wireless that we've had a few bombs of our own. I take it you've heard of the Blitz?"

I came very close to thumping him there and then.

"I'm sorry," I said, "but I have work to do. I have a Combat Report to file. . ."

"My job is important too, you know, whatever you may think," he said. "We might not get the credit, like you chaps, but we can't all be Spitfire pilots, now can we? Now, I have your CO's assurance that you will give me every assistance. And that's an order, by the way."

"OK," I said with a shrug, walking back to where the other chaps were milling about. "What do you want?"

"OK then," he said. "I need you to do the chess scene again. Where's the blond-haired chap you were playing?"

"I'm sorry, but he can't join us, I'm afraid," I said.

"Can't," said the director with a sneer. "Can't or won't?"

"Can't. He bought it half an hour ago."

"Bought it? Oh, you mean. . ." He looked at the other pilots who were sharing a joke as they walked to debriefing. Then he looked back at me.

"Now," I said. "If you'll excuse me. I have that Combat Report to get in."

I was chatting to one of the WAAFs from the Ops Room at the entrance to the base. I'd seen her a few times, but we'd never spoken. Her name was Harriet. "Definitely *not* Hattie," she said. I liked her. I liked her a lot. Despite the fact that she'd nearly run me over on her way in. . .

She had green eyes. I'd never met anyone with green eyes before. I couldn't stop looking at them. I was trying to think of some way of asking her out, but somehow I never managed to get round to the right set of words.

Just then a Hurricane flew low over the base. It banked round and came in to land, but it was wobbling around all over the place.

"He's not going to make it," I said. The Hurricane shot over us at tree height, over the perimeter fence and into the field beyond.

"Hop in," said Harriet. "Let's go and see if he's OK."

I jumped in and she drove like the clappers in the direction we'd seen the Hurricane come down. She'd have made a decent pilot, I reckon. By the time we arrived at the scene, the locals were already there.

The Hurricane had taken a few branches off a willow and pancaked into a field, coming to a halt next to a hump-backed barn. The pilot seemed to be OK, but I could hear him shouting and something didn't feel quite right.

"I think it might be better if you stayed here, just for the minute," I said. I got out of the car and trotted over. A Home Guard with pebble glasses swung round and pointed his peashooter at me. He looked about a hundred years old.

"Woah, tiger," I said, putting my hands up and smiling at him. "I'm on your side!"

He scowled and looked a little disappointed not to be able to shoot me. But he turned away to point his rifle at the pilot who was climbing out of the cockpit and shouting a stream of what were obviously swear words.

When he finally became aware of the crowd around the plane, pointing rifles and pitchforks at him, he smiled. But when no smiles came back he scowled angrily and began to climb down from his plane. He tried to brush a pitchfork away as he walked forward but the farmhand holding it shoved it towards him.

"Stay right where you are, Fritz!" yelled another of the Home Guard.

"Fritz?" yelled the pilot angrily. "You call me German?"

He was going to get shot for sure, so I pushed my way to the front.

"He's not German! Can't you recognize a Hurricane when you see one?"

"How do we know it's not a trick?" shouted one of the farmhands. "You hear about stuff like that."

"He's not English!" yelled another. "How come a Jerry's flyin' a Hurricane?"

"He's Polish, you idiot! He's on our side!"

"Don't you call me an idiot!"

"Useless Poles!" said the farmhand nearest to me. "If it wasn't for them, we wouldn't be in this mess."

"How do you work that out?" I said.

"If those cowards had stood up for themselves, none of this would have started." The Polish pilot lurched forward and it took all my strength to stop him from grabbing the farmhand. "You call me coward, you English pig? I kill you with my bare hands! I kill you with bare hands!" As he lurched forward, pitchforks were levelled and rifles aimed.

"OK, OK!" I yelled. "Let's all calm down, shall we?"

"He threatened to kill me," said the farmhand. "You 'eard 'im, Bill, didn't you? Little so-and-so wanted to murder me."

"No, he didn't," I said, turning to the pilot and making a "let's just humour them and get out of here" kind of face. He spat out another stream of Polish.

"What's he saying? What's he saying? Speaka the English, mate!"

"I said you are ignorant son-of-a-dwarf and I will be happy to teach you some manners."

"Oh brother," I sighed.

The farmhand grabbed a pitchfork from a man nearby and very nearly harpooned us both with it. He was coming in for another go when a gun went off and everyone turned round. It was the old Home Guard chap I'd passed on the way in.

"Let's save it for the Germans, eh boys?" he said.

Everyone held their ground for a few minutes and then they all stepped back a little. The farmhand stuck his pitchfork in the ground and stared off into the distance.

"Having fun, boys?" said Harriet, sauntering over from the car. "Anyone for a lift?"

The Polish pilot smiled. "I would be delighted," he said.

After he had been debriefed and he phoned his base to tell them he was safe, the Polish pilot joined me in the mess. I bought him a drink and we sat down in the corner away from the rest of the lads.

"Gorka," he said, shaking my hand. "Waldemar Gorka."

"Harry Woods," I said. I asked him how he came to be flying a Hurricane so far from home. He looked down at the table, as if he was talking to his glass. He took a deep breath.

"I join flying club at university and learn to fly," he said. "Then I join Polish Air Force. Then I think, 'This is fantastic. This is my life now!'" I nodded and smiled again, but his expression turned grim as he went on. "Then Germans come. Russians come. We do our best, but it is not good enough.

"At end of September I get out. I say goodbye to mother, to father, to my little brother. I want to stay and fight, but father say that there is no use. I would be killed for sure. He is right. I kiss them goodbye. My mother kisses me here –" he pointed to his forehead – "and says she will pray for me. She makes sign of cross and I go.

"I fly my plane to Romania. Romanians are friends but Germans already there. Gestapo already rounding up Jews. Romanians arrest us but guards let us go. I get to Italy, then France and then England. Tell them I am flyer. They train me on Hurricanes. They make me pilot. So here I am."

"And your parents? Your brother?"

"Dead. All dead," he said, taking another drink. I didn't know what to say.

"I'm sorry," I said finally. "It makes me feel even worse about what happened back there with the farm lad. What with you fighting for England after everything that's happened to you."

"I don't fight for England," he said with a wave of his hand. "I fight for *Poland*! I fight in RAF only because English give me plane, give me bullets. Bullets to kill Germans. To kill them like they kill my people." He was wild-eyed now and leaned closer to me to whisper in my face. "Know what I think when they bomb London?" I shook my head. "I think 'Good! Let them see what war is like!' " I looked away. He calmed a little. "How about you? What you fight for, English? King and Country?"

I shook my head. "Someone else asked me that a long time ago," I said smiling. "Then I said I was fighting for my family. Down here, I'd still stay the same thing . . . but up there, I'm not thinking of anyone but me. Up there I'm just fighting for my life, nothing more than that."

He nodded. "Look, English, I sorry if I don't talk like you gentlemen of RAF. I am Polish. Understand?" I smiled weakly and nodded my head, although I didn't really understand at all. How could I?

"Don't apologize for farmer. He think I am German. He want to kill me because I am German. If German pilot lands near me I shoot him dead, and they do the same to me. This I understand." He drained his drink and asked for another. "I hear about German pilot they shot down. He picked up by Home Guard. They take him to pub and buy him drink before taking him in! They buy him drink!"

I laughed. I hadn't the heart to tell him we'd had a German pilot in the mess only the week before when he'd baled out near the base. "We are a funny lot, I suppose," I said. But he didn't laugh.

"Look, war is not cricket match. I hear English pilot talk about dogfight being like – how do you call. . .?" He made a fencing motion in the air.

"Like a fencing match? Like a duel?"

"A duel, yes," he said. Then he banged his fist on the counter. "It is *not* like duel. It is like knife fight in back alley. You dodge your enemy, you avoid his attack, you see your chance, you stick him in guts and run. In. Out. Is it not true?"

"Well," I said, laughing. "I've heard it described more poetically, but you're right, people do talk a lot of rot about jousting and the like. It never feels like that to me. Mostly it's just staying alive."

"And shooting down Germans," he added.

"And shooting down Germans," I agreed, but I couldn't quite compete with his thirst for German blood.

I liked him, though. Admired him too, I suppose. He was a tough nut, that's for sure. For all my months of experience, I felt a kid again next to him.

"Look, I make you a deal," he said. "I fight for you freedom. I fight to keep England free – free for the cricket – free from German dogs. Then we free Poland. No Germans, no Russians – we kick them all out, OK? We free my country. We drink to Poland!"

"To Poland," I said. "To freedom."

"To freedom!"

I arranged to meet and talk to Lenny about the desk job he'd been given. We met up in St James Park in London. He was already there when I arrived and I saw him standing, looking off towards Whitehall. He was wearing his new leg. If you didn't know, you'd never have guessed. Only I *did* know.

"I've brought some of the gang with me, if that's all right?" Lenny turned round, startled slightly from his thoughts, and then his face mellowed and finally cracked into a grin as they all walked up behind me.

"Good grief!" he said. "You're all still alive! Those Germans must be getting slow."

They all came in to ruffle his hair and punch his shoulder. One of the chaps jostled him a little too roughly, and for one awful moment it looked like he was going to fall over. Everyone went quiet as Lenny managed to stay upright.

"Not as steady on my pins as I used to be," said Lenny with a grin.

"So, Lenny," said one of the chaps. "How did you get on with those nurses, then? We all know what nurses are like."

"Hey – watch your mouth," I said, laughing. "My sister's a nurse."

"Whoops! Sorry, Woody. Don't happen to have her number do you?" I thumped him in the shoulder.

"Ow! That hurt, you oaf! That's my bowling arm, too."

"You can't bowl to save your life," said Lenny.

"True. True. So anyway how are you, you old misery?"

"Missing you all dreadfully, of course," he said with a sarcastic raise of one eyebrow.

"Of course. Goes without saying, old chap."

And then we were off. We were more like a group of students than a group of seasoned fighters. The sun shone and golden leaves occasionally fluttered down. As I looked across at them smiling and joking, we all seemed young again.

We stayed quite a long time. I think we were all reluctant to be the first to talk about leaving. Someone produced a hip flask of whisky – something he'd bought on the black market – and tiny glasses were pulled from jacket pockets, with spares for Lenny and me. We waited for a policeman to walk past and then we poured a tot into each glass.

"Absent friends!" said somebody. We raised our glasses and clinked them together.

"Absent friends!" I drank a mouthful and spat it out. Everyone did the same. It was vile!

It really was time to move off then. Lenny shook everyone's hand and he looked almost like his old self. I told him to take care of himself and he told me to do the same. Then, as each man left, he absent-mindedly patted Lenny on the shoulder, just as they used to.

The immediate threat of invasion was gone now, but things were scarcely any easier. We had made the Germans think twice about daylight bombing raids, but that didn't stop them bombing London every night.

At the end of October, we were patrolling along the Thames estuary when I flew over London from the east. It was quite a sight. All across the city there were bombed-out buildings, roofless, with black and hollow windows and walls all scorched and pock marked. Piles of rubble filled the streets.

We were heading back when the Messerschmitts jumped us. They tore down like hawks, scattering us. It was mayhem. The Spit to starboard crumpled in on itself and went down in flames.

They seemed to be everywhere but no matter what I did I couldn't get a clear view of them. That same feeling of frustration, of helplessness. The same feeling of wanting to puke that I'd had since my first patrol.

I told myself to be calm. "Come on, come on," I said, "get on with it. You've done this a hundred times before," as if saying it would make it all right. As if anyone could ever get *used* to this.

It was like standing on a cliff with just your heels touching, leaning out, fear holding you back, Death pulling you on – and we looked over that cliff every day. Every day. Maybe it was only luck that saved you from falling. And maybe my luck was running out.

Suddenly there was a bomber right in front of me. "Pull up! Pull up, you idiot!" I yelled, and my hands obeyed, yanking back on the stick in the nick of time. "Idiot. Idiot," I muttered to myself. "Get a grip!"

Then a dull thud and bump. I was hit. And I never even saw the plane that hit me. I just felt a jolt – and then two more – then a teeth-clenching pain seared through my right leg. I could see daylight through the floor of the cockpit. I could feel cold air rushing past me.

I decided to make a dash for base, but the plane wouldn't respond. The R/T was dead and whistled in my ear. I was losing altitude rapidly and I now could smell burning. Glycol fumes were leaking into the cockpit.

"No, no, please, please. . ." Panic shot through me as I realized the fuel tank might be about to blow. "Please, please. . ."

Then a voice said, "Bale out!" and then again – "Bale out!" But I just sat there staring at the control panel and at the flames that had begun to appear behind it. "Bale out!" a voice screamed in my ear. *My* voice.

This time I took notice. I slid back the cockpit cover, relieved – very relieved – that it slid back so easily, and then I undid my harness and climbed out, remembering at the last second to disengage my oxygen and radio.

I was out, free of my aircraft, tumbling wildly in the air – there was the sky, there was my plane arcing away on a streamer of black smoke, there was the sky again, there was my plane crashing into the sea. I pulled the ripcord.

I was jerked back by the parachute as air punched into it, opening it up to mushroom above me. I swung there like a puppet, winded and gasping for breath. I looked down at my leg. It felt like a bear was gnawing on it but it was still in one piece. For now anyway.

Dogfights growled on above me as I drifted down. As I spun gently, dizzyingly, back and forth, I caught glimpses of the English coast, then the French, then England again. I could hear sirens wailing in the distance, the boom and thud of anti-aircraft fire. I could see the cliffs and the downland beyond. And I could see the huge empty expanse of cold grey water towards which I was heading.

Then I heard it – right behind me. A weird noise droning and roaring and screaming behind me. An Me109 diving towards me with guns blazing, twinkling like stars, clattering like hail on a tin roof.

There was nothing I could do. Nowhere I could go. Shells whistled past me on either side. A kind of weird calm came over me. I thought of Mum and Dad, and Edith, and Lenny. I thought about Waldemar and my lovely green-eyed WAAF. All in those seconds. I just thought, OK then. If this is it, OK. Maybe my turn had finally come.

But then the Messerschmitt shuddered and twitched and banked away.

The pilot had no chance. I saw flames light up the cockpit like a lantern and it spun round out of control. Then there was an explosion and it broke up into a dozen pieces, falling like meteors against the cliffs.

I had hardly taken this in before I realized I had to get my parachute off and fast. I had to release it just before I hit the sea otherwise it would drag me under. I gave the release mechanism a ninety-degree twist and then a hefty thump. Nothing happened.

And then smack – I hit the water. The calmness I'd felt in the face of being shot had left me completely now as I struggled to save myself from drowning. I wasn't going to die a sailor's death – not if I could help it. I hit and tugged and swore and finally the chute came loose and drifted away like a huge jellyfish.

All I had to do now was inflate my lifejacket and hope that someone saw me land and was coming to pick me up. The water was freezing. I could feel my legs going numb and it felt good because it meant I didn't feel the pain any more.

I looked up and the blue sky was scribbled all over with chalk-white vapour trails. In the distance I could hear the hum and buzz of engines, the rattle of gunfire. Again, it occurred to me that this was it for me, that I had swapped the sudden death the Messerschmitt offered, for the far worse fate of slowly freezing in the October sea.

Suddenly, an Me109 tore out of the east, diagonally downwards, belching black smoke. It spluttered and whined and drifted inland to crash out of sight. Then I realized that the pilot had baled out. And he was heading my way. . .

The Jerry pilot landed about a hundred yards away from me and made a much better job of getting out of his parachute. He bobbed in and out of view behind the grey waves, and he seemed to be drifting towards me.

I didn't know what to do at first. I could hardly carry on ignoring him, as we were the only things out here but haddock. And anyway, maybe we were both going to die here. Maybe he was going to be the last person I saw in my life.

"Hello!" I shouted, immediately feeling a little foolish.

"Hello!" he shouted back. "Are you hurt?"

"A little, yes!" I shouted. "How about you?"

"A little, also! You are Spitfire?"

"Yes. And you? You're a 109 pilot?"

"Yes. The Spitfire is good plane?"

"It is. The 109's pretty good, though."

"Pretty good. Yes."

The cold had numbed the pain in my leg, but I knew that if we stayed here much longer, the cold would numb the rest of me too and I'd be a goner. Suddenly, being hit by the Messerschmitt's guns seemed appealingly fast and final.

"It is cold, is it not?" said the German, as if he read my thoughts.

"Yes. Very," I said.

"Are we to die then, Englishman?"

"No!" I shouted.

"Good," he shouted back. "I am not ready to die."

"Who is?" I shouted.

Then I heard the drone of an engine over my shoulder. I turned to see a fishing boat heading for us. I whooped and shouted and waved and shouted and so did the German.

"Over here! Over here!" I yelled. The boat came in close and they hauled me up and on to the deck.

"You'd better get out of those wet things or you'll catch your death," said one of the crew, tossing me a blanket. "How's that wound?" The trouser leg was chewed up and bloody.

"OK, I think," I said, struggling to get out of my flying suit. But out of the water, it started to hurt like hell again.

"Let's go get your friend, there," said the skipper. The boat pulled up alongside the German pilot.

"*Danke, danke!*" he shouted as they reached for him.

"He's German!" yelled one of them.

"I'm not having any Jerry in my boat," said the skipper. "The fish can have 'im if they want 'im. Let 'im drown!"

The boat started to turn for shore, with the German flailing and yelling.

"No!" I shouted, surprising myself, and everyone else, with the violence in my voice. "Pick him up!"

They all turned to face me.

"And why the hell should I? Murdering swine that they are. A minute ago 'e was trying to kill you!"

"I know," I said. "I know that. But we can't just let him drown. We have to be different. If we're going to be as bad as the Nazis then what's the point? If we leave him there, then *what are we fighting for*? If we're just the same as them, then what are we fighting for?"

They all looked at me. A flag fluttered at the top of the mast and the boat creaked and groaned in the swell. The German's cries for help grew fainter.

"OK," said the skipper with a sigh. "Fish 'im out."

The boat turned again and they hauled the German out, though with a lot less care than they had with me. Even so, the crewman who had thrown me a blanket did the same with the German and he duly stripped and wrapped himself up, wincing at some injury to his side.

Someone appeared with a mug of tea and a shot of brandy. We both sat there in silence as the engine chugged and gulls hung in the breeze around us, crying like children. My leg throbbed and I didn't dare look for fear of what I'd see.

"Blasted Nazis," said one of the crew.

"I am not a Nazi," said the pilot. "I am just a German. I love my country."

"Then why didn't you stay there, you swine?" shouted another man. The German looked away, down at the deck, but the man leaned closer and continued. "Look at all this," he said with a wild wave of his hand that took in me, the dogfight above and the whole splintered and bloody world. "Look at it! Don't tell me you love your country, or so help me I'll throw you back in!"

The skipper came over and pulled him away.

"You'll have to forgive us," he said to the German. "We haven't forgotten what it was like picking soldiers off the beach at Dunkirk, with you cowards trying to kill us all for doing it. Most likely we'll never forget it. I don't think I'll ever get the smell of that beach out of this boat."

"I am sorry," said the German.

"Shut up," said the skipper coldly, "Or I'll throw you back in myself."

They left us alone. I could think of nothing to say and so I kept quiet. The German looked away from me and out to sea.

"I flew raids at Dunkirk," he said suddenly. "We fighters gave protection to the Heinkels bombing the beaches and the waiting ships. On 1 June it was different. We flew in low, guns blasting."

It was 1 June when I had shot down the 110. It was odd to think we were all there that day – these fishermen, the German and me.

"As you came in you could see the men below, the lines of men, run for their lives, running for the cover of the dunes. I saw a man turn, and freeze, like a rabbit. As he turned I saw the light glint on his spectacles. Can you believe that? I was so low I saw that, and I saw the shells bursting in the sand in a line towards him.

"The men, they ran for the dunes. But if they stayed in the dunes they could not get off the beach and so they had to come back to their lines and queue for the boats and ships offshore. They came back and so did we. Black smoke rose up everywhere, from burning ships and bombed-out buildings.

"We would fly through these columns of smoke, down towards the men, firing our guns into them." He shook his head. "That was no job for a Luftwaffe pilot. There was no honour in that."

I looked at him but he stayed turned away. In the end I turned away too. I felt like he wanted me to say something, to say it was OK. But I couldn't – no one could. As for honour; was there honour in any of this? And what would I have done in his place? I just didn't know any more.

A kittiwake flew alongside me, only a couple of yards away, its face level with mine. It turned and seemed to look straight at me, its head cocked to one side slightly. Its black eyes glinted and then it banked away from me and glided clear of the boat and out of sight.

I looked back towards the German. At first I thought he was just hanging his head and looking at the deck, but then I realized he was slumped forward. I got up and caught him as he fell and sat him up again. I put my arm around him.

A pool of deep red blood was sinking into the wooden decking below him and the pale grey blanket was soaked with it. His pale hands were cold. I whispered to him. I asked him his name, but there was no reply. He was dead.

He was dead and suddenly I wanted to know his name. Suddenly I had the weirdest feeling that I had more in common with this man than with anyone else I knew. His head rested against my shoulder and I put my arm around him to stop him falling.

And then, in the midst of those staring fishermen, I did something I had never done in the whole course of the war. I began to cry. . .

Epilogue
1941

Anyway, my leg was patched up. They pulled a few pieces of shrapnel out and stitched me up, good as new – or almost, anyway – and before I knew it I was back in the cockpit. I ended up with this rather good scar in my calf shaped like the letter "m" or the way little kids draw birds.

Then one day in April '41, I was lying on my bunk reading a book Lenny had sent me. One of the orderlies came in and gave me a package that had arrived from my folks. I used a letter from Harriet to keep my place, closed the book and opened it up.

There was a copy of a pamphlet the Government had brought out. The cover showed vapour trails against a darkening sky and the words *The Battle of Britain*. Underneath that, across the black silhouette of a building, was written: *August–October 1940*.

The Air Ministry had published it, so it was full of stuff about RAF tactics, with diagrams and the like, and maps covered in arrows. There was a photo of laughing pilots walking across a sunlit aerodrome, hair and scarves blowing in the breeze. I wondered how many of them were still alive.

The pamphlet made it all seem much less of a shambles than it felt at the time. The dawn scrambles and the rabid dogfights had all been smartened up and dusted down. There were little drawings of planes with dotted lines coming from their guns and others with smoke trailing out. It all looked so clean and simple. No blood or pain or burning. No screaming. I couldn't read it then and haven't since.

Mum and Dad wrote and said they were so proud of me. They said I was part of history now. I wrote back and told him so were they. So was Edith. So was Lenny. Harriet. We all were.

But there was truth in it. We had made a difference, we "Few" – I had to admit it. We hadn't beaten the Nazis, but we'd shown they couldn't get everything their own way. We'd given the bully a black eye and winded him a little. And maybe there was honour in that after all. Yes, I think that maybe there was.

Historical note

Officially, the Battle of Britain was fought between 8 August and 30 October 1940 and was the first time that aircraft had played such a decisive role in the War. As well as ensuring that Britain remained free of German control, and free of Nazi deportations to concentration camps, the battle proved to be a major turning point in the War. It helped to convince the Americans to enter the War on the side of the Allies. British resistance also meant that there would be a base from which to bomb German forces (and civilians) and eventually launch an allied invasion of Europe in June 1944.

From the outset, the Germans knew that if they were to invade Britain successfully, they would have to put the RAF out of action first. The German air force (Luftwaffe) began to attack British shipping convoys in the Channel, to disrupt trade, to stop supplies reaching British shores from other countries, and to lure Spitfires and Hurricanes into dogfights over the sea.

During the Battle of Britain, RAF Fighter Command was led by Air Vice-Marshal Sir Hugh Dowding. It was divided into four Groups: 10 Group covered the West Country, 11 Group covered the South East, 12 Group covered the area roughly from London to York, and 13 Group covered the remaining North of England, Scotland and Northern Ireland.

11 Group was commanded by Air Vice-Marshal Keith Park from its HQ in Uxbridge, and was divided into sectors, each with its own Sector Station – Biggin Hill in Kent being perhaps the most famous. As it was closest to German Occupied France, 11 Group was the first line of defence during the Battle of Britain and squadrons in this Group were reinforced from squadrons in other groups to keep them up to full strength. Although Harry Woods is fictional, it is a squadron in 11 Group in which he is seen to serve.

The odds were in favour of a German victory at the beginning of the Battle of Britain. The Luftwaffe were well equipped and had well-trained, battle-hardened pilots and crews and the RAF had experienced heavy losses in France and Norway and during the Dunkirk evacuation. At the end of June it had less than 400 Spitfires and Hurricanes for the defence of the whole country. But Britain did have one secret weapon.

Radar, or Radio Direction Finding (RDF) as it was known, was first developed in 1935. It used shortwave radio pulses to pick up incoming aircraft. The radio pulses bounced back and were captured by a cathode ray tube, showing up as blips of light on a glass screen. By 1939 there were a string of radar stations along the coast from Shetland to the south coast of England.

Information gathered by radar stations (and from members of the Observer Corps dotted around the coast) was relayed by landline to the Filter Room at Fighter Command HQ at Bentley Priory in Stanmore near London. The aircraft were plotted on a large map table and then the information was relayed to the Group Headquarters and then to Sector Stations (airfields). Group commanders decided which Sector Stations to activate. Sector Station commanders decided which squadrons should fly.

Radar had its problems though. Radar picked up all sorts of things – clouds, flocks of birds etc – as well as planes. Height readings were very inaccurate and although it might only take four minutes to warn the squadrons, it only took six minutes for German planes to cross the Channel. Luckily for the RAF, Messerschmitts were at the limit of their range by the time they got to England and Me109s had hardly any fuel in their tanks for dogfights over southern England and could barely reach London.

Radar was a secret and there was a lot of speculation in the country about what the radar stations with their huge masts and antenna were for. The WAAFs, like Harriet in this story, who worked in the airfield Ops rooms, were sworn to secrecy and pilots like Harry would not need to be told. The Germans knew we had it, but failed to put it out of action during their attacks on 12 August.

Germans also failed to follow through on their attacks on RAF airfields. Too often they targeted the smaller satellite airfields rather than the important sector airfields. Even so, they did kill many pilots and ground crew and destroyed valuable aircraft. Though it was terrible for the people of London, it was a let off for the RAF when Hitler changed tactics and started bombing cities instead.

Civilian losses became heavier and heavier as the Luftwaffe's bombs rained down. Over 13,000 Londoners had been killed by the end of 1940 and another 18,000 hospitalized. Thousands more were killed in other cities across the country. Despite this, most people learned to cope with the bombing, and many were eventually able to sleep through it!

Pilot losses were horrendous during the Battle of Britain; at the end of August 1940, RAF pilot losses were approaching 120 men a week. Replacing pilots was an even bigger problem than replacing aircraft, as operational training time was shortened and shortened, with many pilots entering combat never having fired their guns before. Many only flew one fatal sortie.

More than 80% of the 3,080 aircrew listed were British, but those that were not had often volunteered, making their way to Britain at their own cost and often at great personal risk, often escaping from the advancing German army. Six of the twelve top-scoring Fighter Command pilots were from countries other than Britain.

Most Polish pilots, like the fictional Waldemar in this story, were more highly trained than their British counterparts, but as they rarely spoke fluent English, they had British squadron and flight commanders allocated to their squadrons.

Although the Polish squadrons did not become operational until August 1940, they accounted for 7.5% of all the aircraft shot down by the RAF, and the Polish 303 Squadron had the highest score rate in Fighter Command.

Nationality of aircrew involved in the Battle of Britain:

British	2,543	(418 killed)
Polish	147	(30 killed)
New Zealand	101	(14 killed)
Canadian	94	(20 killed)
Czech	87	(8 killed)
Belgian	29	(6 killed)
South African	22	(14 killed)
Free French	14	(0 killed)
Irish	10	(0 killed)
United States	7	(1 killed)
S Rhodesian	2	(0 killed)
Jamaican	1	(0 killed)
Palestinian	1	(0 killed)
Total	**3,080**	**(520 killed)**

The Home Guard

There was a constant threat and fear of invasion in 1940 and the government made a radio appeal in May for any men not already conscripted (because they were too old, for instance) to form platoons of Local Defence Volunteers. Renamed the Home Guard by Churchill, one million men had joined by August – far more than expected. The government could not afford to arm them all and so they made do with whatever they could lay their hands on.

Timeline

30 July 1936 RAF Volunteer Reserve (RAFVR) is formed.

13 March 1938 Germany, led by Chancellor Adolf Hitler, annexes Austria.

June 1938 Spitfires first enter service with 19 Squadron, RAF Duxford in Cambridgeshire.

15 March 1939 Germans invade Czechoslovakia.

23 March 1939 Britain and France declare they will defend Belgium, Holland and Switzerland from German attack.

6 April 1939 Britain, France and Poland sign mutual assistance pact.

28 June 1939 Women's Auxilliary Air Force (WAAF) is formed.

1 September 1939 Germans invade Poland. RAF Reserve & RAFVR called up for active service.

2 September 1939 RAF deployed in France.

3 September 1939 Britain declares war on Germany after it refuses to withdraw troops from Poland.

27 September 1939 Warsaw surrenders.

12 October 1939 British troops sent to France as British Expeditionary Force (BEF).

1 January 1940 Two million British 19-27 year olds are conscripted into the Armed Forces.

9 April 1940 Germans launch full-scale invasion of Norway.

10 May 1940 Germans attack France, Belgium, Holland and Luxemburg. Chamberlain government falls and he is succeeded as British PM by Winston Churchill, who appoints Lord Beaverbrook as Minister of Aircraft Production.

15 May 1940 Germans break through the French line.

25 May 1940 British Foreign Secretary, Anthony Eden, authorizes the withdrawal of the BEF to Dunkirk.

31 May 1940 RAF provide air cover for the evacuation of Dunkirk.

4 June 1940 Operation Dynamo completes the evacuation of 338,000 British and allied troops from Dunkirk.

18 June 1940 Churchill famously states: *"The Battle of France is over. I expect the Battle of Britain is about to begin."*

22 June 1940 France surrenders to the Germans.

7 July 1940 Hitler issues a directive for the "War against England".

10 July 1940 Beaverbrook calls on British housewives

to donate anything aluminium for use in aircraft manufacture. British pilot operational training cut from six months to four weeks.

16 July 1940 Hitler orders "Operation Sealion", his plan for the invasion of Britain by a surprise landing of troops on the south coast.

19 July 1940 Hitler offers peace to Britain but Britain rejects his terms.

1 August 1940 Hitler orders the Luftwaffe to overpower the RAF "in the shortest possible time".

2 August 1940 Commander-in-Chief of the Luftwaffe, Hermann

Goering, orders Adlertag (Day of the Eagles) – a plan to destroy British air power and open the way for invasion.

12 August 1940 German raids against radar stations on the south coast.

13 August 1940 Adlertag begins in poor weather – the German date for the start of the battle.

15 August 1940 British radar stations attacked again.

17 August 1940 British pilot operational training cut again – from four to two weeks. **18 August 1940** German attacks on RAF fighter airfields.

20 August 1940 Churchill makes his *"Never in the field of human conflict"* speech to Parliament.

24/25 August 1940 German bombs fall on Slough, Richmond Park, Dulwich and the City.

25/26 August 1940 nighttime raid on Berlin by Bomber Command in retaliation for bombing of the City.

28/29 August 1940 Germans bomb London suburbs.

29 August 1940 British air raid on Berlin.

30 August 1940 RAF bases bombed.

31 August 1940 Hitler postpones "Operation Sealion".

1 September 1940 RAF bases bombed.

5 September 1940 Hitler switches bombing campaign to towns and cities, including London.

7 September 1940 Mass daylight air raid on London. 448 civilians killed and 1,600 injured.

15 September 1940 Fighter Command destroys 25% of a German air assault on London. (Battle of Britain Day.)

17 September 1940 "Operation Sealion" postponed indefinitely.

18 September 1940 Luftwaffe forced to switch to nighttime raids because of heavy losses.

30 September 1940 Blitz begins – nightly bombing campaign against London.

14 November 1940 Coventry devastated by German bombers.

29 December 1940 Biggest air raid of War with a third of City of London destroyed.

March 1941 Air Ministry publishes a pamphlet called *Battle of Britain*. More than a million sold. The Ministry chooses 8 August as the official start of the Battle and 31 October as the end.

Acknowledgements

All photographs reproduced by the kind permission of the Trustees of the Imperial War Museum, London.

The author would like to thank RAF Duxford, the Imperial War Museum Sound, Film and Video, Photography and Document archives and Tim Collier of the RAF for their generous assistance.

Pilots of a Spitfire squadron dash to their aircraft during a scramble.

Flights of Spitfires on patrol duty in July 1940.

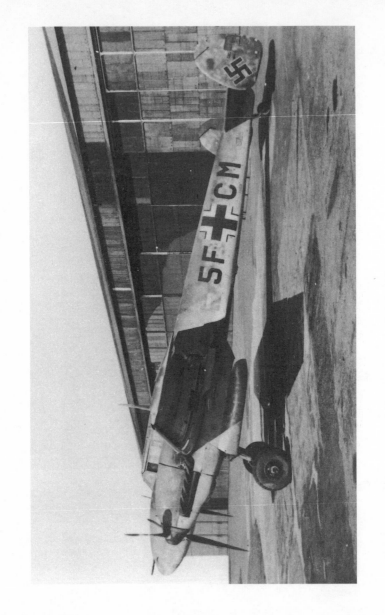

A Messerschmitt 110 fighter-bomber shot down in July 1940.

A Heinkel 111 aircraft over the River Thames, London.

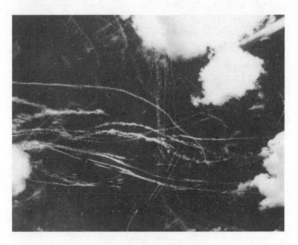

Vapour trails left in the sky by British and German aircraft after a dogfight.

These pilots are coming in to make their reports
after bringing down two Me109s.

A Flying Officer pictured on his aircraft
following a successful mission.

DESERT DANGER

Jim Eldridge

4 April 1942

I was trying to mend the clutch on a police car in my Uncle George's garage, when the bomb went off. One minute I was in the pit under the car, looking at the frayed clutch cable, the next ... BOOOOOOMM!!!... there was an almighty explosion from a few streets away and the garage shook as though it had been hit by an earthquake. My first thought was that the brick roof of the arch was going to come down on top of me; I heard my uncle shouting, "Tim! Get out of there quick!" and I knew he thought so too.

I leapt rather than climbed up the ladder out of the pit and ran for the entrance to the arch, my hands over my head in the hope I'd be able to ward off any bricks if they fell down on me. Uncle George's garage was inside one of the arches at the back of St Pancras railway station, in the centre of London, not far from King's Cross. The arches were like small tunnels that had been built under the railway line, brick caves about 100 feet deep. Small businesses rented out these arches. Some were motor repairers, like Uncle George. There was an electrician, a plumber, and a bloke who sold second-hand furniture – all sorts of businesses. So far the arches had stood up well to the bombing that had been going on since the War started more than two years before; none of them had caved in – yet. But, now that the Germans were dropping bombs on London, and especially as we were so near three of London's biggest railway stations, St Pancras, King's Cross and Euston, our area had become a major target. I think all of us who worked there felt that sooner or later the Germans would score a direct hit on the arches – and then it would be the end for all of us.

I stood in the street next to Uncle George and looked towards Euston. A big cloud of smoke was billowing up from one of the streets near the station.

"I didn't hear any sirens," I said, bewildered. Usually, when there was an air-raid, the sirens went off to tell you the bombers were coming, and you usually had time to get to the nearest air-raid shelter.

"There weren't any," replied Uncle George. "I bet you it was an unexploded bomb from an earlier raid, just sitting there waiting for something to set it off."

That happened sometimes: a bomb would be dropped from the German planes and not go off. Sometimes they'd be buried deep in the ground, and then they'd just sit there, hidden, until one day something would trigger the explosion – a vibration, or something – and the bomb would blow up, destroying everything around it.

"I'd better get over there and see if I can do anything to help," said Uncle George hurriedly.

"I'm coming with you," I told him.

"No," said Uncle George firmly. "There could be anything going on there: a leaking gas main, fires, buildings collapsing. Your mother would have my guts for garters if anything happened to you."

My mother was Uncle George's sister. It was funny really, Uncle George was over six feet tall and built like a shed on legs, with a broken nose from the time when he'd been a boxer, and yet he was scared stiff of Mum, who was small and thin. I suppose it was because Mum had a bit of a tongue on her and didn't hold back when she felt like using it.

Me, I'm Tim Jackson, eighteen years old. My eighteenth birthday had been the week before, on 27 March 1942. I was waiting for my papers to arrive at any time, calling me up into the Army to go off and fight.

"But I'll be going into the Army any day now, Uncle George," I protested. "Anything could happen to me once I go, so I might as well come with you now."

"No," repeated Uncle George firmly. "For one thing, I'm trained to deal with this – you're not. Also, if you go off to war and get killed or injured, that'll be Adolf Hitler's fault. If you go with me now and something happens to you, it'll be my fault. Your mum's not likely to have a go at Hitler, but sure as eggs is eggs she'd have a go at me. You stay here and get on with that clutch. It ain't going to be mended on its own, and that vehicle is needed for vital war work."

"OK, Uncle," I said resignedly.

Uncle George grabbed his bag, which held his gas mask and some tools, and set off towards Euston. With all the bombing that had gone on, lots of the roads had great big holes in them, or were blocked by rubble from collapsed buildings, so if you were going somewhere relatively close by, it was usually quicker on foot than by car.

When Uncle George talked about being "trained to deal with this", he meant that he was an official Civil Defence Warden. He'd wanted to go to war himself, but the War Office told him that as a car mechanic he was in a "reserved occupation". This meant that they needed him to stay at home in England and help keep things on the move. Someone had to keep the fire engines and police cars on the road, so he stayed behind and worked on the vehicles. He also did his bit as a volunteer Civil Defence Warden, going out on emergency calls as an auxiliary fireman, and digging victims out of collapsed buildings after bombing raids. I was his apprentice, learning to be a motor mechanic. I'd been with him for the past four years, since I'd left school at the age of fourteen.

I went back into the tunnel and climbed down into the pit, then I set to work on the clutch of a police car. Most of the vehicles we had coming into the garage were official: police cars, ambulances, fire engines. Because of petrol rationing, very few people could run a car of their own. Most of the vehicles we had in were also pretty badly beaten up from being driven along streets carved up by bombs. London had been especially hard hit in the last two and a half years since the War began. Eighteen months before, during the Blitz, the Germans bombed London every night throughout September and October. It wasn't only London, nearly every other major city in Britain was bombed, but London, being the capital, took the brunt of it. Mrs Jepson, who lived next door to us, told us that Coventry city centre had been completely destroyed in a series of bombing raids in November 1940. She knew because she had a daughter who lived in Birmingham. All I knew about were the raids on London. They reckoned well over one million homes were destroyed, and about 15,000 Londoners were killed in the Blitz. It often struck me and my family that we were lucky to be alive. Everyone knew of people who'd been killed, or had their homes flattened. Every time the bombers came over it was a game of chance: would we be alive in the morning, or would it be our turn to die?

Although some people said the bombing wasn't as bad as it had been in 1940, it seemed even worse to me. Most nights the big German bombers still came over, the air-raid sirens wailed, and we all hurried down into the underground stations that doubled as huge air-raid shelters. Some people actually lived in the underground stations, they even had beds and tables and chairs set up on the platforms. I couldn't stand being in the air-raid shelter. I would just sit there and wait for the All Clear to sound so I could get up to street level again, back to the fresh air. Although when we did come up the air was rarely fresh – it usually smelt of burning.

I think everyone believed things would get better when the Americans had joined the War five months before, in December 1941. Uncle George certainly did. I remember him and Mum talking in our kitchen after they'd heard the news on the wireless.

"You see, Ada, now the Americans have come in, this war will soon be over," he told her, with a big grin on his face. "I give it two months before Hitler surrenders."

"Oh, do you?" Mum had snapped back. "And when did you become an expert on the War, George Wilson?"

"Well, it's obvious, ain't it?" said Uncle George. "The Americans have got all the best weapons. They'll slaughter the Germans."

"The Americans only came into this war because Japan bombed their navy," said my mother. "As far as they're concerned this war is about them against the Japanese. Half of America is German, anyway. Why should they support us against Hitler?"

"Because. . ." began Uncle George, but Mum just gave one of her sniffs and that shut him up.

Like I say, that had been five months ago, and Germany still showed no signs of surrendering. There were those who reckoned the Americans had joined us too late anyway, that we'd already lost the War. With the Germans seeming to get stronger, and the Japanese defeating our armies in Malaya and Singapore, a lot of people thought Hitler would be in London by June. But if anybody said anything like that when Mum was around, she got really mad.

"No way is that squirt Hitler going to set foot in this country," she'd say angrily. "We beat his lot in 1918, and we'll beat 'em again this time round."

I was just putting the finishing touches to the clutch on the police car, when Uncle George came back. As I climbed out of the pit, I could tell by the unhappy expression on his face that it had been difficult.

"Anything bad, Uncle George?" I asked.

He nodded. "Two kids," he said. "Boy and a girl, aged six and seven. Brother and sister. They shouldn't have been out on their own."

"What happened?" I asked.

He sighed, miserably. "They must have been playing and found the bomb poking out of the ground. No one knows for sure what happened, but they must have set it off. Both of 'em blown to bits. Their mum only knew it was them when I found their shoes." He shook his head. "I hate this war," he sighed. "How's that clutch coming along?"

"All fixed," I said.

"Good," he replied. "Let's close up here and go home."

We shut the gates of the repair shop and Uncle George locked up, and then we began to walk home. It wasn't far, only a mile.

As we walked, I asked him: "Uncle George, do you reckon we're going to win this war?"

"Of course we are," he said, surprised. "What makes you even ask?"

"Sometimes I hear the ambulance drivers talking, or one of the fire crews, while I'm fixing one of their vehicles, and all they talk about is how many more buildings have been destroyed, and how many people have been killed. I sometimes wonder if we can last."

"'Course we can," he said defiantly. "We beat 'em last time around and we'll beat 'em again this time."

"You sound just like Mum," I laughed. "That's what she says."

"Well, your mother knows best, Tim," he said.

We walked along Crowndale Road and then up Royal College Street in silence. I could tell from the expression on Uncle George's face that he was thinking about the children whose shoes he had just found. I wondered whether I should start talking to him about something else to take his mind off it, but then I decided it was best to say nothing.

Finally we came to the turning for Plender Street. Uncle George lived six houses further up Royal College Street; Mum and I lived at Selous Mews.

"See you in the morning, Tim," he said. "Unless there's an air-raid, in which case I'll see you in the shelter. Keep an eye on your mum."

"I will, Uncle," I assured him.

Mum was in the kitchen when I got home, boiling a saucepan of hot water on the gas stove so she could do the washing. It was one of the things she was keen on – making sure the two of us had clean clothes. Nearly every day she put dirty clothes to soak in an old bucket in the yard, and then, when most of the dirt had come out, she put a big saucepan on the stove and boiled the clothes clean. I'd come home filthy from Uncle George's garage, so there was a saucepan of water boiling up clean clothes for me every other day.

I'm an only child. My father had been killed in an accident just before I was born, so I never knew him. Mum didn't have any photographs of him, either, so I never found out what he looked like. I guess he looked just like me, because every now and then Mum would look at me and say, "You look just like your father!" I was never sure whether that was a good thing or a bad thing. I don't know why Mum never married again. Uncle George said it was because most men don't want to take on another man's kid, referring to me. Personally, I think the real reason is that Mum's got a very sharp tongue, and she'd scare the life out of most men.

"How was your day, Tim?" she asked.

"All right," I said. "A bomb went off over near Euston. Uncle George went over to deal with it."

Mum lowered the gas under the boiling saucepan, and then asked, "Was he all right?"

"Yeah," I said. "He was upset, though. Two kids got killed."

Mum shook her head and her face tightened in anger. The death of a child always upset her. She said to me once, "Parents should never have to bury their kids. It's not natural."

"A letter came for you," she said. "I put it by the clock on the mantelpiece."

I went over to the fireplace and when I saw the official-looking brown envelope, my heart gave a leap. I hoped this was my call-up papers! I was desperate to get overseas and into the War, to fight for my country and give Hitler a bloody nose.

I opened the envelope excitedly. It was an official letter telling me to report to Number 1 Training Battalion, Royal Engineers, at Napier Barracks, Shorncliffe, Kent on 11 April. Enclosed with the letter was a railway travel warrant, and details of how to get to Shorncliffe. I was to catch the Folkestone train from London Bridge and get off at Cheriton, which was the nearest railway station.

"I've been called up, Mum," I said. "I go for training next week."

Mum simply nodded. She was never one for showing her emotions. "You'll need clean clothes, then," she said.

After we'd had our supper, I sat and read the paper while Mum got out her knitting needles. She was making woolly hats for soldiers. It was part of a scheme the Government had set up, or the Women's Voluntary Service, or some such organization. It struck me that soldiers didn't need woolly hats as much as they needed steel helmets, but I didn't like to tell her so, because it would only upset her. Knitting gave her something to do, especially as she couldn't read, so couldn't pass the time reading a newspaper or a book or anything. I remember how surprised I was when I found out that she couldn't read or write. Mum was angry at my reaction.

"We never had education when we were kids," she told me sharply.

"But Uncle George can read and write," I pointed out.

"That's different," she explained. "He was a boy. Boys got education. Girls didn't."

I didn't think that was strictly true, because I knew lots of women who lived near us who could read and write, but I didn't like to argue with Mum. It didn't pay to argue with her if I wanted a quiet life.

We were sitting there in the kitchen, reading and knitting, when suddenly the air-raid siren screamed. I always hated that sound, even though it saved our lives time and time again. It was a high-pitched whine and it went right through you as it got louder and louder. Mum and I were well practised. We grabbed our coats and gas masks, and rushed out of the front door towards Mornington Crescent tube station, the nearest one to us. All our neighbours were doing the same. Everyone was fully dressed. In these uncertain days, with the threat of an air-raid nearly every night, everyone went to bed with their clothes on, just in case they had to run for cover. Some people even slept with their shoes on, to save them time in case the siren went off.

Usually we had about fifteen minutes from the time the siren sounded to get to the underground station before the bombs fell. It isn't a very long time, especially when you're thinking of those bombers on their way.

We were running along, when Mum suddenly tripped and fell. Luckily I managed to catch hold of her just before she hit the ground. As I held her, I was surprised how light she was. I'd always known she was thin, but I hadn't realized how little of her there was.

"You all right, Mum?" I asked.

"'Course I am," she snapped. "It's these shoes I'm wearing. The buckle's gone on the left one."

"Well you can't run in it," I said. "I'll carry you."

As I went to lift her up, she belted me with her gas mask.

"Get off me!" she ordered. "I ain't being carried anywhere. I'm perfectly capable of getting to the shelter under my own steam."

With that, she took off both her shoes, and then, holding her shoes and her gas mask, she started to run again in her stockinged feet. I ran beside her, watching out in case she fell over again, but we made it to the station with no further problems.

"Hurry up!" shouted the Air-raid Warden who was on duty beside the entrance. "The Germans are coming!" Then he saw that Mum hadn't got her shoes on, and asked: "What's happened to your shoes, love?"

"I'm saving 'em to look nice when I meet the King," she snapped back.

She and I hurried down the stairs towards the platforms. As we did, we met Uncle George, who was hurrying up the stairs the other way.

"There you are!" he exclaimed. "I was worried. I was just coming to find you."

"Mum's shoe went funny on her," I said. "The buckle bust."

"I can talk for myself, thank you very much, Tim Jackson," said Mum sharply. To Uncle George, she said: "Is Ivy here?"

Ivy was George's wife.

"Yes," nodded Uncle George. "She's saving a spot for us on the platform."

"Right," said Mum. "Let's find her. She might have a needle and thread and I can sew this buckle back on."

The three of us hurried down to the platform together, and as we got there I saw a couple of my old school pals, Denny Brown and Chaz Watson, sitting down playing cards. They waved at me to come and join them.

"There's Denny and Chaz," I told my mum. "I'm just going to tell them about getting my call-up papers."

"Your call-up papers?" echoed Uncle George. "When do you go?"

"Next week," I said.

"That's a bit soon," muttered Uncle George, unhappily.

"Not soon enough for Tim," said Mum. "He can't wait to get away." She looked towards Denny and Chaz, and then said to me, "No playing cards with that pair. They'll take your money off you."

"I haven't got any money," I pointed out. "I give all my wages to you."

"Lucky for you I look after 'em," said Mum. "Go on, then. And don't get into trouble."

As Mum and Uncle George went off to look for Aunt Ivy, I went over to Denny and Chaz. They were both grinning broadly.

"Me and Chaz have been called up!" said Denny, and he produced a brown envelope just like the one I'd got.

"Yeah. We're going into the infantry," said Chaz.

"I've been called up, too," I told them. "Royal Engineers. I report for training next Wednesday."

"Me and Chaz go on Monday," grinned Denny. "So we'll be ahead of you, Tim boy! We'll be out there sorting the Jerries out!"

At that moment there was the sound of a huge thud that shook the whole station. Everyone fell silent and instinctively we all looked up at the curved roof above us, looking for any cracks.

"That was a close one," murmured Denny.

"I wonder if our house is still standing," muttered Chaz.

It was the question we all asked ourselves, every time we came down to the underground and listened to the bombs falling outside, feeling the vibration as the walls and roof of the station shook around us. Had our houses been hit? What would we find when we came out of the shelter? Had anyone we knew been killed?

The bombing raid went on for two hours. The whole time, the tube station shook as the bombs struck, but being deep underground, it held.

Finally, after what seemed like an age, the All Clear sounded, and we clambered up the winding staircase to the street. Mum had spent the whole time sewing the buckle back on her shoe, so she could walk normally.

When we stepped outside, the first thing that hit me – as always – was the smell of burning rubber. Whatever got hit, it was always the rubber from things like tyres that had the strongest smell. In the darkness, fires raged and piles of rubble lay where buildings had once stood. The fire engines were already at work, trying to put out the biggest fires, the fire-fighters silhouetted against the red and yellow lights from the flickering flames. Sparks blew about in the air. I put my handkerchief over my mouth and nose to keep the choking black smoke out of my lungs. In front of me, London burned.

I had one more week of this, and then I'd be away, fighting to put a stop to it.

11 April 1942

One week later I was on my way. I packed my bags, said goodbye to Uncle George and Aunt Ivy, and the mates of mine who were still waiting to be called up, and went off to fight Hitler.

Mum came with me to London Bridge station, where I was catching the train to Cheriton. There were a few other blokes standing around at the station, and I guessed they were waiting for the same train. I felt a bit embarrassed, standing there with my mother; it made me feel like a little kid. "I'll be all right on my own now, Mum," I said, trying to be tactful.

Mum looked around at the other young men and nodded.

"Yeah, 'course you will," she said. "But make sure you write and let me know how you're getting on. I'll get your Uncle George to read it to me."

"I'll write as soon as I can," I told her.

She hesitated, then stood on her tiptoes and gave me a quick kiss on the cheek. "Come back alive, son," she whispered. Then she turned and walked away. As I watched her go I felt guilty for making her leave. She was going to miss me a lot – I was all she had.

A tall, thin young chap with ginger hair came over and joined me, and sighed as he watched my mum walk out of the station.

"Mothers, eh?" he said. "Mine wanted to come and see me off, but I begged her not to. She'd only have made a scene – lots of crying. She means well, but I'd never have lived it down." He held out his hand. "The name's Steve Matthews, but everyone calls me Ginger."

I shook his hand. "Tim Jackson," I said. "Are you off to Shorncliffe?"

Ginger nodded. "That's right," he said. "Royal Engineers."

"Me, too," I told him.

There was a yell from a station attendant: "Folkestone train from platform seven!", and suddenly the station was full of blokes, all about my age, all heading for platform seven.

"Where did they all come from?" asked Ginger, stunned.

"They must have been hanging about in the cafeteria, or something," I said. "Come on, we'd better get a move on or we won't get a seat, and I bet it's a long journey to Cheriton."

Ginger and I broke into a run, pushing our way through the crowd. A few of the men gave us annoyed looks as we ran past them, but it was lucky we did. There weren't enough seats for all us, let alone the ordinary civilians who were catching the same train to Folkestone.

Ginger and I managed to grab the last two seats in one of the eight-seater compartments. The six people who were already in it included a couple of elderly ladies, a middle-aged man and woman, and two men of our age.

"Heading for Shorncliffe?" I asked them.

The middle-aged man and woman and the two elderly ladies

ignored me. In fact the middle-aged man gave a disapproving sniff and started reading a newspaper.

The two young blokes nodded.

"I'm Pete Morgan," one of them introduced himself. He was short and tubby, with black hair cropped close at the sides, but sticking up on the top of his head like a carpet. He had a thick Welsh accent.

"I'm Edward White," said the other. He was also shortish, with a mop of blond hair that hung down over his forehead. He added: "Everyone calls me Chalky."

He had a strange accent, which made it difficult to work out what he was saying. It was almost foreign.

"Tim Jackson," I said, pointing to myself.

"Ginger Matthews," Ginger introduced himself. "Have you come far?"

"Cardiff," said Pete.

"Cor, that's a long way!" exclaimed Ginger.

"I haven't come as far as him," said Pete, jerking his thumb at Chalky. "He's come all the way from Newcastle."

Newcastle, right up almost to Scotland. That explained Chalky's strange accent. My Uncle George called them Geordies.

"Newcastle?" I echoed. "Haven't they got any training camps up there?"

"They had one, but it got bombed," Chalky explained. "So that's why I've been sent down here."

"Can't you fellows read?" snapped the middle-aged man angrily.

We all looked at him blankly, and then at one another.

"Why, do you want help reading your newspaper?" asked Ginger cheekily.

The man scowled and pointed a finger at a notice just below the luggage racks. It was a cartoon of two people talking, with Adolf Hitler hiding behind a wooden crate, listening to them. The slogan read, "Careless talk costs lives".

"Careless talk costs lives," announced the man firmly, just in case we couldn't read.

"But I'm not talking carelessly," protested Chalky. "I'm just saying why I had to come all this way to join up."

"You have revealed that your training camp has been bombed," snapped the man, obviously very annoyed. "That's the sort of information that would be useful to the enemy."

"Well as it was the enemy that bombed it, I expect they already know about it," retorted Ginger.

"Are you being cheeky?" demanded the man.

"No, I'm being sensible," replied Ginger.

"Don't talk to them, Eric," said his wife. "They're just hooligans out looking for trouble."

"Hooligans?" I echoed indignantly. "We're on our way to fight for our country, missus."

"Don't you talk to my wife that way, you hooligan!" snapped the man. "And don't you think you can get tough with me, either. I fought in the last war!"

"And he was wounded!" added his wife.

I was going to make a crack back at him, but I caught Chalky's eye and he shook his head, as if to say "Leave it alone. We don't want any trouble." I shut up.

That's the trouble with old folk – they see a bunch of young guys together and automatically think we're out for trouble. And they always think that we're never as good as they were when they were young.

We spent the rest of the journey in an unhappy silence, staring out of the window, watching the landscape and towns go by. Now and then one of us would start to say something, but then Eric the Miserable would glare at us as if we were committing treason and we'd shut up. I was glad when the train finally pulled in at Cheriton.

There was a row of single-decker buses waiting for us outside the station, each one with a piece of paper stuck on the driver's window reading "Shorncliffe Camp". It was a real scramble as we all piled on to the buses, but Ginger, Pete, Chalky and I all managed to get on the same one. When the buses were full, they moved off one by one. I noticed that some of the young men who'd been on the train hadn't been able to get on the buses and were still standing outside the station. When I mentioned it to the driver, he said, "Don't worry, we'll be back for them."

"At least we'll get first choice on the bunks," said Ginger.

The convoy of buses weaved its way through country lanes. It was the first time I'd ever really been out in the country. There were green areas in London: places like Regent's Park and Parliament Hill Fields and Hampstead Heath, but they weren't really countryside. They were large areas of grass with trees, but you always knew they were surrounded by houses. Out here, the countryside stretched for miles. It was trees and fields, with just a few houses. It was so different from being in London.

The buses reached a gate in a tall wire fence. On the fence was a sign reading "Shorncliffe Camp".

"They ought to take that sign down," said Ginger. "Someone might read it and tell the enemy what's behind the fence. Careless talk costs lives, you know."

We remembered Eric the Miserable, and we all laughed.

The buses pulled up, and we all filed off. A tall man, very straight-backed, with a big handlebar moustache and three stripes on his sleeve – which I knew showed that he was a sergeant, was waiting for us.

"Right, you 'orrible shower!" he yelled in a voice loud enough to be heard back in London. "Line up over there in rows of ten!"

Ginger and I looked at each another, and rolled our eyes. I'd spent years at school with teachers who shouted at me, now I was in the Army with more of them.

"Come on, come on!" the Sergeant shouted. "Don't you know there's a war on? We've got to get you trained double quick so you can get out there and take part in it, so hurry up and get in line!"

We scrambled to get into lines of ten, and once we were assembled, the Sergeant bellowed at us: "Right, atten – shun! Stand up straight, hands by your sides. You're in the Army now! On the command you will march forward, keeping in time, beginning with the first row there!"

And he pointed at the line of ten men next to us. "The other lines will follow in single file! Right . . . march!"

And then he set off, the first ten men following, then our line of ten, then the next, and so on, all the time the sergeant shouting, "Hup two three four . . . hup two three four."

We marched until we came to the first in a long line of low wooden huts. In front of every hut stood a uniformed soldier.

"Column halt!" roared the Sergeant, and we all stopped.

"First twenty men fall out!" the Sergeant shouted. Turning to the uniformed soldier, he said: "They're all yours, Corporal Rogers."

"Sah!" acknowledged the Corporal, saluting smartly.

"Column, forward march!" shouted the Sergeant, and the rest of the file of men marched off towards the next hut.

"Right, you men!" bellowed the Corporal at us. "You are A Brigade. This is your barracks. It will be your home for the next seven weeks. You will love it and you will keep it clean and spotlessly tidy! Get in, find yourself a bunk, and then assemble outside in two minutes. Go!"

We hurried inside the hut. There were two long rows of ten beds each against opposite walls. Next to each bed was a small bedside table, with a door and a drawer.

"Grab the beds furthest away from the door," said Chalky, hurrying to the far end of the long room.

Me, Ginger and Pete followed him, and the four of us managed to get the group of four bunks at the far end.

"Why do we want these particular beds?" Pete asked Chalky.

"Because when the Sergeant comes in first thing in the morning and starts looking for things to moan about, he'll see the ones nearest the door first. Being this far away buys us a bit of time."

"Yes, but if anything goes wrong, like a bomb hitting us, we're farthest from the door," pointed out Ginger.

Chalky laughed. "If a bomb hits this place, there'll be no need to worry about getting to the door." He tapped the wooden wall. "This place'll just collapse."

The Corporal appeared in the doorway and began shouting: "Come on, you bunch of old women! Stop all that nattering! I told you I wanted you out here in two minutes! Now MOVE!!"

We hurried outside. As we did so, I whispered to Ginger: "This is going to be worse than being at home, being shouted at all the time, and having to do everything on the double. They'll wear us out before we even get to see the Germans, let alone fight them."

Under Corporal Rogers' shouted orders, we half-marched, half-ran to the Quartermaster's stores, where we were issued with a kitbag, uniform, boots, socks and underwear, toothbrush, comb, boot polish and brushes, all the basic things we were going to need. Then we half-marched, half-ran back to the barracks, where we were told to put on our new outfits.

I thought the khaki uniform looked pretty smart, even if the cloth did feel very rough against my skin. The boots were heavy, but I'd been used to wearing boots with metal toecaps as protection against a rusty old car falling on my feet all the time I was working at Uncle George's garage, so they didn't bother me.

After we'd all got our uniforms on, the twenty of us were marched around the camp by Corporal Rogers, who would stop beside a plain wooden building that looked just the same as every other building on the camp, and he'd shout at us, "Ablutions! Latrine block! Showers! Mess block!" or whatever the building was.

"I'll never remember what all these buildings are," groaned Pete in a whisper.

"Just follow the smell," whispered Chalky. "Believe me, you'll find the toilets soon enough, and the mess hall where they serve the food. Those are the two most important ones."

"Stop talking in the ranks!" yelled Corporal Rogers. Chalky shut up, and we carried on with our tour of the camp.

Then, before we knew it, it was time for our first meal. Mashed potatoes and meat. I wasn't sure what sort of meat it was, and neither were any of the blokes at our table.

"Beef," suggested one bloke near Chalky.

"Never in a million years," retorted Chalky.

"Dog?" queried Ginger.

"Urgh!" exclaimed Pete, disgusted.

"How do you know what dog tastes like?" demanded Pete. "Have you ever eaten it?"

"No," said Ginger. "And this meat tastes like nothing I've ever eaten. So it could just as well be dog."

"I reckon it's horse," said another bloke further down. "They eat horse meat in France."

"Whatever it is, it fills a hole," said Chalky, and he tucked happily into his meal.

As I lay in my bunk that night, listening to the other nineteen men in the long wooden hut snoring and making a cacophony of wheezing noises as they slept, I thought of Mum in our tiny house at Selous Mews, and wondered how she was. It was the first time I'd been away from home in eighteen years. I wondered if she was safe.

"G'night, Mum," I whispered quietly to myself. "Stay safe from the bombers."

12 April – 31 May 1942

The next three days all followed the same pattern: breakfast at an early hour, and on the parade ground under the drill Sergeant, who we now knew was Regimental Sergeant Major Mottram, and who claimed to have the loudest voice in the whole British Army. Three days of marching backwards and forwards – quick march, slow march, left turn, right turn, saluting, foot-stamping loud marching, soft-stepping quiet marching – were all accompanied by RSM Mottram's bellowing voice. By the end of the third day we all either had raging headaches, or had gone deaf.

The fourth day brought something different. After breakfast, and led by Corporal Rogers, we were marched to yet another long wooden hut. Inside it looked like a school room: rows of desks and chairs all facing the front, and a bigger desk at the head of the room.

"We're back at school," muttered Ginger.

"Shut up that talking!" yelled Corporal Rogers. "Find a desk and sit down!"

As Ginger and I made our way to a pair of desks next to each other, I thought how much RSM Mottram and Corporal Rogers, and all the officers we'd come into contact with, reminded me of my Aunt Lou, my dad's sister. Aunt Lou worked in a factory where the noise of the machines was so loud all day long that the women either used sign language to talk to each other, or – if they needed to talk – had to shout to make themselves heard. The trouble was that all of them, Aunt Lou included, carried on shouting when they got outside the factory. When Aunt Lou came to see us she'd sit in our kitchen and yell out even ordinary things like, "Not too much milk in my tea!" so loud that the neighbours four doors away could hear her.

We sat down at our desks, and then the door opened and an officer entered.

"'Tenshun!" shouted Corporal Rogers, and we all got up and stood stiffly to attention.

"At ease," said the officer quietly. "You may sit."

"Sit down!" yelled Corporal Rogers.

We all sat.

"Thank you, Corporal," nodded the officer.

"Sah!" said Corporal Rogers.

With that, Corporal Rogers turned smartly and marched out of the room. All our eyes turned to the officer in front of us.

"My name is Captain James," he told us. "I will be your senior instructor for the next six weeks. You men have been selected for the Royal Engineers because all of you have some sort of engineering skill. We intend to develop those skills to make you a vital part of the Army's efforts to win this war.

"You men are privileged to be joining one of the oldest military units in the country. It began with the military engineers brought to England by William the Conqueror, and has had an unbroken record of service to the Crown ever since. The Engineers have always been at the forefront of all new technological and scientific inventions: telegraphy during the Crimean War, photography during the Abyssinian Campaign of 1867, underwater explosive devices such as the torpedo. It was the Air Battalion Royal Engineers who built the flying machines that led to the formation of the Royal Flying Corps in the Great War. It was also the sappers who designed and built the Royal Albert Hall."

He looked around at us, then asked: "Any questions so far?"

There was the usual sort of silence you get in any classroom when a teacher asks a class that question, and then Ginger put up his hand.

"Please, sir," he asked, "why are the Engineers called sappers?"

Some of the other blokes groaned, just like kids do in class when another kid asks a question, but I was interested in finding out the answer myself.

Captain James nodded. "A good question," he said. "A sap is a trench. In olden days, when a town was under siege, the only way to protect the troops who were attacking it was to dig trenches for them to hide in. The men who dug those trenches, or saps, were the Engineers, and that's how we got the nickname sappers. You will find that very little has changed for the Royal Engineers during the last few hundred years: the piece of equipment you men will be using most will not be a rifle but a spade.

"Much of your training here at Shorncliffe will involve land mines. The different sorts of land mines, how to lay them, and how to defuse them.

"In any battle, sooner or later one side will launch an attack against the other. To prevent our side being caught by a surprise attack, or to slow the enemy attack down, we put mines out between us and the enemy. Two main types of mines are used – anti-tank mines, which explode when a tank track goes over them; and anti-personnel mines, which go off when they're stepped on. Within those two types there are many variations, but these are the ones we'll be dealing with here. We know the way through our minefields, because we have set out our own mines, but the enemy doesn't.

"The enemy, of course, does exactly the same as us to defend their position. So, when our side launches an attack, our tanks and troops have to get through the enemy minefields. In order for that to happen safely, the enemy land mines have to be cleared out of the way and defused. Which is where you chaps come in."

After the lecture, as we walked towards the mess hall for lunch, Pete Morgan shook his head.

"Land mines," he groaned. "I'm going to spend this war finding things that can blow up and kill me."

"Would you rather be in the front line, being shot at by the other side?" demanded Chalky.

"We *will* be in the front line, you idiot," said Pete. "Didn't you hear what the Captain said? That's where these minefields are, right between the enemy and us."

"Oh yeah," said Chalky. "It doesn't sound very safe, does it?"

For the next six weeks we drilled, dug trenches, and learnt about mines.

On our very first day of training we watched from a distance as different sorts of German mines were set off by our training sergeant by fixing a length of string to the trigger of the mine, and then pulling it and setting off the detonator. It was obvious that all of them could do some serious damage.

Over the next two weeks we took apart all different sorts of mines, and then put them back together again, so we would know how they worked and how to deal with them. All of them had dummy detonators and no explosives, so it was completely safe.

Learning about the different types of mine was pretty bewildering though. The Tellermine was mostly used as an anti-tank mine. Inside it was 10 lb of TNT (a high-powered explosive), which was set off when a tank went over it and pushed down the metal plate, setting off the detonator. The S mine (or "The Schrapnellmine 35", to give it its full title) was about the size of a beer can. Inside the beer can – which was really a small gun – was a small canister filled with 350 steel ball-bearings. The mine was triggered by a three-pronged push mechanism and when this was trodden on, the canister was fired about three feet into the air, where it exploded, blowing the steel ball-bearings 160 feet in all directions.

The Schu-mine was a small anti-personnel mine that only used a small amount of explosive, a 200 g demolition charge. The aim of the Schu-mine wasn't to kill, but to blow the feet or legs off anyone who trod on it. It seemed the Germans had worked out that they could cause more problems to our side if they just badly wounded our soldiers, because a wounded man's mates would often try and take care of him while the battle was going on. If he was dead, his body could be left until later.

Then there were the booby-traps the Germans used to stop us from defusing their mines. The typical sort was a wire that went from a pin in the detonator to a peg fixed in the ground. As the mine was lifted, the wire pulled the pin out, and the contraption blew up. The only way to defuse these was to feel for the wire, and then cut it before lifting the mine. It took a long time to clear a field set out with booby-trapped mines.

These mines could be found by using a metal detector, but the Army didn't have many of them. Also, the Germans had come up with a new dodge to make our job even more difficult: a "wooden" land mine. The explosives and the metal shrapnel were enclosed in a wooden casing, to stop metal detectors from finding the mine.

We were also shown how to handle British mines and small bombs.

"Big bombs are dealt with by the Bomb Disposal Unit," our instructor told us. "Their detonators are far more complicated than the ones you're dealing with. They are also much more powerful. The size of mines and bombs we're dealing with may kill or disable a man, or knock out a tank. A big bomb can destroy a whole street. Anyone here who wants to volunteer for the Bomb Disposal Unit and try to defuse something that could blow him into dust is welcome to try."

On the whole, most of us decided to stick with the land mines, though a couple of blokes did volunteer for the UXB (unexploded bomb) brigade. The thing was, most of the work of the Bomb Disposal Unit (BDU) was being done on unexploded bombs that had fallen on Britain. I wanted to get overseas, to where the fighting was going on. All we saw of the enemy in Britain were the German planes when they came over to bomb us. I wanted to fight the Germans face to face.

After three weeks, Captain James made an announcement: "Right, men, you've been playing with toy mines for long enough. It's time to deal with the real thing."

We were taken out to a range and issued with a steel helmet, and a tool kit containing a trowel, a pair of wire cutters and a set of spanners. We also took turns to use a mine detector, which was like a broom handle with a metal plate at the end; a pair of headphones was attached to the plate by a wire attached to the plate. If the plate sensed metal under the surface of the ground, it sent a whining noise through the headphones. The louder and higher the whining noise, the nearer you were to metal. That metal might be a land mine, or it might be just a load of old junk. The only way to find out was to crawl to the place where the metal was hidden, and then scrape away the earth from around it with the trowel and your fingers until you saw what it was.

"Right, men," said the Captain. "In the range ahead of you are land mines, set in rows of four. You will take turns going out in a line of four men, twenty feet apart. When you find your mine, scrape away the earth from around it. If you find a wire, assume this is a booby-trap and it's

151

fixed somewhere in the earth. Cut the wire. Lift the mine out of the earth, and remove the detonator from the explosive charge. Some of the detonators will be held in place by a pin, for others you will need to use a spanner to undo the nut holding the detonator in place. When you've made the mine safe, place it in the two large boxes you will see at the side of the field. Detonators go in one box, the defused mine goes in the other. Remember, these mines are live. Do not knock them, or tread on them, or bang them in any way. Right, first four men . . . forward."

The four blokes in front, Ted Hoskins, Jack Ward, Terry Nutsford and Joe Latimer, stepped forward to the metal detectors lying on the ground.

"Pick up the detector and put the headphones on."

They did so.

"Right, proceed forward. Move slowly, and listen to the noise in the headphones."

The rest of us watched as Ted, Jack, Terry and Joe moved forward, holding the metal detectors in front of them. They advanced about ten yards, and then Joe stopped. Jack moved forward another pace or two, and then he stopped as well. Ted and Terry hesitated when they saw Jack and Joe stop, but then they edged forward, until they, too, came to a halt.

"You will note, gentlemen, that the mines are not in a straight line," said the Captain.

From our observation point we watched as the four men knelt down and began to scrape at the earth in front of them. I saw Jack reach forward, and then lift up a metal mine. He placed it on the ground, took something out of his tool kit, and set to work on it. A few moments later, he stood up.

Joe, Ted and Terry were still working on their mines. Ted was next to finish, then he, too, stood up, holding the mine in his hands.

"It's a con," whispered Pete next to me. "I bet those mines aren't live at all. It's just done to make us feel what it would be like. They wouldn't be stupid enough to take a chance with real explosives that could kill us."

"Sez you," said Ginger. "Me, I'm not taking any chances."

"That's my point," answered Pete.

I turned back to watching our four mates out in the field. Terry reached forward to pick up the mine he'd uncovered, but suddenly he slipped; he automatically put out a hand to stop himself. The next second there was a flash and a deafening explosion, and then there was just smoke and the sound of Terry screaming.

As the smoke cleared we saw Terry rolling around on the ground yelling in pain, one good hand holding his other arm. His hand had gone – blown off, leaving just a bloody stump.

I felt sick.

"Stretcher, Sergeant!" snapped the Captain.

"Sah!" responded the Sergeant.

Already a medical team was hurrying towards the injured Terry, carrying a stretcher.

"You were saying, Pete?" muttered Chalky.

Pete had gone deathly white, and he looked as sick as I felt. One of the other blokes behind us was already doubling over and vomiting.

"Order in the ranks!" called the Captain.

One of the stretcher bearers gave Terry a shot of something to quieten him down, and another started to fix a tourniquet around his arm to stop the bleeding.

"When you go into combat, doing this job will be even harder," Captain James told us. "You will be under enemy fire. It could well be pitch dark. There will often be noise and confusion all around you. Count yourselves lucky you are learning how to do this job under these conditions here in England, rather than in actual battle."

The stretcher bearers had loaded Terry on to the stretcher and carried him away for proper medical treatment. Ted, Joe and Jack were walking back towards us, carrying their metal detectors. An orderly was returning Terry's metal detector, and the remains of his hand. All their faces were pale.

"Right, next four men," ordered the Captain.

"That's us, Tim," whispered Ginger.

I looked round. Ginger was right. The next four in line were me, Ginger, Pete and Chalky.

We each took one of the metal detectors. I put the headphones on, placed my steel helmet over them, and switched on the detector; I heard a humming noise in my ears. I looked down at the metal detector, and realized that it had spots of blood on it. This was the same detector that Terry had been using. I looked across at Ginger on my left, and Pete on my right, and Chalky beyond him. They looked white-faced. I guessed I looked the same. I still felt sick to my stomach.

"Proceed forward," ordered the Captain. "Move slowly, and listen to the noise in the headphones."

I took a deep breath, and moved forward towards where the mines were. It was lucky the mine detector was quite heavy or my hands might have started shaking. I was scared. Defusing land mines when they were already safe was just playing with toys. These were real, packed with deadly explosives.

Keep calm, I told myself as I moved forward. Keep calm. The humming in my headphones carried on the same low whine as I edged forward, keeping my eyes skinned at the ground ahead of me. What if the detector wasn't working after the accident with Terry? If that was so, then it would keep to the same pitch and I could just step on a mine without knowing it was there.

Suddenly the noise in my headphones altered, going up like a musical instrument changing pitch. There was metal ahead – a mine.

Keeping the plate of the metal detector above the surface of the ground so that I didn't accidentally touch the mine and set it off, I edged forward, listening to the noise in the headphones and scanning the ground in front of me. There it was – a tiny button of metal just poking out of the ground.

I put the detector down and knelt near the button that marked the mine, but not too near it: I didn't want to kneel on it accidentally.

The image of Terry and his bloody stump came into my head again, and once more I felt vomit rising up in my throat, but I forced it down. I was a soldier; I had to control my feelings. I mustn't lose control.

The only chance I had of surviving this war was by keeping as calm as I could and obeying orders. I remembered Mum's last words to me: "Come back alive, son." I had to stay calm, which meant putting the image of the injured Terry out of my mind.

I pulled the trowel from my belt. I looked to my left and saw that Ginger was also kneeling by his mine, trowel in hand, looking worried. I looked to my right. Pete was still walking along slowly, holding his mine detector just in front of him. Chalky had found his mine and had started digging around the sides of it with his trowel.

Here I go! I thought. I took a deep breath, and then started scraping away the earth at a distance of about two feet from thesmall metal button, watching all the time for wires in case the mine had been booby-trapped.

I cleared the earth all the way round the mine, and then started to work my way in, scraping the earth away, until finally the mine was revealed. It was an S mine, shaped like a beer can with the detonator sticking straight up from the top like a stick. If the mine went off, 300 metal ball-bearings would explode out of it and tear me in half.

There were no wires attached to it, so it hadn't been booby-trapped. I took a spanner from my belt and set to work to undo the nut holding the detonator in place, all the time aware that if I made one slip I'd set it off. The nut came loose, and very slowly I edged the detonator out, making sure that I didn't trigger the spring that would send the plunger down into the explosives.

Finally it was done: the detonator had been separated from the explosives. There might still be a small spark, but nothing lethal.

I stood up and carried the two parts of the mine, the detonator and the part with the ball-bearings in, over to the large wooden boxes at the side of the field, and carefully placed them inside.

I was sweating like a pig and I had to fight to stop myself from shaking with relief.

Chalky reached the boxes with the two parts of his mine at the same time as me.

"I feel sick," he whispered as he put his mine and detonator into the boxes.

"That makes two of us, mate," I whispered back.

Ginger and Pete joined us, carrying their mines. They also looked pretty shaken, but we managed to force a grin – a mixture of relief and pride at our success – at one another.

We had done it. We had disabled a live mine, and lived. But that had been in controlled conditions. No one was shooting at us. No one was dropping bombs on us. And we had lots of time to disable it. I wondered how I'd cope doing this in a real battle situation, working fast under fire. I guessed it wouldn't be long before I found out.

1 June – 30 July 1942

On 1 June the whole lot of us said goodbye to Shorncliffe and Captain James, Corporal Rogers and RSM Mottram, and set off in a convoy of buses for Folkestone. There, we met our new platoon sergeant, Sergeant Ross, and clambered on board a huge troopship, each of us carrying our kitbags, and set sail for Egypt in North Africa. No one told us what we were actually going to do when we got to Egypt, but I guessed we were going to be defusing land mines.

"You'd think they'd tell us what sort of things we're going to be doing out there," complained Ginger, who felt as annoyed as I did at being left in the dark about what lay in store for us.

"That's the way it is in the Army," said Chalky knowledgably. "They don't tell you anything so that if you're taken prisoner, you can't let on to the enemy."

The cargo holds at the very bottom of the ship, where the tanks and lorries and vehicles and boxes of ammunition were kept, were enormous places, but the areas where we slept were cramped, with low ceilings. Because I was tall I spent most of the first day below decks banging my head against the metal girders, until in the end I learnt to walk everywhere with my head ducked down. Luckily, no one shouted at me "Soldier, stand up straight!" like they did when we were on parade.

Ginger and I sought out one of the ship's crew and questioned him. "How long d'you reckon it's going to take us to get to Egypt?"

"This way round – the long way – about eight weeks," he said.

"What do you mean, 'the long way'?" I asked.

"Right down the west coast of Africa and round the Cape. Then up the east coast of Africa and through the Suez Canal. The shorter way is to go east after the tip of Spain and go across the Mediterranean. That way would only take about two weeks, but of course, we can't go that way."

"Why not?" asked Ginger.

"Because the Med's full of German U-boats and battle cruisers and Italian ships, as well as German and Italian fighter planes bombing every ship that isn't theirs. They're trying to stop supplies getting to our boys in North Africa, which means everything's got to go the long way round. Also, they're trying to put Malta out of action."

"What's Malta?" I asked.

Both the sailor and Ginger looked at me to see if I was joking. When they saw the genuinely puzzled expression on my face, the sailor said: "Don't you know what Malta is?"

"No," I said.

"It's an island in the Mediterranean Sea," said Ginger. "Halfway between the bottom of Italy and North Africa. It's British."

"Right," nodded the sailor. Then, to me, he said, "Didn't they teach you that at school?"

"They didn't teach much at the school I went to, apart from reading and writing and numbers," I said. "We didn't do geography."

"So if you didn't do geography, how come you know where Africa is?" demanded the sailor.

"We did the big places on the map of the world," I said. "Africa, America, the Soviet Union, Europe, China. Places like that. We didn't do small islands."

"Well Malta is very small," said the sailor. "It's also an air base for the RAF. They use the airfields there to bring in vital supplies by plane from England, and then on to North Africa. Plus, we've got fighter planes on the island that attack the ships taking supplies from Italy to Rommel's forces in Africa. If the Germans take over Malta they'll have the whole of the Mediterranean in their pockets, so the Luftwaffe have been bombing it day and night for the past six months, trying to force the island to surrender. The navy have been running convoys across the Med trying to get supplies to Malta for those six months, but most of the ships have been sunk by German fighter planes."

"So what are they doing for supplies on Malta if the convoys aren't getting through to them?" I asked.

"What do you think? They're running out," said the sailor. "No food, no medical supplies, no oil. And all the time the Germans are increasing their attacks. Which is why, with all the German activity there, the Med is definitely a no-no for us on this trip. Otherwise, we could end up being sunk. This route may be longer, but at least you've got a chance of getting to Egypt in one piece."

Ginger and I told Pete and Chalky what the sailor had told us about going to Egypt the long way round.

"Eight weeks!" exclaimed Chalky. "The war in North Africa will be over by the time we get there."

"Yeah, and the Germans will have won," sighed Pete.

"Careful," warned Chalky, "that's treason talk, that is."

"I'm just telling it the way it is," said Pete. "My cousin Mike was in the North African desert and he was brought home in March, just before I got called up. He'd been badly wounded. Lost an arm. He said Rommel's lot are making mincemeat of our boys out there. He said that since last January, our blokes have been pushed right back by the Jerries, right back into Egypt. Mike reckons they can't last much longer, not against Rommel."

"What's all this?" demanded a voice.

We turned to face Sergeant Ross. There was an awkward silence.

"Nothing, Sarge," I mumbled. "Private Morgan was just telling us about his cousin, who was fighting in the desert."

"I heard what Private Morgan said, and I don't want to hear any more talk like that," snapped Ross. "That's the sort of lies and propaganda the Germans want spread about. Well it ain't going to be spread in my unit. Is that clear?"

"Yes, Sarge," I said.

Ross turned to Pete, who looked very shamefaced.

"Is that clear, Private Morgan?" he demanded angrily.

"Yes, Sarge," nodded Pete unhappily. "It won't happen again."

"See that it don't or you'll be on a charge," snapped Ross and he turned and walked off.

We all looked at the very unhappy Pete. "I warned you, Pete," Chalky said.

"I was just saying what Mike told me," said Pete miserably. "And he was there, actually out there fighting in the desert against Rommel and the Jerries. And I bet Mike knows more of what's going on out in the desert than Sergeant Ross, or anyone else on this boat." With that Pete stomped off.

For the rest of that day I couldn't help thinking about what Pete had started to say before Sergeant Ross told him to shut up. That night, just before it was time to turn in, I went looking for him. He was on deck, standing at the rail, looking out over the sea, a thoughtful look on his face.

"You OK, Pete?" I asked.

He turned and saw it was me, and nodded. "Yeah," he said.

"Thinking about your cousin?" I asked.

"What's that supposed to mean?" he scowled.

"Nothing," I said. "I was just curious about what you were saying before Sergeant Ross turned up. About what your cousin told you."

"You heard what Sergeant Ross said," replied Pete. "He told me to shut up about it."

"Yeah, but we'll find out soon enough, anyway," I pointed out. "After all, we're on our way to join the boys out there."

"Then leave it till we get there," said Pete.

"But we've got a right to know what we're going into," I said.

"Then ask Sergeant Ross, or one of the officers," replied Pete. "Maybe they'll tell you what's going on out there. Though I doubt it."

"Why?" I asked. "What's so bad out there?"

Pete hesitated, then he shook his head. "Sorry, Tim," he said. "You heard what Sergeant Ross told me – no talking about it, or I'll be put on a charge. That's good enough for me. My lips are sealed."

With that Pete turned and went back inside. I watched him go, and my head was in a whirl. What was going on in Egypt that was so bad for our side that Sergeant Ross didn't want Pete to talk to us about it?

The next day, at breakfast, I took my tray and sat down on a bench next to Ginger. He was tucking into a bowl of porridge and he had a plate of scrambled eggs waiting. Or, rather, something that looked like scrambled eggs. These days you were never quite sure if what you were eating was what it claimed to be. The "scrambled eggs" were made from powdered eggs that contained some egg, but also had a lot of other things in them to make them bulkier. It was like the sausages we ate – yes, they had some meat in them, but which part of the animal it came from was anyone's guess. Ears and tails and hooves, plus the organs, mixed with oats and water. Still, it was food.

As I ate my porridge, I took a quick look around to make sure we couldn't be overheard by any officers, and then whispered to Ginger: "Ginger, what do you think's going on in Egypt?"

"A war," said Ginger.

"I know there's a war," I said, irritably. "I mean, this business of

Sergeant Ross telling Pete to shut up about what his cousin Mike said. You know, about the Germans pushing our blokes back. And then you think about what that sailor was telling us about why we are having to go the long way round to Egypt: because the Germans are sinking all our ships when they try to go across the Mediterranean."

"So?" asked Ginger.

"Well, what are we getting ourselves into?"

Ginger thought about it for a moment, then he shrugged.

"Maybe it doesn't do to ask too many questions," he said. "Let's just wait until we get there, eh?"

1 – 11 August 1942

We finally docked in Alexandria in Egypt on 1 August, eight weeks after we'd set out. All of us were glad to get off that boat.

It was a shock in so many ways. The first shock was finding I couldn't walk properly. After eight weeks at sea, on a boat that had rolled and heaved in the huge waves of the ocean, I'd become used to staggering rather than walking, trying to stay upright every time the boat lurched. It felt strange to find the ground staying firm beneath my feet. For the first couple of days all of us who'd been packed on the boat walked around as if we were just about to fall over at every step.

The biggest shocks, though, were the heat and the blinding glare of the sun. I'd known sunny days in England when Mum and I had gone on holiday to the seaside, but I'd never experienced anything like this. The sun didn't just shine down on you – you almost felt as if you were inside an oven. This was scorching sun, casting sharp shadows against the white walls of the clay-built buildings. At sea it hadn't seemed as bright as it did here on land, where the glare reflected off every surface.

Alexandria was filled with a strange mixture of people: soldiers and airmen and sailors, all walking around in uniform, all talking in different accents – English, Scots, Welsh, Australian, New Zealand, South African, Indian, Greek. Add in the local Arab population, and it was a complete jumble of languages and noise.

Ginger, Pete, Chalky and I went for a walk on our first day. It seemed odd to see modern army vehicles driving through this ancient city which looked like something out of the Bible, thousands of years old: narrow streets packed with white houses, market stalls, bearded men in long robes shouting and pushing, women covered from head to toe, everything being carried on donkeys. There were camels as well, loaded with huge bags of stuff. It was like going back in time. And the smell! I suppose it came from all those camels and donkeys doing their business all over the place, and the fact that there didn't seem to be a lot of water about. I don't think the toilets were linked to a proper drainage system. If they were, then the outlet of the sewer wasn't far away. We went into the *souk*, which was what they called the market, and there was absolutely everything for sale. It made our street markets at home seem pretty poor by comparison. Back in England we had fruit and veg stalls, and stands selling old clothes, and pots and pans all set out in lines. This market was like a madhouse: a maze of stalls with brightly coloured clothes and carpets, fruit of all sorts, and living animals, tied up or in cages. Meat on the hoof, Pete commented.

As we stepped out of the *souk* and turned a corner, an overpowering smell of stale urine hit us. It smelt like the biggest toilet ever, but it wasn't. We had walked into a large square surrounded by the backs of buildings, and in the square were enormous vats made of clay, with men treading something down in them.

"I hope that's not the local wine being trodden from grapes," muttered Ginger.

"No," said Chalky. "It's a tannery. It's how they make leather here in North Africa. They put animal skins in those vats and soak them in urine. They've been doing it the same way for thousands of years."

"How come you know all these things?" I asked.

"I dunno," shrugged Chalky. "People say things, and I just remember them."

The smell from the vats was really getting to us.

"I don't think I'm going to have any stomach for food," complained Pete, holding his nose.

Chalky grinned. "It won't stop me eating," he said cheerfully. "Our house in Newcastle is near the slaughterhouse. This reminds me of home."

We spent four days in Alexandria, and then we were packed into a convoy of canvas-topped lorries and driven out into the desert. Once we'd left Alexandria behind us, the road changed into a track of rock beneath a covering of soft sand, so the lorries kicked up a trail of dust all the way. I was near the back of our lorry so I got a good view of the landscape as we drove along. It was barren. Empty. Now and then a little bush sprouted up from the rocky ground as if determined that it was going to grow, no matter what, but the overall feeling was that this was a dead place: no water, no plants, just miles and miles of sand and rock as far as the eye could see. The road was bumpy and the lorry shook the whole time.

"Does anyone know where we're going?" Ginger asked.

Most of us shook our heads. We'd been ordered to load up all our gear and get on to the lorries, and that was all we knew. I'd learnt that was the way in the Army – no one told you anything. As a soldier you didn't ask why or what or where, you just obeyed orders.

"A bloke in Alexandria told me we're going to a place called El Alamein," said Tully Ward, a sapper from another unit.

"Where's that?" asked Pete.

"It's about sixty miles west of Alexandria," said Tully. "According to this bloke, it's where our boys have retreated to."

There was an uncomfortable silence in the lorry at the mention of "retreating", and I looked at Pete, thinking of what he'd said about his cousin Mike. Pete shook his head. "I'm saying nothing," he said. "Last time I opened my mouth I nearly ended up on a charge."

We drove on, further and further into the desert, and then I began to notice the flies. There had been flies in Alexandria, but these ones were even bigger. These were huge black creatures that swarmed into the lorries. Soon we were all swatting away at them as they settled on our arms and our faces.

"Ugh!" I exclaimed, as I spat out a fly that had crawled between my lips.

"They're looking for moisture," said Ginger, waving his hands around his head to keep the flies from settling. "Out here in the desert, with our sweat and spit, we're the best chance they have of getting any."

With lots of arm waving, and slapping at the flies with our desert hats, we managed to drive most of them away for a while, but as we went further into the desert, more flies came after us.

Finally, after nearly three hours of bone-shaking travelling, our convoy of lorries pulled up at what looked like an enormous army base. It was larger than anything I'd imagined. It looked like a city of small tents and lorries and tanks that stretched south for as far as I could see.

"This is it, lads," muttered Tully. "El Alamein. The front line."

"How far does it go?" I asked, shading my eyes against the bright sun to look at the line of lorries and tents disappearing into the distance.

"According to this bloke in Alexandria, the front line is thirty miles long, running all the way from the coast down south. This side is us, and about five miles or so in that direction . . ." Tully pointed westwards ". . . are the Germans."

"Right, you lot!" bellowed Sergeant Ross, who'd been riding in the cab of one of the other vehicles. "Stop yapping and get down from those lorries! There's a war on and we won't win it by nattering!"

We hauled our equipment off the lorries, and followed Sergeant Ross to the nearest line of small tents – one of the hundreds of rows, like streets packed with houses.

The men we were replacing had already cleared their belongings out of the tents, and were sitting around outside, waiting to board the lorries to set off back to Alexandria. As Ginger, Pete, Chalky and

I headed for the tent we'd been allocated, I stopped by the four men sitting outside it, their kitbags and tools stacked up beside them.

"What's it like out here, then?" I asked.

The four men looked at each other as if I'd said something stupid, then one of them grinned at me: "It's great, mate," he said. "It's like being on holiday. All the sand you could ask for. If it wasn't for perishing Rommel bombing the life out of us and making us walk backwards for hundreds of miles at a time, loaded down with as much as we can carry, it'd be a great life."

The other three soldiers chuckled.

"Come on, you men!" bellowed Sergeant Ross. "Less talk, more action!"

As Sergeant Ross moved on to chase up the rest of the unit, the soldier who'd spoken shook his head. "More action!" he echoed sarcastically. "You'll all get action soon enough."

"Right," nodded one of the other men. "Rommel and his army are just five or so miles away, getting ready to attack as we speak. He's pushed us a thousand miles back to here, right across North Africa. He only needs one last push. If he can get through our position here at Alamein, then what's left between him and Alexandria?"

"Desert," said Ginger.

"Exactly," nodded the man. "Nothing but sand. You lot are our last hope."

Just then a sergeant appeared. "Come on!" he bellowed at the four men. "Get on board the lorries. You lucky people are having a rest you don't deserve!"

The soldiers got up, gathered their kitbags and tools, and headed for the waiting lorries. One of them stopped and turned, then gave me a wink.

"Do me a favour, mate. Stop the Germans getting through for as long as you can, will you? After what we've been through, I've promised myself a few days of fun in Alexandria before Rommel gets there."

With that he laughed, and then hurried after his mates.

Over the next few days we got ourselves used to being at the front-line position at Alamein. We were now part of the Eighth Army – the name given to the Allied forces in the desert. It wasn't just a British Army, it was a mixture of regiments and battalions from the different countries of the Empire, mainly Australia, New Zealand, South Africa, India and Rhodesia. The British officers did their best to stop us British soldiers from having too much to do with the other nations, especially the Australians. I found out why one day when three Australian soldiers came into our part of the camp, saying they were trying to set up an international rugby tournament among the soldiers of the Eighth Army.

"The idea is every country puts together a team: you Brits, us Aussies, the Kiwis, the South Africans, and we all put a bit of money into the kitty, and the winners take the loot," announced their leader, a tall, muscular guy who introduced himself as Eddie Kelly. He grinned. "Of course, we Aussies will win, there's no doubt about that. But we need someone to beat to make it interesting. The Kiwis say they'll join in if we can get a few more teams. So, what do you say?"

Chalky shook his head.

"We don't play rugby," he said. "Our game's football."

One of the other Australians sneered. "Football!" he scoffed. "That's a game for pansies. No wonder you Poms need our help in beating this Hitler bloke – you're all soft."

"Some Brits play rugby," said Ginger. "It's just that those who don't are more intelligent than those that do. We think you have to be pretty stupid to play a game where you get your head trampled on."

"Who you calling stupid?" snapped the Australian, and for a second I thought there was going to be a fight between him and Ginger. Then we heard Sergeant Ross's voice calling out: "You men! What do you think you're doing?"

Immediately Ginger, Chalky, Pete and I snapped smartly to attention. The Australians looked at us, then at one another, shaking their heads.

"Proper little toy soldiers, ain't they?" grinned Eddie Kelly.

Ross had joined us and he glared at the three Australians. "What are you men doing in this part of the camp?" he demanded. "And stand to attention when you're talking to a non-commissioned officer."

The three Australians laughed out loud.

"An officer?" chuckled the man who'd been about to fight Ginger. Then he pushed his face close to Ross's and said, "That's the trouble with you Brits. You'd salute a camel if it had an officer's hat on. Well that's not the way we work. Show me a man I respect and I'll salute him. If he buys me a beer first, that is."

Ross's face grew purple with rage. "How dare you!" he spluttered. "What is your name and regiment, soldier? I'll have you on a charge."

The soldier shook his head.

"No you won't," he said. "No Pommie gives me orders."

Kelly put his hand on his mate's shoulder to calm him down.

"Let it go, Sean," he said. "We're all in this war together, remember. If they don't want to play a game of rugby, forget 'em."

With that the three Australians ambled off, heading towards their own separate camp.

Throughout this exchange Ginger, Pete, Chalky and I had remained standing stiffly to attention. I was shocked at the way the Australian had spoken to Ross. No man in the British Army would have dared to say anything like that, not unless he wanted to face a court martial on a charge of insubordination.

Ross stood glaring after the three Australians, a nerve in the side of his face twitching angrily, and then he became aware of the four of us.

"At ease!" he snapped.

As we relaxed, Ross addressed us, his face grim. "You men are to have nothing to do with those Australians, besides fighting beside them and working with them. I will not have their bad influence spreading through the ranks of my platoon. Is that clear?"

"Yes, Sarge," we said.

When Ross had gone, I turned to the others. "Did you hear the way that Australian spoke to Sergeant Ross?" I said, still shocked. "That was amazing!"

"I heard the Australians have their own way of doing things," said Chalky. "Someone said the ordinary soldiers call their officers by their first names, sometimes even by nicknames. They're like all mates together."

Ginger laughed. "Can you imagine us being mates with Ross and having a beer with him?" he grinned.

"Only if he bought the round of drinks," laughed Pete.

The flies out in the desert took some getting used to. There were no mess tents, which meant that all meals were taken out in the open, and the flies just loved that. I learnt to drink a mug of tea with my hand over the top to keep them out, sipping the tea between my fingers. In an effort to solve the problem of the flies, an order had been issued that every man was to kill 50 flies every day. With them hovering around us by the million, that was easy, you could kill 50 in the space of a few minutes while you were drinking tea. But it didn't stop them, they just kept coming.

The main topic of conversation among the men was the leader of the German Army in the desert, Field Marshal Rommel.

"He's clever," announced one of our mates, Jez Cromer. Jez had been out in the desert for eighteen months, and from him we learnt what had been going on. It was a similar story to the one Pete had told about his cousin Mike, but his time we were hearing it from the horse's mouth.

"When I was first out here there was only the Italians we were fighting," Jez told us. "That was January 1941. There were about 40,000 of us under our Supreme Commander General Wavell, and half a million Italians, but we wiped the floor with 'em. In just two months we took 150,000 Italian prisoners, and almost the whole Italian Army surrendered. Great. As far as we were concerned, that was it, the War was over. And then Hitler sent out Rommel to help the Italians. He brought over a division of tanks – Panzers, they call them – and before we knew what was happening, Rommel started to attack. Not a big all-out attack, but small attacks where he thought we were weakest. And he was right.

"Before we knew it, we were retreating. He was catching us unawares, coming out of the desert where no one expected him. Very cunning. That's why he got the nickname 'Desert Fox'. By July 1941 we'd been pushed right back about a thousand miles, almost to this point here at Alamein."

"And you've been here ever since?" said Ginger.

"No," said Jez, shaking his head. "Wavell was replaced by General Auchinleck, we call him 'the Auk'. He said we were going to fight back. And we did. Last November we went on the offensive and this time it was Rommel's turn to be pushed back a thousand miles, right back to the other side of Libya. Him and his Germans and Italians."

"So what happened?" asked Chalky. "Why are we back here?"

Jez shrugged. "I don't know," he said. "Except that just when we thought Rommel was finished, he launched a counter-attack. January, it was, nearly eight months ago. And try as we might to stop him, he just kept pushing us further and further back, until we landed here." Jez shook his head and sighed. "He's a clever general, that Rommel. He knows what he's doing when it comes to fighting a war. And so far no one seems able to stop him."

12 – 29 August 1942

The big job that Ross had for me and the lads was filling sandbags and building defensive walls with them. All day long we shovelled sand into sacks and tied them up. When we had a big pile of them we built a wall along the front line of our position. This wall would form a line of defence if the Germans launched an attack and managed to get through the minefields. It was hot, hard and boring work. Still, it was safer than being out in the minefields.

We'd been in the desert for nearly a week, when word came through that a new set of commanders were taking over the Allied Army in North Africa.

"The Auk's been sacked," Tully Ward told me and Chalky.

"Why?" I asked.

"Because he hasn't been able to beat Rommel," said Tully, "and we're back here in Egypt after retreating halfway across Africa, instead of kicking Rommel and his army out."

"Who's taking over from him?" asked Chalky.

"According to my sources, Field Marshal Alexander," said Tully.

"What's he like?" I asked.

"No idea," Tully shrugged. "Never met him. He's going to be the new commander-in-chief of everything. Plus, he's bringing a new commander for the Eighth Army. A general called Montgomery."

"What's he like?" asked Chalky.

Again, Tully shrugged. "No idea," he repeated. "Though I do hear he wasn't first choice for the job. Everyone wanted General Gott. He's been out here before and knows what desert war's like."

"So why didn't they send Gott?" I asked.

"Because he was killed," said Tully. "Didn't you hear?"

I shook my head. "How?" I asked.

"He was on his way here when the Germans shot his plane down. Killed him." Tully shook his head. "So instead we've got a bloke taking charge who's never been out in the desert. What a way to run a war!" As he turned to go he stopped and said, "A word of advice, Tim. Always try and keep up with what's going on. Who's in charge and who's about to get the push. It's all part of staying alive in this war."

"So," said Chalky after Tully had gone. "We've got a new commander. I wonder what he'll be like?"

"Tully doesn't seem to think much of him," I commented.

"Yeah, but Tully's never met him," Chalky pointed out. "He might be good."

"He'll need to be," I said with a sigh. "So far none of them seem to have been able to stop Rommel and his gang."

It was the next day, 13 August, that we got our chance to meet our new commander. We'd just finished breakfast when the signal bugles sounded for Assembly, and we all hurried out to the area of stony earth that was our parade ground. Sergeant Ross was already there when we arrived.

"Right, you lot! Form ranks! Get in line!" he shouted. "Your new commander's coming to see what sort of men he's taken on! Let's try and impress him! Come on, hurry up!"

We all shuffled into our lines beneath the desert sun. Ginger, Pete, Chalky and I were in the line at the front. We'd been standing there for about fifteen minutes, wondering what all the fuss was about, when a jeep pulled up and a thin-faced man with a small moustache got out. He was wearing shorts and a woolly jumper, but what was most noticeable was that instead of wearing a general's cap, on his head was an Australian bush-hat with metal badges stuck in it.

"Are you sure he's a general?" whispered Ginger.

"Quiet in the ranks!" bellowed Sergeant Ross. "'Tenshun!"

We all snapped smartly to attention and Montgomery walked along the lines of soldiers, inspecting us. When he'd finished he returned to his jeep and climbed into the back of it.

"That was a quick inspection," muttered Pete.

But Montgomery didn't sit down. Instead, he turned to look at us, and I realized that he was using his jeep as a platform so he could see us, and all of us could see him.

"Men!" he announced. "I am General Montgomery, the new commanding officer of the Eighth Army in North Africa. So far the fighting here in the desert has been a tug-of-war, with first our side pushing the Germans and the Italians back, and then Rommel and his army pushing you men back to this spot here at El Alamein. Rommel believes that he needs only one more push and he will drive through us and reach Alexandria. If that happens, the war in North Africa will be over and we will have lost. We cannot allow that to happen.

"My orders from the Prime Minister are to destroy Rommel and his army. There will be no further retreating. We will fight on the ground that we now occupy here at Alamein, and if we can't stay here alive then we will stay here dead."

As these words sank in, I could feel a change in every man standing in the lines. No one said anything, no one reacted with words, but we all knew from Montgomery's tone that he meant what he said. No surrender. No more retreat. We stand firm, and we win or we die.

"I intend to drive Rommel and his army completely out of Africa," Montgomery continued. "But we shall do it in our own good time, when we are ready. When we are strong enough to launch an attack, and be able to follow it through.

"But first, we have to be ready for the battle that is about to happen. We know that Rommel is preparing to launch an attack against our position here. It may come in a week, it may come in two weeks. It may come tomorrow. But when it comes, we will stand firm. The Germans must not get past this position. It is up to you men to make sure of that."

With that he nodded to the officers, saluted all of us, and sat down in the back of his jeep. His driver immediately jumped behind the steering wheel, started the vehicle, and they drove off across the shimmering desert.

Sergeant Ross turned to face us. "Right, you men!" he bellowed. "You heard what the new commanding officer said! It's up to you! Orders will be issued later. Dismissed."

As the lines broke up and we walked away, Pete shook his head. "Stay here alive or stay here dead," he grimaced. "It's not our choice, is it?"

"I like him," I said. "He seems to know what he's doing."

"That's the way of generals," said Pete gloomily. "They all have the air of knowing what they're doing. The problems come when they try to put it into practice. I mean, it's all very well him telling us we're going to beat Rommel, but I bet right now Rommel's saying exactly the same thing to his men."

Despite what Pete said, there was no doubt that Montgomery had made an impression on the Army. I found out later that he'd driven round to every division and regiment along the whole Alamein front, giving the same speech about there being no more retreat, and "if we can't stay here alive we'll stay here dead". It seemed to put a bit more backbone into the men and improve morale, as well as scaring the living daylights out of everyone.

The first real impact it had on us sappers was when we were assembled by Sergeant Ross and told we were to enlarge the minefields in front of our positions.

"General Montgomery isn't joking when he says we're not going to retreat any further," he informed us. "So, to make sure that Rommel and his army don't have it easy when they launch their attack, he wants bigger and stronger minefields. Thousands of mines. He wants every German tank that tries to attack us blown to smithereens. Every German foot soldier put out of action before they get to our front lines. So, lads, spades out and let's get digging. And remember, the Germans booby-trap their mines, so let's booby-trap ours. Trip-wires hidden in the ground, every trick you can think of. It's our job to make sure that when the Germans launch their attack, their troops never get as far as us."

And so we set to work. Knowing that the Germans would be watching us through telescopes, and from the air, we started to expand the minefields. Although it wasn't the same as finding and disabling an enemy land mine, it was still dangerous work. Every time you picked a mine out from the vehicle, you were aware that you were holding something that, if dropped or handled wrongly, could blow up and kill you.

We placed the mines like we were sowing plants in a field. The lorry carrying the mines and equipment rolled forward in a straight line, which we kept clear of mines so that we had a track to follow to get through our own minefield. We dug holes, then took the mines from the lorry and sunk them just below ground level across a vast area. We marked it out with lengths of tape so we knew where the mines were.

We set the booby-traps: a length of wire attached to the detonator pin, the other end of the wire fixed to a large pin hammered into the ground. When the German sapper tried to lift the mine clear, the wire would pull the detonator pin and – bang! It was dirty, but they were doing the same to us.

We mixed the different types of mine in the same minefields: anti-tank mines (which were sunk deeper) as well as anti-personnel mines. The German sappers wouldn't find them all. They'd even be able to walk over the anti-tank mines without setting them off.

It took us a week to set out all the mines. Thousands and thousands of them. We needed so many that eventually we began to use German and Italian mines that had been captured. Many of the British ones we were putting down weren't actually made in Britain at all but were what were known as EP mines, or "Egyptian Pattern". The problem was that these were less stable than the ones made in Britain. Metal springs were a vital component of the detonators in British mines. In Egypt there was a problem making them, so they used a chemical fuse inside a glass phial instead. This meant that EP mines were much more fragile, and had to be handled very carefully.

All the time we were setting out the mines, we kept alert, half-expecting the Germans to attack. But they didn't.

"It'll be night when the Germans attack," said Ginger. "They won't hit us during daylight."

"Rommel's launched attacks during the day before now," Chalky pointed out.

"Yeah, but those were skirmishes," said Ginger. "Like Monty said, Rommel needs just one more big push to get to Alexandria.

That means a huge offensive, and he'll want to try to catch us off-guard. Trust me, it'll be at night."

By 25 August all our mines were in place and we sappers joined the rest of the Army in sitting behind our defensive front line, waiting for the Germans to attack. There was work to do for us, of course: making sure our big artillery guns and tanks were all in good working order; checking the supply vehicles over. But mostly we just waited.

30 August – 7 September 1942

It was 30 August and night had begun to fall. Our squad had spent the day laying out even more land mines to defend our front line. Counting the mines the Germans had put out in their own line, there must have been a million land mines between us and the Germans. The gap between the two front lines was a solid mass of minefields over thirty miles long, except for a strip a mile wide between the German minefield at the very front of their position, and ours.

We had finished our work for the day, and Ginger, Pete, Chalky and I were settling down for a quiet game of cards outside our tent, when the alarm sounded and someone shouted, "The Germans are coming!"

Immediately I rushed into our tent and grabbed my binoculars. As I was coming out I bumped into Sergeant Ross.

"Where you going, Jackson?" he demanded. "Bird-watching?"

"No, Sarge, I wanted to see the German advance up close."

Ross stared at me as if I was mad. "How close do you want to get, you idiot?" he snapped. "We're right at the front!"

"Not right at the front, Sarge," I pointed out. "Our tanks and big guns are in front of us."

"Be thankful they are, otherwise the Germans would be using you for target practice," said Ross. "Get your equipment and get with the others. If our guns take a hammering there'll be some nifty repairs needed."

"Yes, Sarge," I said.

With that Ross hurried off. I was still determined to see what was going on, so I put my binoculars to my eyes, and as I did so there was an enormous explosion just to my right, and the force of it knocked me over. A shower of sand and rocks rained down on me.

"Tim, you twit!" I heard Ginger's voice yell.

Then I felt myself being hauled to my feet.

"Here!" said Ginger, and he thrust my steel helmet towards me.

I put it on.

"If one of those rocks, or some shrapnel, had hit you on the head you could have been killed!" he shouted.

He had to yell to make himself heard because the German big guns had opened up now, and heavy shells were either exploding near us, or whistling over our heads and blowing up behind us. Our own big guns and tanks were returning the heavy fire.

"I wanted to see the attack up close," I shouted at Ginger.

"You'll be able to see it close enough if they get through!" yelled Pete.

He pointed out into the minefields we'd laid just that afternoon. Through the drifting smoke, and the light of our searchlights, I could see the German sappers trying to carve a way through the minefields. Their tanks loomed huge and menacing behind them.

"They've reached our minefields already!" shouted Chalky.

Gunfire opened up from our side, tracers poured into the minefields and cut down the German sappers at the front.

"Poor swines," muttered Pete.

"They'd do the same to us if the positions were the other way round," said Chalky.

"The positions will be the other way round soon," said Ginger grimly. "And then we'll be the sappers being shot at."

I put my binoculars back up to my eyes, and found that one of the lenses had been smashed when the rocks had fallen on me. I lowered them and just watched, every now and then ducking down behind the walls of sandbags as German bullets and shells came hurtling towards our position.

The noise was incredible! All thought of talking vanished. Ginger opened his mouth to say something, but I couldn't hear a word. All I could hear was the crashing and booming of explosions as German shells blew up, and the thunder of our own heavy guns returning shellfire and the metallic scream of our machine guns firing.

Behind the barricading walls of sandbags, we were joined by a platoon of infantrymen with rifles ready, bayonets fixed. Sergeant Ross appeared and gestured to us to follow him. The four of us slipped away from the cover of the wall, crouching low as bullets and shells whistled over our heads. As we did so, more infantrymen appeared and joined their mates behind the barricades. They also had their rifles – ready for hand-to-hand fighting if the Germans broke through our defences.

We followed Sergeant Ross to where one of our six-pounder guns had taken a direct hit. Two of the gun crew were lying on the ground and even in the darkness I could see the blood soaking their uniforms. Sergeant Ross pointed at the six-pounder and we set to work, taking off the parts of the big gun that still worked. The idea was that if any other six-pounders took a hit and were wrecked, we might be able to build a replacement from the cannibalized parts. Providing there were the men to man it, of course.

As we worked, a medical team arrived to tend the wounded men. It was obvious from the shake of the head of the medico who examined the two men lying on the ground that both were dead. Meanwhile, the rest of the team set to work to patch up the four other men from the gun-crew as best they could. The seriously injured who couldn't walk were taken off in an ambulance.

As Pete and I worked at unbolting the twisted gun barrel from its mounting, I was suddenly aware of the droning noise of aeroplane engines above us, barely audible above the noise of the gunfire. I looked up and saw a fleet of planes flying from behind our lines towards the Germans. As they reached the German positions, I saw what looked like hundreds of tiny parachutes falling from the planes . . . and then suddenly they burst into flames. Parachute flares. Hundreds of burning torches falling down on the Germans, lighting up the night sky as they fell, turning the night into broad daylight.

Another wave of planes followed the first, and they began to bomb the brightly lit targets below. I stood there, awed by the enormity of it, and imagined what it must be like for the advancing

Germans: to be caught inside the minefields in the bright lights and beneath the bombs.

But the Germans hadn't given up. There were more whistling sounds above me as their shells came over, and more explosions behind and beside me as they blew up, shaking the ground beneath my feet.

Pete tapped me on the shoulder and jerked his thumb at the twisted gun barrel. I nodded and went back to work with my spanner, loosening the nuts and bolts that held it in place. All the time I was aware that we were under fire with the crash of guns. The air was now thick with black smoke.

I took out the last bolt and Pete and I used brute force to heave the gun barrel away from its mounting. The direct hit on the barrel had pushed it back into the mounting at an awkward angle, but finally we managed to get it free.

Meanwhile, Ginger and Chalky had taken a good gun barrel off the damaged mounting of another six-pounder. Pete and I found them, and the four of us carried this undamaged gun barrel to the good mounting of our battle-hit gun, and bolted it into place. One good gun put together from two damaged ones.

We carried on working in this way, stripping the good parts from damaged guns and stacking them together in neat piles, while the battle continued around us. There was no sign of the enemy troops breaking through our front line.

At 0200 hours, Sergeant Ross came down the line and gestured to us – it was still too noisy for us to hear him speak – to return to our tents and get some sleep. A replacement team of sappers was with him, all kitted up, ready to take over from us.

As I hit my bunk the battle was still going on. The noise should have kept me awake; the fear of being hit by German shells should have kept me awake, or of German troops breaking through our front line and catching me asleep. But the sheer physical exhaustion of the hard work under those conditions meant that within a few minutes of my head hitting my pillow, I was fast asleep.

The next morning, as we all struggled out of our tent to answer the "Reveille" bugle call, the first thing that struck me was the smell of burning metal. It was everywhere, in the hazy smoke that hung in the bright sunshine of the new day in the desert.

As we walked to the parade ground, we passed a unit of Engineers heading back to their tents, finishing their shift and going to bed. Their faces were blackened with smoke and their clothes were stained with oil and sweat. I recognized one of them as Joe Johnson, a sapper from another unit. He looked absolutely worn out.

"Morning, Joe!" I greeted him. "Looks like we won, then."

"No thanks to you lot, all safely tucked up in bed," retorted Joe.

"We were out there before you," Chalky countered. "We were stripping guns under enemy fire while you lot were having supper."

"Anyway, it don't look like we've won yet," said Joe. "One of the tank drivers told me the Germans are massing by that big ridge, getting ready for another go." Joe left us to it, and I looked at the others.

"It's not over," Pete said gloomily. "We've got to go through it all again."

"That's just Joe Johnson winding us up," said Chalky confidently. "The Germans can't have stood up to the hammering we gave them last night. Remember the planes dropping those flares on them? And the bombers? Not to mention our big guns. And just listen. . ."

We stood there and listened. Nothing – just the background buzz of an army going about its business, mending its machines.

"See," grinned Chalky. "If the Germans were still going to attack us, we'd have heard about it by now. Trust me, it's over. We've won."

The smile was wiped off Chalky's face as soon as we lined up on the parade ground, and Sergeant Ross addressed us.

"Right, men!" he bellowed. "You did well last night. Those minefields kept the enemy away from our front lines long enough for our big guns and the RAF to do them some damage. But the word is that the Germans are going to try again. It looks like this one will be a daylight attack. So, I want everyone standing by in units as before. Our job will be the same as before: strip and repair all damaged weaponry. If we're going to stop the Germans breaking through our position, we're going to need every gun we've got."

Just as he said those words, we heard a series of dull thuds from the German positions, followed by the whistling sounds of flying shells.

"Incoming!" yelled Sergeant Ross. "Take cover!"

We ran to the low walls of sandbags that offered us protection – just in time as it turned out, a series of explosions erupted as the German shells landed behind our lines.

Immediately our own guns responded, the deafening THUD THUD THUD of their gun-barrels sliding backwards and forwards as they burst into flame and smoke, punching shells towards the Germans.

"Right, men!" hollered Sergeant Ross. "Action stations!"

And so the battle started again, and once more we were up to our sweaty armpits in smoke, fire and explosions and dead and injured men.

It went on like that for five days. Day after day and night after night. The Germans would launch an attack with their big guns and their tanks, while their sappers tried to force their way through our minefields. Our own defences poured red-hot metal at them, keeping their sappers and tanks pinned down, while the RAF flew bomber sorties against them.

As we lined up on the parade ground on the morning of 7 September, surrounded by drifting smoke from the previous night's battle, Sergeant Ross made a different sort of announcement. Instead of telling us, as usual, that the Germans were massing for yet another attack, he bellowed at us: "Good news, lads. The word from our observers is that the Germans are pulling back. We've held them. Well done."

8 September – 14 October 1942

The battle we'd been in for the last seven days became known as the Battle of Alam Halfa, because the main point of the German attack was aimed at the Alam Halfa ridge to one side of El Alamein. Once it had sunk in that the Germans really had withdrawn and it wasn't just a clever ruse on Rommel's part, I felt an amazing feeling of elation – a sense of wonder at the fact I was still alive. We had been in battle, and we'd won. Or, if we hadn't won, at least we hadn't lost. We'd held off the German attack. The minefields that the rest of the boys and I had laid had done their job and slowed down the Germans long enough for our artillery to take good aim at their tanks and advancing infantrymen. The big question now was: what would happen next? We all reckoned that Rommel's forces had taken such a hammering from our defences that it was unlikely he'd launch another attack too soon after the first one had failed. So, when would Montgomery launch his own offensive?

"The end of September," said Pete.

"Why the end of September?" asked Chalky.

"Because of the full moon," replied Pete.

"What, you reckon he's one of those lunatics who's driven mad by the full moon?" asked Chalky, bewildered.

"Maybe he turns into a werewolf," I grinned.

"No, you idiots," said Pete, irritated. "Haven't you noticed that most of the big attacks come when there's a full moon? That's so there's enough light for the attackers to see what they're doing and where they're going."

It had never struck me before, but once I thought about it, I realized that Pete was right. Rommel had launched his attack against us when there was a full moon. So, if Montgomery was using the same tactics, then we'd be launching our attack against the Germans at the next full moon, which, as Pete said, was in the last week of September.

But the end of September came and went, and there was no sign of preparations for an all-out attack.

"Maybe Montgomery doesn't believe in waiting for a full moon," suggested Ginger. "Maybe he's going to go when everything's at its darkest."

"Or attack in broad daylight, when the Germans aren't expecting it," added Chalky.

Pete shook his head. "Mark my words, we'll go when there's a full moon," he said. "Anyone like to place a small bet on it?"

"Yeah," said Chalky. "How much?"

"Two pounds," said Pete.

Chalky shook his head. "Too steep for me," he said. "Five bob?"

"You're on," said Pete, and the two shook on it.

As we moved into the first few days of October, our unit received an order from Sergeant Ross to repair a tank that had been damaged going over a mine.

"What sort of tank is it?" I asked. "I need to know what tools to bring with me."

"No tools that you've got in your box will fit this thing, Jackson," said Ross. "It's a Bitsa."

"A what?" asked Ginger.

"Bitsa this, bitsa that," explained Ross, with a grin. "Its official name is a Scorpion. It's basically a Matilda tank with lots of bits and pieces added."

The Matilda was a two-man tank, a bit smaller than most battle tanks, but with very thick armour.

"What sort of bits and pieces, Sarge?" asked Pete.

"You'll see when you get there," he said.

We loaded our tools into a truck and Chalky took the wheel, heading north under Sergeant Ross's directions. We drove for about five miles, and then we came across a tank sunk into the sand. I could see at once that its offside track had been buckled. What was odd about this tank was that instead of having a large gun mounted on it, it had what looked like a big round drum with lots of long chains hanging down, sticking out the front between two long shafts.

We all got out and gathered round it. The driver of the tank was waiting for us and he grinned as we reached him.

"Hello, mates," he said cheerily. "I've had a bit of an accident with your invention."

"It ain't our invention," said Ginger.

"Well, it was put together by your lot – the sappers," said the tank driver. "Trouble is, when I was giving it a go, I must have missed a mine with the flails."

"What are the flails?" Chalky whispered to me.

"Driver," ordered Sergeant Ross, "start the engine and demonstrate the flails for this lot of ignoramuses here."

"Right, Sergeant," said the tank driver. "Only it won't clear anything because the tank won't move with the busted track."

"We'll fix the track in a moment," said Ross. "Just show them how this thing works."

"Yes, Sarge," nodded the driver, and he clambered up on the tank and disappeared through the hatch inside it.

We all stood and looked at this weird machine for a moment, wondering what it was going to do, when the engine of the tank fired up, and suddenly the drum between the shafts began to turn and the lengths of chain began to spin out, crashing into the ground in front of the tank, beating at the sand and rocks and sending up a cloud of dust.

We all began coughing, and I put my hands over my mouth and nose to stop myself from choking. Luckily, the tank driver turned off the engine, and then his head popped out from the hatch.

"See it?" he asked.

"And tasted it!" coughed Ginger, and he spat on the ground to get the dust out of his mouth.

"There you have it, lads!" grinned Sergeant Ross. "The Scorpion anti-mine tank! As it moves forward the chains hit the ground and set off any mines lying in front of it."

"So why is it sitting there with one of its tracks buckled, Sarge?" asked Ginger.

"Because the driver can't drive straight," said Ross.

"I *was* driving straight!" protested the driver. "One of the mines must have been deeper in the ground than the others, so the chains didn't touch it."

Pete let out an admiring whistle.

"Well, if they can get this thing to work, it'll put us out of a job," he said.

"That's wishful thinking, Morgan," scoffed Ross. "There is one major problem with this machine which is why it'll never replace you men."

"What's that, Sarge?" asked Chalky.

"If it does hit a mine it stops in its tracks, which means the tanks coming behind it can't get past. On the other hand, if one of you gets blown up by a mine while trying to disable it, the tanks behind you can just roll right over you."

It wasn't a comforting thought.

"Right, you lot," ordered Ross. "I want the track put back on this vehicle, let's get it rolling again. And make a careful note of how you do it, because you're going to be mending an awful lot of these machines before this war's over, or my name's not Ross."

We set to work, first checking to make sure the area around the tank was clear of other mines. As he got out his tools, Ginger looked at the Scorpion anti-mine tank and grinned.

"This is one of the weirdest machines I've seen since I've been in the sappers," he said. "We'd have to go a long way to find anything odder than this."

As it turned out, Ginger didn't have to wait too long to find something stranger than the Bitsa. The day after we'd got it rolling again, Sergeant Ross came into the mess tent as we were finishing our breakfast.

"Jackson, Matthews, Morgan and White," he snapped. "There's a convoy of tanks and lorries heading to the southern position. Grab your kit, get yourself on one of those lorries and once you're there report to Captain Maskelyne, A Force, Royal Engineers. You're joining the Magic Gang."

"The what, Sarge?" asked Ginger.

"The Magic Gang," repeated Ross.

"What's that?" I asked.

"You should know by now, Jackson, that you don't ask questions in this army, you just carry out orders," said Ross crisply.

"How long are we going to be there, Sarge?" asked Pete. "How much kit should we take with us?"

"That depends on how long Captain Maskelyne wants you for," replied Ross. "Just take your usual pack and equipment. Come on, get a move on! This war won't wait for you!"

As we watched Sergeant Ross walk smartly out of the tent, Pete shook his head. "You know, half the time I haven't got the faintest idea what Ross is talking about," he said.

"What's the Magic Gang?" I asked, still puzzled.

"It's a new unit not long been put together," said Chalky. "I heard some bloke in B Unit talking about it. It's a mixture of Royal Engineers and wizards."

"Wizards?" I laughed. "We're going to use magic to defeat the Jerries?"

"That's right," nodded Chalky.

"Here!" said Pete suddenly. "This Captain Maskelyne. Is he the same man who used to be on the stage before the war? The Great Maskelyne, the master illusionist?!"

"That's him," nodded Chalky. "Jasper Maskelyne. He volunteered to help the war effort and they sent him out here to entertain the troops. But then he started to come up with ideas about how he could use his trickery to beat the Germans, so they made him a captain in the Engineers and set up this new unit, A Force. Known as the Magic Gang."

"What do they do?" I asked.

"According to this bloke, they make tanks and things disappear, and then reappear in the middle of nowhere."

"Pull the other leg, it's got bells on!" jeered Ginger.

"It's true," insisted Chalky.

"Rubbish!" I snorted.

"I saw him performing on stage just before the War," said Pete.

"He was brilliant – fantastic! He really did make things disappear. And he sawed a woman in half, right before our eyes. It was incredible!"

"So?" I said. "It's one thing to do conjuring tricks on a stage, it's quite another to make a full-size tank disappear and reappear in the middle of the desert."

"Not just one tank," said Chalky. "He does it with hundreds of tanks. And lorries. He even makes planes disappear."

Just then the tent flap opened and Sergeant Ross looked in and glared at us.

"Are you lot still here?" he demanded crossly. "I gave you an order. Now get your kit packed and get south, or I'll have you all on a charge!"

The convoy was enormous: about a hundred lorries and fifty tanks, all heading south in a long line. The four of us sat in the middle of it, in the back of a lorry. Above us, every now and then, we heard the sound of German planes circling us, like vultures hovering over their prey.

"If the Jerries attack us now, we'll be a sitting target," said Pete. "In a long line like this, and in broad daylight, we're like a line of ducks, waiting to be shot at."

"They won't attack," said Chalky. "Reconnaissance only, I bet you. Seeing what we're up to."

"Don't you believe it," said Ginger. "Pete's right. At this speed they could pick us off. They could knock out three or four tanks and the same number of lorries easily."

"Ah, but then the Jerries could lose their planes as well," Chalky pointed out. We all looked at the machine guns set up on the backs of the lorries; the gunners that moved them watching the skies determinedly. "Remember, with all this desert, our gunners have got a clear line of fire at any plane that comes close."

"That's assuming they use fighter planes to attack us," pointed out Ginger. "They could use bombers from a higher altitude. Our machine guns wouldn't be able to touch them."

"At the first sign of their bombers, our RAF boys would be up there, no problem," said Chalky confidently. "I tell you. . ."

He was cut short as the air around us erupted into gunfire as the machine gunner on the back of the lorry behind ours swung his weapon and let off a burst; streams of bullets poured upwards. I heard the scream of a plane's engine as it came in low and the chatter of bullets from its guns.

"Down!" yelled Pete, and we all threw ourselves on to the wooden floor of the lorry. Not that it would do much good, I thought. The lorry covering was made of canvas and bullets would just tear right through the fabric. However, when you were under attack it was safer to be lying down.

The machine gunners on the lorries swung their guns round and kept up a stream of fire after the German plane as it disappeared into the distance. "All right, alarm over," said Ginger.

The sound of the guns stopped. We all got up off the floor of the lorry and took our places on the crates. As we did so, Chalky went as white as his name.

"Oh my lord!" he said, and for a moment I thought he was going to pass out.

"What's the matter?" I asked. "You've been shot at before."

"Yeah, but not when I've been sitting in a lorry full of explosives," he said. He pointed at the crates we were sitting on. They were marked "AMMUNITION" and "DANGER. EXPLOSIVES".

"Of all the lorries to choose to sit in, we've picked the most dangerous!" groaned Pete.

"Anyway, Chalky," said Ginger, pointedly. "Tell us again how we're not going to be attacked."

Chalky shook his head and wiped his brow. "OK," he said. "A bloke can't be right all the time."

As we journeyed south, we all kept an eye on the sky, watching out for another barrage from more German fighter planes, but they seemed content with just watching us.

I kept thinking about what Chalky and Pete had said about Captain Maskelyne. I'd never seen him perform, but I'd heard about him, of course. Just before the War the papers had been full of stories about him, with photographs showing him on stage pulling a string of razor blades out of his mouth, or standing around in an evening suit looking handsome. He looked like a film star: he was tall and slim, with black hair slicked back, a centre parting, and a neat pencil-thin moustache. All the women went mad for him. He could do amazing tricks – not just sawing a woman in half and then showing her to be perfectly all right afterwards, or doing incredible card tricks in which he read the mind of the person who'd chosen a card – but once I'd read he even made an elephant disappear from a stage in front of everyone. It was obviously all trickery, but I wondered what sort of magic he was going to use here in the desert, and how that trickery was going to help beat Rommel. The whole idea seemed impossible.

After about fifteen miles we drove past a gang of sappers who were busy digging a trench in the middle of nowhere. Near them were stacks of metal pipes, which were obviously going into the trench.

"Poor blokes," muttered Chalky as we passed them, leaving the sappers behind to carry on digging. I looked out of the back of the lorry and watched the men drop a length of pipe into the trench, then set to work digging up the next section to drop another length of pipe in.

"Why are they laying pipes out here in the middle of nowhere?" asked Ginger.

Pete shrugged. "Looks like they're putting in a water pipeline," he said.

"If they're running a water pipeline to the southern end, it's going to be a long job," I commented. "They're still only halfway there."

Finally, we came to the southern end of the Allied position. The place was buzzing with activity. Men wandered around, there were tanks and lorries, and crates and crates of ammunition and supplies piled one on top of the other. It was obvious that things were building up to a major offensive.

We asked a soldier where we could find Captain Maskelyne,

and he pointed to a tall slim figure standing beside a mountain of wooden crates of ammunition. He was holding a piece of paper and talking earnestly with a corporal. As we walked towards him, I realized that we hadn't really needed to ask. Maskelyne looked exactly the same as he did in his photographs, except for the khaki uniform and captain's cap.

Ginger, Pete, Chalky and I walked up to him just as he was stabbing his finger at the piece of paper and telling the corporal: "The point is, Wilson, this thing won't work unless the Jerries *believe*. We have to make them think these things are tanks and not just stacks of crates piled one on top of the other beneath camouflage nets, and for that we need tank tracks coming out from the netting. Tracks that look like this. You can make them with a long broom-handle. OK?"

The corporal nodded. "Will do, sir," he said, and he went off, taking the piece of paper with him.

"Captain Maskelyne?" asked Ginger.

Maskelyne turned to us. "Yes?" he queried.

"Privates Jackson, White, Morgan and Matthews, Royal Engineers, reporting for duty, sir," said Ginger.

We all stood stiffly to attention and saluted.

"Yes, that's quite enough of that," said Maskelyne dismissively. "If everyone spent less time saluting and more time getting on with actual work, this war would be over a lot damn quicker. Engineers, eh? Good. What tools have you brought with you?"

"Just our packs, sir," I said. "Spades for digging, and between us we've got wrenches and hammers and screwdrivers."

"That'll do," said Maskelyne. "Right, you men are going to be privileged to learn the secrets of the magician's trade – something that very few people are privy to. And you are going to help me pull off the biggest illusion of all time."

"Make tanks and planes disappear?" I said.

Maskelyne must have caught the note of disbelief in my voice, because he jerked his head towards me and fixed me with a steely look.

"And you are. . .?" he demanded.

"Private Jackson, sir," I answered.

"Well, Private Jackson, the answer to that is yes. For the past few days we have been making tanks and lorries disappear from this point and reappear thirty miles away at the northern point of the Allied position."

We stood in awkward silence. Finally I said, "We've just come from the north, sir, and we haven't seen them."

"Of course you haven't, Private, because they are invisible," said Maskelyne curtly. "And at the same time we have been keeping the non-existent tanks and lorries here in full sight of the Germans so they know they are still here. Even though they are not."

I caught Ginger's concerned expression and I knew he was thinking the same thing as me: we were dealing with a madman. The Great Maskelyne has actually gone mad with all this talk about tanks and lorries being "invisible".

Maskelyne looked at us, his fixed steely look scanning the faces of all four of us as we stood there in stunned and awkward silence, and then suddenly he burst out laughing.

"Oh my, if you could see your faces!" he roared delightedly.

We looked back at him, bewildered.

"Sir?" asked Chalky, baffled.

Maskelyne waved his arm around. "What do you see," he demanded, "all around you?"

We turned and looked at the bustling camp, and then turned back to Maskelyne. "Lots of soldiers," answered Pete. "Thousands of them."

"And?" prompted Maskelyne.

"Hundreds of tanks," said Chalky.

"Thousands of boxes of ammunition," I added.

"Like this one?" asked Maskleyne, and he pointed to the large crate next to him.

"Yes, sir," I nodded.

"Tap it," said Maskelyne.

I looked at him, puzzled. "Pardon, sir?"

"Bang your knuckles against it," he said.

I reached forward and did as he said. The knocking of my knuckles against the wood made a hollow sound.

"It's empty, sir," I said.

"As are most of these," said Maskelyne. "They're brought down by the lorryload, day after day after day, and stacked up, in full view of the German reconnaissance planes."

Then he pointed to a line of tanks hidden beneath camouflage nets.

"What do you see there?" he asked.

"Tanks, sir," said Pete. "Hidden by camouflage nets."

"Go and take a closer look," Maskelyne instructed us.

Puzzled, we went to the camouflage netting, and looked at the tank. Chalky reached through the netting, and tapped its side.

"Wood," he said in surprise.

"Wood and canvas," said Maskelyne. "Did you drive from the north?"

"Yes, sir," said Ginger.

"Did you pass a party of Engineers digging a trench?"

"Yes, sir," nodded Ginger. "About fifteen miles north of here."

"Why were they digging the trench?" asked Maskelyne.

"To lay a pipeline, sir," I replied. "They looked like water pipes to me."

"And where is this pipeline going to?"

"To here, sir," said Chalky. "At least, that's what it looked like. The trench was being dug from north to south."

"Excellent," nodded Maskelyne with a smile. "In fact you may be interested to know that at night they dig up those same pipes, and the next day, when the German planes are flying over to check on the progress, they carry on digging the trench even further south, laying the same pipes again. There is no pipeline, gentlemen. We are simply creating the illusion of a pipeline. As far as the Germans are concerned, their air reconnaissance tells them that a pipeline is being laid to this position to bring much-needed water here. Their same air reconnaissance also tells them not that we have lots of empty boxes and constructions of wood and canvas hidden under camouflage nets, but that there are masses of crates of ammunition and thousands of tanks here. What sort of message do you think that sends to Herr Rommel?"

"That a major attack is going to be launched from here involving thousands of men," I said.

Maskelyne nodded. "Correct, Private Jackson," he said.

"But . . . but what about the tanks up north being invisible?" I asked.

"Simple," said Maskelyne. It was obviously giving him great pleasure explaining the mystery behind these great tricks to us. "Next time you go back north, have a close look at some of the piles of crates stored there. You will find that many of them aren't piles of crates at all, but shelters made out of the sides of crates. Inside them are tanks, which can burst out of those shelters in a second. Also, many of the lorries up north are really tanks dressed up with wooden and canvas coverings to make them look like lorries from a distance. And some things that look like mess tents from the air, when seen from the ground actually have tanks inside them."

I had to admit it was brilliant. It was the biggest conjuring trick of all time, and if it worked, it could save hundreds of soldiers' lives. Rommel would think that Montgomery was going to launch his attack in the south, and so he'd put most of his troops there to defend it. When Montgomery actually attacked in the north, there'd be fewer Germans. In theory, it was a great plan.

My three friends and I worked with Captain Maskelyne and his Magic Gang for ten days, building lots of dummy tanks out of wood and canvas. We even made up fake soldiers to make it look like there was some kind of action going on around these "tanks". Every time a German reconnaissance plane came over, we moved the dummies to different positions, so it looked like there were hundreds of soldiers at work, getting ready for the assault.

While we were there, I found time to write a letter home to Mum. Or, at least, a letter for Uncle George to read to her. I'd only written to her a couple of times, once while I was training at Shorncliffe to let her know that I was all right, and once while we were on the boat. I hadn't had a reply from her yet, but I knew that was because she would have to ask Uncle George to write it for her, and Mum wasn't the kind of person who liked to ask for help or to let others see how she felt so I guessed she'd write back in her own good time.

The problem with writing a letter when you're in the Army and there's a war on is that your correspondence is checked by a senior officer to make sure you're not giving away any secrets that might "help the enemy", as they put it. So, we were not allowed to write about where we were, or what we were doing, or if there was any fighting going on, or if any of our mates had been wounded or killed, because any of that information might, apparently, be useful to the enemy.

Also, you were not allowed to write home and complain about anything, such as the food being lousy, or the flies in the desert making life a misery, because that might have "lowered morale", in the Army's words.

Which meant that about the only type of letter you could write home was one that said, "Dear Mum, I'm OK, everything is fine here, we're going to win the War any day now. Love from your son, Tim." Still, at least a letter from me would let her know that I was still alive and well enough to write. So, I wrote and told her I was out in the desert (though I expected the officer who'd be checking it would cross that out), and that I was well, and I was thinking of her, and hoping she was keeping safe, and I was looking forward to seeing her at home soon.

About the middle of October the lads and I got orders to return to the north, back to El Alamein itself. This time round, our journey with the convoy was safer, travelling at night, with no lights, moving slowly enough to see the vehicle in front so there was no risk of a collision. A hundred lorries and a hundred tanks, moving back to the northern position under cover of darkness, at a time when the German reconnaissance planes wouldn't be up and flying and able to see what we were up to.

"So, what do you reckon to the Great Maskelyne, Tim?" asked Ginger as we travelled north.

I shook my head in admiration. "He's a genius," I said. "To hide a whole army in one place, and have a pretend army in another, and in the middle of a desert where the Germans can see what's going on. It's absolutely fantastic!"

"Beats making an elephant disappear on stage at the Palladium," nodded Pete.

"It's only fantastic if the Germans fall for it," said Chalky.

"We fell for it, and we were right up close," I pointed out. Pete and Ginger nodded in agreement.

"Yeah, but we're not Rommel," said Chalky. "He's a clever one, that Desert Fox. I bet he's got a few tricks up his sleeve as well. Maybe he's got his own magician working for him. What do you think about that?"

I fell silent and thought about what Chalky had just said. It was a good point. Rommel was clever, there was no doubt about that. They didn't call him the "Desert Fox" for nothing. So far he'd outwitted every British general who'd come out to the desert to try and beat him. Montgomery was being very clever using Maskelyne the Magician to decoy the Germans into thinking the major attack was going to come from the south. But what if Rommel didn't fall for it? What if he had his own sneaky plans, which at that very moment he was putting into operation without us knowing about it?

15 – 23 October 1942

As soon as we got back to the main Alamein position, we realized that the easy-going days with Captain Maskelyne and the Magic Gang were over.

"Right, you lot," bellowed Sergeant Ross in greeting. "Your life of leisure is over! You're back among the workers now, so, get yourself equipped with a long-handled shovel from the stores and report back to me."

"A long-handled shovel," groaned Pete. "This is going to mean some serious digging."

"Not at this hour, surely!" exclaimed Chalky. He checked his watch. "It's nearly nine o'clock at night. I bet he's just going to give us our orders for first thing in the morning."

As so often, Chalky was wrong.

We reported back to Sergeant Ross and he pointed to an area marked out with tape. "We're digging trenches," he told us.

"At night, Sarge?" asked Chalky.

"Of course at night!" shouted Sergeant Ross. "We don't want the Germans watching us and knowing what we're up to, do we?"

"I bet this is another of the Great Maskelyne's tricks," Ginger whispered to me out of the corner of his mouth.

"You are going to dig trenches deep enough and long enough for a platoon to hide inside," continued Ross. "As you will be the men hiding in it, I'd advise you to make sure the walls are strong and won't collapse on you when you're inside. These trenches have got to be deep enough for a man to stand up inside them without his head poking over the top, because we're going to put canvas roofs on them so the Germans won't spot them when they fly over. Any questions?"

"Yes, Sarge," said Ginger. "What are these trenches for?"

"When I say 'any questions', Private Matthews, I am simply being civil. I do not expect you to ask one! Now, get to work."

We started digging a series of trenches eight feet deep. It was hard work. The ground was rocky and tough in some places; in others it was just loose sand. Although the sand was easier to dig, it was impossible to make a wall from it that wouldn't collapse, so we had to shore it up with timbers. The rocky ground was even worse, because when you dug the rocks out, it was just sand again, which also collapsed.

We spent the next week resting during the day and digging every night. As we dug, we talked about what the trenches might be for.

"Montgomery's hiding the Army up here," said Ginger. "Like I said, I bet this is one of Maskelyne's tricks. The soldiers up here hide in the trenches under the canvas roofs and they're invisible from the air. So, Rommel thinks the bulk of the Army is down south, where all those dummies are."

"But Ross said that *we're* the ones who are going to be hiding in these trenches," pointed out Chalky.

"Of course he'd say that," countered Ginger. "He wants to make sure that we make these trenches safe enough for us to stay in."

We finally found out what the trenches were for on the morning of 23 October. The whole of our division of Royal Engineers were assembled on the parade ground, and Captain Medley, our commanding officer, came to address us.

"Men," he began, "I have been authorized by our commander-in-chief, General Montgomery, to tell you that tonight we will be launching a major offensive against the Germans. We have kept this information secret until this moment to prevent the Germans finding out.

"Late this afternoon you will go into the trenches you have dug at the front of our position. The RAF will fly covering actions to prevent any German reconnaissance of this movement. You will take with you all your equipment, and a packed dinner. You will be there for some hours, concealed beneath the canvas roofs.

"At 2140 hours, our artillery will open fire on the positions of the enemy's big guns, which are to their rear. It will be one of the biggest bombardments there has ever been and we intend to put the German big guns out of action. This bombardment will last for twenty minutes.

"At 2200 hours our artillery will switch the bombardment to the very front of the German positions. You men will then come out of the trenches and advance through our own minefields, clearing a path for our infantry and tanks, which will be close behind you. You will continue advancing until you reach the defensive minefields laid by the enemy. You will clear a path through the enemy minefields in order that our infantry and tanks following you can get clear sight and attack the enemy."

I felt a knot in the pit of my stomach as what Captain Medley said sunk in. In less than twelve hours, we were going right into the enemy firing line. I couldn't help but give a little shudder at the thought. I hoped no one noticed.

Captain Medley continued his address to us, but now his voice took on a much more serious tone.

"I know I'm speaking to young men, some of you only eighteen or nineteen years old, but I have to give it to you straight," he said. "Some of you will be killed, or lose an arm or leg, because Jerry will be trying to stop you. There will be mortaring, Stuka dive bombing and plenty more besides. But you have to open a path through the minefields for our tanks and our infantry, or else this battle will be lost. And if we lose this battle, gentlemen, there is a strong possibility we shall lose this war. And that must not be allowed to happen. We cannot let the evil code of the Nazis rule this world and destroy everything that we hold dear.

"I will now hand over to Sergeant Ross, who will detail the tactics that will be used to open pathways through the minefields tonight. Sergeant Ross."

"Thank you, sir!" thundered Sergeant Ross. "Right, lads, this is the plan for tonight's attack. In order to get the tanks rolling, we need to clear a series of paths twenty-four feet wide through the minefields, and we need to do it fast. The boffins at the top reckon a team of six men can clear a gap eight feet wide using a metal detector. By their way of thinking, that team of six should be able to move forward at the rate of nine feet a minute. Which is three times faster than clearing mines by poking a bayonet in the ground and trying to find them. The six are: one man using the metal detector, one who'll lift and disable the mine, two men who'll be marking the side of the cleared path with tape so the tanks can see where they're going, and two men in reserve. So, three teams of six men each should be able to clear a gap twenty-four feet wide at the same speed, nine feet a minute. Any questions?"

Ginger put up his hand.

"Yes?" demanded Sergeant Ross.

"If it's going to be dark, how will we see to clear the mines at that speed, sir?" he asked.

"Because, you lucky lads, you will have searchlights on you the whole time. It will be like daylight out there."

Pete put his hand up.

"When I asked for questions I didn't expect everyone to put their hands up," complained Ross. "This will be the last question. Yes, Morgan?"

"If we're going to be lit up by searchlights so we can see, then won't the enemy be able to see us as well, Sarge?" asked Pete. "I mean, if they can, they'll have a clear target for shooting at us."

"If I may answer this question, Sergeant," said Captain Medley.

"Certainly, sir," said Ross.

"As I said earlier, before you go out and start clearing the minefields, our heavy artillery will launch a bombardment of the enemy positions to protect you," said the Captain. "It is unlikely the enemy will have any chance of shooting at you while that bombardment is going on."

"Thank you, sir," said Ross. "I think you have put any concerns the men may have had to rest." Looking at Pete, he snapped, "And even if the Germans do shoot at you, Morgan, you can't have everything. This is war, remember." Turning back to Captain Medley, Ross asked: "Are there any further points you wish to make to the men, sir?"

Medley nodded. "There is just one last point, Sergeant," he said, and he produced a sheet of paper. "The Commander-in-Chief, General Montgomery, has written a personal message to all the men in this Army. It gives me great pleasure to be able to read it to you all."

At this, Sergeant Ross stamped to attention. "Right, squad!" he yelled. "You are about to hear a personal address from General Montgomery. You will all pay careful attention."

"Thank you, Sergeant," said Medley. "These are the words of General Montgomery himself, addressed to every one of us," Captain Medley informed us. Then he began to read from the sheet of paper:

"When I assumed command of the Eighth Army I said that the mandate was to destroy Rommel and his army, and that it would be done as soon as we were ready. We are ready now.

"The battle which is now about to begin will be one of the decisive battles of history. It will be the turning point of the War. The eyes of the whole world will be on us, watching anxiously which way the battle will swing. We can give them their answer at once, 'It will swing our way.'

"We have first-class equipment: good tanks; good anti-tank guns; plenty of artillery and plenty of ammunition; and we are backed by the finest air striking force in the world.

"All that is necessary is that each one of us, every officer and man, should enter this battle with the determination to see it through – to fight and to kill – and finally, to win. If we do all this there can be only one result – together we will hit the enemy for six, right out of North Africa.

"The sooner we win this battle, which will be the turning point of this war, the sooner we shall all get back home to our families. Therefore, let every officer and man enter the battle with a stout heart, and with the determination to do his duty so long as he has breath in his body.

"And let no man surrender so long as he is unwounded, and can fight.

"Let us all pray that the Lord mighty in battle will give us the victory."

Captain Medley folded up the sheet of paper and put it in the pocket of his tunic. "That is the message from our commander," he said.

"Bear those words in mind when you go into battle tonight." Turning to Sergeant Ross, he said: "That is all, Sergeant."

"Thank you, sir!" bellowed Ross. To us, he yelled "'Tenshun!"

We all sprang to our feet and stood stiffly to attention.

"Squad, dismissed!" roared Ross.

1700 hours 23 October – 24 October 1942

That afternoon, RAF fighters zoomed around in the sky above us to keep away German planes, and lorries drove backwards and forwards throwing up dust clouds to stop the Germans seeing what was going on through their telescopes. At 1700 hours we climbed down into the long slit trenches right at the very front of our position, and sat down on the seat-shaped sections of rock and sand. We were in groups of six, just like Sergeant Ross had told us we would be. Our team of six included Ginger using the metal detector, me as the one who'd be down on his hands and knees disabling the mines, Pete and Chalky laying the tape to mark the way for the tanks, with Billy Paul and Joe Johnson as reserves in case something bad happened to any of the four of us. Billy and Joe also had rifles ready with bayonets fixed to act as probes if the metal detector packed up, or got blown up.

By 1740 hours we were all in place; the trenches were filled. The lorries stopped their mad skidding around on the desert and outside the trenches the dust clouds died down. Above us the sheet of canvas that hid the trenches from the German telescopes flapped slightly in the afternoon breeze.

"Four hours to go before the bombardment starts," said Ginger, checking his watch. "What shall we do?"

"We could play I-spy," suggested Pete.

"That shouldn't take long," said Ginger with a laugh. "I spy with my little eye something beginning with S."

"Sand," said Pete.

"Exactly," grinned Ginger.

"I don't know about you lot, but I'm going to eat my packed dinner," said Chalky. And he started to unwrap the greaseproof paper from his sandwiches.

"How can you eat at a time like this?" demanded Pete.

"Because I don't know if I'll feel like eating later," said Chalky.

That made sense. Ginger nodded and began to unwrap his own sandwiches.

I left mine untouched. I felt too sick to even think of food. In my head I kept seeing the images of those German sappers when Rommel had tried to launch his big attack at Alam Halfa. Saw them falling as our machine guns cut into them, or being blown up as they lifted a booby-trapped mine. Was it going to be the same for us? Captain Medley said the bombardment from our big guns would keep the Germans down. But then, he would say that, wouldn't he?

I wished I had more than just a steel helmet to protect me from the bullets. I was wearing shorts and a cardigan. They were the right clothes to wear against the cold of the desert night, but not against bullets. And not against exploding mines.

But Captain Medley had been honest with us. Some of us were going to die. Some of us were going to be seriously wounded. Would one of them be me? I wished I'd written more in my letters to Mum. More about how grateful I was to her for bringing me up on her own, and how much I missed her. If I was going to die, I wanted to see her one last time and tell her I loved her. But now it was too late.

As I watched Ginger and Chalky munch their sandwiches, I felt around in my pack for a stub of pencil and a piece of paper. Then I wrote, "Always thinking of you, Mum. Thanks for everything. You are the best Mum in the world. Your loving son, Tim." I folded the piece of paper over and wrote her name and our address on it. Then I nudged Ginger, who was sitting next to me.

"What's up?" he asked.

"Will you do me a favour?" I asked.

"Sure," he said. "What?"

"If I don't make it out of this, and you do, will you give this note to my mum?"

I offered him the piece of paper. Ginger nodded, took it, and tucked it away into his breast pocket. "Sure," he said. "But you'll come out of it all right. The Germans haven't got you yet, have they?"

But even though he said the right words, I could tell from something in his voice that he didn't really mean it. None of us knew what was going to happen to us tonight. None of us knew if we were still going to be alive tomorrow. We sat there in the trench as darkness fell.

The hours passed. As the hands of my watch ticked nearer to zero-hour, I could hear some of the blokes in the trench muttering to themselves, and I realized that they were saying prayers. Some were praying for themselves, others were praying for their families back home. Most of them, though, were like me, just sitting in silence and waiting.

And then, right on the dot, the barrage from our big guns started, and it was like nothing I'd ever heard before. It was huge. No, huge was too small a word for what was happening, for the sound and the vibration of the earth around us. It was as if the whole world had suddenly gone into one enormous explosion as we pounded the enemy, sending shell after shell overhead, the earth lifting and falling with the incessant thudding. For a moment I was worried that the trench was going to fall in on top of us.

With all that noise there was no way we could have talked even if we'd wanted to. For twenty minutes the barrage went on and then there was a sudden switch in the noise as our guns turned their attention to the German front line. I looked at my watch – 2200 hours.

I felt a tap on my knee and looked up. Ginger was standing up and gesturing to me that it was time to go. I tapped the man next to me for him to pass the signal on, and then I followed Ginger and the long line of men. Up the steps we went, out of the trench, and into a night that could have been daylight. Above us was a bright full moon, and I remembered what Pete had said. He was right about generals attacking by full moon. He had won his bet with Chalky. Searchlights from our own side blasted dazzling light into our defensive minefields, and on towards the German lines.

Here we go, I thought.

We were five miles from the German front line, so I calculated we should be out of danger from their machine guns until we reached their minefields.

Clearing our own minefield wasn't too bad. We knew where the mines were – we'd already marked them all in preparation for this – but we still used the system that Sergeant Ross had explained: six men working as a team to clear a gap eight feet wide using a metal detector. To our left another team of six were working to clear their own eight-feet wide gap, and to our right another team of six was doing the same. Eighteen men making a gap of twenty-four feet. Wide enough for a tank to get through.

Because we knew where the mines were, Billy Paul and Joe Johnson joined me in defusing them and putting them in a trench to one side of the minefield. Ginger still worked with the metal detector, and Pete and Chalky laid the lengths of tape to mark the edge of our cleared section.

I was lifting one of our mines when there was an explosion from the team to our right. I only heard it because there had been a momentary lull in the barrage from the big guns. We all looked, and saw that the man lifting the mines had handled one incorrectly, and it had exploded. Luckily for him, the charge in the mine wasn't big enough to kill him, but I could see that his leg had been blown off.

He was thrashing around on the ground and screaming in agony. Then the big guns of our artillery opened up again. I turned back to my own mine-clearing and tried to forget the image of the wounded man. I had to keep my hands steady and my nerves calm. I had to get this right.

Our team worked its way forward, the earth around the mines being scraped away, the detonators taken out, then the mines lifted clear and put to one side in the trench behind the marking tape.

The ground around me was shaking now, and I looked behind me to see our infantry, their bayonets fixed, following us. Behind them came our tanks, which was why the ground was shaking.

Yard after yard we cleared, and then suddenly we were out of our own minefields and heading across the patch of no-man's land towards the barbed wire that marked the beginning of the German minefields. Ginger went ahead first with the metal detector. Although there should have been no mines in this patch of ground, we couldn't afford to take anything for granted.

Behind us there was the constant sound of firing as our artillery and tanks kept up their bombardment of the German front-line positions, shelling them to stop them firing at us, but the Germans fought back. Tracers of bullets came from their lines, smacking into the ground in front and around us. The terrifying thought struck me that if one of those bullets hit a mine near me, I'd be dead, but I did my best to push the thought away. It was as Captain Medley had said, we had to force a way through their minefield for our troops to be able to attack the Germans. If we didn't, they'd win this battle – and maybe even the War. We had to go on.

We reached the German barbed wire and I knelt down on the ground, took out my wire cutters and cut through the strands of wire to open up my section. The guys on either side of me were doing the same. All the time there was the sound of machine-gun fire and bullets picking at the ground or going over our heads. Frantically I tried to remember our lessons on the maximum range of German machine guns. It was supposed to be no more than a mile, but bullets were hitting the ground around me. The German barbed wire was supposed to be two miles from their most forward position, so either they had machine guns that could fire further than we thought, or Rommel had moved some of his defensive machine-gun posts a long way forward, right into the middle of their minefields.

Behind me the infantrymen began to open fire over our heads and through the spaces between us, aiming at the unseen German lines ahead. Our tanks also began to launch their shells and they hurtled over us into the darkness. The noise was excruciating.

As we worked, the gunfire got more intense. I felt a glancing blow on my head, and heard a metallic "ping!" as a bullet from a German machine gun ricocheted off my steel helmet. I was glad I was wearing it or that bullet would have taken off the top of my head.

We kept low now: Ginger on his knees, holding the metal detector in front of him, while I crawled along the ground, trying to keep below the stream of bullets from the Germans. Now and then one of our tanks got a hit on a machine-gun post, and the firing from the German lines stopped. But it was a momentary relief: soon a replacement crew would pick us out and the firing would start again. Bullets tore at the rocky ground, sending slivers of rock and sand up into my eyes.

I heard a thud and a gasp from my left and turned in time to see Ginger crumple and collapse. In the light from the searchlights and the moon, I could see a dark stain spreading across his shirt. I hurried over to him to see where he'd been hit, but one of the infantrymen grabbed me and pointed ahead towards the German lines. Billy Paul was already hurrying forward to pick up the metal detector that had fallen from Ginger's grasp as he was hit. I hesitated, not wanting to leave my pal, then realized that the infantryman was right: the troops and tanks had to get through.

Billy had taken the headphones off Ginger's head and put them on, and now he moved forward, holding the metal detector in front of him. He stopped and pointed at a small bulge in the ground. I nodded. A mine was there, hidden just below the ground. I set to work with the trowel, scraping the earth away as quickly as I could, but carefully in case it was booby-trapped. It was. A wire went from the detonator to a spike in the ground. I cut it with my wire-cutters and then went on to disable the detonator. I wanted to go back and see how Ginger was. Had he been killed? If he hadn't – if I helped him – could I save him? But if I did that I'd slow down the whole process, and we had to get the paths through the minefields cleared before the Germans had time to react fully. I clenched my teeth and moved on with Billy, both of us on our knees. All the time our soldiers kept up a stream of gunfire over our heads into the German positions, with the tanks behind us loosing off a shell every now and then, blasting away at the Germans.

I had no idea how long we'd been working; it all seemed to merge into a blur of noise and death, and I was caught in the middle. There was no way back, all I could do was go on.

We kept moving, going as fast as we could. All around us were explosions. I didn't know if they were mines going off as they were lifted by our men, or mines accidentally stepped on, or explosions from German artillery being fired at us.

We reached a German machine-gun post. The crew were all dead, lying around the blasted remains of their gun. The gunfire from the German lines was getting heavier. We were getting closer every step. And then suddenly there were no more mines. There was the wreckage of guns and machinery, burning tanks and lorries and vehicles, and dead bodies lying on the ground, but no more mines. We had cut our path through the German minefield.

The artillery men behind us began to pour forward at speed, firing as they went, sending a hail of bullets into the German positions.

Pete, Chalky, Billy, Joe and I moved to one side as our tanks surged past us and began to roll through behind our infantrymen, into the German stronghold.

We had broken through.

24 October 1942 – April 1943

While the main attack by the infantry and the tank regiments continued, we sappers pulled back to our base. The Germans were still firing, loosing off artillery shells and stray machine-gun bullets, which meant we had to keep our heads down, but at least we could move faster, sure that the ground in front of us was clear of mines. Not that there was a lot of room for us to move, with the infantry surging forward and tanks rumbling past us and nearly running us down.

As I moved back towards our own lines, ducking my head and crouching low the whole time, I scanned the ground, looking for Ginger, but there was no sign of him. I saw a couple of stretcher-bearers carrying away a wounded man and thought it might be Ginger, but when I got near them I saw it wasn't. I tapped the nearest stretcher-bearer on the shoulder. With all the gunfire and explosions going on it was hard to make myself heard, but I put my mouth close to his ear and shouted: "Have you seen a wounded bloke with ginger hair? One of our mob? A sapper?"

The stretcher-bearer shook his head sadly.

"Wounded blokes are all I've seen, mate," he said.

"He was shot somewhere round about here," I said, gesturing at the area around us.

The stretcher-bearer shook his head. "Sorry, mate," he said. "Someone else might have picked him up."

I made my way back through the lines of advancing infantry and rumbling tanks, looking all the while in case I could see Ginger. But by the time I got back to our own positions, I'd seen no sign of him.

The first person I ran into when I got back was Chalky.

"Where have you been, Tim?" he asked. "We thought you'd been caught out there."

"I've been looking for Ginger," I said. "I wondered if the first-aid people had found him."

Chalky's face fell. He nodded.

"Yeah," he said, dully. "They found him. They brought him in."

"Where is he?" I asked urgently.

"In the morgue tent with the others," he said. "He's dead, Tim."

I felt as if I'd been hit by a hammer. Ginger, dead. I felt so guilty. I wondered if I'd stopped and helped him instead of going on, clearing mines, he'd still be alive.

Chalky must have seen what I was thinking from the expression on my face, because he said: "He died straight away. Bullet through the heart. There was nothing any of us could have done to save him, Tim."

I nodded, but it didn't make me feel any better.

The attack continued for the rest of the day. While our infantry and tanks pushed forward, we sappers went into the minefields and collected up the mines and detonators we'd discarded the night before, and loaded them on to lorries. There were hundreds of thousands of them. All different types – British, German, Italian, and some I'd never seen before.

As I lifted the mines and packed them into the lorries, I thought of Ginger, and how there was no sense in any of it. Who lived and who died. It was all chance. Ginger and I had been side by side, but it had been Ginger who died and me who lived. Why? You did your best to keep yourself safe, but in the end it was all down to luck.

I kept thinking of that first day I'd met Ginger, at London Bridge station. I'd liked him straight away. He was friendly and honest and open and cheerful. And clever. Much cleverer than me. And now he was dead at eighteen years old. It didn't seem right.

Although we'd broken through their minefields, the Germans held firm. For the next week we threw everything we had at them: tanks, heavy artillery, the RAF bombing them day and night, the infantry, but still we couldn't get past them, and they wouldn't retreat – they just stayed there and took a blasting. And then, on 4 November, the news came that the Germans were retreating. But it took a lot longer before it was over. They only retreated about 50 miles, and then they started to set up their defences. Although there were fewer of them than there had been at Alamein, they did everything the same as before: laid out minefields in front of their front-line position, dug in their heavy artillery, and kept their tanks ready to defend against attack.

We all thought that Montgomery would go straight after Rommel and not give the Germans time to dig in like this, but he didn't.

"I don't understand it," I said to Pete and Chalky one day in the mess tent, as we listened to reports from the RAF reconnaissance planes that said how the Germans were building up their defences. "Why don't we go after the Germans now, straight away?"

Jez Cromer, who was just along the table from us, answered: "That's because Monty's learnt from where things went wrong before."

"How?" I asked.

"Remember I told you we pushed Rommel right back, and then he pushed us right back?" he asked.

I nodded.

"Yeah," I said.

"Well that's because every time we thought we'd got him down and out for the count once and for all, he came back at us and knocked us out. What Rommel'd do is sit tight, then he'd send out a skirmishing squad of his tanks to attack us. Then they'd turn and run, and we'd go after them, set on getting them before they got away. That's what Rommel was waiting for. As soon as our tanks and attack force was out in the open – wham! He'd hit us and knock us out, and then he'd counter-attack and send his tanks into the hole he'd made in our defences.

"Mark my words, Monty's not going to play into his hands like that.

Remember what he told us before Alam Halfa? That he was going to wait and attack the Germans when he was ready, not before. The Germans may have lost a lot of men and equipment at Alamein, but so did we."

Yes, I thought. Ginger among them.

"We've got more men and tanks and ammo due in from Alexandria," Jez continued. "My bet is Monty's going to wait until we're back up to strength before attacking Rommel."

Jez was right. And not just about attacking the Germans at their new position. We hit them hard there, and they pulled back again. And once again, Monty waited until we were up to full strength before he launched his attack.

It took another six months of battles fought in this way before we finally forced the Germans to surrender. Six months of us attacking, the Germans retreating and digging in, then us waiting until we were strong enough to launch another attack. Each time it was the same form: our side opening with an enormous barrage from our heavy guns and tanks on the German positions; then we sappers would go in and clear the minefields the Germans had laid out; then our infantry and tanks would attack and force the Germans back another fifty miles or so, where they would dig in again. Each time there were fewer of them. Each time Monty would wait until he'd got more reinforcements of men, more supplies of ammunition, before attacking again.

May 1943

How those Germans held out, I don't know. By the end they must have been down to just a few thousand men, but they were fighting every step of the way as they retreated. The end came on 12 May 1943 at a place called Tunis on the North African coast, 2,000 miles west of Alamein. The Germans must have been hoping that the enemy navies would take them off the harbour at Tunis and get them home, but the RAF kept up such a force of bombing on the German and Italian ships that in the end what was left of Rommel's army had no place left to go, so they surrendered.

The rest of the boys and I carried on under Monty's command, across the Mediterranean Sea to Sicily. By now we had teamed up with the Americans, who'd been fighting their way across Africa from the west, and our joint force launched an attack on Sicily where the Germans and Italians still had a strong base. I say we had "teamed up", but to tell the truth it was like a race between two bitter rivals: Monty and the American General Patton. Both of them wanted to be the first to reach the city of Messina on Sicily, and be seen as the victor. The trouble with this rivalry between the two generals was that it spread down to the ordinary troops, so that instead of working together as we should have done, just fighting the Germans and Italians, we were encouraged to try and keep one step ahead of the Americans, and Patton encouraged his men to keep one step ahead of us.

In the end the Americans won the race: on 17 August 1943 they entered Messina, and when we arrived they cheered us and called out "Here come the guys who came second!" and "Welcome to the tourists!" Monty was furious; not because of the way the Americans acted towards us but because we British hadn't got to Messina before Patton and the Americans.

In September we moved on to Italy. Again, it was a joint attack with the Americans, but our offensives were concentrated on different parts of the Italian coast. Our target was the Calabria region. Although the Italians surrendered pretty quickly, on 8 September, the German troops in Italy fought so hard that it took the whole winter to defeat them. We suffered a lot of casualties during the Italian campaign, and one of them was Pete. He was shot dead by a sniper while out defusing mines. First Ginger, then Pete. Our gang of four was now down to two – just me and Chalky.

In March 1944, with the battle in Italy still raging, Chalky and I were sent home on leave. Chalky went back to Newcastle to see his folks, and I went home to Camden Town.

It felt strange at home after being away for so long. As I walked along Selous Mews towards our house, my kitbag over my shoulder, our cobbled street seemed so narrow. Even though it was my home, the place where I'd grown up, after all this time away from it, it felt foreign to me. I suppose the desert and the huge amounts of space in North Africa, and the fighting in Sicily and Italy, had changed me.

I knocked on our front door, and when Mum opened it I was shocked to see how tiny and frail she looked.

"So, you've come home, have you?" she said, almost grumpily. It wasn't the welcome I'd expected.

"Yes," I said.

"Make sure you wipe your feet," she told me, stepping back to let me in. "I've just washed the passage."

I felt like a giant in our tiny little house.

"I'll put the kettle on for a cup of tea," said Mum. "Have you eaten?"

"No," I said.

"I'll make you a sandwich," she said. "We're still on rations so I haven't got much. It'll have to be spam."

Spam was a sort of pressed meat that came in tins. It was supposed to be pork, but none of us were ever sure what was really in it. "Spam would be great," I said.

I put my kitbag in the front room and walked into the kitchen, where she already had the kettle on.

"How have you been?" I asked.

"As well as can be expected when there's a war on," she said. "You got through safely, then?"

"Yes," I explained. "I was one of the lucky ones." I thought of Ginger and Pete, and all those thousands of other men who'd gone off to war just like me, and were never coming back but were buried in a grave far from home.

"How are Uncle George and Aunt Ivy?" I asked.

"Your Uncle George is dead," she said, matter-of-factly getting two slices of bread and buttering them for my sandwich.

I stood there, stunned. "Dead?" I echoed.

Mum nodded. "He was out fire-fighting when a bomb hit the building he was trying to save, killing him outright. Ivy's hair turned white overnight when she heard the news, but she's surviving. Nothing else she can do when something like that happens."

Mum finished making the sandwich, put it on a small plate, and placed it in front of me.

"There," she said. "That'll keep you going till supper."

I sat at the kitchen table, looking at the sandwich, and thought about Uncle George and Ginger and Pete, and everyone else I knew who'd died in this war, and suddenly I lost my appetite.

"I'm sorry, Mum," I said. "I'm not hungry."

Mum bridled, upset. "Not hungry?" she said, angrily. "After you've stood there and watched me make it. With food in short supply as well! You eat that sandwich, and be grateful! They may be dead, but the living have to eat. Life goes on."

And so I did. I picked up the sandwich, and did as I was told. It tasted terrible, and it took a lot of chewing, but I ate it. Like Mum said – life goes on.

Epilogue

Chalky and I didn't stay at home on leave long. In June 1944 we were part of the invasion force that landed on the beaches of Normandy. We were both wounded soon after we landed and were invalided back to England. For both of us, that was the end of our war.

After we came out of hospital, Chalky and I kept in touch by letter. He offered to put me up if I visited him, but I was kept busy trying to start up my own business in Uncle George's old garage. Plus I met a girl and we were talking about getting married. Still, one day me and her will go up north and see Chalky.

Yesterday, 8 May 1945, they told us the War was over. As I heard the news on the radio, I couldn't help but think of all the people I'd known who'd died during the last five and a half years, and I thought: let's hope that something good comes out of this, let's hope that they didn't die in vain.

Historical note

The battle in North Africa was one of the most crucial in the whole War. In the words of the British Prime Minister at the time, Winston Churchill: "Before Alamein we never had a victory; after Alamein we never had a defeat."

Rommel said later that he believed the destruction of his army in North Africa by Montgomery's Allied troops resulted in Germany losing the War. Rommel believed that if he had been able to get his army back to Italy they could have re-formed.

Astonishingly, neither of the two opposing generals took any part in the opening stages of the Battle of Alamein. On 23 October Rommel was in Austria undergoing medical treatment for blood and liver problems. The entry in Montgomery's diary for that day reads: "In the evening I read a book and went to bed early. At 9.40 pm the barrage of over one thousand guns opened and the Eighth Army went into the attack. At that moment I was asleep in my caravan. There was nothing I could do and I knew I would be needed later."

The "British" Eighth Army in North Africa was not exclusively British. In fact, many of the soldiers in the Eighth Army came from Australia, New Zealand and South Africa, with units from England,

Scotland, India, France and Greece. One third of Rommel's army was made up of Italian soldiers, although his major force was his German Panzer (tank) Divisions.

The destruction of Rommel's army in North Africa meant the way was clear for a combined British-American force to cross the Mediterranean Sea from North Africa to Sicily, and then on to Italy, to force the country to surrender.

The minefields of Alamein

The Battle of Alamein saw some of the largest uses of land mines in the whole of the War. Rommel described the minefields ordered to defend his front-line position as "The Devil's Garden". The largest was five miles deep and had half a million mines laid in two long fields. In the middle of these Rommel positioned anti-tank guns and infantrymen. Rommel believed that The Devil's Garden was impenetrable – that there was no way the British could get through it without suffering so many casualties that the attack would fail.

Because the British were aware of the enormous size of these minefields, and the huge number of deadly mines underfoot (many of them booby-trapped), the opening attack on the night of 23 October was called, with black humour, "Operation Lightfoot".

The attack used both sappers on foot and Scorpion "flail tanks" to try to clear the mines. A lot of the flail tanks broke down and it was left to the sappers to clear the mines by hand. Although many sappers used metal detectors to find mines, most were uncovered by prodding the ground carefully with a bayonet attached to a rifle.

The sappers

The role of the sappers in warfare stretches right back in history: in 52 BC Julius Caesar wrote a detailed account of the military engineering techniques he used in his war in Gaul. He ordered his soldiers to dig long trenches as a defence against the attacking Gauls, and into these trenches he had iron hooks and sharpened stakes fixed, hidden beneath twigs and brushwood.

The sappers have used the same basic system ever since: dig defensive trenches and fill them with objects that will slow down an enemy attack: in modern warfare, these are usually land mines, although in Vietnam in the 1960s and 1970s, the Viet Cong dug deep trenches with sharpened bamboo stakes, some with poisoned tips, as traps for American infantrymen.

Land mines

The earliest exploding land mines, which used gunpowder, first appeared around 1530 in southern Italy. They were called "fougasses". They were actually cannons placed underground and covered with small rocks and debris. A long trail of gunpowder was placed over the ground from the hidden underground cannon to a hiding place, from where – once the attackers were seen approaching – the cannon was set off by igniting the trail of gunpowder. The problem with this method was that gunpowder absorbs water from the air and loses its explosiveness. This meant that the trail of gunpowder could only be laid shortly before the cannon was fired.

Major changes in land mine technology occurred during the American Civil War (1861–65), and they were particularly used by the southern Confederate side. Electrical firing mechanisms were introduced, which meant the mines could be detonated from a distance without the need for gunpowder trails. The pressure-mine also came into operation during the American Civil War. This was partly buried beneath the surface and was detonated by someone stepping on to it and triggering an electrical charge, or simply by breaking a glass container which made a chemical connection, setting off the gunpowder.

During the wars of the twentieth century the use of land mines, particularly those intended to injure or kill an individual, was widespread, with technology becoming evermore sophisticated.

By the end of the twentieth century the human cost among civilians as a result of land mines – with many hundreds of thousands of people killed or maimed – made some nations realize that the use of land mines had got out of hand. For example, after the first Gulf War many land mines were left in place, and by 1993 1,700 civilians had been killed by them, with many more badly injured. It was calculated that in 1994 there were at least ten million active land mines left in the ground in Afghanistan.

The result was an attempt to control the use of land mines, and also carry out Land mine Clearance Programmes to remove mines left in place after the end of a war. In December 1997 in Ottawa, Canada, an international treaty to ban anti-personnel land mines was signed by 121 nations.

Timeline

1 September 1939 Germany invades Poland in defiance of Allies.

3 September 1939 Britain, France, Australia and New Zealand declare war on Germany.

13 September 1940 Italians advance into Egypt.

December 1940 British counter-attack in Egypt.

7 February 1941 Italian forces surrender.

12 February 1941 Rommel takes over Axis forces in North Africa. Launches offensive.

November–December 1941 Operation Crusader by Allies forces Rommel back.

7 December 1941 Japanese attack US fleet at Pearl Harbor, Hawaii.

8 December 1941 USA enters the War.

May–June 1942 Rommel's counter-attack forces Allied retreat.

23 June 1942 German forces cross into Egypt. Allies dig in at El Alamein.

August 1942 Field Marshal Alexander made Commander-in-Chief of Allied forces in Middle East. Montgomery takes over command of Eighth Army.

31 August–6 September 1942 Battle of Alam Halfa: Rommel launches attack.

31 October–4 November 1942 Battle of Alamein. Allied victory.

November 1942 Operation Torch: combined British-American landings in North-West Africa.

March 1943 Rommel leaves North Africa for Europe.

12 May 1943 Remnants of Rommel's army surrenders. War in North Africa ends.

July–September 1943 Allied invasion of Italy. Italy surrenders.

6 June 1944 D-Day: Allies land on Normandy beaches

20 July 1944 Attempt on Hitler's life by German generals fails. Many German officials arrested by Gestapo.

14 October 1944 Rommel, suspected of being part of German generals anti-Hitler plot, forced to commit suicide by Nazi SS.

30 April 1945 Hitler commits suicide.

7 May 1945 Unconditional surrender of German forces.

2 September 1945 Formal surrender of Japan.

Picture acknowledgements

P250 Map of North Africa and the Mediterranean, Michelle Strong

P251 Rommel and his plans © Mary Evans Picture Library

P252 Montgomery and Churchill © British Pathe – ITN Archive

P253 Allied Sappers © British Pathe – ITN Archive

P254 A Sapper lays a land mine © British Pathe – ITN Archive

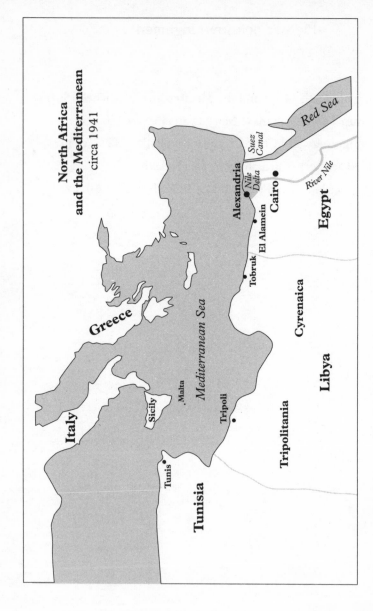

A map of tNorth Africa and the Mediterranean c.1941.

Rommel, Commander of the Afrika Korps, and nicknamed the "Desert Fox", consults battle plans with his staff.

Field Marshall Montgomery, Commander of the Allied Eighth Army, welcomes Winston Churchill to Tripoli, Libya, in February 1943.

Allied sappers use mine detectors to locate mines on the desert track.

An allied sapper lays a mine in the desert near El Alamein

D-Day

Bryan Perrett

December 1945

My name is Andrew Pope. Eighteen months ago, while commanding an infantry platoon, I took part in the Normandy Landings on 6 June 1944, a date that has now become known as D-Day. This is my story of how we prepared for D-Day, which was the greatest amphibious military operation in the history of the world, and of the fierce battles that took place once we were ashore, ending in the complete destruction of a German army. . .

1942–1943

I do not come from a military family although my great-grandfather, whose photograph we have, served as drummer boy during the Crimean War. He later served in India and other places around the world and retired as a sergeant major. During what is now known as the Great War my father served as an infantry officer. He was badly wounded on the Somme and again at Passchendaele, and he still has a slight limp as a result of his injuries. He rarely speaks of that war, which he regards as a horrible diversion from normal life. As he had seen almost all his friends killed or wounded, I can understand how he feels. When he left the Army he joined a firm of solicitors in Branchester, which is our county town.

I left school in 1942, shortly before my eighteenth birthday, having obtained good grades in my examinations. I was pleased that I had done particularly well in French and German, as these were my favourite subjects. It was then that I decided to volunteer for the Army rather than wait to be called up, because it seemed wrong to me that I should sit around doing nothing while the current war was going on, and anyway all of my school friends were doing the same. The war news was depressing. In North Africa, the British Eighth Army had sustained a serious defeat, Tobruk had fallen and the German Afrika Korps' runaway progress had been stopped with difficulty at a place called El Alamein, only 60 miles from Alexandria. On the Eastern Front, the German armoured divisions were carving their way deep into the Soviet Union and nothing the Russians did seemed able to stop them. At home, people talked about the opening of what they called the Second Front, which meant our army returning to France. Everyone knew that Hitler would only be beaten once this happened, and they looked forward to it because it would pay back the defeat we had suffered during the German invasion of France in 1940, followed by the Dunkirk evacuation. However, on 17 August 1942, a British and Canadian raid on the port of Dieppe was repulsed with heavy losses and it became clear that there would be no Second Front for a long time to come.

At the recruiting office that afternoon in 1942 I was told I would be sent joining instructions within a few days. My parents, of course, expected me to be called up sooner or later and I wondered how they would react when I told them I was going early. In the event, I didn't have much choice in the matter.

"Well, what have you been doing today?" asked my father after we had finished dinner.

"I've joined up," I said. "I was told that volunteers get a choice where they can serve, so I've asked to be sent to your old battalion, the 4th Branchesters, when I've finished my training. The sergeant said that there shouldn't be any difficulty because of the family connection. I was told that the battalion is on anti-invasion duties in East Anglia – having a rather dull time of it, apparently."

Father continued filling and lighting his pipe, regarding me in a way he had not done before.

"You've done the right thing," he said at length. "Just the same, I wish that you'd volunteered for something other than the infantry."

I knew what he was thinking. There had been times during the Battle of the Somme when the average life expectancy of a junior infantry officer in the trenches was two weeks.

"Things are different now, Dad," I said, little knowing what lay ahead. "We don't fight like that any more."

"Maybe," he replied, reflectively. "Nobody has used gas this time, thank God, but weapons are much more efficient than they were in my day."

He paused for a minute and I could see that he was thinking of the past.

"You'll meet some fine men, you know, fine men," he continued. "You'll go for a commission, I suppose? You've had a good education and gained some experience in the school cadet corps, so in a way it would be shirking if you didn't put yourself forward as a potential officer."

"Yes, Dad."

"Good."

He puffed quietly on his pipe for a while, then looked me straight in the eye.

"You're right, of course, many things have changed a lot – but two haven't. First, remember that an officer's responsibility is to perform the task he has been set. Second, he'll never be able to perform it unless he has the trust and respect of his men. The only way he can earn that is by looking after them, seeing that they get fair treatment and being careful with their lives. Having said that, loyalty is a two-way street, you know. If three of my chaps hadn't taken terrible risks to bring me in from no man's land when I was wounded at Passchendaele, I wouldn't be here today."

There was nothing I could say to this, because he had seen a terrible war at first hand, whereas I had not. Seeing my serious expression, he gave one of his rare smiles.

"Don't worry, Andy, you'll be all right. Just don't go chasing medals or you'll give your mother a fit!"

Three weeks later I reported to a basic training unit. I found myself sharing a barrack room with men from many parts of the country and all walks of life. There were factory workers, farm labourers, clerks, tram drivers, accountants, builders and many more. Being away from home didn't bother me too much as, in a way, it was like starting a new term at school. I did, however, feel a little out of place among my companions at first. My own experience was confined to school and home, whereas they knew a great deal about life in the outside world. I asked them about their jobs and most of them seemed quite pleased that I was interested, telling me about their families, wives and girlfriends as well. They knew that I was classified as a PO (Potential Officer) and sometimes made fun of me. Some said they wouldn't want the responsibility of being an officer. Others that I was a fool looking for an early grave, but they were good-humoured and helped me out when I couldn't clean my kit when I was on fatigues (that is, in a working party, in the cookhouse or elsewhere). In return, I was able to help some of those who couldn't read or write properly with letters to and from their families. Because of my experience in the cadets I had no difficulty with such things as drill, weapons training and map reading. Physical training, constant exercise on the drill square, runs, route marches and the assault course made me fitter than I had ever been in my life.

In due course the squad completed its basic training and its members were posted to their various regiments. I was sorry to see them go. While I was waiting to go before a WOSB (War Office Selection Board) I was given a short driving course. I was worried by the thought of the WOSB because it was a big hurdle and had the reputation of rejecting half of those who appeared before it. When I did attend I was subjected to three days of mental and physical tests during which my responses were carefully noted by officers on their clipboards. I did not think I had done at all well, but at the end of it I was summoned before the President of the Board and, to my relief, told I had passed. I felt as though I had won a major prize and telephoned my parents with the good news.

While all this was going on, the War had taken a turn for the better.

General Montgomery's Eighth Army had defeated Rommel's Afrika Korps at El Alamein and was pursuing it across North Africa. It was beginning to look as though we might win the War after all.

In December 1942 I reported to the Officer Cadet Training Unit (OCTU) from which I hoped to pass out with a commission. On the first morning my company of new arrivals paraded wearing the white cadet bands around our forage caps. We all felt rather pleased with ourselves but were, in fact, about to enter the most ruthless phase of the selection process. For the next sixteen weeks we had barely a moment to ourselves. Our drill and uniform turnout had to be perfect at all times. As most of us were bound for the infantry, we had to learn the organization of an infantry battalion by heart. The battalion was commanded by a lieutenant colonel and consisted of six companies, each commanded by a major. Headquarters Company was responsible for administration and transport, while Support Company contained the battalion's mortars and anti-tank guns. The remaining four companies, lettered A to D, were rifle companies, each consisting of three platoons. Each rifle platoon was commanded by a lieutenant or second lieutenant, with a sergeant as his second-in-command, and contained three rifle sections.

Our cadet training began with our taking it in turns to command a section in attack and defence, and then a platoon. When we progressed to company tactics I began to realize that as future platoon commanders we were also being trained above that level so that if our company commander became a casualty we could at least take over for a while. We learned to dig slit trenches and the art of camouflaging ourselves and our positions. We learned about the different sorts of patrols we would have to lead and practised carrying these out after dark. Then there was advanced map and compass work, learning the basics of co-operation with tanks, artillery and engineers. There were lectures on army administration, our soldiers' pay and welfare, the enemy's weapons and tactics, current affairs, and how to give lectures ourselves when the time came. We were introduced to the relevant sections of King's Regulations, which govern how the Army is run, and the Manual of Military Law. There were many other subjects and throughout the course we were tested regularly to see how much we had absorbed.

The instructors, the company sergeant major and his sergeants harried us constantly, recording our progress in minute detail and discussing it among themselves. During one exercise, held in January, we were soaked by incessant rain by day and frozen when we tried to sleep in our slit trenches at night. I was sharing a trench with a former stockbroker named Guy Unsworth, who complained constantly. When we were told that the exercise would continue for another week, he gave full vent to his feelings.

"You got something to say, Mr Unsworth, sir?" snapped one of the sergeant instructors.

"Well, I mean to say, this just isn't on, is it Sergeant?" replied Unsworth in an aggrieved tone. "We're frozen stiff, soaked to the skin, and when the rations get to us they're stone cold. As if that isn't enough, when we try to eat them, our mess tins fill with rain. This whole thing has been badly organized in my opinion."

"That a fact, sir?" said the sergeant, eyeing him shrewdly. "I'll make a note of what you say."

In fact, when the exercise ended the following day, I realized that the instructors had simply been testing our reaction to bad news. Shortly after, Unsworth and a few others disappeared. I asked the sergeant where they had gone.

"RTU cases, the lot of them," he replied. "That stands for Return To Unit. They've been sent back to their regiments as private soldiers, considered unsuitable as officer material. Ask yourself this – if you were a squaddie, what would you think if your officer went whining on because he was cold, wet and hungry all the time? That reminds me, Mr Pope, sir, there was a spot of blanco powder on one of your belt buckles at inspection this morning – so sharpen up or you'll be following them!"

After that, the dreaded letters RTU haunted all our waking hours. Next to go were those who were inclined to panic, followed by those who seemed indecisive. I could understand that, too, as we had been taught that sometimes our decisions would have to be made quickly in difficult and dangerous circumstances. After that, some who were unable to master important subjects also left.

By the middle of March 1943 the numbers on the course had shrunk to a hard core. There had been no departures for a while and we were told that we could order our officers' service dress uniform from the tailors. We were warned that this would be entirely at our own risk as the course had four weeks to run and any slackness would still result in our being returned to our units. As a result we tried all the harder.

During our passing-out parade we were inspected by a general who made a speech and then took the salute as we marched off the square. It had been hard work but we were now second lieutenants and felt a real sense of achievement. As I had requested, I was posted to the 4th Battalion, The Branchester Regiment, but given a week's leave before I had to report. I felt highly conspicuous in my service dress, shiny Sam Browne cross-belt and peaked cap and was genuinely surprised when I was saluted for the first time. Father looked me over, grunted his approval and said, "Well done!" Mother refused to let me change into comfortable civilian clothes and, although she had not been at all keen on my joining up, kept inviting her friends round to see her soldier son, which made me cringe with embarrassment.

By now, the news from the various war fronts was even better. In Tunisia the Germans and their allies, the Italians, had been penned into a narrow coastal strip. One evening during my leave, while we were sitting listening to the Nine o'Clock News on the radio, the announcer described how the Russians were liberating huge areas of their country.

"Hmm, there'll be no stopping them now," said Father, thoughtfully. "It will take time, but Stalin has mobilized millions of men. Hitler made

266

a big mistake when he invaded Russia. Napoleon tried it and came to grief, and he was a lot brighter than Hitler."

"D'you think it will all be over before I get a chance to do any fighting?" I asked, having very mixed feelings on the subject. Part of me badly wanted to do my bit in bringing the War to a successful end, but part told me that, the risks of death or serious injury apart, active service would, at best, be most unpleasant.

"Don't be in such a hurry," he replied. "There's a long way to go yet. We have France, Belgium and the rest to liberate yet. Jerry's a good soldier and he won't make it easy for us."

He lapsed into silence for a while.

"I don't know how you'll find it, Andy," he said at length, "but my experience of war is that it's ninety per cent boredom and ten per cent sheer naked terror."

April 1943

The board outside Temple Marton camp gates read *4th Battalion The Branchester Regiment* and showed the regimental badge, a crowned dragon inside a laurel wreath, surrounded by battle honours inscribed on scrolls. The sentry directed me to Battalion Headquarters, where I reported to the adjutant, Captain Henry Dodsworth. I handed over my documents, which he glanced at briefly.

"Ah, yes, you're expected," he said. "I'll take you in to see the Colonel. I'm afraid he can't spare you much time as he only took over yesterday."

He knocked on the connecting door to the next office and opened it.

"Mr Pope, Colonel," he said, ushering me in. I saluted and was confronted by a stocky, muscular man whose battledress blouse bore the ribbons of the Distinguished Service Order and the North African campaign. A nameplate on his desk said Lieutenant Colonel JC Armitage, DSO. He rose to shake my hand.

"Glad to have you with us," he said. "Andrew, isn't it?

"It's Andy, usually, Colonel," I replied.

"Right. Just out of OCTU, I believe. Well, whatever they taught you there, I like things done my way, because it produces results, got it?"

"Yes, Colonel."

He stared at me intently, as though he had just spotted something.

"How old are you, Andy?"

"Eighteen, Colonel."

"Hmm. Well, just the same, I'm giving you Number Three Platoon in A Company. I'm trusting you to do a good job with it."

"Yes, Colonel."

"That will be all, Andy," said the adjutant.

I saluted again and followed him back to his office.

"You'd better get along to A Company HQ," he said. "Let them know you've arrived. Nigel Wood is acting as company commander for the moment."

Captain Nigel Wood was tall, fair-haired and genial. He made me feel welcome at once. He was about ten years older than me and told me that his family farmed near Branchester. He had joined the battalion as a Territorial in 1938.

"Mind you, there's only about half the original members left," he said. "A lot were sent as reinforcements to the regiment's battalions overseas. Again, some of the older officers and Non Commissioned Officers (NCO) were no longer fit enough for an infantryman's war, so they were sent to less demanding jobs like training depots and guarding prisoners of war. They've been replaced by chaps from all over the country. You'll find that they're a good lot."

"What happened to my predecessor?" I asked.

"He's gone to the 1st Battalion. Should be joining them in Tunisia about now."

At that point the door opened and two cheerful-looking lieutenants strolled in.

"Spot of lunch, Nige, old bean?" asked one.

"I'll thank you to show your acting company commander some respect," replied Nigel, who did not seem in the least put out. He introduced them as John Crane and Tony Walters, who commanded, respectively, Numbers One and Two Platoons. John was tall, dark and wore a constant half-smile, while Tony was shorter and had a mass of curly fair hair.

"John is going to be our first casualty," said Tony, amiably. "You see, whatever we're doing, the CO (the battalion's Commanding Officer) picks A Company first, and the company commander picks One Platoon. Stands to reason, doesn't it?"

"Pay no attention to him," replied John. "He lives in a world of his own. Always late for everything – if he ever finds a girl willing to marry him, she'll have gone off with someone else by the time he gets to the church!"

"By the way, how old are you, Andy?" asked Nigel.

"I'm eighteen."

"I was eighteen once," mused John.

"Surprised you can remember that far back," commented Tony, then turned confidentially to me. "He's twenty-four, you know. And as for Nigel, no one has ever found out how old he is. Could even be thirty!"

"Your platoon sergeant, Sergeant Warriner, will meet you in the company office at two o'clock, Andy," said Nigel during lunch.

"He's mustard – regular soldier, wounded serving with the 5th Battalion at Alamein. You're lucky to have him."

It was clear from the moment I set eyes on him that Sergeant Albert Warriner was a highly professional, no-nonsense sort of NCO. His turnout was immaculate, from his gleaming cap badge to his shining boots. His tunic bore the Military Medal and North African Campaign medals. Of middle height, he gave the impression of lean, muscular hardness. His sandy hair was brushed back. His angular face contained a long nose above a rat-trap mouth. His eyes were level, shrewd and never seemed to blink. I had the impression that he had summed me up at a glance. He could have been any age between thirty and forty. When he spoke it was in short bursts, with an edge of menace in his voice. He threw up a salute that quivered with precision.

"Mr Pope, sir?" he said. "I'm Sergeant Warriner. You're taking over Number 3 Platoon, I believe."

"That's right," I replied, returning the salute and shaking hands.

"Let's take a turn round the camp, sir. Show you what's what."

It sounded more like an order than a suggestion. We left the office and talked as he indicated what the various buildings were used for. When I asked him about himself he said that he had been in the Army for fifteen years, was married and had a family.

"I understand that you were wounded at Alamein," I said. "And I see that you've been awarded the Military Medal."

"Ha!" His face remained completely expressionless when he laughed. "Ha! Ha! Shouldn't wonder if they had one spare and decided I needed it, sir! There's better men deserved it and didn't get it. Now, how about you, sir? Just out of OCTU, I'm told. How old would that make you?"

When I told him, his only acknowledgement was a small upwards nod which could have meant either that he disapproved or simply that he had absorbed the fact.

"You'll be inspecting the Platoon at morning parade tomorrow, sir?" he said at length.

"Yes, Sergeant, and after Colonel Armitage has addressed the battalion I'd like to see them one at a time in the platoon office."

"Very good, sir. I'll set them to weapon cleaning while that's going on."

I suddenly found myself at a loss for what to say next. A hint of a friendly smile appeared at the corners of his mouth.

"Difficult time for you, this, sir. Just remember – you command the Platoon and I run it for you. If you need advice, just ask. All my young officers have turned out well, I'm glad to say. You'll be all right."

"Thank you, Sergeant. I appreciate what you say."

I felt a great sense of relief, knowing that I would have the backing of such an experienced man.

"There's four Fs you must remember when dealing with the men," he continued. "Be Fair, Firm and Friendly, but never Familiar. Now, if you'll excuse me, I've things to attend to, so I'll see you on morning parade, sir."

He saluted and marched away smartly.

I spent the rest of the afternoon settling in. It had alarmed me that I had been asked how old I was so often. I looked in the mirror. Aware that I did indeed appear young for my age, I wondered what the Platoon would think about being commanded by me.

At morning parade next day the order was given for platoon commanders to inspect their men. As I walked towards Number Three Platoon, Sergeant Warriner marched forward to meet me, halted with a crash of boots and saluted.

"Number Three Platoon ready for your inspection, sir!"

"Thank you, Sergeant Warriner."

I was conscious that over thirty pairs of eyes were watching me curiously. Sergeant Warriner fell in beside me as I walked towards the ranks.

"Take longer than you usually would to inspect each man, sir," he said in an undertone. "They're sizing you up, so let 'em know you're sizing them up, too. And remember – praise where it's due, blame where it isn't."

Halfway along the front rank I stopped in front of a large man with a broken nose. His boots shone, his belt buckles and cap badge gleamed and his trouser creases were sharp.

"Name?"

"Baker, sir."

"A good turnout, Baker. Well done."

"Sir."

So far so good, but in the rear rank I came across a man whose turnout was passable but whose chin was covered in stubble. Instead of staring straight ahead, he regarded me with something like a contemptuous leer.

"Name?"

"Grover, sir."

"Why haven't you shaved this morning?"

"I have, sir."

"You have not. Why not?"

"I have, sir. Must have used an old blade. If you shave you'll know you can't get new ones often, 'cos there's a war on, sir."

He was, in fact, suggesting that I was a boy who was too young to shave and therefore unfit to give orders to older men like him. I had been warned that, sooner or later, someone would challenge my authority, but I had not expected that it would happen so soon. I was horribly nervous but knew that I must win this confrontation if I was to establish myself as the platoon commander. His leer became wider and more self-confident. I was suddenly very angry and surprised myself with my response.

"When I want a lecture on current affairs from you I'll ask for it, Grover! Appear in front of me again like that and you're in for serious trouble – and you can cut out the dumb insolence, too!"

"Charge him, sir?" asked Sergeant Warriner.

A formal disciplinary charge would mean that Grover would be marched in front of Nigel Wood, who would sentence him to be confined to barracks for a period, a punishment known to the soldiers as "jankers". This involved performing numerous extra fatigue duties and parading at the Guard Room at various times in full equipment. However, I had dealt with the incident and did not want to exaggerate its importance.

"No, not this time, but he's had the only chance he's getting. Find him some extra duties."

"Be a pleasure, sir. Grover – report to the Provost Sergeant after tea tonight. He wants the grass round the Guard Room cutting. Should take you about three hours if you're lucky."

"Yes, Sergeant," replied Grover, his face sullen and resentful.

After the inspection we were to be addressed by Colonel Armitage. I ordered Sergeant Warriner to march the Platoon to the camp cinema and made my own way there. When the whole battalion was assembled the officers filed into the front row of seats. As Colonel Armitage began to walk down the aisle, followed by the adjutant, everyone was called to attention by Mr Ash, the red-faced, fiercely moustached Regimental Sergeant Major (RSM). The Colonel mounted the stage, motioning us to sit down.

"Since 1940 this battalion has been engaged on anti-invasion duties here in East Anglia," he said. "That was a necessary job. It was also a boring job, and now that Hitler is firmly on the defensive and there is no prospect of our country being invaded, the job has come to an end. You will no doubt have wished at times that you could be playing a more active role in the War, because everyone knows that until the enemy has been beaten none of us will be going home. Well, the moment for you to play that role has now come."

You could have heard a pin drop in the short pause that followed.

"My task is to turn you into a fit, efficient, hard-fighting battalion, ready to take the field. I can tell you that something very big indeed is being planned. I do not know what, when or where it is to take place because I have not been told myself, but I have been told that you will be a part of it. Now, some of you will have made yourselves very comfortable here over the years. I can promise you that you will find the next few months very uncomfortable, but at the end of it you will be leaner, harder and capable of tackling the toughest of enemies."

He paused again to let this sink in.

"No one will be excused. Not even the clerks, storemen, batmen, cooks and the others who somehow manage to stay out of the rain when the rest of us are getting soaked!"

There was much laughter at this.

"That's all I have to say for the present. Carry on, please, Mr Ash."

The RSM called the battalion to attention and we filed out of the cinema.

It took the rest of the morning and the whole of the afternoon to complete my interviews with the Platoon, during which Sergeant Warriner stood behind me. I recorded the personal details of my men in a notebook. These included their home town, their civilian occupation, whether they were married and had families of their own, their hobbies, sports and interests. I also asked them whether they had any personal problems.

I saw the junior NCO first. The three section commanders, Corporals Gray, Morris and Sherwood, had been in the Territorial Army before the War. In civilian life, they had been, respectively, a plasterer, a milkman and a refuse collector. They were all married and seemed solid and reliable. The Lance Corporals were newer arrivals but showed promise. I then saw each of the privates. The Platoon had its characters and it was them who interested me most. Grover I had already encountered. Now properly shaven, he glared resentfully at me. He said he was an orphan, had no fixed address and had worked as a casual labourer since he left school at twelve. He had no interest in sport, or anything else for that matter. His record revealed a string of civilian convictions for petty theft, brawling and drunkenness. His military charge sheet contained a long list of offences, including insolence, insubordination, failure to obey orders, and many more.

"Why don't you sort yourself out?" I asked.

"Not my fault, sir," he replied, glowering at Sergeant Warriner. "They've got it in for me, the lot of them."

I asked him why and he simply shrugged. When I asked him if he had any particular problems he gave vent to a sudden flash of anger.

"Oh, yes, I got a problem, sir. My problem is the whole piggin' Army! Why should I fight for my country? What's the country ever done for me? This war's nothin' to me."

"Want a reason, do you?" shouted Sergeant Warriner. I thought he would explode with fury. "Then think of the innocent women and children killed in the Blitz! And there'll be more before this lot's over. You'll fight for your country and like it, like the rest of us! Now get out of my sight!"

"I'm sorry about that, sir," he said when Grover had gone. "He's a bad 'un. He'll be over the wall at the first sign of trouble, mark my words."

"Can we get rid of him?"

"Ha! Don't think I haven't tried. Easier said than done, sir, because no one wants him."

"Isn't he a bad influence on the rest of the Platoon?"

"They ignore him, sir. Weighed him up as soon as he arrived. Can't name one of them you could say was his friend."

"I'm not surprised. Seems to hate everyone, including himself. Can we make anything out of him, d'you think?"

"I've met his type before, sir. Sometimes they'll surprise you and buckle-to when the going's rough, but don't count on it in this case."

Then there was Baker. He was married with two boys, had been a coalman, and was an amateur middleweight boxer who, because he was light on his feet, had also won ballroom-dancing contests. He gave every appearance of being a good soldier, but his crimesheet showed that he had been punished regularly for going absent without leave.

"Why?" I asked him.

"Personal reasons, sir."

"If you've got a problem then tell the platoon commander," said Sergeant Warriner. "But for this you could have had a stripe on your arm, maybe two."

"Prefer not to say, Sar'nt."

"Pity," Sergeant Warriner said when Baker had gone. "Ten to one it's wife trouble. Corporal Gray knows, I'm sure of it, but I can't get it out of him."

Private Joseph Haggerty was Irish and came from Liverpool. He was short, dark, had a shifty expression, but was good humoured and played football for the battalion. He described his civilian occupation as general dealer. I asked him what he dealt in.

"Oh, whatever comes me way, sir," he replied, grinning broadly. "I'll sell it on, like, for the best price I can get."

"He means he's a burglar, sir," commented Sergeant Warriner.

"Ay, come on, Sarge!" protested Haggerty. "Yer know I don't nick off me mates! I've gone straight since I joined up."

"Keep it that way!" snapped the Sergeant.

Haggerty leaned confidentially towards me, smiling like a conspirator and tapping the side of his nose.

"Mind you, sir, if ever yer need anythin', like nylon stockings an' such as are in short supply, I do know a coupla helpful fellers."

"That will be all, Haggerty," I said.

Private Adrian Helsby-Frodsham was about thirty, of sturdy build and dapper appearance with a gold watch chain stretching between the pockets of his battledress tunic.

"How do you do?" he said in a cultured voice.

"Never mind how d'you damn well do!" bellowed Sergeant Warriner. "It's your platoon commander you're talking to! And get rid of that watch chain – I've told you about that before! This is your signaller, sir, when he's not putting on his Posh Charlie act."

"I see from your documents that you were an artist in civilian life," I said.

"Oh, I do the odd dawb, sir," he replied. "Portraits mostly – keeps the old body and soul joined together, what?"

"And what are your interests?"

"Principally, painting the pretty wives of rich men, sir. That's rather rewarding. Then there's fast cars, good food and wine and the occasional holiday in France. Simple things, really."

"I don't know, of course, but it's possible we might all be taking a trip to France. Can you speak French?"

"Yes, I studied in Paris for three years, so I'm reasonably fluent."

It occurred to me that he could be a useful member of the Platoon in a variety of ways.

"Can you draw cartoons?" I asked.

"I can, sir – lots of good subjects hereabouts," he replied, looking pointedly at Sergeant Warriner, who responded with a stony stare.

"Perhaps you could do some of the Platoon," I suggested. "You know what I mean – the things that happen while we're training and so on. We can put them on the notice board for a week, then keep them in a platoon scrapbook."

He agreed, and Sergeant Warriner clearly approved of the idea, commenting that it would do some people good to see themselves as others saw them.

Last to appear was my batman – that is, soldier servant – who also acted as my runner in the field. Private Timothy Allen, whom I had already met briefly in the Mess, had been a valet at the Savoy Hotel in London and it was natural that a former commander of the battalion had initially taken him as his batman. However, Allen could not stop talking about the royalty, aristocrats, admirals, generals, film stars and politicians whom he had looked after at the hotel, driving everyone to distraction. He had therefore slid down the battalion's hierarchy, through the majors, captains and senior lieutenants, and as I was the most junior officer for the present I was landed with him.

"I imagine that you find the Army very different from your earlier occupation," I said, and instantly regretted it.

"Oh, yes, sir," he replied. "It's not that I don't approve of the War or the Army, sir, because I believe we're right to fight against Hitler – he and his crowd were never gentlemen, sir, so the dreadful things they've done came as no surprise to me. That's why I joined up. No, sir, the main difference is financial, you see. Many of the people I looked after at the hotel were generous, sir, very generous. Now take Mr Niven, sir – Mr David Niven, the actor, that is. . ."

"Stop talkin'!" snapped Sergeant Warriner.

"You know that your duties involve digging a slit trench for us both, don't you?" I asked.

"Indeed I do, sir. I dig a very fine slit trench, even if I do say so myself. Apart from the two of us, I'm always very fussy who I invite into it. After all, one wouldn't invite just anyone into one's home, would one? I like to keep up standards, sir, even in the field. There are some people. . ."

I could see Sergeant Warriner raising his eyes to heaven in despair.

"Thank you, Allen, that's all," I said, but he continued talking as he made his way to the door.

"Oh, by the way, sir, I've buffed up the buttons on your service dress, creased your trousers, and polished your Sam Browne belt and shoes. And as soon as you're back, sir, I think I'd better give those boots you're wearing a bit of attention. And you'll need more handkerchiefs, sir. I like my gentleman to have a clean handkerchief every day, and you've less than a week's supply left. . ."

There was a sense of deep and enjoyable silence after he had gone.

"Well, that's that," I said, closing my notebook.

"Mixed bunch – is that what you're thinking, sir?" asked Sergeant Warriner. "They rub along together pretty well, considering. Handled right, they won't let you down."

Just then the door opened and Nigel poked his head round.

"Spot o' news, Andy," he said. "The new company commander arrives next Monday. Name's Duncan Flint, Distinguished Service Order and Military Cross, no less. Bit of a hot shot by all accounts."

"Ha!" Sergeant Warriner gave one of his mirthless laughs. "Knew him pre-war. When the 2nd Battalion was forced to surrender at Tobruk last year, he refused to give up until Jerry promised his company the Honours of War. Then he escaped from a prisoner-of-war train in Italy and made it home. No disrespect intended, gentlemen, but he'll make you earn every penny of your pay. You may even hate his guts at the end of it, but we'll have a damn fine company!"

April – September 1943

The following Monday I was conducting a map-reading class when Company Sergeant Major Darracott appeared.

"Sorry to interrupt, sir, but Major Flint, the new company commander, has arrived," he said. "He'd like to see you in his office at 11:00 prompt."

I reached the office at the same time as John. We strolled in and saluted the figure seated behind the desk. He was looking down at some papers, so all that I could see was that he was well-built and had iron-grey hair. Nigel stood behind him, looking ill at ease. I could hear Tony's feet hurrying along the corridor. He entered the room and saluted. Only then did the man at the desk look up. He had a clipped moustache and the most piercing eyes I have ever seen.

"Get out and come in again – all of you!" he snarled. There was a frightening edge to his voice. We did as we were bidden, halted in front of his desk and saluted together. He regarded each of us minutely in turn.

"Now let us get one thing straight from the start," he said. "When I say eleven-hundred hours, I mean precisely that. It is now thirty seconds past eleven and I regard that as being very late indeed. If you are thirty seconds late attacking after the barrage has lifted you will have given the enemy time to man his machine-guns and you will lose a lot of men. Do we agree, gentlemen?"

"Yes, sir," we said in chorus.

"Good. I also want you to know that I regard any hesitation or surliness in carrying out an order as disobedience, that half-hearted effort is a sign of laziness and that if you knowingly communicate inaccurate or incomplete information to me that is the equivalent of lying. Do we understand each other?"

"Yes, sir," we said again.

"I am glad that is clear. I shall require the pleasure of your company for a drink after dinner, gentlemen. You may now return to your duties."

We saluted, turned about and left the office.

"Phew!" said Tony. "I think I've just been run over by a steamroller!"

Dinner in the Mess was usually a pleasant, relaxed affair, but on this occasion Nigel, John, Tony and I were more concerned with what lay in store for us than with what we were eating. Later, when we had settled ourselves in armchairs in the ante-room, Major Flint joined us and instructed one of the Mess staff to bring us drinks from the bar. It was soon apparent that this was not a friendly gesture, but one made for the same reasons I had interviewed everyone in my platoon. He asked each of us a series of searching questions and was obviously making up his mind about us. As our interrogation drew to an end, Nigel asked him about the fall of Tobruk.

"Yes, I thought that would come up, so I'll tell you now and get it out of the way," he said. "We had no tanks left and when Jerry broke through the defences and reached the town, the general in command, a South African named Klopper, didn't have much choice other than to surrender. Our battalion was holding an area of the eastern defences, near the sea. With Jerry tanks crawling all over them, the rest of the battalion obeyed the order to surrender. I didn't, because my company was lucky enough to be holding a position between two wadis, that is, steep-sided, dried-up river courses, with a cliff covering our rear. The only way Jerry could get at us was across a stretch of ground between the wadis, and I had covered that with a minefield. At the time I believed that the Eighth Army wouldn't stand for the loss of Tobruk and would counter-attack, so all we had to do was hold out until they arrived. What I didn't know was that the Army had taken a real beating and was retreating across the frontier into Egypt."

He paused for a moment, remembering what had happened.

"Well, we held 'em off for two days," he continued. "They lost three tanks on the minefield, and the rest couldn't get past them. They shelled us time and again, but we beat them off every time their infantry attacked and caused them a lot of grief. We also lost a lot of good men. By the morning of the third day the company was down to the size of a platoon. The riflemen had about five rounds left apiece, and the Bren gunners less than a magazine. We had no food and what water was left we saved for the wounded. Anyway, a Jerry colonel appeared with a flag of truce. He said we'd put up a terrific fight but if we didn't surrender he had orders to exterminate us. I told him that if he tried that every one of us would take two or three of his men with us. I knew it was hopeless, so I said that I would surrender on two conditions – first, that he granted us the Honours of War, and second, that he arranged for our wounded to be attended to immediately. He was a decent enough sort and agreed.

"We spent the morning smartening up and making the wounded as comfortable as possible. At noon, the agreed time, I led what was left of the company through a gap in the minefield. Then we formed up, fixed bayonets, and marched between two lines of Jerries. They presented arms and their officers saluted. When we halted I thanked the men for all they had done and ordered them to ground arms. I watched them being marched off under guard. That was the worst day of my life and I have no intention of repeating it."

We all sat silent for a moment. I think we were all a little surprised that he had cared so much about his men.

"You managed to escape, though, sir," said Tony, breaking the silence.

"Yes. I was flown to Italy and held in an Italian prisoner-of-war camp until August. The guards were a sloppy lot and I managed to pinch a tyre lever when one of them was working on his lorry. I suppose I thought it would come in handy as a cosh. Anyway, it was decided that the British officers would be sent to Germany and we were put aboard a train consisting of cattle trucks. I began working on the truck's floorboards with the tyre lever. I got one up, then more, until I had made a hole big enough for me to drop through on to the track. I could see through the ventilation slits in the side of the truck that we were getting closer to the Alps. The train made frequent stops, but I decided to wait until it was dark and we were in open country. The right moment seemed to arrive and I dropped through. I think others would have followed, but just then the train began to move again. Maybe some of them tried it later. Anyway, I lay between the rails until the train was out of sight."

"What happened next, sir?" I asked.

"I became a thief. At various times I stole bicycles, clothes, food and money. By moving only at night and staying hidden during the day, I somehow got over the mountains into France. The Jerries weren't occupying the south of the country at that time, but the French government, located in a town called Vichy, were collaborating with them and would have handed me over like a shot if their police had got their hands on me. I was sitting in a café in Nice, looking like a scarecrow, when two characters put a revolver in my back and marched me down an alley and into a house. They belonged to the Resistance, and while they suspected that I was an escaped British POW, they were worried that I might be a German posing as one. So, for the next three days I was grilled over and over again. At length London confirmed my details over their short-wave radio link. From that point on, it was plain sailing. I was spirited across southern France to the Pyrenees, where I was handed over to the group's Spanish friends. They had been on the losing side during the Spanish Civil War and they had no love for General Franco, who, as you know, is one of Hitler's best pals. To cut a long story short, I was taken through some pretty remote areas of

Spain until we reached the frontier with Gibraltar. I was taken across in a coffin in the back of a hearse. Pretty creepy, I can tell you. In Gibraltar they found a space for me in a homeward-bound destroyer."

We had all listened in silent wonder and admiration as Duncan Flint told his story. Suddenly, he stood up and his manner changed abruptly.

"I'll wish you good night, gentlemen. I shall be joining you for a run at 06:00."

"Er, you remember you've ordered a company run for 08:00?" asked Nigel, startled.

"Quite right – you should be nicely warmed up by then!" was the reply.

It soon became clear that Major Flint intended sparing his officers nothing. At the morning parade following the company run he addressed everyone.

"It won't be too long now before we find ourselves on active service. I intend working you hard, but no harder than I work myself and your officers. We have a heavy programme of exercises ahead of us. During those exercises I shall sometimes tell platoon commanders or their sergeants that they have been 'killed'. That will mean that corporals may find themselves commanding their platoons for part of an exercise. Likewise, lance corporals may find themselves acting as platoon sergeants and private soldiers commanding sections. Why are we doing this? Because I intend encouraging you to use your personal initiative. It has been my experience that soldiers who use their initiative survive, and those who don't, don't."

He now had everyone's undivided attention. I exchanged glances with Nigel, John and Tony. It was apparent that none of us had expected this.

"I want you to remember a few things at all times, no matter how tired you are," the Major continued. "Always expect the unexpected. Think of everything the enemy might possibly do, then it's no surprise when he does it. Treat him to a dose of the unexpected, because he doesn't like it. If you are in contact with him, never move without covering fire if you can avoid it. Learn what you can about the enemy's weapons – you may have to use 'em in a tight spot. And if that spot is so tight that you think things couldn't get worse, keep giving the enemy a hard time. You'll be surprised what you can get away with."

Duncan Flint certainly kept his promise. There were early morning runs three times a week and we were sent over the assault course whenever there was a spare moment. Fortunately, I was still as fit as I had been at OCTU and didn't experience too much difficulty, but many of the others found it hard going until they toughened up. Then there were platoon, company and battalion exercises, sometimes carried out in company with tanks. These included attacks, occupying a defensive position, withdrawals, street fighting in a dummy village, and patrolling at night. During these, the "enemy" consisted of one or other of our brigade's battalions. As we progressed, a friendly rivalry began to develop between A Company's three platoons. Colonel Armitage and Major Flint, who both had personal experience of war, could often be seen arguing fiercely with the exercise umpires and directing staff, who had not. This caused Sergeant Warriner much wry amusement.

"Ha! They're supposed to teach us," he said. "Now we end up teaching them! All they know is what they read in tactical manuals!"

I knew what he meant because Warriner's practical experience had become evident on the first day of the exercises. I had turned up with my issue map case and binoculars slung round my neck.

"Looks as though I'll be needing a new officer ten minutes after we go into action, sir," he remarked after giving me a cursory glance.

"What do you mean, Sergeant?"

"Your map case, sir. Reflects in the sun. Jerry sniper spots it, takes a look through his telescopic sight, sees that you're wearing binoculars. Puts two and two together – map case plus binoculars means you're someone important. Draws a bead on you and the platoon has lost its officer. My advice is ditch the map case, keep the map in your trouser-leg pocket and tuck your binoculars into your battledress tunic."

I did as he suggested. A few minutes later Major Flint walked over.

"I see you've been taking survival lessons, Andy – well done," he said, and nodded approvingly at Sergeant Warriner.

In fact, this was one of the few occasions on which I received any praise. When I did well I was called Andy, but I seemed to make one mistake after another and so most of the time it was Mr Pope.

"Mr Pope," the Major would say, "your two leading sections came over that crest like a line of tin ducks at a shooting gallery! Learn to use the ground as cover, for God's sake!"

291

Or, "Mr Pope, you failed to identify that machine gun post to your left. You and your platoon headquarters have been wiped out!"

Or, worst of all, the dreaded phrase, "See if you can get it right this time, boy!"

To be fair, the Major always made these comments out of the men's hearing and explained the nature of the mistakes to the Platoon in a general way so that they would learn not to make them themselves. He also encouraged us platoon commanders to be more flexible in our approach to tactical problems.

"You have got to win the fire-fight before you even think of attacking," he said. "The German light machine gun, the Spandau or MG34, is a belt-fed weapon theoretically capable of firing over 800 rounds per minute. Your Brens, on the other hand, are magazine-fed and can only produce a theoretical 450 rounds a minute. So concentrate *all* your Brens into a single fire base and take out his MG34s one at a time. You'll find that once his machine-gunners have gone, the average Jerry rifleman tends to give up."

Likewise, he had his own ideas about using the PIAT (Projector Infantry Anti-Tank), which launched a hollow-charge bomb capable of penetrating a tank's armour, three of which were issued to each company.

"Don't think you have to wait for a tank to use your PIAT," he told us. "If the enemy's holed up in a house, use it to bring it down round his ears."

Tactics such as these, based on his own experience, were to prove invaluable when the time came for action. Even so, there were days when I hated him, and I know that Nigel, John and Tony felt the same. The odd thing was, Duncan Flint had an uncanny ability to read my thoughts, which I found disturbing. When, without saying a word, I had decided to do something, he would suddenly bark at me to do exactly what I had intended. This happened quite a lot and was very annoying. Once, after he had given me a real dressing down, I was glaring with dislike at his retreating back when he unexpectedly halted, wheeled round and fixed me with his terrifying stare.

"I don't give a damn what you think, laddie!" he snarled. "Now, let's get one thing straight, shall we? My intention is that one day this company will earn a name for itself in history, as did my last company – and you're part of it, whether you like it or not! Have you got that?"

"Yes, sir," I replied, somewhat shaken. This was just what he might have said if he had known what I was thinking about him, which was far from pleasant.

My father had told me that a young officer's education is completed in the Sergeants' Mess, as the sergeants' long service has given them a wide understanding of human nature. It was the custom for the orderly officer of the day (a junior officer who was responsible for mounting the camp's Guard which provided sentries during the night, inspecting the cookhouse and many other things) to be invited into the Sergeants' Mess after his ten o'clock inspection of the Guard. On one such occasion, after paying my respects to Mr Ash, I found myself sitting on a bar stool between Company Sergeant Major Darracott and Sergeant Warriner.

"Bit of a hard time for you, just now, sir," said the Sergeant Major, who was a Dunkirk veteran.

"Well, if there's a way of doing things wrong, I usually find it, don't I, Sergeant Major?" I replied ruefully.

They both laughed.

"Don't let it get you down, sir," said Sergeant Warriner. "We've all of us had bad patches at one time or another. They come to an end."

"Maybe you'd be surprised to know that during the exercises there wasn't a platoon leader in the battalion who didn't get strips torn off him by his company commander or even the Colonel, sir," added the Sergeant Major. "True, Major Flint is taking more trouble with you, but he wouldn't be wasting his time if he thought you were useless, would he? You'd have been long gone to some depot for the unwanted."

"Maybe you're right," I said, feeling somewhat reassured. "I dare say I'll get used to him in time."

They exchanged knowing glances.

"Fact is, sir, the Major's seen more than his fair share of scrapping in this war," said Sergeant Warriner. "Seen most of his old friends killed or badly wounded. That hurts – I know because I've had some."

"What we're saying is this," continued the Sergeant Major. "Friends are for peacetime. Being friendly is the way to make friends – he doesn't want 'em, so he isn't. That doesn't stop him being a damn fine officer. D'you get my drift, sir?"

"Yes, I think so," I said. "I'll bear in mind what you say, and thanks for the advice."

I felt much better after this. At first, my handling of my platoon during the exercises had been stiff and awkward, and the men sensed it. However, as my confidence grew they became used to me and we began to work as a team. Grover continued to give trouble in a minor sort of way but was under control. Baker, however, went absent without leave once more. On his return he offered no excuse and was sentenced to fourteen days confined to barracks. I warned him that if he committed the offence again he would probably be sent for a spell in a detention barracks.

Curiously, it was Baker who was responsible for my getting to know the men better. During the inter-company boxing contest, A Company was level-pegging with D Company. Everything depended on the last match, in which Baker was fighting. He had the measure of his opponent from the start, but during the last round a strange look came over his face and he continued raining blows on him after the bell had rung. After he was pulled off he seemed to come to, went across and apologized to the other man, saying that he didn't know what had come over him. Needless to say, he was disqualified and we lost the match. Major Flint had wanted A Company to win and he was furious.

"Baker is *your* man," he snapped at me as he stalked out of the gymnasium. "Sort him out!"

Sergeant Warriner had said that Corporal Gray knew what was troubling Baker, but when I approached him he was reluctant to discuss the matter. I said that it was in Baker's interest that he should, because if Baker went absent without leave again he would be sentenced to detention. That meant his pay would be stopped and his wife and family would suffer because of it. He thought about it for a minute, then told me the story.

"Ron Baker and I have been friends for years, sir," he said. "Well, one night before the War we were at a dance. That's where he met Mary. Well, being a boxer, Ron's light on his feet and a good dancer. The two of them won plenty of competitions. They got married and now they've got two boys. Ron thinks the world of them. Well, just after the War started, Mary fell ill. She's never really recovered and if anything she's got worse. Her doctor says an operation would set her right, but every penny they've got goes to paying his bills, buying medicine and looking after the boys. There's nothing left to pay for the operation, nor will there ever be on a private's pay. Ron's worried sick about it, and that's why he keeps going absent without leave. What makes it worse, sir, is that he's a proud man who won't take charity from anyone."

"Thank you, Corporal, I'll see what we can do," I replied. "In the meantime, don't mention any of this to Baker."

I reported this to Duncan Flint and together we went to see Colonel Armitage.

"You say that in every other respect Baker is a good soldier with the potential to become an NCO?" asked the Colonel after he had considered the problem.

"Yes, Colonel," I said. "If we can't help he'll keep going absent without leave. He knows he'll get detention next time, but it won't stop him, and nobody will be any better off."

"I will support that, Colonel," added Duncan Flint.

"Quite so," said the Colonel. "Andy, find out who is the family doctor, will you? While you're doing that, I'll talk to the Secretary of the Regimental Benevolent Fund."

Corporal Gray gave me the doctor's name, which I passed on. A couple of days later I was called into Duncan Flint's office.

"Your man Baker," he said. "The Secretary of the Benevolent Fund has spoken to his doctor. He, in turn, has spoken to the specialist who will carry out the operation. In the circumstances, the specialist will reduce his fee, which will be paid by the Fund. Nevertheless, I want you to verify Mrs Baker's situation for yourself. You can borrow my jeep on Sunday morning and drive over to see her – take Baker with you."

I told Corporal Gray that we might be making some progress, and that Baker should meet me at the Guard Room at 08:30 next Sunday, but not the reason why.

That Sunday, I found Baker waiting for me at the Guard Room, wearing a puzzled expression.

"Where are we going, sir?" he asked as we turned out the camp gates.

"What's your home address?" I asked.

"22 Webber Street, Donby, sir. Why?"

"Then that's where we're going."

"Someone's been talking," he said, his face flushing with anger. "I'll deal with him when I get back."

"No, you won't. He was thinking of your boys. He says they're proud of their dad – how d'you think they'd feel about you ending up in detention barracks and no money coming in?"

He remained silent, but I could see that he understood.

"And another thing," I added. "Your wife needs an operation – let's see if we can get her one, shall we? That way, she gets better, the boys get looked after, and you stay in the Platoon."

"I'll take charity from no man," he said stubbornly. "I've never had 'owt but what I've earned, fair and square."

"It's not charity. The Regiment looks after its own and the Benevolent Fund exists for just this sort of situation. Besides, I know you wouldn't want your wife to suffer longer than she had to, or become so ill that she couldn't look after the boys. Apart from which, we both know that if the War hadn't broken out, you'd have earned enough to deal with the problem yourself."

"Happen you're right, sir," he said with a sigh. "Seems I'd best put my pride in my pocket, then."

About an hour later we drove into the small industrial town in which he lived. He directed me into a street of terraced houses and asked me to pull up outside one of them. As he got out of the jeep two small boys who had been playing football ran towards him with delighted yells. When they had calmed down a little he brought them over.

"These are my lads, sir. This is Jack, he's nearly seven, and this is Tom, he's five. This is Mr Pope, boys – he's my officer, so mind your manners, the pair of you. I'll just let your mam know we're here."

"Hello," I said. "Ever sat in a jeep before? Jump in."

A few minutes later I joined Baker in the house and was introduced to his wife. She would have been good-looking but for an expression of pain that had become etched on her face, and she moved slowly and with difficulty. It seemed obvious to me that she couldn't go on much longer like that. I told her what had been decided and that she should contact her doctor, who would arrange for the specialist to carry out the operation.

"I don't know what to say, sir," she said, and burst into tears. Nothing in my training had prepared me for this and I was horribly embarrassed.

"Just get well, that's what we all want," I mumbled, and told Baker I would wait for him in the jeep outside.

"You've taken a ton weight off my shoulders, sir," he said when I dropped him off at the Guard Room. "Thanks – we're both very grateful to you."

It was now approaching lunchtime. I found Duncan Flint reading a newspaper in the ante-room. He barely glanced up when I told him the result of my visit.

"Good," he said at length, turning a page. "If there are any more personal problems in Three Platoon, see that you sort them out before they become this serious."

He was right, of course, but his manner infuriated me. The following week Mrs Baker had her operation and made a good recovery.

After that more of the men came to me with their problems. I found myself arguing with Duncan Flint about their leave entitlement, with the Paymaster about their pay and with the Quartermaster about their kit. I arranged compassionate leave when members of their families died and saw to it that they had legal advice when they needed it.

I had been advised that it was sometimes wise to be blind to minor faults and deaf to chance remarks that one might overhear. One day, however, I heard some of the men talking about me when they thought I was out of earshot.

"He's all right, is Mr Pope," said one.

I felt as though I had grown a foot in height.

October 1943 – May 1944

During the months that followed we still remained in ignorance about where we would be sent. Duncan Flint refused to speculate, but Nigel felt that because we trained a great deal with armoured regiments, it was unlikely to be Italy – the Italian campaign had become an infantry war in which tanks had only a limited role to play. More than ever, therefore, we became convinced that we were being trained for the invasion of France.

This seemed to be confirmed when, in October, each company was sent to the Battle School at Thetford. There, we carried out live ammunition exercises and completed a stiff assault course during which constant explosions simulated shellfire and machine guns fired inches above our heads as we crawled through or jumped over the numerous obstacles. I was extremely nervous, for I knew that people had been injured and even killed during this sort of training. Fortunately, nothing of that sort happened, and I suppose it gave us all an idea of what to expect. However, looking back, I now know that it could not possibly duplicate the sheer naked fear we experienced when we were faced with the real thing.

We were getting our breath back when Nigel pointed to a group of officers in unfamiliar uniforms talking to the Directing Staff.

"Americans," he said. "Come to see how it's done, I expect."

Being based in East Anglia we had met plenty of American airmen, but these were the first soldiers we had seen, although the United States had entered the War on the side of the Allies in December 1941.

"I like their waterproof uniforms," said John. "They call them combat fatigues, I believe. Those round helmets of theirs must be easier to keep on than the ones we've got – mine bounces all over the place."

"That's no surprise," commented Tony. "You've got a pointed skull like a Martian. Sometimes I think you are a Martian."

"Frankly, old chap, yours wouldn't stay on at all if you hadn't got so much hair," retorted John. "Better not visit the barber's – no one would recognize you when you came out!"

"Uh-oh! Looks as though we're getting a visitor," observed Nigel as Duncan Flint walked towards us with an American officer whose helmet had the single white star of a brigadier general on the front. The Sergeant Major called the company to attention and we officers saluted. The American was portly and wore rimless glasses. I thought he looked like a banker in a Hollywood film. A white identification label saying FASSBINDER was sewn on to his tunic.

"At ease, men," he said, grinning broadly. "I've been watching you this morning and I consider that you gave a fine display of fitness, speed, stamina and determination. I guess that you guys are just about combat ready."

The men were obviously pleased. Then, to my horror, Haggerty, the joker from Liverpool, spoke up.

"You goin' to have a go yourself, then, sir?"

Duncan Flint's eyes flicked angrily from Haggerty to me and I expected to be called to account later. Fortunately, the American took it in his stride.

"Hell, no, son," he replied, chuckling. "You fellers have been at this since the War began – we're just getting started! When the time comes, though, we'll be right in there pitching alongside you!"

When the American had gone, Duncan Flint turned to face the company, hands on hips. I think we all knew what to expect.

"Now I'll tell you what I think," he said. "By my standards you were satisfactory – just. I've seen you move much faster but the only reason I'm not sending you round again is that when you really come under fire you'll discover you have a turn of speed you never thought possible!"

The men laughed. I think they liked his style, which was more than we did at the time. Telling the Sergeant Major to dismiss the company, he turned to us.

"And as for you four, I expected more from you!" he snapped. "You should have set the pace, not conformed to it. You're paid to lead, so lead!"

"Miserable so-and-so!" muttered John angrily as the Major stalked off. "Nothing we do ever seems to satisfy him!"

I could see that Nigel was angry, too, but as the company's second-in-command he had a duty to support Duncan Flint, whatever he thought privately.

"He's doing his job as he thinks best," he said. "Remember, he's had a lot more experience than we have. What's more, though he's older than us, he still got round the course first, and that gives him the right to criticize."

"It wouldn't hurt him to say 'well done' now and again, would it?" I commented.

"You know, he's never said as much, but I think he's rather pleased at the way the company is coming on," Nigel replied. "Just the same, I don't think he'll let up until he's satisfied he can take us into action. That's when I think he'll ease off."

"He's still a miserable so-and-so," said Tony.

Nigel rounded on him sharply.

"That's enough! He's your company commander and don't you forget it! And get your hair cut – you're starting to look like one of the girls who serve in the men's canteen!"

A fortnight after we got back from Battle School, a naval commander gave the whole battalion a lecture, with slides, in the camp cinema. He told us that as a result of the landings in North Africa, Sicily and Italy, the Royal Navy had accumulated a great deal of experience and was preparing to mount the largest seaborne landing in its history, of which we would be part.

"Obviously, I don't know where you'll be going, and I wouldn't be allowed to tell you if I did," he said. "However, as far as you are concerned, the drill will be as follows. First, you will board an LSI,

304

which is short for Landing Ship Infantry. Most LSIs are former passenger liners or cross-channel ferries converted to carry LCAs, that is, Landing Craft Assault. You will remain aboard the LSI until you are seven miles from the objective, then transfer to the LCAs, which will be lowered into the sea. Once you are all afloat, the LCAs will line up and head for the beach. The operation will be controlled by someone like me from a motor launch, the advantage being that he has radio contact with the overall commander of that landing sector and knows the situation on the beach ahead.

"If the weather is bad, you won't find the LCAs comfortable – they're almost flat-bottomed and they pitch and roll a lot. As if that isn't bad enough, they are blunt-bowed because of the landing ramp you'll use to get ashore, and a lot of spray comes inboard in any sort of choppy sea. We call them 'kipper boxes' for obvious reasons, but they'll get you there and give you some protection against the enemy's fire as well. Are there any questions so far?"

"What about our supporting armour?" asked Colonel Armitage. "And when can we expect our Support Company's heavy weapons to arrive – the anti-tank guns, mortars and so on?"

"Most of the tanks will come ashore directly from Landing Ships and Landing Craft Tank," replied the Commander. "The idea is that they will touch down some minutes ahead of you. That way you'll find that Jerry's attention will be fully occupied by the time you put in an appearance."

A murmur of approval went round the hall. I was a little puzzled by his use of the word "most" and it would be some months yet before I understood why he had used it.

"As for your own heavy weapons," the Commander continued, "you can expect them to arrive in the follow-up wave. Your transport lorries have a lower priority and will be landed as soon as you've captured sufficient ground ashore."

He went on to describe some of the specialized landing craft that the Navy had produced to accompany our amphibious assault. There were landing craft armed with guns, rockets and bomb-throwers, all designed to deal with some aspect of the enemy's defences. In fact, there seemed to be a landing craft for every conceivable job, including one fitted with stretchers that could ferry casualties out to the waiting hospital ships.

"Nevertheless," continued the Commander, "we're not letting you and the landing craft crews have all the fun. Before you go in, the enemy's defences will have received one almighty battering from our battleships, cruisers and destroyers. As if that isn't enough, bombers from the RAF and US Army Air Force will give them another battering, and you'll have continuous fighter cover all the way. I can promise you this – it's going to be a very noisy party indeed! Anyway, we're going to give you a dry run next month – give you a chance to get some good sea air into your lungs and play about in the sand a bit!"

This produced laughter and a mutter of approval. I think we all looked forward to this exercise as a break in the training routine.

In the middle of November 1943 the battalion made a day-long journey by troop train, reaching Cardiff docks in darkness. I could just make out the name *Countess of Antrim* on the stern of the LSI we were boarding. Everything went like clockwork, for the ship's crew had done this many times, although none of us had been aboard a Royal Navy ship before and it showed immediately. Unfortunately, Three Platoon tried to walk down the steep companionways as though they were stairs. Inevitably, someone's hobnailed boot skidded on a steel tread, and the result was that those below him were swept away by his fall. The tangle of protesting bodies at the foot of the companionway caused the seamen much amusement, as it did to those of us who were not involved. As it sorted itself out I felt a certain amount of guilty pleasure that Grover was at the bottom of the pile. Winded and bruised, he picked himself up, swearing horribly that someone had done it on purpose to spite him.

Shortly after, the ship moved out into the Bristol Channel. I managed to get some rest on one of the bunks in the officers' quarters, but when the steady thump of the ship's engines slowed I knew that we were somewhere off the Welsh Gower Peninsula, where our landing was to take place. A moment later the Tannoy loudspeaker crackled into life, telling us to report to our allocated landing-craft stations. I reached the deck to find a sleet-laden wind blowing. I made my way forward in total darkness to No 4 Port Side, where Sergeant Warriner had just finished calling the roll.

"All present and correct, sir!" he reported.

"Get your troops aboard the landing craft, if you please, gentlemen!" shouted a petty officer.

We clambered over the ship's rail and into the craft. I made my way to where the craft's commander, a young midshipman, was standing beside the small armoured structure in which the coxswain, responsible for steering the craft, stood behind his wheel. When the midshipman was satisfied that everyone was aboard he gave the order to lower away. As we were lowered down the ship's side into the sea, the craft's engine burst into life and we moved away into open water. The men settled themselves in a crowded huddle on the deck. The craft was pitching and rolling in a series of sharp jerks and whenever the blunt bow smashed into a wave, spray flew back at us. This, together, with the sleet, meant that we were soon soaked to the skin. A light blinked to starboard.

"Control launch," explained the midshipman. "Everyone seems to be lined up, so let's go. Full ahead, coxswain, steer oh-one-oh."

"Oh-one-oh it is, sir," replied the coxswain.

The engine note rose to full power as the craft headed for the distant shoreline, still invisible in the darkness. The journey took longer than I had expected and it was obvious that the men, drenched with flying spray from time to time, were not enjoying it. Looking over the side, I could see the bow waves of the other landing craft on either side. It all looked most impressive. At length the sky to the east began to lighten. Ahead lay a low black smudge that I took to be land. The details of this became clearer as the light strengthened into a grey twilight. I knew that this was only an exercise, but it was as close to the real thing as we would get for a while, and it was exciting.

"Touch down in five minutes," said the midshipman. "We'll get you up the beach as far as we can – save you getting your feet wet."

"Stand by," I said as I made my way forward to the ramp through the huddle of packed bodies. Soaked, cold and cramped as they were, the Platoon seemed only too glad that an end to their misery was in sight.

The craft slid smoothly up the sand and the ramp dropped.

"Come on!" I yelled, dashing across it with the Platoon streaming after me. We had been given a full briefing before we left camp and I quickly identified the landmarks that indicated the position of our first objective. We charged across the beach and into the sandhills, where we worked round the flank of the "enemy" position, then attacked it. Knowing that one day we would be doing this in the face of a real enemy, I hoped that it would be as easy. After taking the objective, we moved inland, eliminating pockets of "resistance," then started digging in as C and D Companies passed through to take their own objectives. The "opposition" was provided by a local Home Guard unit who fired blank ammunition and threw thunderflashes at us. They were middle-aged men, most of whom wore Great War medal ribbons. Their commander, a captain about the same age as my father, also wore the ribbon of the Military Cross.

"Bit of a lark, really," he said to me. "Still, it does get you familiar with your landing drills, I suppose."

I had a feeling that he wanted to tell me something, but wasn't quite sure what.

"Have you been involved with an amphibious landing before?" I asked.

"Yes, I was at Gallipoli in 1915," he replied. "Came ashore in unprotected ships' boats, we did. The Turks just fired into the mass of us with their machine guns. So crowded together we were, you never knew whether the man next to you was alive, dead or dying. Still, we got the job done."

I already knew that some of the Gallipoli landings had been a bloodbath and did not know quite what to say. He regarded me with kindly but shrewd eyes and must have seen my concerned expression.

"Now don't you go worrying about that," he continued, patting me on the shoulder. "We've all learned a lot since then. You're better trained and better equipped than we ever were, and you've got proper landing craft, too. All I'm saying is, when the day comes, don't take anything for granted."

At the de-briefing, everyone seemed pleased with the way the exercise had gone. Even Duncan Flint was in an affable mood and congratulated us. When I complained that according to the exercise umpires my platoon had sustained eighteen casualties as we came ashore, he simply laughed.

"Well, they've got to award you something, haven't they?" he said. "After all, yours was one of the first platoons to cross the beach! Still, it's better than being wiped out, isn't it?"

Once they had dried out, even the troops seemed to have enjoyed themselves. Returning from the de-briefing, I found my platoon sitting round in groups, laughing and joking among themselves.

"Well done, Three Platoon," I said. "The umpires say that some of us were killed, but those who survived did a great job."

"Bit of a doddle, really," said Helsby-Frodsham, when the laughter had died down.

"If the real thing's as easy as that, sir, then let's get on with it, that's what I say," added Corporal Gray.

"Just one thing, sir," chimed in the irrepressible Haggerty. "Them landing craft are a disgrace – can't you get someone to fit 'em with nice comfortable seats?"

I had some reservations about the exercise, partly because of my conversation with the Home Guard captain, so as we route-marched into Swansea, where a train was to take us back to East Anglia, I asked Sergeant Warriner what he thought of it.

"As an exercise, very good, sir," he answered in his flat, matter-of-fact way. "Very good indeed. Can't be faulted."

"But?" I said, knowing that he was holding something back.

"It was an exercise, that's all, sir," he replied, glancing at me sharply.

"And if it had been the real thing?"

"We'll know about the real thing when it happens, sir. Until then, neither of us will be any the wiser."

And with that I had to be content.

I was lucky enough to be sent on leave with half the battalion at Christmas, the other half going at New Year. Turkeys were in short supply, but Mother had managed to find a duck. One day, I thought, there would be better Christmases, but before that happened I would have a war to fight.

In January 1944 we all attended another lecture in the camp cinema. It was given by a senior officer of the Royal Engineers and the subject was Hitler's Atlantic Wall, which was the term used for the German coastal defences stretching from Denmark to the Spanish frontier. Much emphasis was placed on the French coast, which was another indication of where we would be going. Below the high-water mark there were obstacles intended to impale landing craft. These obstacles consisted of wooden stakes or "hedgehogs" made from pieces of angle-iron welded together. Both were fitted with explosive charges. The beaches were mined and, where a sea wall did not exist, concrete walls had been built to prevent tanks leaving them. Then there were the coastal artillery batteries, their huge guns encased in massive steel and concrete bunkers. More bunkers, sited to sweep the beach with their fire, contained anti-tank and machine guns. Behind the beach defences there were anti-tank ditches. These seemed to be covered by fire from concrete pillboxes and trenches nearby, most of which were surrounded by barbed wire and minefields. Every building overlooking the sea had also been turned into a miniature fortress. In addition, we were told that the German field artillery batteries, located some way inland, would add the weight of their fire to the beach defences.

The engineer officer could not have given us more to worry about if he had tried, but suddenly the whole tone of his lecture changed.

"Yes, I agree that it looks like a very tough nut to crack," he said. "However, since the Dieppe raid we have produced the means of dealing with every single aspect of these defences. I cannot tell you what they are, but they have been thoroughly tested and they work. Everyone knows that in this sort of operation it will be you, the infantry, who will be most at risk, and everyone is working hard to ensure that your casualties will be kept to an absolute minimum."

After the lecture, Nigel, John, Tony and I discussed what form these mysterious means might take. Sergeant Warriner had told me that, at Alamein, gaps in some of the enemy's minefields had been cleared by flail tanks. These were old Matilda tanks on the front of which was a revolving drum fitted with chains. When it turned the chains flew out and battered the ground, exploding the mines ahead of the tank. We all agreed that similar tanks would probably be used, but had no idea how the other problems were to be dealt with.

The following week we were given our objectives, although we did not know their names or even where they were. After crossing the beach and the sea wall, A Company was to take three houses about 100 yards inland. On our left, B Company had a similar task. We were then to take a hamlet half a mile inland. A mile beyond this, we were to take a large chateau, its outbuilding and nearby cottages, then C and D Companies were to go into the lead. When they had taken their objectives, another of our brigade's battalions was to pass through while we reorganized and consolidated our gains.

Everyone – officers, NCOs and privates alike – studied the objectives in great detail. We made sand-table models of them and constructed full-scale replicas on the training area. Every so often the RAF would send us their latest batch of air-reconnaissance photographs, some taken from high above and others at low level, and we would incorporate any changes that seemed to have been made in the defences. We also received some pre-war picture postcards of the area, with the names carefully concealed. I got to know the location so well that I could have found my way round it blindfold. We practised attacking the objectives from every direction, with and without tank support, until we had worked out the best possible plan.

During this time we also received more lectures. The first was from another naval officer who told us how the warships lying offshore would continue to give us gunfire support long after we had landed. This would be controlled by a specially trained observer who would accompany us and identify targets by radio. He also showed us some slides to illustrate the devastating effect of naval gunfire on land targets. Next, a Royal Artillery officer described how, once the guns were ashore, it was possible not only to focus the fire of several batteries, or even regiments, on to a target, but also switch it around the battlefield at short notice, as required. Then, an RAF wing commander told us how we would be given close air support. This would involve a forward air controller, an RAF officer who could see the target from a pilot's point of view and relate it to landmarks on the ground. These skills enabled him to "talk in" a strike by ground-attack aircraft. More often than not, he said, they would be rocket-firing Typhoons. Each rocket, he told us, was as powerful as an 8-inch shell. We were all very encouraged by what we had been told.

It was at the end of February 1944 that we learned that Field Marshal Rommel had been appointed commander of the enemy's Army Group B in north-west France. Everyone was aware of Rommel's reputation as a dashing commander during the desert war in North Africa. However, as Sergeant Warriner pointed out, he had been decisively defeated at El Alamein by the very man who was to lead our army when it invaded France, General Montgomery.

In his own way Private Allen, my batman, was also preparing for the invasion. One day he asked me for seven shillings and six pence. When I asked him why, he replied: "I have purchased a small stove and a supply of paraffin tablets from a friend who used to go camping before the War, sir. It occurred to me that in quieter moments we would enjoy a cup of tea. I remember Mr Boris Karloff saying how much he enjoyed my tea. Mr Karloff, you'll remember, sir, played Frankenstein's monster in films. He's English, you know, and Karloff is not his real name, of course. He always said he couldn't get a decent cup of tea in Hollywood, and. . ."

"Well done. Good idea," I said, hurriedly handing over the money. I little thought then that Allen and his little stove would earn a paragraph in the regimental history.

Early in April 1944 we were sent on a week's embarkation leave, which meant that we would soon be going overseas. I can't say that I enjoyed it, because while my parents tried hard to seem cheerful I could see that they were worried, and I simply wanted to get on with whatever lay ahead. Shortly after I returned to camp we received orders to move. The stores were piled on to our own lorries and the troops clambered aboard a convoy of Royal Army Service Corps (RASC) troop transport lorries. Apart from a handful in battalion headquarters, none of us knew where we were bound, and the RASC declined to comment. I could tell from the sun that we were heading steadily west and then south, but as all the signposts had been removed when it was thought the country might be invaded, I had no idea where we were. During the journey we saw many other convoys, American as well as British, consisting of lorried infantry, tanks, Bren carriers, towed guns, self-propelled guns and vehicles from every branch of the army, their progress carefully regulated by the Military Police in their red caps. Sometimes a convoy would join ours for a while, then turn off along a side road, and sometimes we would join someone else's convoy before turning off. I began to marvel at the organizational skill that enabled thousands of vehicles and tens of thousands of men to travel simultaneously towards their given destinations.

It was dusk when we passed through a checkpoint, on either side of which a barbed-wire fence stretched out across the countryside. In the distance I could see armed patrols moving along the fence. I guessed that we were somewhere in the south of England. We travelled on for another 30 minutes before turning off into a large field, surrounded by more barbed wire, in which a tented camp had been set up. Before we dispersed to our tents, we were formed into a hollow square and addressed by Colonel Armitage.

"We are now in the assembly area for the invasion of France," he said. "We are, therefore, considered to be on active service. For security reasons, all of southern England has been sealed off from the rest of the country. No one will be permitted to leave, for any reason whatsoever. The boundary of the secure area is under constant watch by armed patrols and the police. Anyone attempting to breach this cordon will be tried immediately by court martial and I do not have to remind you that desertion in the face of the enemy is a crime for which the death penalty can be imposed. It is no longer possible for you to make telephone calls. You may write letters, although these will be censored in the usual way and will not enter the postal system until we have left. Incoming mail addressed to our old camp in East Anglia will be delivered here.

"We have all trained hard for this moment. We have studied the enemy's defences and decided how they can be overcome. We already know that we can expect maximum support from the Royal Navy and the RAF, but during the next few days we are going to meet some more people who can help us smash a hole right through Hitler's Atlantic Wall."

My feelings on hearing this were mixed. I felt as though a door had closed behind me and that I would not go through it again until the War was over, assuming that I survived. I also felt that I had become a tiny cog in a machine so huge that I could not begin to understand its size.

Next morning I could see that every field stretching to the horizon was occupied by infantry, tank, artillery and engineer units. Overhead, fighter aircraft patrolled ceaselessly, keeping the prying eyes of German aircraft at a safe distance. That afternoon we marched along the road to a copse in which Sherman tanks were parked under camouflage nets. I could see at once that they were nothing like any of the Shermans we had seen before, for they were fitted with two propellers low down at the back and surrounded by a girdle of what looked like folded canvas. We gathered round a cheerful captain who was standing on the engine deck of one of the tanks.

"Let me introduce us," he said. "We are half of C Squadron, The Flintshire Yeomanry, and we'll be going ashore at the same place you are. In fact, we'll be going ashore just ahead of you to make sure that Jerry's attention is fully occupied by the time you arrive. Our tanks are Sherman DDs, which stands for Duplex Drive, or just DDs for short."

He turned towards the next DD with a shout of, "Right-ho, Sergeant Morris!" There was a hiss of compressed air and the folded canvas suddenly rose into a screen that concealed all of the tank except the tracks. There was a murmur of surprise.

"That is our floatation screen," continued the Captain. "When it's erected, we can float, and the propellers drive us along in the water. As soon as we reach the beach, we collapse the screens, engage the drive and fight like a normal tank."

He paused for a moment.

"The idea is that we are launched from our Landing Ship Tank, or LST, some way out to sea. The tank itself will be under water, suspended from the floatation screen. From the shore, we will simply look like a group of ship's boats – rather smaller, in fact, as there are only a few inches between the top of the screen and the water."

"Doesn't that mean you're in danger of being swamped if there's any sort of rough sea running?" asked Colonel Armitage.

"Yes, Colonel, it has been known," replied the Captain, grinning. "That's why we'll be wearing life jackets. If conditions are too rough, we'll just have to land direct from our LSTs, but we'll still give Jerry an unpleasant surprise."

"Either way, you'll still have to get through the beach obstacles, won't you?"

"True, Colonel, but they will have been dealt with by naval demolition teams – that is, frogmen. They will time their swim to reach the obstacles when they are covered by high tide. They will neutralize Jerry's own charges, then clear gaps in the obstacles for the rest of us to go through. The gaps will be clearly visible at half tide."

The DDs were a revelation to me, but there were more surprises in store. That evening I wandered into a large wood where I found more unfamiliar armoured vehicles, all heavily camouflaged. I was met by a Royal Engineer officer of about my own age who told me that they belonged to the assault squadron that would overcome the fortifications on our sector. He pointed out some flail tanks, which I recognized from Sergeant Warriner's description of those used at El Alamein, although these were based on the Sherman and known as Crabs. He told me that once they had cleared a path through the minefield they would stop flailing and fight as conventional tanks. He then pointed out as strange a collection of vehicles as I have ever seen.

"These are our AVREs," he said proudly. "AVRE stands for Assault Vehicle Royal Engineers."

"What kind of gun is that?" I asked, indicating the stubby barrel protruding from the front of the turret.

"It's a mortar, actually," he replied. "It fires a bomb, called General Wade's Flying Dustbin, to a range of 90 yards. It's designed to crack open the steel and concrete of the enemy's bunkers."

Next, he pointed to two AVREs, one with a large iron-girder bridge attached to its front and the other carrying an enormous bundle of brushwood wrapped round with chains.

"Here's one of our bridgelayers," he said. "We can lay the bridge against a sea wall so that other vehicles can cross it. The AVRE next to it is a fascine carrier. The brushwood bundle, or fascine, can be dropped into an anti-tank ditch and becomes a causeway that other tanks can cross. The AVRE can be used for all sorts of other jobs, too."

I was astonished by these wonderful machines. Their existence, known only to those who manned them and very few others, was one of the best-kept secrets of the War.

The following day all the battalion's officers spent time with those of the DD and assault squadrons. We learned that they too had practised on mock-ups of the enemy defences. We worked out which areas would cause each of us problems and how we could solve these by working together. The commander of the assault squadron told us how his teams would operate. First, the Crabs would flail a path through the minefield to the sea wall, then turn to one side. Then, AVREs would lay their bridges against the sea wall, to create ramps. Next, the fascine AVREs would climb the ramp and drop their brushwood bundles into the anti-tank ditch beyond. The DDs would follow, providing fire support for our attack on the houses and strongpoints. In addition, the assault team possessed armoured bulldozers that could uproot obstacles and fill in craters. When he was asked what would happen if one or more of the vehicles in his assault teams was knocked out he replied that this had been allowed for and sufficient numbers would remain to complete the task.

During the night I heard the DDs and the assault squadron moving off and guessed that they were being embarked aboard their LSTs. Later in the day we were issued with ammunition and rations for the landing, and that afternoon the Support Company's vehicles and anti-tank guns left for the embarkation area. The rifle companies were told they would be leaving next.

As it happened, it was my turn to be orderly officer. I was walking around the camp's perimeter fence at about midnight when I saw movement in the distance. As I ran towards it I saw a figure laying a plank across the barbed wire. Obviously, someone was trying to desert.

"Stop where you are!" I shouted, loosening my revolver in its holster.

The figure turned and I recognized it at once.

"Where d'you think you're going, Grover?" I asked.

He loomed out of the darkness, full of menace.

"Get out of me way!" he snarled. "I told you – I'm not gettin' me head blown off in any bleedin' invasion, not for you or anyone else! So you'll just clear off, sonny, if you know what's good for you! Try and stop me and I'll kill you!"

"No you won't," I replied, drawing my revolver. "For a start, I'm armed and you're not."

He paused warily, but was obviously waiting for me to drop my guard before he pounced.

"Think about what you're doing," I continued. "Once you're over the fence you stand a good chance of being picked up by one of the patrols. If they're American, they might be trigger happy and shoot you on sight. If they're British, you'll face a court martial and a firing squad. But let's suppose you get through, what then? You've no papers, you won't get work or a place to live. You'll spend years on the run and at the end of it you'll still be caught and face a court martial. Is it worth it?"

I could feel his hatred as though it was a physical force.

"Yeah, it's fine for your sort," he said. "Had it made from the moment you were born, didn't you? You make me sick. And what have I got to come back to? Nothing!"

"Let me tell you something," I replied. "Once we're over there, Jerry couldn't care less where we come from or anything else about us. To him, we'll just be targets to be shot at, and as far as that goes we'll all be equal. At least you'll come home with a bit of respect for yourself and that's better than looking in the mirror and seeing a coward."

He swore horribly and looked away. All the aggression seemed to have evaporated. At that moment I was sick of him and everything about him.

"You can desert if you want to, Grover," I said. "I won't stop you. You're no use to me, you're no use to the rest of the Platoon and you're no use to yourself. We'll all be better off without you. Suit yourself."

With the odds stacked so heavily against him, I was reasonably sure that he would stay, but I was taking a calculated risk. If he went, his departure would be welcomed by everyone, but if it ever became known that I had let him go I would be in serious trouble for breaking the disciplinary code. The best I could expect was a severe reprimand from the divisional commander, and the worst a court martial. Against this, if he stayed I would have done my duty and he might just pull himself together.

"Very clever, aren't you, Mister Bleedin' Second Lieutenant Pope?" he said after a moment's indecision, then turned and disappeared among the tents. I was suddenly aware of Sergeant Warriner emerging from the shadows.

"Been expecting this," he said. "Had my eye on him. You handled it well, sir. You can charge him with attempted desertion and gross insubordination if you want to."

"I don't," I replied. "Any other time I'd have thrown the entire book at him. Just now, however, I had the impression that he'd looked himself in the face for the first time and didn't like what he saw. So, either we lose a deadbeat or we get someone who'll pull his weight. Can't lose, can we?"

The Sergeant gave one of his short laughs.

"Ha! Nineteen now, aren't you, sir?"

"Yes, why?" I replied, irritated by the question.

"Nineteen going on thirty – you'll do all right for me, sir!" he said, turning away. "Good night."

I wondered if I *would* be all right when the time came, or whether I would be found wanting. If I made a mistake, the result would not just be another roasting from Duncan Flint, but lost lives. For a moment I felt the heavy burden of responsibility, then realized that there was no escape from it.

3 – 6 June 1944

During the early afternoon of 3 June a convoy of RASC lorries arrived to carry the battalion to Southampton, its port of embarkation. The journey was slow, with frequent halts caused by the volume of traffic heading for the port, so that it was not until evening that we reached the quayside. After a roll call, we marched along the line of moored LSIs. We halted alongside our old friend the *Countess of Antrim* and were directed aboard. Everything seemed pleasantly familiar. Hardly had the last man set foot on deck than the embarkation gangways were removed, the mooring lines were cast off, the engines began to throb and the distance between the ship and the quayside began to widen steadily.

I was startled by the speed at which it happened. I had expected something like a band to play us off or a rousing speech from a general, but instead there was only the bustle of quiet efficiency. However, if I was surprised by the speed of our departure, I was equally surprised when we dropped anchor only a mile or two off the English coast. In the gathering dusk I could see the outline of many other ships anchored nearby, but not their details. A full gale was blowing and there was no incentive to remain on deck. Obviously, it would be impossible for us to make an amphibious landing in those conditions.

After dinner, Duncan Flint distributed maps to his officers. I saw that we would be put ashore at the southern end of the seaside resort of St Grégoire-sur-Mer, that the name of the inland hamlet we were to take was St Grégoire Le Petit and that the château was called Flambard-Chambourcy.

"We're going to Normandy!" exclaimed Nigel, running his finger along the line of coastal resorts. "I've already been to some of these places."

"Normandy?" I said in surprise. "But I thought that we'd use the shortest crossing, and that's from Dover to Calais!"

"That's what Jerry thinks, too," said Duncan Flint. "So we're going in somewhere else!"

I remembered the Major's advice about treating the enemy to a dose of the unexpected.

"Now listen," continued the Major. "I know I've pushed you very hard since I arrived. I expect that there have been times when you've called me a name or two among yourselves."

"Yes, that's right," murmured Tony. The Major ignored him.

"Well, I hope the one thing I've taught you is to think for yourselves. As you'll have gathered, we have been planning this operation for years and every possible contingency has been allowed for. Yet my experience has always been that however carefully an operation is planned some things start to go wrong from the very beginning. If that weren't the case, there would be no need for officers. As it is, we'll have to sort out whatever does go wrong, and quickly too. So, within the context of the battalion and company plans, use your initiative. Now go and brief your platoons."

The gale continued throughout the following day, with the ship pulling hard against her anchor chain. Her officers said that even if we crossed the Channel they would not be able to get us ashore, so we would have to make the best of it until the weather improved. On 5 June the weather began to moderate, but was still very unpleasant. The troops, who had been keyed up for the assault, began to grumble at being confined below decks. Then, at about 14:00, the anchor came clattering up, the engines began their steady thumping and we headed slowly out to sea. By late evening we had reached a point in mid-Channel and slowed to a standstill, surrounded by hundreds more ships of every type, including more LSIs, LSTs and many types I could not identify. Destroyers fussed around the lines like sheep dogs, shepherding vessels into the correct order. I spotted the midshipman who had commanded our landing craft during our exercise off the Gower Peninsula.

"Does this mean we're going in, then?" I asked.

"Looks that way," he replied. "The forecast for tomorrow promises some improvement, but there'll still be a nasty sea running. Still, Jerry won't be expecting us in this sort of weather, and that's a bonus."

"Won't he have lain minefields off the French coast?"

"Oh, yes, but they'll be some way out. Anyway, our minesweepers will be clearing lanes through them, if they haven't done so already."

Shortly after, we received official confirmation that we would land at 07:35 next morning, which meant that we would start boarding the landing craft at 05:00. Now that we knew what was happening, everyone's spirits rose. "Good. Let's get on with it – we're fed up waiting around out here," was the Platoon's general view when I passed on the news.

Towards dusk, the whole mass of shipping began moving slowly southwards in the direction of Normandy.

I had grown used to the almost permanent presence of our fighter aircraft during daylight hours, and to the drone of heavy bombers at night. On the night of 5 June, however, that drone was multiplied many times over. I did not know it then, but one British and two American airborne divisions were about to parachute on to what would become the northern and southern flanks of the beachhead.

At about 04:30 Sergeant Warriner and I inspected the Platoon's equipment, arms, ammunition and rations. A cheerful sailor came round, handing out cans from a box.

"Self-heating soup, mate," he explained. "You'll have a long cold run in and you'll be glad of it. Instructions are on the can. You'll be pleased to hear that the RAF has started beating the daylights out of Jerry."

I had been conscious of the constant roar of aircraft engines for over an hour. Even so, everyone was feeling on edge, so it was a relief when we were ordered to our landing craft stations. Because of an overcast sky it was still dark when we reached the deck. The French coast was invisible, but I could see the flash of explosions and the glow of fires in that direction. As I clambered aboard the landing craft I saw that three lightweight ladders had been stowed along one side of the craft, as we had been promised. These were intended to help us cross the sea wall and the section commanders had already detailed the men who were to carry them.

We were lowered into the sea without incident, but not even the exercise off the Gower had prepared me for the sea's ugly movement when we left the ship's side. The gale had certainly abated, but there was a huge swell moving crossways beneath us, so severe that in addition to the motion I'd expected (and the clouds of flying spray), the craft seemed to slide sideways down those heaving mounds of water. As the light became stronger I could see more of our landing craft forming up into an assault wave. The sea was covered with ships as far as the eye could see, many of them flying large silver balloons trailing thick wires to deter low-level air attacks. Overhead, I could hear more bombers heading for the coast to continue their remorseless battering of the enemy's defences. Then came the squadrons of fighters, ready to pounce on any intervention by German aircraft, though none appeared.

After a while, I was conscious that we should have commenced our run in towards the coast. However, we remained more or less stationary, although the midshipman occasionally manoeuvred the craft to allow for the tide having carried us away from our correct position. I had hoped to reach the beach with a fit, aggressive platoon, and the longer we remained afloat the less likely this became. In fact, some of the men had already begun to vomit and many of the rest were looking green and sweaty.

"What's happening?" I asked the midshipman at length.

"I don't know," he replied. "Some sort of hold-up ahead. Maybe the LSTs have had trouble getting in."

As I watched the last of the bombers making their way back to England, there was a sudden distant flash far away to our left. I could see a battleship, wreathed in smoke, and seconds later the roar of her guns reached us. Then, every warship in sight seemed to open fire – battleships, monitors and cruisers, all filling the air with furious sound and blasting the enemy's defences with tons of high explosive every minute. I knew I was watching history being made, but at that precise moment I felt too sick to care.

"Here we go," said the midshipman in response to some unseen signal. The engine note rose to full power as we pushed steadily ahead. I glanced over my shoulder at the fast-receding *Countess of Antrim*, conscious that we were leaving our last link with home.

The craft's motion eased somewhat now that we were moving. I began to feel better and took more interest in what was going on. The lines of landing craft forging ahead were themselves an impressive sight. As the coast came into view I could see explosions and fires raging ashore. We passed through destroyers pounding away as hard as they could. Shells began to burst round us, sending splinters clattering off the hull. Minutes later we passed a craft of some sort, on fire and sinking, with men floundering in the water. I was horrified, but there could be no question of our stopping to pick them up without becoming a target ourselves, and in any event people were depending on us to do our own job.

"It's not all one-sided, is it?" I said.

"Never is," replied the midshipman levelly.

The incident made me realize that we were only minutes away from sustaining casualties of our own. During the months we had been together, I had grown to like the men of Three Platoon, and now it was inevitable that some of us would not live to see the end of the day. I looked round their stolid, friendly faces. Some were seasick, but all were impassive, keeping their fear locked away from the others. I knew that I was doing likewise, because my own fear had begun to grip me in its icy hand.

We passed a Landing Craft Rocket just as it sent salvo after salvo of its missiles streaking whoosh-whoosh-whoosh towards the beach minefields. Now I could see the three houses we were to take, instantly recognizable from our constant study of air photographs. I could also see the lines of semi-submerged stakes and iron hedgehogs and, beyond them, lines of LSTs crowded together at the water's edge. Nearby, a Landing Craft Gun was banging away at the beach defences. On our own craft a seaman was manning a machine gun, rattling away at an unseen target. The combined level of noise was such that we barely heard the enemy's rounds striking the ramp. The seaman slumped behind the gun mounting with a dark stain of blood spreading across his left shoulder.

"Starboard ten!" said the midshipman sharply, then "Midships!"

I could see a light flashing from the control motor launch and that the battalion's landing craft had all turned on to this new heading.

With growing alarm I pointed out that this was taking us away from our objective. The midshipman explained that because of the congestion he couldn't get us in where we should be, but would drop us as close as he could.

"Port ten – take her in!" he said a moment later, then turned to me, a smile creasing his normally dour expression.

"Away you go – give 'em hell!" he said as we shook hands.

As I made my way forward I suddenly remembered the Home Guard captain's description of Gallipoli and wondered whether the landing craft's interior would be swept by machine-gun fire when the ramp went down, turning it into a shambles of dead and dying. Chilling fear fought with the residue of seasickness in my stomach. My legs felt so leaden that it was an effort of will to get them to move.

"We've come in too far to the right!" I heard myself shouting to the Platoon. "Bear left as soon as we're ashore and run like hell! The sooner we get under the cover of the sea wall the better!"

The men, their faces set, nodded dumbly. There was a screech of tortured metal as we scraped past one of the obstacles, an iron framework known as Element C. I was horrified to see that a large explosive charge was attached to it. To my intense relief, the charge did not detonate, but I had no time to reflect on the subject as the craft slithered to a standstill on the sand and the ramp went down.

"Come on!" I yelled as I ran down it, then slopped through a few yards of water to reach dry land. As I pounded over the beach I could see the entire shoreline. The rest of the company, and B Company beyond, were all running hard for the sea wall. Here and there a man dropped. Others were being helped to safety by their comrades. In the distance a DD was burning, but more DDs were pumping shells into the fire slits of the concrete beach bunkers. A bridge AVRE leaned at an angle, its track shot off. Crabs were flailing paths up to the sea wall and more vehicles were pouring out of the LSTs. Green tracer from an enemy machine-gun post began to flash past me from left to right, about thirty yards ahead. I thought I would die when I reached it, but kept running. It stopped, possibly because one of the DDs had neutralized the post. Mortar bombs began to explode nearby. Behind me I could hear Sergeant Warriner's bellow as he urged the men on:

"C'MON, MOVE YOURSELVES! MOVE! MOVE! MOVE! D'YOU THINK WE'VE BROUGHT YOU TO THE SEASIDE SO YOU COULD MUCK AROUND IN THE SAND?"

I found the going hard, and for those who were worse affected by seasickness it must have been torture. I reached the sea wall panting and estimated that I had run approximately 350 yards. To my left a Crab had finished flailing its lane and was moving to one side as a bridge AVRE approached. The wall itself was covered in barbed wire and would have been impossible to climb without the ladders. Gasping, the Platoon arrived. In their wake I could see two or three of them sprawled on the sand, and two more helping a third towards the wall.

I ran up the first of the ladders to be placed and jumped over the promenade railings. The whole area beyond was pitted with craters from the naval bombardment.

"Head for the anti-tank ditch!" I shouted as more of the men joined me. "Use the craters for cover and move in short rushes."

We were still too far to the right of the three houses, from which the flashes of machine-gun fire had commenced as soon as we appeared. I was shocked to see Corporal Gray flung backwards by a burst just as he reached the top of the ladder. Then we were alternately running and crawling towards the anti-tank ditch, into which we dropped to recover our breath.

"The Major's calling, sir," said Private Helsby-Frodsham, my signaller.

I took the headset from him but all I could hear was mush, broken now and then by an unintelligible word in Duncan Flint's voice.

"Unreadable, out," I said, returning the headset. "What's wrong with this thing? It was working perfectly when we left the ship."

"I got drenched a couple of times in the landing craft," replied Helsby-Frodsham. "There must be salt water in the connectors – I'll dry them off as soon as I get a chance, sir."

Things began to happen very quickly indeed. An AVRE carrying a huge fascine clambered over the ramp placed by the bridgelayer and began crawling towards the anti-tank ditch. From low down in the right-hand house there was a flash and a blast cloud of dust.

"Anti-tank gun in the cellar!" shouted Sergeant Warriner. "Look – you can just see the concrete reinforcement above the window!"

The German gunner could never have seen anything like the AVRE and its fascine in his life, and his shot passed harmlessly through the fascine itself. Getting the fascine into the ditch was critical if the DDs were to support our attack on the houses, so I ran along the ditch, telling each section to concentrate its fire on the anti-tank gun's fire slit. The AVRE continued to waddle forward, halted with a jerk, and the fascine tumbled neatly into the ditch. Our fire must have been having some effect as the anti-tank gun's second shot was off-line and simply grazed the side of the AVRE's turret. The AVRE crossed its fascine, trundled forward for a few yards, then fired its mortar. I could see the bomb for most of its flight and realized why it was called a flying dustbin. The tremendous explosion caused the front of the building to collapse like a house of cards. I saw two machine-gunners who had been firing from an upper window go down with it to be buried under a mound of brickwork and beams that also covered the anti-tank gun's fire slit. My men cheered lustily.

Two DDs were now over the wall. They opened fire on the two remaining houses, eliminating one source of enemy fire after another. I now had to do some quick thinking. The three houses were to have been taken by the company in a frontal attack, but my own platoon's objective had already been eliminated by the AVRE and anyway we were too far to the right to take part in the attack on the other two houses. I decided to swing round the now burning ruin and cut off any of the defenders who tried to escape.

"Right flanking – come on!" I shouted. As we sprinted across the open space I was conscious of the two DDs crossing the fascine and the rest of the company rising from the ditch, bayonets fixed. Once past the houses we swung to the left and, sure enough, about twenty men in field-grey uniforms and coal-scuttle helmets were running from the rear doors.

"Put a long burst into the ground ahead of them!" I shouted to the nearest Bren gunner.

This, together with the levelled bayonets of the Platoon charging towards them, convinced the enemy that they should drop their weapons. They were a sorry lot, most of whom were covered in brick and plaster dust. Many had obviously been shaken by their ordeal, including their officer, who seemed anxious to retain some of his dignity.

"We will counter-attack and throw you back into the sea!" he shouted hysterically in English.

"Shut yer gob or I'll throw you into the sea, mate!" said Haggerty, stripping the man of his Luger pistol and handing it to me.

The rest of the company appeared, grinning. The prisoners were pushed into line and marched off to the beach by two slightly wounded men.

"What's the matter with your radio?" snapped Duncan Flint.

I told him.

"Then how come you carried out my order?" he asked belligerently.

"I didn't receive your order," I replied, irritated. "It seemed like the right thing to do."

"It was. You used your head. Well done. Now let's get on – we're falling behind our timetable."

We began to move inland, accompanied by the two DDs. It did not take us long to reach the hamlet of St Grégoire Le Petit, which had been badly knocked about by the bombardment. We approached it warily, expecting more fighting, but instead the civilian population came out, waving French flags and cheering.

"*Ah, les braves Anglais!*" they shouted. They told us that the Germans had gone, offered us wine and cheese and hugged us. With difficulty we extricated ourselves and continued towards our next objective, the château of Flambard-Chambourcy, passing the wreckage of a German artillery battery, strewn with bodies, on the way. In my ignorance of war I actually began to enjoy myself for a while.

This ended abruptly as we topped a rise. Some 500 yards down the slope lay the château, a large country house flanked by lower wings on either side, with a stable block at the rear. Nearby were the estate's home farm and the cottages of the workers. Extensive woodland stretched across the hillside beyond. No sooner had we appeared than the entire position seemed to sparkle with machine-gun fire coming from every window and many places in the grounds. It was apparent that any attempt to advance further would be suicidal. Instinctively, the Platoon ran for the cover provided by a hedge and ditch just ahead of us. Looking round, I saw that three of my men were down. Almost immediately, mortar rounds began to explode around us. The two DDs arrived, halted and opened fire on the building. After a few rounds one gave a convulsive lurch as it was penetrated by return fire. It began to belch smoke. Four of the five-man crew tumbled out, not a second too soon, for as the last of them hit the ground the tank burst into flames that roared from the hatches like a blowtorch. The second tank reversed back from the crest until only its turret was showing and continued to engage the enemy, changing its position from time to time.

Using my binoculars, I began to examine the German position in detail through the lower branches of the hedge. As well as machine guns and mortars, the enemy had three tracked vehicles in the position. They each seemed to be armed with a powerful anti-tank gun protected by armour plate. I remembered what they were from our recognition lectures on enemy equipment.

"B Company are pinned down on the left, too," said Duncan Flint's voice at my elbow. "Spot anything?"

"Yes," I replied. "The Jerries haven't dug in, so all this must be a bit of a surprise to them. They seem to have three tracked tank-destroyers – one by the summer house, one in the entrance to the stable yard and one by the manure heap in the farmyard."

"Too tough a nut for us to crack on our own," he said after surveying the position himself. His tone was almost friendly. "Just the sort of place Jerry would use to rally troops retreating from the coast as well as feeding in reinforcements from elsewhere, don't you think? A kind of 'hold at all costs' job while he pulls himself together."

Colonel Armitage arrived. After taking in the situation he told us that C and D Companies were coming up and that he would push them round both flanks to take the château from behind. During a pause in the firing I went back to our casualties. One was dead, but with the assistance of Baker, who had been promoted to Lance Corporal shortly before we left East Anglia, I managed to bring in the other two. One's arm was shattered and the other had serious chest wounds. While we bandaged them with field dressings, the other two companies started their attack. They made progress for a while, but were then halted by determined resistance in the woods.

At this point the brigade commander arrived, bringing with him a lieutenant commander who wore his naval insignia on a khaki battledress and was accompanied by a naval signaller. I began to feel that my part of the front was becoming seriously congested with senior officers.

"What the devil is going on here?" snapped the Brigadier testily to Colonel Armitage. "You should be two miles further on! The divisional commander wants results and he wants them now!"

While the Colonel explained the position, I couldn't help chuckling to myself. Everyone in the Army, it seemed, had someone hounding him. I hounded the Platoon, Duncan Flint hounded me, the Colonel hounded Duncan Flint, the Brigadier hounded the Colonel, the Divisional Commander hounded the Brigadier, and so on, right up the chain of command.

"This is one for you, I think, Toby," said the Brigadier, turning to the Naval Gunfire Support Officer (NGSO).

"Just my sort of party," replied the Lieutenant Commander. He settled himself down beside me with his signaller and transmitted the map co-ordinates of the château and the farm.

"We've got HMS *Norseman*," he explained. "She's a cruiser with eight 8-inch guns. Ever seen an 8-inch shell explode?"

I shook my head.

"Then you're in for a treat. First one should be arriving in about 35 seconds." He obviously took enormous pleasure in his work.

There was a sound like ripping cloth as the shell passed overhead. Then a huge fountain of earth, flame and smoke erupted some distance in front of the château.

"Short. Add four hundred," commented the NGSO into his microphone.

The next round exploded beyond the château.

"Down two hundred."

"How many salvos will you give us?" asked Duncan Flint. I could see that a plan was forming in his mind. "And how long between salvos?"

"Five should do the job," replied the Lieutenant Commander. "Assuming that they're nippy aboard, say between 30 and 45 seconds between each. Why?"

"I think that after the second salvo the Jerries will be so stunned and blinded by smoke and dust that we should attack. If you give us six salvos we should be in among 'em before they can recover their wits – those of them that are still alive, that is."

"Good idea, Duncan," said Colonel Armitage. "I'll warn B Company. They can take the farm while you deal with the château."

"Six rounds gunfire, commence, commence, commence!" said the NGSO into his microphone.

The first salvo passed overhead with a gigantic tearing sound. Huge explosions erupted around and among the enemy-held buildings. I saw walls tumbling and roofs collapse. Before the dust had settled the second salvo landed. The whole area was obscured by smoke and flying debris.

"Come, my lucky lads!" shouted Duncan Flint. The company set off at a brisk walk down the long slope. To my relief, there was little or no response from the enemy. I began to count the salvos mentally. After the third the buildings vanished beneath the spreading pall of smoke and dust. As the fourth came in something began to burn, adding thick smoke to the fog. By the time the fifth landed we had quickened our pace to a trot and were approaching the bottom of the slope. The sixth erupted as we reached the balustrade fronting the château's ornamental gardens.

"Charge!" I yelled, vaulting the balustrade. Yelling like fiends we tore across the garden. Great holes had appeared in the walls and roof of the house, through which broken beams and sagging floors were visible.

Somewhere, a fire was raging. Field-grey bodies lay half-buried in rubble. With shouts of *Kamerad!* (*Friend!*) more Germans staggered out of the wreckage, their hands up. They seemed completely dazed, with all the fight knocked out of them.

My responsibility was to clear the wing of the house on the right. We went through the usual house-clearing drill, but met no resistance. The tank destroyer in the entrance to the stable yard had taken a direct hit and been reduced to a tangle of torn metal. As I entered the yard itself, however, a burst of sub-machine gun bullets cracked into the brickwork near my head. I caught sight of a figure in an upper window of the stable block. It dodged out of sight. Mindful of what the AVRE had done to the defenders of the house near the beach, I decided to bring the PIAT gunner forward. While several men kept the window under fire, I directed him to aim his bomb into the wall beside it. The whole room seemed to explode. We charged across the yard and into the stable. One of the Bren gunners fired bursts through the ceiling into the rooms. There was a scream and the sound of a body falling. Blood began to seep through the plaster above. I heard boots running towards the head of the stairs.

"Don't shoot – we surrender!" shouted a voice in German.

"Hold your fire!" I said.

Three frightened German soldiers clattered down the stairs, their hands raised. They were almost incoherent with fear, and I gathered that their sergeant had refused to let them surrender earlier. Now he was dead, and so was one of their comrades. They also told me that the chateau had been used as a regimental headquarters. I ordered them to be frisked and put with the other prisoners. Of the two remaining tank destroyers, one had been knocked out in the farmyard by the DD and the other, having made a run for it, had overturned into a ditch bordering the narrow lane behind the château. There was no sign of the crew.

I may not have liked Duncan Flint, but I had to admit to myself that he was a first-class soldier, as the company had sustained virtually no casualties in the attack. Colonel Armitage said that the resistance experienced by C and D Companies in the woods had melted away as soon as the château fell and that we were to follow on as soon as we had reorganized.

Duncan held a quick orders group. I had not seen John since the previous evening and felt a chill of apprehension when Sergeant Brumby, his platoon sergeant, turned up in his stead.

"Where's Mr Crane?" I asked.

"I should think he's probably on his way back to England by now, sir," replied the Sergeant. "Stepped on a stray mine while we were running for the sea wall. He'll lose one leg for sure, and the other's a mess."

I couldn't look at Tony Walters, who had always joked that because John commanded One Platoon he would be our first casualty.

"I wish I'd kept my mouth shut," I heard him mutter.

"I dare say you do," snapped Duncan Flint harshly. "In future, just keep your idiotic forecasts to yourself and remember that what happened to John was rotten bad luck, nothing more. Now let's get on."

We followed up C and D Companies and dug in around the crossroads that had been their final objective. As we did so, the brigade's reserve battalion, accompanied by Sherman tanks, passed through us to continue the advance.

"Where've you been?" shouted Haggerty. "Did you get lost?"

"What are you doing, sitting round here?" they yelled back. "You should be halfway to Paris by now!"

Shortly after, the sounds of battle told us that they were in action. I had lost all track of time and was astonished when my watch revealed that it was still early afternoon. A lifetime seemed to have passed since we left the *Countess of Antrim* and England seemed another world away. Our anti-tank guns and mortars arrived. Peter Gresley, the anti-tank platoon commander, told me that the landing beaches looked like a disturbed anthill with men and vehicles travelling in every direction, yet everyone seemed to know what they were doing and where they were going. At about 16:00 the concentrated booming of tank guns could be heard some miles to our left. It rose to a crescendo, fell, rose again and finally ceased. Later, we were told that the enemy's 21st Panzer Division had twice attempted to drive through the beachhead to the sea, but had been beaten off. Suddenly aware that I was ravenously hungry, I gulped down my can of self-heating soup, having forgotten about it until that moment.

Shortly before dusk, the first of the battalion's jeeps and transport vehicles appeared, enabling us to replenish our ammunition. We stood to in our slit trenches for an hour, but nothing happened. Sergeant Warriner had already given me our casualty return – three dead, including Corporal Gray, four seriously wounded who required evacuation, and five slightly wounded: a total of twelve.

"We've got away with it very lightly indeed, believe me, sir," he concluded.

"Yes," I replied, unable to grasp what he had said for a moment. "That's a third less than they gave us during the Gower Peninsula exercise."

Then the full impact struck me. That had been a statistic and this was reality. The slightly wounded would probably come back to us, but the dead had gone for ever and it was unlikely that we would see the seriously wounded again.

I took a turn on guard, then settled into my slit trench. I had seen history made, but just then it seemed less important than the hour or two's sleep that lay ahead.

7 June – 16 August 1944

I cannot remember the details of everything that happened in the weeks after D-Day, for the simple reason that they are all jumbled together in my memory and, for most of the time, I was too exhausted to absorb the sequence in which events took place. I remember hearing that the Americans had sustained heavy casualties getting ashore on one of their landing beaches, and that all our beachheads were now linked together so that we had a continuous front facing the enemy.

I learned, too, yet more secrets about D-Day. After the Dieppe raid, the planners had recognized that we would not be able to capture a French port in working order when we invaded, so under the codename Mulberry we had brought two prefabricated harbours with us. These consisted of large, hollow iron and concrete structures together with lines of old ships that were towed into position and sunk to form breakwaters and protect the harbours from gales. Each harbour contained three floating piers, connected to the shore by floating roadways. Every tug in the country, and more from the United States, had been required to tow these across the Channel. Then there was PLUTO, standing for Pipe Line Under The Ocean, which was an undersea pipeline laid from England to Normandy, that kept us supplied with fuel.

By landing in Normandy, we had certainly taken the Germans by surprise, but there was a price to pay. To the south-west of Caen was a large area of countryside that the French call *bocage*. It consisted of small fields, narrow lanes and high hedgerows growing from earth banks. It was ideal defensive country that enabled the enemy to conceal himself until the last possible moment before opening fire. It also stopped our tanks from giving us their full support, for as soon as they attempted to climb a bank an anti-tank gun would put a round through its exposed belly plates. It therefore became an infantryman's war in which we fought from hedgerow to hedgerow, just as my father's generation had fought from trench to trench in the Great War. We suffered serious casualties, but the enemy, lacking air power and exposed to our terrible naval gunfire and artillery, suffered far more. We now know that Hitler had insanely forbidden them to yield a single yard of ground and we grew to respect their discipline and fortitude. For our part, deadly tiredness was our constant companion. There was little sleep to be had in the short summer nights, for we stood to for an hour after dusk and again for an hour before dawn, and in between we would take our turn on guard.

Even when we were resting out of the line we were still within range of the enemy's heavy guns, which would sometimes send over a shell or two to remind us that they were still there. Much of my time was spent writing letters to my parents or to the next of kin of men who had been killed. The fine sunlit days were mocked by the devastation caused to this pretty countryside. Farms stood ruined and the bloated bodies of cattle caught in the crossfire lay stinking horribly in the fields. Sometimes, Helsby-Frodsham would go foraging in his amiable way and return with cheese and bottles of wine that would be shared among the Platoon.

It was in the *bocage* that Three Platoon won its first decoration. One day at the end of June 1944 we were advancing up a slope towards a hedge when two machine guns opened up, one from each corner of the field, so that their fire overlapped. We dived for cover at once. The slope was concave and, to my relief, the machine guns' fire could not do us much harm as long as we remained pressed to the ground.

Haggerty was lying some yards in front of me, to the right. I saw his pack twitch several times as it was hit. A stain began to spread over his battledress and I feared the worst. Then, he was up and running at the nearest machine gun, a look of berserk fury on his face. His feet seemed to be swept from under him by an unseen hand. As the German shifted his fire to another target, he scrambled up and sprinted the last 20 yards to the gun, which was dug into the earth bank below the hedge. Throwing himself to one side of the fire slit, he posted a grenade through it. Its explosion was followed by screams and the gun fell silent. Meanwhile, the Platoon's Brens, as well as those of Two Platoon, had suppressed the fire of the second machine gun.

"Come on!" I shouted. "Don't leave it all to Haggerty!"

As we charged up the slope I saw Haggerty toss a second grenade into a rifle pit, then fire from the hip into another with his rifle. Caught between him and the advancing company, the surviving Germans emerged with their hands raised in surrender.

"Are you hit?" I said to the panting Haggerty as we began turning round the captured trenches.

"They shot the piggin' heel off me boot, sir," he replied, examining his damaged footwear. There was a strong smell of whisky about him. Duncan Flint arrived, having witnessed the whole incident.

"More to the point, are you drunk?" he asked.

"No, sir!" replied Haggerty indignantly. "Just take a look at this."

He opened his pack to reveal the shattered remains of two whisky bottles. Printed on the soggy labels were the words GOVERNMENT STORES – NOT FOR SALE.

"And how did you come by these?" asked Duncan Flint suspiciously.

"Did a bloke in the Service Corps a favour once, sir," said Haggerty, grinning. "He dropped them by one night when we were out of the line. I was going to share them with the lads. That's why I got mad when Jerry smashed 'em."

We all thought that the truth might be a little different, but despite this he received the Military Medal on Duncan Flint's recommendation.

Once we had fought our way out of the *bocage*, progress should have been easier, but by then the enemy had rushed reinforcements to the front and was resisting fiercely. On one occasion we were holding one side of a hill and the Germans the other. They did everything in their power to stop us taking the crest, which overlooked their positions for miles around. Once they tried a night attack in an attempt to dislodge us. It was led by Tiger tanks, followed by infantry. Our defensive artillery barrage stopped the infantry, but the Tigers came on and began wandering about the battalion's positions. By then, we all knew that tanks were all but blind in the dark and that without their infantry they were almost useless, so we simply lay in our narrow slit trenches, which were invisible to tank commanders within their closed hatches. Allen, oblivious to what was going on, had just brewed tea. A Tiger halted beside our trench, its weight causing the wall to crumble. To his intense annoyance, some of the soil dropped into Allen's steaming mug.

"Really! Some people have no manners at all!" he said. "I'm going to give that man a piece of my mind!"

Before I could stop him, he had clambered out of the trench and aboard the Tiger. Obviously, in the dark he had mistaken the tank for one of the Churchills with which we had worked so often. At that moment the enemy commander opened his hatch in an attempt to get his bearings.

"You really should have more consideration for other people!" shouted Allen before he realized who he was addressing. The two stared incredulously at each other for a second, then Allen flung the scalding contents of his mug into the German's face. With a yell of rage and pain the commander drew his pistol and began blazing wildly into the darkness, but by then Allen had leapt back into the trench.

The Tiger moved off with a lurch, only to fall victim to a PIAT bomb fired into its thin stern plate before it had covered 100 yards.

"He was a German, sir – a German!" said Allen in a shocked voice when he had recovered from the surprise. I'm afraid I was too helpless with laughter to offer him any sympathy, as was the rest of the company when the news of his exploit spread. Private Allen was to become a legend as the only man in the regiment to have attacked a Tiger with a mug of hot tea.

There was, in fact, very little to laugh at on that hill. On the morning after the Tiger attack we had just finished the dawn stand-to when I glanced in the direction of Two Platoon. I saw Tony stand up and stretch in his slit trench. He gave me a cheery wave. Then came the rising scream of an incoming heavy calibre shell. The explosion obliterated the trench and no identifiable trace of Tony was ever found. I was deeply saddened and very shaken by the incident, for Tony had been a good friend and now I was the last of A Company's original platoon commanders. I was left with a horrible feeling that it would be my turn next.

"Doesn't work like that, sir," said Sergeant Warriner in his flat matter-of-fact voice. "His number was on that one – yours wasn't, so best leave it at that."

Sometimes Warriner's casual acceptance of death annoyed me, but he was right, of course. Death was our constant companion and our concern had always to be for the living.

We had a short rest period after we were relieved on the hill, then returned to another part of the line. At various times throughout the campaign we received replacements for our casualties, including two officers almost straight from OCTU. Neither of them lasted more than a few days. One took a sniper's bullet through the head when he stood up to read his map. The other lost his way while leading a night patrol and was listed as missing. The trouble with the replacements generally was that they were neither as thoroughly trained nor as experienced as we were. They were lonely, lost souls and although I did my best to make them feel at home they were not accepted by the rest of the Platoon until they had proved themselves in a couple of actions. One of them, a man called Phillips, was indirectly responsible for the most unlikely of recipients winning our second decoration.

When we returned to the line we took part in a brigade attack. The battalion on our right was unable to capture some high ground, and we were therefore unable to make progress because we were overlooked and under fire from two directions. Duncan Flint ordered us back to our trenches, covered by a smokescreen laid by our 2-inch mortars. Despite this, the enemy continued to rake the area with mortar and machine-gun fire. As the smoke cleared I looked back and saw three members of the Platoon lying in no man's land. Two were not moving but the third, Phillips, was writhing in agony from the wounds he had received. For the moment I estimated that it would be suicidal for anyone to go out and get him. I shouted that he should remain still to avoid losing more blood and that we would bring him in when things quietened down a little. Either he did not hear me or was too frightened to understand, for he continued to try and get up, only to collapse in a heap.

Suddenly a figure ran from our lines towards him. It was Grover. Machine-gun bullets were kicking up the earth round him and mortar rounds were exploding constantly nearby. I could not see how he could possibly survive, but he did. He reached Phillips, heaved him on to his shoulders in a fireman's lift, and ran back.

"What made you do it?" I asked him later.

"'E was like me – no mates," he said, a look of defiance in his eyes. "Could 'ave been me out there and you lot couldn't 'ave cared less. Just thought I'd show the piggin' lot of you."

"That's not true and you know it," I replied.

After that, however, the Platoon's attitude towards Grover changed. Ever since D-Day he had been an unremarkable soldier and I suspected that he had hung back during one or two attacks. Now, however, the men began to regard him with something like respect and shared their jokes and other things with him. As a result of this, he seemed to mellow and began to pull his full weight.

"If your parents had been alive they would have been proud of you," I told him on the day we learned that he had been awarded the Military Medal. "One day you'll have a family of your own. They will be proud, too, because it isn't every kid whose dad has won the MM."

"Yeah, mebbe," he said thoughtfully, as though he had just seen a future for himself. "That would be a turn up."

He looked at me suspiciously, as though I had the power to spoil it for him.

"I said a few things to you before we left England, sir," he said at length. "I was wrong, an' I admit it. What worries me is that you always cracked down on me before, but you didn't for that. Why?"

"I don't remember any such discussion, Grover," I lied. "Whatever it is you're thinking of is best forgotten."

He gave a huge sigh of relief. What passed for a smile crossed his harsh features.

"Thanks, Mr Pope, sir," he said. "I'll not let you down."

A week or two later we had advanced another mile or so and our front lay along a narrow stream in a shallow valley. I was told to report to Duncan Flint, who had set up his company headquarters in the cellar of a cottage.

"Take a look at this," he said, handing me an air-reconnaissance photograph. It showed the long gentle upward slope on the enemy side of the stream, leading to the woodland at the crest, which we knew was the enemy's front line. At first I couldn't see anything remarkable.

"As you know," he continued, "there are several hummocks about 500 yards up the slope. Look closely at this one, under the tree. There are signs of digging. Could mean Jerry has a standing patrol or an observation post there. The brigadier wants us to take a look tonight – better still, go and get a prisoner! I suggest you move out at 23:45. Right, Andy, off you go – and don't mess up!"

I spent the rest of the day examining the route I would take. I decided to leave Sergeant Warriner in command of the Platoon and take Corporal Baker, Haggerty, Grover and six other men whom I knew I could rely on. During the evening stand-to we blackened our hands and faces, changed from boots into gym shoes and pulled on woollen cap comforters. In addition to our usual weapons we carried trench knives and coshes made from soil-filled socks that would stun rather than kill.

At 23:45 we moved quietly across the shallow stream. Patrolling can be a terrifying experience, because you are literally moving through darkness into unknown territory where the slightest mistake can cost lives. Clouds were passing across the moon and I had decided to take advantage of the shadow cast by a hedge that climbed the slope. Both sides were sending up flares as a matter of routine. When these burst above us we stood stock still, for even in semi-darkness any movement draws the eye. Consequently, our progress was very slow. I led the way, gently swinging a thin stick ahead of me. It touched something. Bending down, I felt a wire stretching in both directions. It was either connected to a flare or a grenade that would have exploded when someone tripped over it. I suppose that the route I had chosen was an obvious one and the enemy was bound to have placed such booby traps along it. By following the wire we located the stake to which it was attached, enabling us to disarm the device. We encountered three more trip wires before we were level with the suspected enemy post. We then crawled across the slope for about 100 yards to avoid being seen by those on the crest. I found myself on the edge of a trench that became deeper and finally entered the back of the hummock.

Just then, Corporal Baker touched me lightly on the shoulder and pointed towards the crest. The trick when trying to identify something in the dark is to look just above it. I saw a figure carrying something walking down the slope towards us. I signalled the patrol to spread out, which they did silently. Then I positioned myself near the start of the trench and stood up.

"*Halt! Wer da?* (Halt! Who's there?)," I hissed, in my best German.

"*Bauer – mit abendessen* (Bauer – with supper)," came the answer.

"*Ach das, gut! Geben Sie es mir.* (Ah, that's good! Give it to me.)"

Obediently, Bauer handed me a box. In an instant he was surrounded and Grover had a knife across his throat. His eyes rolled in terror.

"Keep him quiet," I whispered, then turned to Baker. "Come on, let's take a look inside."

Drawing the Luger pistol I had captured on D-Day, I led the way down the trench. A canvas door covered the entrance to the dugout. Pulling it gently away, I peered inside. The roof and walls had been reinforced with timber beams. An officer was looking through a pair of huge periscopic binoculars that disappeared into the roots of the tree above. Nearby, a second man sat in front of a gently humming radio, the aerial of which also disappeared through the roof, presumably into the branches of the tree. On a table was a field telephone, an artillery plotting board and a number of papers. It was all very ingenious.

"*Guten abend, Herren!* (Good evening, gentlemen!)," I said, pushing my way inside. "*Hände hoch – schnell!* (Hands up – quickly!)"

The pair of them spun round. The officer began reaching for his pistol, saw my Luger and Baker's Sten, thought better of it and raised his hands as he had been told. I could see from their badges that they belonged to the Waffen SS, who were Nazi troops fanatically loyal to Hitler. The ordinary German soldier fought by the rules (and we respected them for it), but these people did not. They would play dead in their foxholes until we had passed, then shoot us in the back, or pretend to surrender then open fire again, or shoot our stretcher bearers when they were attending to their wounded as well as our own. We showed them no mercy on these occasions and they did not seem to want it.

"Take half the patrol and escort the prisoners back to our lines," I said to Corporal Baker. "And send Haggerty in, will you? He can help me carry some of this stuff back."

"Yessir," replied Baker. "Just a thought, but if they turn funny and we have to shoot them, that could mean trouble for you back here."

"Yes, you're quite right, given their reputation," I said. "Tell you what, cut their braces and trouser buttons, then they'll have to keep their hands in their pockets. They'll not be much of a threat with their pants dangling round their ankles!"

Grinning, Baker did as I suggested. The officer, whose SS rank I took to be the equivalent of major, was about to make a vigorous protest but quietened down when Haggerty put the point of a trench knife under his chin. As the prisoners and their escort faded into the darkness, I took a look through the binoculars. Even in faint moonlight I could see every detail of our positions. For the past few days any movement on our side of the lines had immediately attracted accurate shellfire; now I knew why. The binoculars and their stand were too big to move, so I contented myself with smashing the lenses. While I did so, Haggerty opened the box that Bauer had delivered.

"Scoff, sir," he said. "It's not bad. Try some."

The box contained a flask of coffee, coarse grey bread, sausage and two boiled eggs. The coffee, which I believe was made from acorns, was dreadful, as was the bread, but the sausage and eggs weren't too bad. As I collected together the enemy's range tables, code books and list of radio frequencies, Haggerty did a good job of putting the radio out of action. Suddenly the field telephone gave a muted buzz. I wondered whether I should answer it and decided that it would seem strange if I didn't. I guessed that in such close proximity to our lines its users spoke in a whisper, which made it less likely that I would be identified. I picked up the receiver.

"*Ja?* (Yes?)"

"*Ist Bauer da, Herr Sturmbannführer?* (Is Bauer there, Major, sir?)"

"*Ja, ja, Bauer ist hier* (Yes, yes, Bauer is here)," I lied. No doubt they were wondering where he had got to.

"*Gut. Hauptsturmführer Klinger wird mit Ihnen in fünf minuten Sein.* (That's good. Captain Klinger will be with you in five minutes.)"

"*Danke* (Thanks)," I said, and rang off, not wishing to prolong a risky conversation.

"There'll be an SS captain arriving in five minutes," I told Haggerty. "My guess is that he's the Major's relief and if so he'll be bringing his radio operator with him. Tell the chaps outside to let them through, then close in behind them."

Five minutes later the canvas curtain was pulled aside.

"*Alles in ordnung?* (Everything in order?)," said a cheery voice.

"*Für mich ja - für Sie, nein!* (For me, yes – for you, no!)" I said in German as I spun round, thrusting my pistol into the startled officer's face.

Before the look of bewilderment had left their faces, the Captain and his radio operator were grabbed from behind. While their braces and trouser buttons were being cut, I gathered up the various books and papers I had assembled, stuffing them into a briefcase the Major had left behind.

"Come on, let's go," I said. "We're in danger of outstaying our welcome."

The return journey did not take as long as our outward march, partly because the moon was setting and partly because we had already cleared the trip wires off our path. Our standing patrol on the bank of the stream confirmed that Corporal Baker had come in and taken his prisoners to company headquarters. I did likewise, and from there they were marched off to be interrogated by the battalion's Intelligence Officer, who was also greatly interested in the documents I had brought in.

Duncan Flint was grinning from ear to ear, a sight I had never seen before.

"Can't do a darn thing right, can you, Andy?" he said. "I told you I wanted a prisoner and you walk in with five!"

"Thought you'd be glad of the company," I replied.

"Well done – it won't be forgotten, I promise you. Now go and get some sleep."

During the next few days the enemy's artillery fire was noticeably less intense, and certainly less accurate. A week after the patrol I was summoned again to company headquarters, where I found Colonel Armitage and the Brigade Commander.

"Ah, the young man himself," said the Brigadier as I entered. "You've done well, Andy. In fact you've been Mentioned in Despatches. I thought you deserved more but the divisional commander is a bit old-fashioned – believes that officers don't need medals to perform their duty."

I was handed the citation which said that a patrol led by Second Lieutenant Andrew Pope had eliminated an enemy artillery observation post, taken several prisoners and captured a number of important documents as a result of which the artillery fire-plan and signals network of the SS Panzergrenadier Division *Nibelungen* had been severely disrupted.

"That's just the way it worked out, sir," I said. "We were lucky, that's all."

"Results are what counts," replied the Brigadier. "Anyway, the Divisional Commander has agreed to bring forward your promotion, which isn't due for several months yet. Well done."

"Keep it up, Andy," said the Colonel, patting me on the back as he followed the Brigadier out.

"You're improperly dressed," said Duncan Flint, handing me a pair of pips. "Put these on – you're a full lieutenant now. Apart from which, I don't much care for second lieutenants."

"So I gathered," I replied. For a moment I almost liked him.

17 – 19 August 1944

By the beginning of August 1944 there had been definite signs that our efforts were beginning to pay off. We learned that Rommel had been evacuated to Germany after being seriously wounded, and that Hitler had narrowly survived an assassination attempt by some of his generals. The Americans had broken out of their beach-head and were swinging round the German left flank, which was being bent steadily backwards. Using new tactics, the British and Canadian armies began to push back the enemy's right flank to the north of Caen, so that by the middle of August both ends of the enemy line had been bent back so that the line itself resembled a sack. The Germans were now struggling desperately to hold open the neck of this so that they could escape eastwards.

We were enjoying a spell out of the line when the officers were called to a briefing by Colonel Armitage. He told us that the battalion had been ordered to seize a village called St Marc les Trois Ponts, situated directly on the enemy's escape route. The village lay on a hill enclosed in a loop of a river. Bridges crossed the river into the village on its east, south and west sides. During a night attack, we were to enter the village from the north, riding in Armoured Personnel Carriers (APCs).

The attack would be spearheaded by tanks moving behind a heavy artillery barrage while the RAF suppressed opposition on the flanks with carpet bombing. Once a hole had been punched in the enemy front we would pass through it, enter the village and hold it against all comers until we were relieved. The result would be that a block would be placed across the enemy's escape route.

"Ha! It's a Death or Glory job, sir!" remarked Sergeant Warriner after I passed on the orders to the Platoon. "Difficult enough with a full battalion, but we're badly under strength."

That was true enough. The company now numbered about 80 men. My platoon, 25-strong, was the largest, but of those who had landed with me on D-Day only 15 remained, and some of them had returned to us after being wounded. I had also lost most of the original NCOs, either as casualties or because they had been sent to make up losses in other platoons. I had an uneasy feeling about this operation, but if someone higher up the chain of command had decided that we were expendable, there was nothing I could do about it.

We climbed aboard the APCs as dusk was falling on the evening of 18 August. For once, A Company was last in the battalion column. The attached artillery Forward Observation Officer (FOO), a Captain Paddy O'Connor, tagged on behind us in his Stuart light tank. Two squadrons of Shermans clattered past to deploy across the head of the column. We began to move forward, slowly but steadily. The artillery was already at work, pounding the enemy's front line. Right on time, flights of heavy bombers droned overhead to release tons of bombs on farms, woods and other possible strongpoints on either side of our route. Few could have survived in those rectangles of erupting earth flames and smoke as more and more aircraft released their bombs into the same target areas. Now I knew why the RAF called it carpet bombing.

The column came to a standstill. From ahead came the noise of tank guns. Distant flames indicated burning tanks, but whether they were our own or the enemy's I had no idea. From garbled talk on the APC's radio I gathered that the Shermans had run on to a newly laid minefield and were being engaged by the enemy's anti-tank guns and tanks. Time passed without any further movement forward. As the bombers turned for home it began to seem as though the operation would fail before it had really begun.

"ALL STATIONS ONE – FOLLOW ME!" Duncan Flint's voice cracked like a whip in my earphones. "SHELLDRAKE CONFORM! OUT."

Shelldrake was the codename for the FOO. As the company's five APCs swung off the road to the right, I looked round and saw that his Stuart was following us. It seemed that the Major had studied his map and spotted a route to the objective across country, using farm tracks and minor roads, although this took us through one of the areas that the RAF had subjected to carpet bombing. I heard him call Colonel Armitage to advise him of this, but there was no response. We did not know it at the time, but in trying to work his way round the tank battle, the Colonel's APC had struck a mine and the shock of the explosion had thrown his radio off the frequency we were using. If we had known, we would probably have halted instead of proceeding deep into enemy territory on our own.

As soon as we reached the devastated area, the APCs began to buck, pitch and roll in the bomb craters. It took all the drivers' skill to get us through this smoking lunar landscape. Those of the enemy who had survived were too dazed to offer resistance. Some disappeared into the darkness, but most stood with their hands raised. Ignoring them, we pressed on, making better time along the farm tracks. The winding course of the river came into view, shining in the moonlight. At length we halted just short of the road leading into St Marc from the north and left the APCs, which Duncan Flint ordered to return by the way we had come.

As we entered the village I could hear the sound of many wheels and horses' hooves on the cobbles. At the top of the main street a steady procession of horse-drawn enemy supply wagons was crossing the little square by the church. It was obvious that they had entered the village by the bridge to the west and would leave it by that leading east. Duncan Flint wasted no time. He instantly ordered the whole company to make a bayonet charge up the street. Confronted by a swarm of yelling figures emerging from the darkness, the transport drivers surrendered at once. I was instructed to continue the attack down the street leading to the western bridge, where we captured more wagons and their drivers. Across the river I could see a long stream of traffic was waiting to cross, including more horse-drawn wagons and a number of motor lorries. I opened fire on these. When the fuel tank of one of the lorries exploded, the light of the blazing vehicle revealed frantic men running in every direction for cover.

I attended a quick orders group at the church while Sergeant Warriner put the houses nearest the bridge into a defensible state by barricading the windows and doors. The FOO's Stuart was parked alongside the church vestry, which was now Company HQ. Duncan Flint said that he expected the rest of the battalion to join us soon. In the meantime, each platoon would guard one of the bridges and contribute five men to cover the way we had entered the village. The horses were to be turned loose and the wagons used to form barricades across the streets.

"What about the prisoners?" I asked.

"We haven't the manpower to guard 'em, so send them back where they came from. Chances are they'll say there are more of us here than there are. You can expect probing attacks, but because the river is on three sides of the village these can only be directed at the bridges."

"What about behind us?" asked Nigel.

"My guess is that the people to the north of us already have their hands full," the Major replied. "Nevertheless, I'm keeping an eye on the situation."

The probing attacks began an hour later. There were bursts of firing from Sergeant Brumby's One Platoon at the southern bridge, followed by more firing from Sergeant Mason's Two Platoon at the eastern bridge. I guessed that it would be our turn next. The burning lorry was no longer giving much light so I sent up flares from time to time.

One of these showed a score of crouched figures running across the bridge. They were caught in the crossfire of our three Brens, the leaders being cut down at once. None of those who tried to escape across the bridge reached the other side. Quiet descended once more on the village. The thought struck me that our situation was similar to that of the position held by Duncan Flint's company at Tobruk, which had been protected by two wadis and a cliff. An hour before dawn I was summoned to another orders group. As I hurried up the street the frightened faces of the village's inhabitants peered at me from their cellar windows.

Duncan Flint was standing on the church steps when the rest of us arrived.

"There has been an unfortunate development, gentlemen," he began. "The battalion has been heavily counter-attacked and I do not know how long it will be before it will join us. Meanwhile, we are sitting right on one of Jerry's lines of retreat and, his probing attacks having failed, he will try and use some of his armour to dislodge us. I believe that you'll be hit first, Andy, and—"

His words were drowned by the scream of an incoming salvo of shells. There was an explosion in the church doorway and I remember being hurled through the air – then blackness. I do not think that I was unconscious for more than a few seconds. I was aware of running feet and the sound of Sergeant Brumby's voice.

"Take 'em down to the crypt under the church, lads. Joe, have look at Mr Pope."

I opened my eyes to see Sergeant Mason looking down at me.

"You hit, sir?" he asked.

All my limbs seemed to be in working order but I had a splitting headache. Soldiers were carrying bloodstained figures down the steps into the crypt. More figures were sprawled on the cobbles. There seemed to be blood everywhere. I sat up slowly, shaking my head.

"What's happening?"

"The Major's been badly hit, sir," answered Sergeant Mason. "So has the Artillery Officer. I'm afraid Captain Wood is dead, so is Sergeant Major Darracott and Barnes, the Company Signaller."

I stood up unsteadily. Obviously, those who had been standing on the other side of the orders group had absorbed the worst of the shell's effects.

"You're in command, now, sir," said Sergeant Brumby in a matter-of-fact voice.

The shock of our loss was bad enough, but suddenly I felt crushed by the immense weight of the additional responsibility thrust upon me. I was commanding an under-strength company that was doing a battalion's job behind enemy lines, and whatever happened had become my responsibility. The two sergeants were looking at me expectantly.

"Send someone to fetch Sergeant Warriner," I heard my voice say. My ingrained training and discipline were asserting themselves automatically. "Tell him to bring Corporal Baker and Helsby-Frodsham with him – at the double!"

Sporadic shelling continued to strike the village, so I moved the orders group to the narrow space between the vestry and the parked Stuart. Shortly after, the others arrived.

"Sergeant Warriner, you'll take over as company sergeant major," I said. "Corporal Baker, you are now commanding Three Platoon. Helsby-Frodsham, you are responsible for the company signals net."

They nodded, obviously aware of what had happened.

"Now, the Major's opinion was that we would be attacked by armour shortly," I continued. "I agree with that, and also that Three Platoon is most likely to be hit first. This is what we are going to do. There's a china shop round the corner. It contains a supply of round, earthenware casserole dishes. Lay them upside down in a pattern across the square. With any luck Jerry will think they are anti-tank mines, especially if we get someone to paint a sign saying ACHTUNG – MINEN! Sergeant Warriner, would you attend to that?"

"Sir!" Sergeant Warriner did not bat an eyelid at the changed circumstances.

"What about us, sir?" asked Sergeant Brumby.

"Collect as many bottles and jars as you can and make Molotov cocktails with them. Use the petrol in the Stuart, but leave enough for the engine to charge the tank's radio batteries or we're sunk. Supplement it with paraffin, lamp oil, any liquid that will burn.

"When the attack develops, keep your men out of sight. Jerry may think we've pulled out – if so, well and good. With any luck, his leading vehicle will halt at our 'minefield'. At that point, your PIAT will knock it out, Sergeant Mason. Simultaneously, Corporal Baker, your PIAT will knock out the last vehicle in the column. That will leave the rest of them trapped between the two. At that point, and not before, we tackle them with our Molotov cocktails, as well as any infantry who happen to be escorting them. Any questions?"

They shook their heads.

"All right, we'd all better get on with it. I calculate that we've only 30 minutes of darkness left."

No sooner had they left than Helsby-Frodsham reported that the company's radio linking us to the battalion was smashed beyond repair. We therefore decided that he would operate the company's internal radio net while we tried to establish a new link using the artillery set in the Stuart.

I clambered aboard the tank, where the FOO's operator, Bombardier Seward, a very capable and experienced NCO, was sitting beside his set. He told me that, subject to my orders, he could probably get us fire support when we needed it. He showed me a map board already marked by the FOO in which the three bridges had been given codewords, as were various crossroads, farms and woods in enemy territory.

"All I have to do is send the codeword and the guns will do the rest, sir," he said. "It may not be as accurate as it would be if Captain O'Connor was controlling the shoot, but it will be near enough."

He also said that a message could be relayed on the artillery's radio frequency to brigade headquarters and then to our battalion, although it would take time. I handed him a scribbled note to send:

ONE FOR NINE. SUNRAY DOWN ALSO SUNRAY MINOR AND
SHELLDRAKE. AM PROCEEDING WITH MISSION BUT EXPECT
MAJOR ATTACK SHORTLY. OUT.

"One" was the A Company callsign and "nine" was the battalion
control set, while the words "Sunray" and "Sunray Minor" indicated
the company commander and his second-in-command.

I climbed the church tower just as day was breaking. Looking south,
I could see a long line of enemy traffic that had by-passed the village
moving across country. It included horse-drawn transport and guns
as well as motor vehicles of every type. A massive jam was building up
where it attempted to join another traffic stream heading east. Further
south, I could see shells bursting and guessed that they were probably
fired by the Americans as they strove to close the enemy's escape route
from their side. A roar of powerful aero engines signified the arrival of
a squadron of rocket-firing Typhoons that pounced on the stalled lines
of vehicles. Explosions erupted along the columns and fires sprang
up. Through my binoculars I watched tiny figures running across the
fields. It seemed that we were doing our job and I was determined to
see it through.

"Sir, Sergeant Brumby says there's a Jerry officer with a flag of truce
at the south bridge," shouted Helsby-Frodsham up the belfry ladder.
"Wants a word with whoever is in charge."

I deliberately took my time walking down to the bridge, in the middle of which stood an impatient-looking German colonel and a soldier with a white flag on a stick. We exchanged salutes.

"What do you want?" I asked.

"I wish to speak with your commanding officer," he replied in clipped, precise English. "This is not a matter for a mere lieutenant."

"Well, he's having his breakfast and doesn't want to talk to you," I lied. "By the way, I think my German is better than your English, so let's converse in that."

It wasn't, of course, but saying so gave me a slight advantage and clearly annoyed the Colonel.

"I am here to offer honourable surrender terms," he said. His face wore a haggard, desperate expression that I decided to exploit.

"Splendid, Colonel," I replied. "If you would kindly get your men to throw their weapons in the river and form up in that field we shall deal with them in due course."

His face went purple with rage.

"You young fool, don't you understand? I am here to demand *your* surrender!" he bellowed.

"Out of the question," I said, feigning astonishment. "And we both know that you're not really in a position to demand anything, are you?"

"Very well, you have had your chance, *Herr Leutnant*," he snarled. "When your men are slaughtered the responsibility will be yours!"

"Good morning to you," I replied, turning on my heel.

Sergeant Warriner was waiting for me when I returned to the church.

I gave him the details of my conversation with the German, at which he gave his short laugh.

"You can't blame him for trying, sir!" he remarked. "By the way, I've found a French doctor who is willing to look after the wounded, sir," he said. "Two of the women have nursing experience and they're willing to help, too."

"Do they know that Jerry will probably shoot them if things go badly for us?"

"They're willing to take a chance, and we'll need 'em." He stood looking thoughtful for a while before he continued.

"Couple of things bothering me, sir. We've only enough ammunition for one good engagement, and we're holding too much ground for a company."

"Well, there are plenty of captured weapons lying about, so we'll use those first. I agree about our perimeter, though. My plan is to deny the enemy the bridges for as long as possible, then fall back on the square. That way we'll still be able to stop them using the route through the village."

"Very good, sir." The Sergeant's tone was non-committal. "I'll have the men collect the abandoned Jerry arms and ammo. Rations aren't a problem – there's a baker's round the corner, and a butcher's too, so I've requisitioned some of their stock and distributed it."

Bombardier Seward appeared in the turret of the Stuart.

"Your message has been acknowledged, sir," he called. "I'll let you know as soon as the reply comes through."

I climbed up beside him, consulted my map and scribbled a six-figure grid reference on a message pad.

"This is our position, including the church, the churchyard and the square," I said, handing it to him. "Get your chaps to add it to their list of targets. The codeword will be VENICE. Use the Slidex code when you send, of course."

I had learned the Slidex code at OCTU and knew that if enemy operators were listening it would be almost impossible for them to crack it on the basis of one transmission.

"Are things that bad, sir?" Seward replied, eyeing the pad dubiously. Normally, one only called down artillery fire on one's own position in extreme circumstances.

"No, but we may as well be prepared."

Helsby-Frodsham poked his head out of the vestry door.

"The Major's asking for you, sir."

In the crypt the French doctor and his volunteer nurses were doing what they could for our wounded. The doctor told me that Duncan Flint was drifting in and out of consciousness at the moment and was very seriously injured. His back, left arm and left leg were swathed in bandages through which blood was soaking.

"Ah, Andy, there . . . you are," he said. It was obvious that speech was difficult and painful for him. "Now listen carefully . . . this is what you've to do. . ."

"I'm sorry, Major, but I'm in command now. You've been badly hurt and must get all the rest you can."

He glared at me balefully.

"In command . . . are you? What . . . are your plans . . . then?"

"I'm going to hold the village as long as I can. If we look like being overrun I'm going to pull everyone back here into the crypt, then call down an artillery strike on top of us. When that's lifted we'll break out and rejoin the battalion."

"Good . . . I would have . . . done . . . the same. Not altogether . . . wasted my time with . . . you, it seems. I've seen . . . my company . . . march into captivity once. Don't want . . . to see it again. Just don't . . . mess up, laddie."

It was hardly a vote of confidence, but he was drifting into unconsciousness and I bit back a sharp reply. I climbed the tower again. To the south the American shell bursts seemed much closer and our aircraft were harrying the enemy columns without mercy. I was witnessing the death of the German Army in Normandy. From the north came the sounds of intense fighting as the rest of our battalion tried to break through to us. I began to wonder whether the German Colonel's threats had simply been bluster, although from time to time salvos of shells continued to land in the village, wrecking houses and setting one ablaze. Sergeant Warriner joined me. By shouting instructions to Seward, we were able to bring down our own shells on areas in which the enemy might be forming up for an attack.

"Slidex message, sir," said Helsby-Frodsham from the top of the belfry ladder. He handed me the message pad. "The Bombardier's decoded it for you."

375

The message read: CRUMPETS FOR TEA USUAL TIME EARLIER IF POSSIBLE.

"What's it mean, sir?" asked Sergeant Warriner.

"I think it means that the battalion will have broken through to us by 16:15. That's the time we used to have tea in the Mess. It's coming up to noon now, so we've about four hours to wait, unless Jerry decides to attack us after all."

"He has, sir! Take a look!" Warriner exclaimed, pointing.

A large force of enemy infantry were moving stealthily along the north bank of the river, using trees and hedges for cover. They obviously intended attacking the open end of the village, using the same route we had entered it by. It was here that our defences were weakest.

"Tell Sergeant Mason to send one of his sections across to the north end of the village!" I shouted down to Helsby-Frodsham, then turned to Sergeant Warriner. "Go and take charge there yourself. There's only a narrow gap between the two bends in the river and I don't think Jerry will be able to deploy his full strength for an attack there. I'll reinforce you if necessary."

I had the sickening feeling that somehow I had made a terrible mistake. The sounds of heavy fighting still came from the north, so where had this attack come from? I glanced quickly at the map and saw that a weir was marked two miles downstream. Obviously the enemy had crossed there on foot. I cursed myself for not noticing it earlier. Yet, they could not have known that the north end of the village was our weakest point, and would have been aware that they could only attack on a limited frontage. If this was a diversion where would the main attack be delivered?

Seconds later I knew the answer. Four low-slung assault guns were moving along the road towards the west bridge. Behind each trotted a squad of infantry, with yet more infantry beyond them. I rejected at once any idea that our Stuart should engage them, for its little 37mm gun was no match for the assault guns' long 75mm cannon, apart from which its radio was our only link with the outside world. I shouted for Seward to bring down shellfire on the west bridge, and for Helsby-Frodsham to tell Corporal Baker to keep his men hidden in accordance with our plan. Already I could hear the crackle of rifle fire and the stutter of Brens as Sergeant Warriner's men began beating off the diversionary assault.

The assault guns passed through the rain of shells apparently unscathed. The leading vehicle fired in turn at each of the overturned supply wagons we were using as barricades, then pushed its way through the splintered wreckage. As it reached the square its driver, spotting our "minefield", halted, uncertain what to do. Immediately, a PIAT bomb slammed into the side of the vehicle, its blast killing those within. A second bomb hit the rearmost vehicle, which shuddered to a standstill with smoke pouring from its engine compartment. Then all hell seemed to break loose. Three Platoon appeared at the windows of houses on both sides of the street, hurling Molotov cocktails and blazing away with their weapons. The assault guns' infantry escort were cut down, as were the crews attempting to escape from their burning vehicles.

377

The west to east route through the village was now successfully blocked, but as our artillery concentration on the west bridge lifted, more and more of the German infantry swarmed across, fanning out to the right and left so that they outflanked the positions held by Sergeant Brumby and Sergeant Warriner. I descended the tower just as Corporal Baker signalled that he had lost two houses near the bridge. I told Helsby-Frodsham to call the platoon commanders and tell them that they should fall back slowly on the church, but make the enemy pay for every yard of ground. He was to add that on hearing three long blasts on my whistle they were to break contact and run for the church.

"MAKE SURE EVERYONE KNOWS WHAT YOU'RE DOING," said a sudden voice in my head. I put it down to fatigue, but it was just the sort of annoying remark Duncan Flint would make when I had already decided to do something.

It had now become a soldier's battle. There was nothing more I could do at this stage, so I snatched up a machine pistol and several magazines from a dead German lying beside an assault gun, and visited each platoon in turn. I cannot recall the details, but the fighting was bitter. It raged in the streets, through houses, from barricade to barricade and across gardens. The Germans were fighting to break out of a trap, but we were fighting for our survival and that gave us an edge.

Heavily outnumbered, we were forced back slowly, which was good in one way as we had less ground to hold. On the other hand, we were losing men steadily and had fewer to hold it with. During each lull I

378

managed to gather half a dozen men together as a reserve and used it to recapture a house or barricade with a counter-attack. I lost track of time but at length it became apparent that we would be overrun. Sergeant Warriner's group had already fallen back to the north wall of the churchyard. Corporal Baker and Three Platoon were already pulling back to the west wall. One and Two Platoons were retreating doggedly but were being pressed hard. The danger was that they would be swamped by the next enemy assault, and that would leave us with too few men to hold the churchyard. Worse, this was the moment I should have called down our own artillery, but I could not leave them exposed to it. I already had my whistle in my mouth when I heard the voice again: "NOW! BRING 'EM IN BEFORE IT'S TOO LATE! YOU HAVEN'T A SECOND TO SPARE!"

I blew three long blasts. The men came streaming in, pursued by the enemy's fire. I saw Sergeant Brumby run to the leading assault gun, which had been knocked out in the centre of the square. He clambered on to the superstructure, where a Spandau machine-gun was mounted beside the commander's hatch. He immediately opened fire on the Germans massing in the streets leading to the south and west bridges, scything through them and forcing them to dive for cover.

"Back to the church!" I yelled at the two platoons. "Barricade the doors when everyone is inside and go down to the crypt!"

As they ran past me I turned to Sergeant Brumby. "Come on – you've done enough!" I shouted. "Get inside – I'm calling down an artillery strike!"

"I'll just see the lads safely inside, sir!" he replied as he continued to blaze away. "Don't worry about me!"

Bullets were already ricocheting off the gun shield and the assault gun's armour as I ran to the Stuart.

"Call for VENICE now!" I yelled at Bombardier Seward. "Then get out of there and into the church!"

As we squeezed through the last gap in the church's big double doors I glanced across the square. Sergeant Brumby was lying slumped across the machine-gun, his blood running down the assault gun's side. The doors slammed shut and were barricaded with anything we could lay our hands on. In the crypt, we did likewise with the door connecting it to the church. The doctor and his nurses were hard at work in the hot, over-crowded space. A small door in the wall of the crypt gave access to a flight of steps leading up to the churchyard. I ordered the fit men to assemble by it and told them that as soon as our bombardment had lifted we would use these to assemble behind the north wall of the churchyard.

"We'll go over it together," I said. "I'm counting on Jerry being too dazed to do anything, but don't stop for anyone or anything. The rest of the battalion is heading this way and we should be able to break through to them."

From above came the sound of the enemy battering on the church door, together with the tinkle of breaking glass and explosions as they flung grenades into the building. I went over to Duncan Flint and to my horror saw that his face was now covered by a blanket. Shaking his head sadly, the French doctor told me that he had died only minutes after my last visit. The men had liked him, and I decided to keep this news to myself for the moment. Although I had never really liked him, I felt a terrible sense of loss, for A Company was his creation and now he had gone.

I glanced at my watch. It said four o'clock. I felt bitterly disappointed that we had not been able to hold out for another fifteen minutes, because the rest of the battalion would have arrived by then. Then came the scream of the first salvo of shells. What followed seemed to go on for ever. The earth round us seemed to heave as salvo followed salvo. From above came the sound of crashing masonry and the shattering of glass as the huge windows were blown in. In the crypt, dust was shaken from every crevice and hung in the air like a fog. I expected the church floor to collapse on to us any minute, but the stout stone Norman columns continued to support it. Then there was silence.

"Come on!" I yelled, wrenching the door open and charging up the steps. I emerged into a scene from hell. Part of the church wall had collapsed, bringing much of the roof down as well. German bodies, many of them dismembered, lay everywhere. Shattered gravestones and monuments littered the ground. Skeletal remains could be seen in some of the craters. The occupant of an uprooted coffin grinned bonily at me as I ran past. I reached the north wall and heard the thud of boots as the others joined me. I peered over. The enemy, severely shaken, had pulled back into the surrounding gardens to regroup and reorganize. To my surprise, shells began to burst among them.

"Look, sir!" shouted Sergeant Warriner, pointing.

A squadron of Sherman tanks, deployed in line, was approaching the village, firing as they advanced. Some way behind was the battalion's leading company, riding in APCs. As the enemy turned to face this new attack, two strange vehicles detached themselves from the tank squadron and closed in on the end of the street. Through my binoculars I was able to identify them as Churchills, although they were towing armoured trailers. Suddenly a great tongue of flame belched out of one. It lasted for several seconds and stretched half the length of the street, setting everything in its path ablaze. I had heard of the terrible Crocodile flamethrowers, but never seen them before. Smashing their way through the barricades, they advanced slowly and with infinite menace. I could see the enemy's fire ricocheting uselessly off their armour. Another belch of flame, this time reaching the edge of the square and sticking to anything it touched. Many of the enemy fled, but most flung down their arms and surrendered.

Beside me, our men were cheering and waving their helmets. The Crocodiles reached the square, shunted the derelict assault gun aside and turned south to cross the bridge into what had been enemy territory. The Shermans followed in their wake. Then came our own B Company, the commander of which, Major James Masterson, stopped briefly beside me.

"Ye gods, young Andy, what's been going on here?" he asked, looking around the scene of carnage and desolation. "Anything I can do to help out?"

"I'd be glad if you'd drop off a few of your blokes, sir," I replied. "We've a lot of wounded and there's prisoners to guard."

"Will do," he said. "Sorry I can't stop – got an appointment with our American cousins. Seems they've closed the enemy's last escape route and it's just about all over."

The rest of the battalion passed through. The wounded, the enemy's as well as our own, were taken out to a fleet of ambulances that had arrived. The prisoners were marshalled and I made arrangements for our own men to have a brew of tea and a hot meal. The church tower was still more or less intact, so when these administrative tasks had been attended to Sergeant Warriner and I climbed to the top. We watched in silence as, to the south, British and American red and green recognition flares went up and white flags began fluttering along the stalled enemy columns. Typhoons flew overhead, ready to pounce on any remaining signs of resistance.

"Damn fine show, Andy, damn fine!" said a voice. We turned to see Colonel Armitage clambering out of the hatch. "You can tell A Company how proud I am of them – and so is the Brigadier and the General!"

"Thank you, Colonel, they'll appreciate that," I replied. "I'm afraid there are less than fifty of us left on our feet."

"That's hard to bear, I know," he said, looking out at the surrendering German Army. "Nevertheless, several thousand of those people could have made their escape through this village during the time you've been here, then been used to fight against us again. You must balance your loss against that."

He paused for a minute, looking down at the ambulances moving off.

"I'm sorry about Duncan, Nigel and the others," he continued, turning to look me straight in the eye. "Duncan was a difficult man to command and I'm sure he was a difficult man to serve under, but he produced results and that's what counts. He thought that you showed great promise, by the way, although he'd never have told you so."

I was surprised but did not think it appropriate to comment, so I simply nodded.

"Oh, one other thing, Andy," said the Colonel as he began to descend the ladder. "If you care to give me a list of names for suitable awards I'll give it my full backing."

"Too bad about the Major, sir," commented Sergeant Warriner after a few moments' reflection. "I suppose that last effort was too much for him. Should have stayed in the crypt with the rest of the wounded."

"What do you mean?" I asked, taken aback.

"As we ran in I saw him standing behind you in the square."

I felt the hairs rise on the back of my neck.

"Major Flint had been dead for nearly four hours by then. The doctor will confirm that. Did you see him after we'd pulled back into the church?"

"No, sir," replied the Sergeant, a look of bewilderment crossing his face. "But I did see him standing behind you in the square just as clearly as I'm seeing you now. I'll take my oath on it!"

Warriner was an honest man, not given to too much imagination, and I knew that he was telling the truth.

"Wouldn't let go, would he?" I said, at length.

"Looks that way, sir," he replied, in his matter-of-fact way. "Wanted to be sure the company was in good hands, that's all. When he was satisfied, he left us. That's the only explanation I can offer. Now I don't know where soldiers go when they die, sir, but wherever it is he'll be grateful to you."

Shortly after, another battalion from the brigade arrived to take over the village from us. I marched what was left of A Company to a nearby field where we spent the night. I found it difficult to sleep until I realized why. For the first time since D-Day the sound of the guns was absent. The silence was uncanny.

Epilogue

To my sorrow, A Company was never re-formed. Following the great Allied victory in Normandy, our armoured divisions swept north to liberate Belgium while the Americans embarked on a whirlwind advance to the German frontier. During this period we were told that our entire division was to be disbanded and used to reinforce other divisions. The problem was that the United Kingdom's manpower resources had become stretched to their limits.

My recommendations for awards won during the battle for St Marc were accepted in full. Sergeant Brumby, but for whose self-sacrifice we might have been overrun, received the posthumous award of the Victoria Cross. Sergeant Warriner, who had commanded the most difficult sector of the defences as well as acting as company sergeant major throughout, added a Distinguished Conduct Medal (DCM) to his Military Medal (MM). As he had been involved in active service throughout the Desert War and from D-Day onwards I felt that he had done enough and this was also accepted. He was confirmed in the rank of sergeant major and posted to a training regiment in England. I am not sure whether he was grateful or not. Sergeant Mason, later killed in Holland, received the MM, as did Corporal Baker, who rose to the rank of sergeant. He has recently been demobilized and returned to his family. A recommendation was passed to the Royal Artillery that Bombardier Seward, who had carried out his dead officer's task and ensured that we received artillery support when we needed it most, should receive the DCM, and I am pleased to say that this was approved. Several more men were Mentioned in Despatches.

Of the old Three Platoon hands, Grover has reached the rank of corporal and decided to remain in the Regular Army, where, at last, he seems to have found his niche in life. He is said to be a strict disciplinarian, but then he knows his own tricks best. Haggerty was promoted to lance corporal twice and lost his stripes on both occasions because of his illegal business activities. I am told that, but for his MM, he would have spent time in detention barracks. He has now returned to Liverpool, apparently a great deal richer than when he left it. Helsby-Frodsham received a serious leg wound during the closing stages of the action, rendering him unfit for further service in the infantry. Rather than have him idle his time away in some depot, I produced several brilliant water-colour sketches he had made of the fighting in Normandy and suggested that he was appointed an official war artist. The appointment was sanctioned and he recently came to see me with the news that he had been commissioned by the Regiment to paint the final stages of the battle for St Marc. I took Allen with me when I started my present job, fearing that no one else would put up with him. He has now returned to the Savoy Hotel and is probably driving its guests to distraction with his endless chatter.

As for myself, I was sent on a course to learn my duties as an Intelligence Officer, then joined my new brigade, of which the newly promoted Colonel Armitage is second-in-command. After a while, I was sent on a short leave to England. My parents accompanied me to Buckingham Palace, where the King presented me with the Military Cross. A shy, quietly spoken man with a slight stammer, he had obviously been briefed about the action at St Marc and asked me several well-informed questions about it. One could not help but like him.

For the rest of the War, most of my duties involved the interrogation of prisoners. When the fighting ended, I found myself interrogating Nazi Party officials, members of the Gestapo, and SS concentration camp guards. They were all guilty of horrific and inhuman acts. I do not know which of them I detested most – those who claimed that they were only obeying orders, or those who showed no shame at what they had done and went smirking to the gallows. They were evil personified and it had been worth fighting a war to rid the world of such men.

Historical note

The Allied invasion of Normandy, Operation Overlord, was the largest amphibious operation in history. It involved no less than 1,213 warships, 4,126 landing ships and landing craft, 736 support vessels and 864 merchant vessels, plus two pre-fabricated Mulberry harbours, which Andy mentions in his story. Air cover was provided by the combined might of the British and American tactical air forces, supplemented by the heavy bombers of the US Strategic Air Force. Prior to launching the invasion, elaborate deception measures successfully convinced the Germans that the Allied landings would take place in the Pas de Calais, which offered the shortest sea route between the United Kingdom and France. As a result, most of their armoured divisions were held back in this area. As the Allied troops moved to their embarkation ports, southern England was sealed off from the rest of the country for security reasons. Simultaneously, French Resistance groups attacked road and rail communications in northern France to hinder the movement of enemy reinforcements into the battle area.

After postponement due to bad weather, the date of the invasion, codenamed D-Day, was set for 6 June. Shortly after midnight, one British and two American airborne divisions were dropped to secure the flanks of the invasion area. The seaborne assault, under the overall command of General Sir Bernard Montgomery, commenced at 06:30, when the tide would leave the German beach obstacles exposed. On the right, Lieutenant General Omar Bradley's US First Army landed on two beaches designated Utah and Omaha; on the left, Lieutenant General Sir Miles Dempsey's British Second Army, including a large Canadian element, landed on beaches designated Gold, Juno and Sword. As Andy narrates, on the British and Canadian sectors the specialized armoured vehicles developed by the 79th Armoured Division proved invaluable in overcoming the enemy's beach defences and casualties were far lighter than had been expected. The Americans, however, lacking such vehicles, sustained over 3,000 killed and wounded on Omaha Beach alone. Nevertheless, by midnight, 57,000 American and 75,000 British and Canadian troops, plus their equipment, had been put ashore and the process of linking the beach-heads had begun. Allied losses amounted to 2,500 killed and 8,500 wounded; the full extent of German losses remains unknown.

The Allied strategy during the Normandy campaign was for the British and Canadians to maintain constant pressure on the enemy, thereby preventing the transfer of German reserves to the American sector, where the great breakout from the beach-head was planned. This meant that much of the fighting took place in close *bocage* country, where the Allies could not make full use of their armour. Consequently, losses among the infantry were high, sometimes approaching the level sustained during the Battle of the Somme in World War I. For their part, the Germans, who also lacked air cover, were handicapped by Hitler's "no withdrawal" orders and forced to endure the terrible effects of naval gunfire.

On 1 August the Americans broke out of the beach-head and began swinging round the enemy's left flank. Simultaneously, the British and Canadians began forcing back the enemy right flank, so that by the middle of the month the German armies in Normandy were trapped inside a shrinking pocket south of Falaise. The exit from the pocket was finally closed on 19 August. Some 10,000 Germans had died within it and 50,000 were captured. Also captured or destroyed were hundreds of tanks, self-propelled guns, armoured cars, artillery weapons and motor vehicles.

The episode involving Andy's batman, Private Allen, and the Tiger tank is based on a real incident that took place during the bitter battle for Hill 112. The operation to close an enemy escape route from the pocket is based on the actions fought at, respectively, St Lambert-sur-Dives and Mont Ormel, during the last stages of the campaign.

Early in his story Andy mentions that one of his ancestors, Michael Pope, served as a drummer boy during the Crimean War. Michael's adventures can be found in another *My Story* book, *Crimea*.

Timeline

19 August 1942 British and Canadian raid on Dieppe obtains much useful information regarding the nature of the German coastal defences.

6 June 1944 D-Day. US First and British Second Armies secure five beach-heads on the coast of Normandy.

7–12 June Beach-heads joined to form continuous 50-mile front.

19–22 June The Great Storm. American Mulberry harbour seriously damaged.

26 June–1 July Operation Epsom, the British Second Army's offensive across the Odon and Orne rivers south-west of Caen.

29 June Americans take Cherbourg.

9 July British take Caen.

18–21 July Operation Goodwood, the British Second Army's offensive south-east of Caen.

20 July Realizing that he was leading Germany to a terrible defeat, a group of senior German generals attempt to assassinate Hitler with a bomb planted in a briefcase. They fail to kill him. He takes a ferocious revenge on them.

25 July Operation Cobra, the American break-out west of St Lô begins.

30 July Beginning of Operation Bluecoat, the British Second Army's offensive towards Mont Pincon and the Vire river, pinning down German troops ordered to oppose the American breakout.

6–7 August Americans beat off weak German counter-attack at Mortain. US Third Army turns German left flank. British capture Mont Pincon.

8–11 August Operation Totalize. First Canadian Army's offensive towards Falaise, Phase I.

14–16 August Operation Tractable, the First Canadian Army's offensive towards Falaise, Phase II, pushes in the German right flank. The German armies in Normandy are now trapped within a shrinking pocket south of Falaise.

17–19 August Trapped German armies struggle to escape eastwards but surrender when the last exit from the pocket is closed.

17–26 September Allied airborne operations in Holland secure bridges at Eindhoven and Nijmegen but end in gallant failure at Arnhem.

16 December 1944–16 January 1945 A major German counter-offensive in the Ardennes is defeated.

8 February–10 March The Allies secure the left bank of the River Rhine in Germany. The Americans capture the bridge at Remagen intact on 7 March.

22 March The Americans cross the Rhine in force at Oppenheim.

23 March The British cross the Rhine at Wesel.

30 April Hitler commits suicide in his bunker in Berlin.

2 May Berlin falls to the Russians who have arrived from the east. Advancing British and Russian armies make contact.

5–8 May Unconditional surrender of German armies in western Europe.

Picture acknowledgements

All photographs reproduced by the kind permission of the Trustees of the Imperial War Museum, London.

P398 Map of the D-Day Landings, Andras Bereznay

Every effort has been made to trace the copyright holders and we apologize in advance for any unintentional omissions. We would be pleased to insert the appropriate acknowledgements in any subsequent edition of this book.

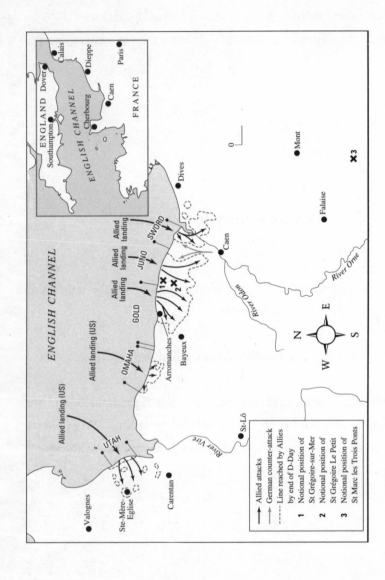

A map of the D-Day landings, 6 June 1944.

Allied troops going ashore in Normandy on 6 June, 1944. DD (Duplex Drive) Sherman tanks are already on the beach along with other armoured vehicles.

LCAs (Landing Craft Assault) transport Allied infantry from the LST (Landing Ship Tank) to the beach.

Allied troops landing. As the tide rises some have a longer wade ashore than others.

German prisoners beside a knocked-out Sherman Crab tank. The tide is rising but they are still standing where they have been told to.

Allied infantry of the follow-up wave prepare to leave the beach on D-Day.

Amphibious lorries bringing supplies ashore. The barrage balloons, which can be seen in the distance, provided a defence against attacks by low-flying aircraft.

A 'Kangaroo' Armoured Personnel Carrier (APC) with infantry aboard. Like the real kangaroo, which carries its young in its pouch, this vehicle carried its passengers in a central compartment.

Allied infantry and tanks forming-up for an attack.

An AVRE (Armoured Vehicle Royal Engineers) carrying a fascine. Fascines would be used to fill anti-tank ditches so that vehiles could cross them.

Infantry and tank action in the *bocage*, a large area of countryside in Normandy.

Experience history first-hand with My Story –
a series of vividly imagined accounts of life in the past.

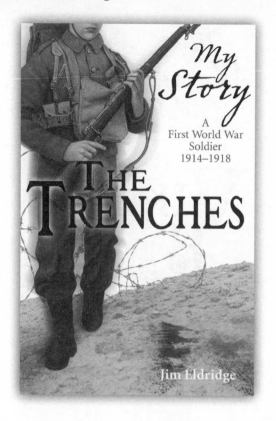

It's **1917** and **Billy Stevens** is a telegraph
operator stationed near Ypres. **The Great War**
has been raging for three years when Billy finds
himself taking part in the deadly **Big Push** forward.
But he is shocked to discover that the **bullets**
of his **fellow soldiers** aren't just
aimed at the **enemy**...

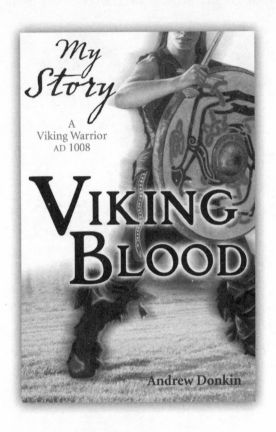

It's AD 1008, and after being injured in a raid
that goes horribly wrong, Tor Scaldbane
is devastated at losing his chance to be a
legendary warrior.

But then he discovers the sagas of his ancestors; glorious,
bloody battles, ancient heroes, powerful gods ... and
realizes that all might not be lost after all...

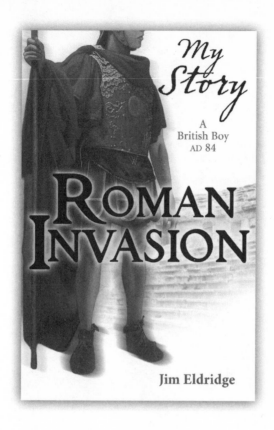

My Story

A
British Boy
AD 84

ROMAN INVASION

Jim Eldridge

It's AD 84 when **Bran**, **a prince** of the **Carvetii tribe**, is **captured** by the **Romans**. **A legion of soldiers** is marching east, to build a **military road**. It's **hostile** country, and **Bran** is to **go with them** as a **hostage** to ensure the legion's safety ... but **no one is safe** in newly **conquered Britain**.